The Dark Inside

ROD REYNOLDS

FABER & FABER

First published in 2015
by Faber & Faber Ltd
Bloomsbury House
74–77 Great Russell Street
London WC1B 3DA
This paperback edition first published in 2016

Typeset by Faber & Faber Ltd
Printed and bound by CPI Group (UK), Croydon CR0 4YY

Author's Note: Certain buildings have been moved from their real-world locations for
narrative purposes.

A CIP record for this book
is available from the British Library

ISBN 978–0–571–32305–0

FSC
www.fsc.org
MIX
Paper from
responsible sources
FSC® C101712

2 4 6 8 10 9 7 5 3 1

To my mum, Margaret, my wife, Claire,
and my daughter, Elodie. My love always.

CHAPTER ONE

MARCH, 1946

I arrived in town four days after the latest killings. Tall pines lined the road in. They only petered out the last mile, where the Texas-Pacific line ran parallel to the blacktop, gunmetal rails running off into the distance. A sign at the town limits read TEXARKANA, U.S.A. is TWICE AS NICE. A dog cocked its leg and took a piss against it as I passed.

There were farmhouses sprinkled across the landscape. The road carried me close by one of them, a single-storey affair with unpainted walls. Alongside it was a dilapidated barn, bales of hay peeking out from inside; its lopsided tin roof sat atop walls constructed with red planks, and the gaps and missing boards gave the structure the appearance of a mouth full of broken teeth. A man in bib-and-brace overalls was driving a horse buggy down a track towards it. When the highway curled around the property and gave me a view of the far side of the barn, I saw a flatbed Ford from before the last war, rusting and covered in dried mud, sitting on blocks.

White clapboard houses with pitched roofs and narrow windows dotted the outskirts of town, the distances between them vast by Manhattan standards – patches of open country as big as city blocks. Some had swing seats and picket fences – signs of civilisation. But dirt tracks to shotgun shacks branched right off the highway; one had no front door, and five shoeless Negro children sat outside it on a crumbling porch, watching my car as I travelled down the road.

Three days travel and a million miles from New York. A bullshit assignment.

Exiled.

Highway 67 took me downtown. A train horn droned somewhere in the distance, getting louder as I drove. I passed an out-dated war bonds poster still affixed to a telegraph pole; the print was faded and weathered, but legible: *Save To Beat The Devil! Buy Victory Bonds.* The image was Hitler's face, complete with pointed ears and red horns, looking worried. I'd bought two hundred bucks' worth of bond notes back in forty-four – my contribution to Uncle Sam's war effort. Seeing that poster now, after the fact, was like a rebuke: *did you do your part?*

I tried to slow my thoughts down. I'd flown from New York Municipal to Atlanta, my exit ordered with such haste that I'd had to organise my own rental car when I landed. From there it was still a six hundred-mile drive across three states – Tom Walters so desperate to run me out of New York he'd put me on the first flight south. It just underlined what we both knew: he didn't give a damn about the story he was sending me to cover.

Neither did I, for that matter. It wasn't that I had no feeling for the three that had been killed – it wasn't that way at all. Fifteen years of working crime beats – in Los Angeles and Chicago before New York – taught me that murder stays with you, and I could list out the name of every victim in every killing I ever covered. It just smarted that after clawing my way to the pinnacle – crime reporter at the *Examiner* – I was being sidelined onto this story as a punishment. More than that: as a way to keep me out of mind while Walters worked on getting rid of me for keeps.

Walters was the news editor of the *Examiner*, and an up and comer in the Greenbeck Corporation, the company that owned the paper. We'd rubbed along fine until my accident in forty-three – an automobile wreck that shattered my legs and had me in and out of hospitals for a year. When I finally got back on the job, his opinion of me had soured, blaming me for what had happened. He took me to task over everything – my expense account, my word counts, the stories I filed; along the way, I found out he nixed three consecutive pay rises I was due. Never had the moxie to have it out with me like a man, though; scheming behind your back was his way.

Things had come to a head a month ago. One of the subs, Nelson Hunter, had spiked a story of mine. Wasn't his fault – he was just doing what Walters had told him to do, the boss man coming at me in his sly way like he always did. I'd stormed over to Hunter's desk, and matters got out of hand; a shouting match at first, getting rough when he shoved me. I swung for him in retaliation, busting his lip. He came back at me, and it was about to turn into a donnybrook, but the boys watching got between us and pulled us apart. When they did, I was still so hot, I picked up Hunter's typewriter and tossed it through Walters's office window. The memory of the glass shattering was still clear in my mind, as if it'd happened an hour ago. Ditto the silence that followed. Then the panic that rushed through my chest when I realised what I'd done.

Walters hadn't been in his office at the time. It was that and my friend Sal's intervention that saved me. Sal brazened it out and told a specially convened meeting of the board, including

Walters, that he saw Hunter throw the first punch, and the window got broke in the scuffle. They knew he was covering for me, to some extent or another, but Sal was a heavyweight, had enough juice with the Police Commissioner's office that they couldn't afford to get on the wrong side of him by calling him a liar. They sent Hunter and me home for a month, him suspended with pay, me without.

When they'd let me back on the job last Tuesday, the travel orders and airline ticket had been waiting for me on my desk, along with a memorandum from Walters: I was off the City crime beat. Didn't have guts enough to tell it to my face. Twenty-four hours later, I was on an Eastern Air Lines flight to Candler Field in Atlanta, via a stopover in DC.

I'd driven right through the night to get from Atlanta to Arkansas. I wasn't in a rush – the first victim had been dead for eleven days, and with no suspects for any of the murders, the story had gone cold. It just felt better to be on the road than pass another night awake in a strange bed, thinking about how bad I'd left things in New York. Truth was, the incident at the *Examiner* would never have got out of hand like that, save for the fact my marriage had just gone to hell. My wife, Jane, had turned me out of our apartment a month before the fight. It came as no big surprise; she'd been unhappy for a time by that point – ever since the car wreck. She said it changed me; that there was anger in me all the time afterward. She was right, but I wouldn't have it back then, and we quarrelled round the clock. Even so, it damn near broke me the day she told me we were through.

Four weeks later, on that first afternoon when they'd sent me home after the fight, I sat alone on an upturned crate in a two-room rental in a tenement on the Lower East Side; no furniture, bare walls, a threadbare brown carpet and my belongings in five cardboard boxes piled in a corner – and that's when I finally got wise. Damn temper had already cost me my marriage and my home; now it had cost me my career too.

I blinked and focused on the road. I stopped at a red light, the signal swaying on its wire above me, mine the only car at the crossroads. I pulled out the address Walters had given me, checked it again: *Texarkana Chronicle, 315 Pine St, Texarkana.* The boss man didn't bother with a map. His one-liner, scrawled underneath: Ask for Jimmy Robinson.

I drove two more blocks then parked outside a coffee shop called Wendell's, thinking to go in for directions. Before I got out, I reached into my jacket and pulled out the photograph I'd picked up on the newswires before I left, looked at it again: Alice Rose Anderson, the female victim of the first attack. The survivor. I turned it over in my mind, sorted through the little I knew.

I'd spent Tuesday afternoon culling everything I could off the wires, but the Associated Press stories were thin. The first attack had occurred the weekend before last, sometime in the early hours of Sunday morning. Alice Anderson and her sweetheart, Dwight Breems, were parked in his car on a rural road on the outskirts of town. He'd been killed but she'd survived. It mentioned the killer having a gun, but the cause of death wasn't confirmed. The question that had stuck in my mind when I was reading through: did the killer allow her to live? If so, why?

A week later, sometime in the small hours of last Sunday, there had been another attack: Patty Summerbell and Edward Logan, murdered in what the story described as a lovers' lane. Both of them had been killed, gunshot wounds stated as the cause of death. A man and his son on the way to their hunting stand had stumbled across the scene the next morning. Police had appealed for anyone with genuine information to come forward. There was no mention of a suspect in either case.

The part that really stuck in my throat: Patty Summerbell and Alice Anderson were only seventeen years old.

I looked again at the picture in my lap. She was pretty, had fair, shoulder-length hair and an easygoing smile, her front teeth slightly apart. She was looking at something to the side of the camera, her eyes big and bright; a carefree expression, like nothing in the world could ever hurt her.

I set the photograph on the seat next to me and stepped onto the sidewalk.

*

'Y'almost there already, hun – *Chronicle* building's just down the street.' The waitress smiled at me. Her name badge read *Martha*; she had dark circles under her eyes and her apron was covered with grease stains. 'Take a left out the door and it's three blocks down, on the Texas side. Behind the Hotel Mason. Can't miss the Mason.'

'Thanks.'

She didn't move, kept watching me, wiping a semi-circle on the counter with a dirty grey rag. 'You a reporter?'

I looked up from the counter, nodded.

'I knew it. Where you from?'

'New York.'

'New York?' The rag stopped in front of me. 'Lord, that's a trip. I knew a fella went there once. Take you a long time?'

I went to speak, but she leaned in close, cut me off. 'You here because of the killings?'

I took a sip of coffee. 'Yes, ma'am.'

She straightened up, nodding. 'Such awful business. Those poor young people.' She gripped her side of the counter. 'My daughter knew Patty Summerbell, you know, was in her class at Texarkana High. When she heard Patty and Mr Logan was dead, my Clara was just . . .' A shake of the head to finish the sentence.

I fished a dollar from my pocket, slipped off my stool. 'I'm sorry. It must be hard.'

'It is. So hard. And that poor Anderson girl—' She splayed her fingers over her mouth. 'Jesus spare me for saying it, but there's folks say she'd be better off dead, and I don't know they're wrong. I know I shouldn't say it, but to go through that, I mean to live through that, must be . . .'

I turned back to her. 'Mind if I ask what you mean by that, ma'am?'

She stared past me, hands working the hem of her apron, a world away. Something in her expression made me pull my notepad out.

As I set it on the counter, a bell rang and a fat counterman leaned through a swing door from the kitchen. He eyed me, then glared at the waitress. 'Martha, you working today or aren't you?'

She blinked, then in a quiet voice said, 'Excuse me.' I watched as she disappeared into the back. I gathered my things up, dropped the dollar on the counter and went back to the car.

*

The sun had dipped behind a low bank of clouds. The main drag was State Line Avenue; it ran north–south, following the state borderline, splitting the city between Texas and Arkansas. Businesses made a gimmick of it: The Lone Star Diner faced Arkansas Liquor. Traffic was light, but parked cars jammed the street, more than I'd seen since I first hit Dixie.

I hung a U-turn and headed south, past a cluster of hotels, and a theatre called the Saenger. It had a classic-revival facade, its sign framed with flashing bulbs – looked like a second-rate Broadway. Beyond that, the road split around the Federal Courthouse building, a granite monster sitting by itself on an island in the middle of the street. The Arkansas and Texas flags flew on their respective sides. When the road rejoined, the red sign on top of the Mason was an easy spot; the hotel must have run to ten storeys, dwarfed everything around it. I pulled up round back and spotted the *Chronicle* building across the street. It looked like a meat warehouse.

*

'Mr Robinson, this is Charles Yates, from *The New York Examiner*.' The secretary flashed me a tight smile, then retraced her steps across the newsroom.

Robinson was playing hunt-and-peck on a typewriter. He looked me up and down, then stood to offer his hand. 'Jimmy Robinson. Good to know you.' He had an oversized rectangular head with a thinning patch of blond hair on top.

'Charlie.' We shook. 'Tom Walters told me to look you up, said you'd be my contact.'

Robinson glanced over his shoulder to an office in the

8

corner; stencilling on the door read *S.J. McGaffney, Editor*.
'Yeah, Gaffy said something about it. Tell the truth, I thought
he was joking.'

'Joking?'

'We don't get many visitors from New York is all.'

I shrugged. 'We go wherever the story is.'

'The story?'

'The attacks.'

'Long way to come for a story.' He flashed a sly grin like he
knew it was bunk.

'Readers love a bogeyman,' I said. 'Long as he's on the other
side of the country. Murder sells.'

His face changed. He crossed his arms.

I held up both palms. 'No offence—'

'Word to the wise: most everyone in town knows one of
these young people.' His voice had turned gruff. 'Or their
families.'

'I didn't mean anything by it.'

He didn't flinch or move. 'This ain't about selling papers.
Not here.'

'Understood.'

He held my stare for a second, then turned around and went
back to his typewriter.

I stood there for a moment like I had my thumb up my
ass. Typewriter keys clattered all around me, and Robinson was
working at his like I'd never been there. I shook his shoulder.
'There a telephone I can use around here?'

He pointed behind without looking at me. 'Girls at reception will fix you up.'

I tramped back to the front desk wondering what the hell

his problem was. When I got there, the secretary fell over her-self to be helpful – took her all of two minutes to get me a line to New York. The telephone was on a counter behind the desk, looking out onto the main newsroom. I pressed the receiver to my ear and waited for Sal to pick up.

'*Examiner*, this is Pecorino.'

'Sal, it's me.'

'Charlie?' Static crackled down the cable. 'It's a bad line, where are you?'

'Dixie.'

'What the hell?'

'Walters sent me.'

'Nuts to that. What happened?'

'I came looking for you yesterday. Walters didn't tell you?'

'You're kidding, Walters wouldn't tell me the time right now if I asked him. I just assumed—'

'I'm someplace called Texarkana.'

Sal whistled. 'Jesus, Charlie, that somewhere past nowhere? You screwed up good this time.'

'Goddamn Texas, Sal. I'm in trouble.'

Sal chuckled to himself. 'Yeah, sounds like it. Then again, you had to see that coming, right?' He sniffed, waiting for me to disagree with him, but I couldn't. 'What story you working?'

I picked at a splinter on the wooden countertop. 'Two bod-ies in a lovers' lane last weekend.'

'Cross-country for a couple stiffs?'

'Yeah. Possible link to another murder a week before. Same thing, man and his girl in a car – except the girl survived that time. Something and nothing.'

'Sounds like a whole lot of the latter, you ask me. Dead bodies in Dixie . . .' There was a rustling sound as he changed ears, buying himself a second. 'You anywhere near New Orleans?'

'Why?'

'Just thinking out loud. You can work a voodoo slant into it, you might get it to play. Otherwise . . . I mean, what's your angle?'

'Right now, I don't know. What am I supposed to do, Sal?'

'File some copy, I guess. Better to keep Walters sweet than sit on your thumbs down there.'

'Yeah, I know it.' I turned away from the secretaries at the front desk, feeling like I had something to hide. 'Sal—'

'Here it comes.' He exhaled a deep breath.

'Hold on, would you? All I was gonna ask is you keep your ear to the ground, clue me in on what Walters is saying about me. I'm really worried, Sal.' I had a nasty sensation as I said it, the feeling like I was holding onto a ledge by my fingertips, about to fall. It was all slipping from my grip – my career, my marriage – and there wasn't a thing I could do to pull myself back up onto that ledge. Especially not stuck on the other side of the country.

Sal must have detected a note of it in my voice. 'Just work the story, you'll be back before you know it.' It was a throwaway line – no conviction in it.

I glanced out over the main newsroom. No-one was in earshot, but it felt like everyone was listening to my conversation. I tried to quash it, told myself this wasn't New York – no-one knew my business here. 'I'm serious, Sal. I think he's trying to get me to walk so he don't have to push me. Why the hell else did he send me all the way to Texas for three bodies?'

There was a pause before he said spoke again and I knew he'd been distracted by something at his end. 'You worry too much, Chuck; you're getting paranoid because you're at arm's length. Forget it – what's done is done.'

We both knew there was more to it than that. 'Look, just let me know what you hear, would you?'

He muttered something away from the receiver, his attention fully elsewhere now, then came back on the line. 'Sure, sure, Chuck. Listen, I gotta go.' He hung up.

I couldn't blame Sal if my credit line with him had run out. Already, I felt like yesterday's man.

I made my way back over towards Jimmy Robinson's desk, wondering if this town could manage a hot shower and a decent bed. When he saw me coming, he picked his hat up and jammed it onto his head. 'C'mon, I'll take you out to the scene,' he said. A changeup – the willing tour guide all of a sudden. I couldn't get a handle on the man; I wondered if he was a drinker.

'Now?'

'Before the light goes.'

'My things are in my car. And I need to get a room—'

'All taken care of,' he said, heading for the doors.

I glanced around the newsroom again, seeing maybe thirty people. The *Chronicle* was one of dozens of newspapers owned by the Greenbeck Corporation, but had almost nothing in common with the *Examiner*. The outfit in Texarkana was small, everyone on one floor; the whole operation would have fit into the canteen back home. There was a single row of rewrite men, telephone receivers jammed against one ear as they scribbled on notepads, and the rest of the desks were only half-filled – the beat writers out on the street. Size aside, it was just

like every other newspaper outfit I ever saw – cramped by nec-
essity, every man within shouting distance of the rest of the
room, the different departments arranged in rows. A factory
assembly line, churning out newspapers instead of cars. The editor's door was ajar now, and a man with a thick moustache
was watching me. Everyone else was business as usual – typewriters and telephone calls, a weird intensity, like they didn't
want to make eye contact. It felt like they were talking about
me, snatched whispers – but I nixed the thought, put it down
to being today's feature attraction. The stranger from the big
city. I buttoned my coat. 'Robinson, wait up.'

Robinson was out front climbing into a black Ford by the
time I caught him up. 'Get in,' he said, waving me over from
behind the wheel. 'And call me Jimmy.'

*

A mile outside of town, Robinson pulled off highway 82 onto
a dirt track hemmed in by trees. The sky behind us was already
getting darker, deep blues turning black, like a creeping bruise.
He followed it for a short way, then stopped in a small clearing,
turned the engine off.

I squinted through the window. 'This is the place?'

He nodded. 'Last Sunday. Sometime in the early hours.'

He climbed out and lit a cigarette. He walked a little way,
the tip of his smoke glowing in the dusk. I stepped out onto
soft mud, my heel sinking down. I stood so the car was between
us, a barrier. The temperature had dropped and I felt my skin
gooseflesh. The headlamps threw some light across the ground.

'Patty Summerbell and Edward Logan. Car was parked right

13

about where you're standing. That's where they found them.'

I sidestepped like I was standing on a grave. A bird screeched, a jagged sound in the quiet clearing, and a cold wind blew through, carrying the smell of pine and wet earth. Robinson squatted down, elbows on his knees. 'Logan was found in the front seat, and she was face down in the rear. Killer shot them both in the back of the head.'

'What were they doing out here?'

'They's courting. Lot of young folk come round here to park up together.' He flicked his smoke away into the dark and reached down, scooped up a handful of dirt. 'Didn't kill them in the car, though. Soil over here was soaked with blood. The sum'bitch shot them then stuffed them back in. Then he stuck Patty in the gut with a piece of broken glass. Three times.' He let the soil run through his fingers. 'Why'd he do that, you think?'

'I don't know. Maybe . . .'

Robinson walked behind me. I turned to face him, but he pushed me back round again.

'I mean think on it.' He put a finger to the back of my head. 'I pull you out of your car, put a gun to your head, and say, "Go".' He shoved my shoulder, motioned for me to walk in front of him. 'Go on, go.'

I started towards the patch of soil. Cold sweat trickled down my back. We walked slowly, his finger touching my skull the whole time.

'The girl's screaming, crying, begging. And Logan, he's . . . what? He's bargaining, trying to make a deal? Or is he begging too? Trying not to piss his britches?'

'What's your point, Robinson?'

'Just want your perspective, New York.'

My pulse thundered in my ears.

'Then we stop. Right here.' He leaned in close. His lips brushed my ear. 'Then . . .'

A click.

'. . . I blow your brains out.'

I jerked and spun around, heart thumping.

He was holding a revolver, but he wasn't looking at me. His eyes were glazed over, focused on something beyond the trees. The gun was by his side, pointed to the floor.

'I mean, can you imagine the terror?' he said. 'Your last seconds, stumbling in the dark, nothing but black night and screaming hell . . .' His jaw was shaking, veins popping in his neck. He looked at me. 'Eddie Logan was a war hero. Navy discharged him two months ago. Fought the Japs for his country, and this is what it got him.' He stepped closer, his hot breath on my face. 'Patty Summerbell was seventeen years old. A goddamn kid.'

I backed up, watched his hands. I felt trapped, the trees a cage.

'This ain't a story, Yates.' He hacked his throat clear, spat on the floor between us. 'This ain't filler for you sum'bitches to read over your eggs in the morning.'

'I never meant to—'

'Some goddamn madman killed our kin like dogs and he's still out there. How the hell you think that makes us feel?' His face verged on purple. His eyes glistened with tears.

'I never meant to disrespect them, Jimmy.'

He lifted the gun to his temple and pulled the trigger two, three, four times. All clicks. 'Don't worry, it's empty.'

He turned and walked back to the car.

CHAPTER TWO

We drove in silence. Adrenaline had me twitchy and raw. If there were any other way back to town I would have taken it – anything to get away from this maniac they'd saddled me with. His attitude changed as quickly as the wind, and he acted like a man stretched to breaking point. I knew the signs; I saw shadows of my own past in the way he behaved.

There was something else though. I thought I'd feel only fury, but Robinson's righteous anger hit me in the gut. The killings were strange and brutal. Homicides ran at five hundred a year in New York City. Three dead youngsters in Texarkana should be a story for the local boys – but Robinson's pain was overflowing. The people here were taking it hard; everyone I'd met so far was torn-up by this killer.

Sal was right – I couldn't see an angle to make this play in New York. But a new thought formed now: work the story anyway. Tom Walters sends me across the country just to get me out of his newsroom? To hell with him. Cover the story anyway, do it right. Those kids deserved that much.

We turned back onto the highway. Opposite the turnoff, a neon sign cut through the night, read CLUB DALLAS. The scrub lot out front was filled with cars, and music boomed from inside. The location was miles from anywhere. I wondered if Logan and Summerbell had been there on the night they died. I pulled my notebook from my pocket, scribbled the name down – call it instinct over anything concrete. Robinson didn't say anything, didn't seem to notice, eyes locked on the road ahead.

*

He stopped the car outside the *Chronicle* building just past ten o'clock. I rubbed my eyes, feeling displaced. I thought about Jane and realised it was for the first time that day. 'You said something about a room?'

Robinson motioned with his head to the building behind us. 'Reservation in your name at the Mason. Best hotel in the South.'

I nodded, an acknowledgment. I climbed out of the car, adrenaline-drained and dog tired.

Robinson leaned across the seat, the streetlight above casting his face in shadow. 'I know what you think, New York. And you're wrong. You ain't better than us. Watch yourself, hear?'

He pulled the passenger door towards him.

I grabbed it, yanked it open again. 'That a threat?'

'Friendly advice.'

I held the door, held his stare. 'Listen, I know babysitting me is the pits – I've been in your shoes, I don't want this gig any more than you do. And I'm sorry about those kids, Jimmy; no-one deserves to die like that. But don't ever pull a gun on me again.'

*

The Mason's lobby was cavernous, people milling all around – busy even at that time of night. Most of the noise came from a long bar running along the far wall to my left. I recognised a couple of faces right off: third-stringers from the *Dallas Morning News* and the *Houston Chronicle*, sipping whiskies, glad those kids got themselves killed on their side of the state line. Texas didn't pay much attention to the rest of the country, but the bodies were found in Bowie County, Texas – so the story got ink, and the boys got expense accounts.

The rest were strangers to me; drunk, talking too loud, wearing bad suits. The combination screamed amateur hour; local hacks, out of their depth even in this shallow pool. One of them was passed out on the bar, his hat flopped into the bowl of nuts next to him.

The clerk passed me a pen and a paper to sign. I scrawled my name, then followed a bellhop towards a bronze-plated elevator. Cutting across the floor, I noticed two cops had joined the crowd at the bar.

The bellhop followed my stare. 'They been here every night,' he said.

'What?'

'The law. Since the killings. They make it so all the reporters stay here, figure it's easier to keep an eye on them that way.'

'Keep an eye on them?'

'That's my guess.'

'The cops always take a keen interest in hacks round here?'

He looked at me and shrugged, then stepped into the elevator.

On the third floor, we came out into a long corridor. Somebody had spent money on the place: black marble wainscoting offsetting white marble floors; ornate ceilings and ugly chandeliers. The grandeur of the hotel was out of kilter with the town. From what I'd seen, Texarkana wasn't even half the size of Manhattan. A nowhere railroad junction that got fat on money from lumber.

My room was more of the same opulence – mauve velvet drapes and matching carpets. There was a writing desk in one corner, a walnut chest of drawers against one wall, and a picture frame above it holding a photograph. It was taken at the opening of the hotel – a man in a suit mugging for the camera as he cut a ribbon across the entrance. The caption underneath read, *Principal investor Mr. Winfield H. Callaway commemorates the grand opening of the Hotel Mason.* The bellhop placed my case at the end of the bed and offered to show me around.

'I'll figure it out.' I forked over a dollar. 'There a telephone I can use somewhere?'

'Yessir, there's a bank in the lobby. Take a left out the elevator and around the corner.'

He half-bowed and slipped out. I sat down on the edge of the bed, all the hours catching up with me. My clothes smelled of stale sweat. I loosened my tie and put my head in my hands, noticed the dirt caked on my shoes as I did. I closed my eyes and the murder scene swirled in my mind. Bloody soil in the clearing, Alice Anderson's face where Patty Summerbell's should have been – the gap-toothed kid from the photograph screaming, pleading, clawing at the red dirt—

A noise jolted me straight.

The door was open, the bellhop standing there. 'Better lock it, sir.' He stared at me, unblinking. 'Nobody knows any more.'

'Hold, please.'

The operator had said ten minutes to put me through to New York, but it had been more like thirty. I cradled the telephone and checked the clock across the lobby. The crowd at the bar was thinner than half an hour ago, but still going. Two clusters had formed, one around each cop, and the boys greased them with liquor – cats fighting for scraps. The officers soaked in the attention, took every drink that was offered.

The line buzzed into life. My pulse jumped a fraction and the booth got stuffy and close. The dialling sound droned on in my ear, and it was only then I started to get nervous, realised I hadn't even thought what to say when Jane answered. I wished I'd had one drink, enough to lift me up to that sweet spot between charming and confident.

In the end it didn't matter; the operator came back on the line, stated the obvious when she said there was no answer. I checked the clock again; eleven at night – midnight New York time. I tried not to think about where Jane might be at that time of night.

CHAPTER THREE

Banging on the door woke me the next morning. The sheets were cold on my skin and damp with sweat. I opened up, found the same bellhop from last night slouched on the other side.

'Morning, sir. Message for you from Mr Robinson at the *Chronicle*. He said to wake you.'

He handed me a note. Jagged writing, sharp angles. It read, *'Police briefing at eight this morning.'*

I glanced at my wrist; no watch – still on the bedside table. 'What's the time?'

'Just past seven, sir.'

'Police far from here?'

'Which police, sir?'

'How many are there?'

'Plenty. Texarkana-Texas City Police, Texarkana-Arkansas City Police. Bowie County Sheriff's—'

I crumpled the note. 'Wherever they brief the press.'

'That's Sheriff Bailey's office, sir. It's two blocks away, just off State Line.'

'Thanks.' I nodded and closed the door.

I went to the bathroom and splashed cold water on my face to try to wake up. Leaning on the sink, I lifted my head and caught sight of myself in the mirror, water still running off my chin. My face was carrying a week's stubble. More salt than pepper these days.

Police headquarters was a four-storey redbrick just south of the *Chronicle*. The girl at the front desk pointed me to a directory sign near the bottom of the main stairway. I traced down the list until I found Sheriff Bailey's office; on the way, my eye skimmed entries for both Texarkana City Police departments, and for Sheriff Landell of Miller County – all on different floors of the same building.

The sheriff had converted a squad room for the briefing; I smelled it before I saw it – old whiskey and cigarettes, a roomful of hacks trying to smoke away their hangovers. No-one was talking, bleary eyes trained on the doorway.

Notable by his absence was Jimmy Robinson.

There were more chairs than bodies. The smart ones had got the lowdown in the Mason's bar the night before; this crowd was young and green – too far down the food chain to get the skinny from someone else.

And me. Looking for a grounding, someplace to start.

Sheriff Bailey walked in at eight on the dot. He was big – Texas big – and flanked by two officers in a different uniform, one a head taller even than him. I recognised the light tan colours they wore, same as the police in the Mason bar the night before, but couldn't tell if it was the same men.

Bailey stood behind a desk at the front of the room. A small brass sign, which was the only adornment on it, read *'Sheriff Horace J. Bailey, Bowie County, Tx.'* He crossed his arms. 'Gentlemen, thank you for joining us this morning. From the look of some of you boys, I might say it's been a chore getting here.'

That was greeted with grunts and some shuffling paper noises.

'Alright, to business. As of this morning, Friday, we are still actively pursuing all leads in the search for the killer, or killers, of Patricia Summerbell and Edward Logan both late of Texarkana, found murdered Sunday last on a dirt track off of highway 82. Y'all know there's limits to how much we can share with folks right now, but I can say we're holding a number of men for questioning...'

A look passed between Bailey and the other two officers.

'... and with the full co-operation of Sheriff Landell's office, we are tracking further persons of interest in the Miller County area.'

From the middle row: 'In other words, same old, same old.' Laughter passed around the room.

Bailey was stony-faced. 'On the record: we are making good progress and we are damn sure gonna get our man.' He sidled over to where the hack with the big mouth sat, put his boot on the man's chair and leaned over his knee. 'Off the record: buckle your mouth.'

The room held its breath. The hack pulled back, slouched low in his chair. The two officers at the front smirked. The taller one cracked his knuckles.

Bailey just stared. The silence dragged. Even the smoke seemed to hang still.

The hack's eyes darted around the scuffed beige walls, trying to land anywhere but on the sheriff.

Finally Bailey straightened again. A low grunt came from the back of his throat: 'Good.' Then he turned, walked back to the front and re-took his position behind the plaque. 'Y'all have questions?'

Hesitation. Eventually a hand went up in the corner – slow, uncertain. 'What can you tell us about the men you're holding?'

'They all from Texarkana.'

'Can you give us some names?'

Bailey glared at the man. 'You know I can't, son.'

'At least what led you to them?'

Bailey: 'Police work.'

Another hand went up. 'Some people saying this man could be a drifter, left town after the killing – can you comment to that, Sheriff?'

'If we don't already have this man in our cells – and, son, you write down that *if* – then there ain't no sense in denying it's possible. Because if he ain't cleared out already, then we'll have him presently. Ain't nowhere to hide in Texarkana.' Bailey took his hat off and flattened his thin grey hair. 'But if he's running, make no mistake: ain't the same as getting away.'

I jumped in then. Three pairs of eyes flicked to me as soon as I opened my mouth. 'Sheriff, can I confirm you're hunting the same man for the attack the weekend prior?' I skimmed my notes. 'On Dwight Breems and Alice Anderson?'

The tallest cop cupped a hand to Bailey's ear and whispered something. Bailey's expression didn't change. He licked his lips. 'Accent like that, you gotta be Mr Yates from New York City.'

Someone was talking about me. Figure word had got around because I'd come all the way from the big city – but still, it felt strange to be newsworthy. 'That's right.' Two reporters from the row in front looked at me over their shoulders.

Bailey fixed me with a stare. 'Mmm-hmmm.'

I waited for him to answer my question. More heads turned as the silence dragged. I held his gaze; for a second it felt like I was behind bars in a cell.

'Ain't no evidence to link the two,' Bailey said.

'The stories I saw on the newswires suggest there are circumstantial similarities—'

'I hope you ain't expecting me to repeat myself, Mr Yates.' He looked away, pointed to another raised hand.

I spoke first. 'If this man's still on the loose, isn't there a chance he could strike again?'

Bailey glared at me. I watched his face; the room was hot and close, cigarette smoke cloying in my throat. I forced myself not to tug at my collar, but when I shifted in my seat Bailey took it as me blinking first. 'I ain't gonna speculate on the mind of a killer, Mr Yates.' He dropped a hand to the holster on his hip. 'But I will say this . . .' He ran a finger over the butt of his revolver. 'He'd be a damn fool to try.'

*

The briefing broke up shortly afterwards. Bailey waved his arm to signal the finish, then led the other two officers out the door without saying another word.

When I got outside

uncrossed his arms as I approached. 'Jack Sherman, Mr Yates. Texarkana City Police.'

I shook his hand. 'Officer.'

'Lieutenant.'

'What can I do for you, Lieutenant?'

'New in town, right?'

'Arrived yesterday.' I put my hands in my pockets. 'But you knew that already.'

'That's right.'

'Did I see you at the Hotel Mason last night?'

He nodded, looking past me, down the street. 'That was me.' He looked away, talked out of the corner of his mouth. 'That stunt you pulled with the Sheriff just now.'

'What stunt?'

'Talking about more killings.'

'It's a fair question.'

'It's reckless to excite folk with that kind of talk. I don't want to hear it being advanced around town.'

'Because it's a possibility?'

He turned his head, looked me over like he was examining rancid meat. 'Right there's why the Sheriff don't like reporters. You twist people's words.'

'I've asked twice and I still haven't got a straight answer.'

e was . . . ' know this town, Yates.' He spoke slowly, like
ings don already ds one at a time. 'I ain't saying bad
ough You're worried is different. Folk here's scared
I'm talking about ... you've g   ng them up.'
f you're sure you've g

He took my tie in his hands and adjusted it slowly until it was flush with my throat. 'Report what the Sheriff tells you.' His breath smelled of tobacco juice and there was brown saliva on his teeth. 'Report *only* what the Sheriff tells you.' He clapped me on the shoulder, big hands like catcher's mitts. 'Understand?'

I said nothing, seething on the inside but knowing better than to argue with him. Sherman straightened his hat and took off back towards the police building. The sun had disappeared behind a grey cloud, taking all warmth with it. I hooked my finger under my collar, pulled it away from my neck. A half-grin formed on my lips. First Robinson acting weird, now Sherman trying to warn me off. Could be there was a story here after all.

CHAPTER FOUR

I walked back to the *Chronicle* building, Sherman's voice still rattling around my head. The sidewalks were busy, filled with GIs in green uniforms, tote bags slung over their shoulders. Texarkana: another transfer point on the journey home. Seeing them took me back; to forty-two, troop ships docked at piers in Brooklyn and Manhattan, gung-ho crowds giving the boys a roaring send-off, the silent tears the real story, almost too hard to write. Now, four years and a thousand miles away, I saw the circle complete. Some of the men were delirious, de-mob joyous. One group ran along the street playing horse, whooping, carrying each other on their backs and passing a bottle of bourbon. Another GI trailed behind them looking punch drunk. A big man with a child's features – a country kid heading back to Oklahoma or Texas. He had the same face I'd seen time and again: weary grey, the dark circles under his eyes no disguise for the horror they held.

A thought hit me, spiked with guilt even as it formed: *What if it was one of them?* No telling what these men had seen and endured. It wasn't a stretch to imagine an unhinged GI who got too used to killing, the power in holding a gun too potent for him to put it down for keeps.

*

28

Robinson wasn't at the *Chronicle*. The girl at the front desk said he hadn't been in all morning. I went through to the office anyway, looking for McGaffney, the editor. The noise level dropped a peg when I walked in, and a group standing around a table in the far corner all looked up and stared at me.

McGaffney's door was shut. I could see two silhouettes behind the frosted glass. A woman was talking – animated, but not shouting; I only made out one word – 'Robinson'.

The glass pane rattled when I knocked. A man to my left said, 'He's busy.' The voices inside stopped. I reached for the knob, but the door flew open. A redhead with eyes the colour of emeralds barged past me, her hat under her arm. I did a double-take – she had a resemblance to the victim in the photograph, Alice Anderson.

She stopped and turned back towards the office. She was raging, her cheeks red. 'You can't treat people this way.'

McGaffney held his hands up to pacify her. 'You have my sympathies, but we got a job to do. We working at the behest of the police—'

'Behest? I'd say in cahoots.'

'Ain't that way.'

She closed her eyes and composed herself. 'I'm asking you as politely as I can stomach: please keep that man away from her. It benefits no-one.'

He frowned, his stare never leaving the redhead. 'Do what I can.'

'It's not right, Mr McGaffney. You know it's not right.' She stalked off towards the street.

McGaffney was behind his desk, his hands flat on the

tabletop now. When the woman left, his eyes flicked to me, the rest of him unmoving.

'We haven't met yet. Charlie Yates.' I stepped into the office and stood behind the chair opposite him. The room was hot, smelled of ink and cigar smoke. An ashtray on the desk held two dead stogies.

'Know who you are,' McGaffney said.

'Okay.' I coughed, clearing my throat. 'Know where I can find Robinson? He sent me to a briefing this morning but didn't show.'

McGaffney grunted. 'Heard you went along. Careful vexing Bailey's boys like that.'

'News travels fast here. The Sheriff doesn't like reporters, huh?'

'Likes us just fine.' McGaffney stared at me.

I sat down and he frowned. 'I had some questions.' I took out my notepad. 'You mind?'

McGaffney inclined his head to one side. 'Tom Walters asked you be extended every courtesy.'

The idea of it brought a doubtful smile to my face. 'That how he put it when he got in contact?'

'Nope.' He laced his fingers. 'Your Mr Walters got himself some powerful friends with the Greenbeck people. Made that much clear, didn't need to sugar it none beyond that.'

I could picture Walters brow-beating McGaffney, flaunting his connections with the high-ups. A thought crossed my mind: how much did he tell McGaffney about me? I shook it off, turned to a fresh page in my pad and took the top off my pen. 'Sheriff Bailey thinks you're dealing with separate incidents here. That's not how it reads to me.

Chronicle's close to this, what's your take?'

McGaffney leaned back in his chair and searched the ceiling.

'McGaffney?'

'Sheriff's office isn't linking the two. Not for me to say otherwise.'

'But there are similarities.'

'Some. Differences too.'

'Because the killer let the Anderson girl live?'

McGaffney shook his head. 'Sheriff doesn't want folk jumping to conclusions. They overrun with "tips" already. Last thing they need is people's imaginations running away with themselves.'

'What happened to her out there?'

'You seem plenty informed already.'

'I read what I could before I came down, but the wire stories were short on detail, though. Figure you can fill in the blanks.'

He took a deep breath, then blew it out, puffed his cheeks. 'Alice Rose Anderson and Dwight Breems. Friends saying she been sweet on him a couple months. Courting. Attacker ambushed them when they were parked out near New Boston Road. All the young'uns go out there.' He picked up a pen and tapped it against his thumb as he spoke. 'Best the police could get from the girl, they's in the front seat, fooling around, when this flashlight beam comes through the window. Blinds them. Then she sees him, the killer. Wishes she didn't. He's got on this white hood.' McGaffney gestured at his eyes with the pen. 'Two holes to see through.' He put the pen down, took a long breath. 'He smashes the window with a gun, tells them to get

31

out or he'll kill them. She's screaming now, don't remember too much after that. Covered in glass.'

I scribbled notes as he spoke.

'Breems, he gets out of the car, forks over his billfold, but this maniac pistol whips him.' McGaffney held a finger against his forehead. 'Fractured his skull in three places. The girl heard it so loud, she thought it was gunshots. Next thing she knows, sum'bitch drags her out the car and tells her he's gonna kill her too. Tells her to run. She don't move, so he sticks her in the gut . . .' He tapped a spot just under his ribs. 'She thought it was a knife, but the docs say it was glass. From the window.' McGaffney locked his eyes on mine as he said it. 'Hell of a thing, ain't it?'

A similarity to Logan and Summerbell – Patty stabbed in the stomach three times after she'd been shot. An image of Alice Anderson formed, her dress torn and bloody. I blinked, willed it away.

'So she takes off, blood pouring out of her gut. He's behind her – she thinks; she's so scared she can't hardly see – but she makes it back to the road and flags down a car. Driver damn near runs her down. He picks her up, takes her to the hospital. Says he didn't see no-one else.'

McGaffney watched my face when he finished. His moustache was black and bushy, worked with the lines around his eyes to give him the look of an old gunslinger.

I met his stare and tried to figure why he was lying to me. The story was too slick, like a speech he'd rehearsed. His face said that was all I was getting.

'I want to speak with her. Miss Anderson,' I said.

He rubbed his face. 'Can't. She's in Pine Street Hospital and she's been sedated ever since it happened. When she's awake, she's either screaming or talking gibberish.'

'I'd like to see her anyway.'

He shrugged. 'Ask the Sheriff's office. They'll tell you the same.'

'What about the driver who picked her up? Got a name?'

'Police already talked to him.'

I held my pen over my pad, waiting.

McGaffney picked at a hangnail. 'Likesay, he didn't see nothing.'

'I'll get it from the write-up. How about you make it easy for me?'

He stood and walked to the window. He cracked two of the blinds apart, gazed out at the street. 'We done here, Mr Yates. Jimmy'll help you, anything else you need.'

'You know where I can find him at?'

'He's out on a story.'

I smiled at the brush-off and flipped my pad shut, got up to leave. At the door, I turned back. 'What did you do to upset that redhead was in here before?'

He picked up the telephone and dialled a number as if I wasn't there.

*

Wendell's coffee shop was close to full. I ordered a cup at the counter, feeling grease on the surface under my fingers, and listened to the conversations swirl around me, loud enough that they all but drowned out the Wurlitzer in the corner. Five days on from Logan and Summerbell, it was clear the locals

33

were deep in shock still, and the murders were the main topic of conversation. People talked over each other.

I took in the array of faces. Seemed like no-one would meet my eyes – but then why would they think to? I was a stranger in a place full of people who knew each other at least enough to chew the fat with. I couldn't see the waitress from the day before. Didn't matter; eavesdropping for ten minutes had told me everyone was saying the same as her.

My last glance around the room, I noticed a face along the counter from me, been watching me the whole time. A kid, dark bruises around his eyes. His bottom lip was busted up. He had a military cut. He had a fork in his hand, hadn't touched the plate of biscuits and gravy in front of him.

I watched him watch me. His mouth moved like he was talking to himself. I slipped off my seat, started towards him. The kid worked his jaw, still watching me.

Then conversations around the room stopped. Heads turned one after the other, all looking in the same direction – behind me. The redhead I'd seen at McGaffney's office walked up to the counter, ignoring the looks, eyes straight ahead. Everyone watched, the atmosphere suddenly tense. She set her bag down in front of the counterman, gripped it with both hands. 'Martha working today?' Her voice carried around the now-silent room.

The counterman shook his head. 'Not today.' I made the connection in my head – *Martha*, the name badge on the waitress I was looking for, from the day before.

The redhead glanced around the room, unsure. 'Kindly tell her I stopped by?' She leaned over the counter, spoke so soft I almost missed it. 'And to keep her gossip to herself.'

The fat manager raised himself upright. 'Lizzie, now—'

'Don't "Lizzie" me. Where're your manners?'

The counterman gritted his teeth, the muscles in his face and neck tensing. I shot him a look as a warning not to lose his cool, shifting my weight so I could slip off the stool quicker if need be. He glanced at me and then back to the redhead. 'I'll talk to her some, but this ain't Russia. She's free to speak her mind.'

'Yes she is. But she doesn't know anything, so my advice would be she save her breath.' She turned away from him, caught my eye as she did. For a moment I thought she recognised me; she looked about to say something, a hesitation that passed in a heartbeat. Then she made for the door.

The room breathed again when she left. The manager was leaning on the counter, on his fists. I snatched some coins from my pocket and dumped them on the counter, then rushed out after the woman. In the doorway I stopped, checked back. The kid with the bruised face was gone.

*

'Ma'am—'

The redhead ignored me and kept walking. She wore a fitted skirt that finished just below her knees and made her take clipped steps, her hair bobbing in time as she went. Two GIs wolf-whistled as she passed them, their heads swivelling to watch her go. She flat ignored them – the exact same thing Jane would have done, even though she'd be mad inside. Thinking about Jane like that, the way she kept her dignity in every circumstance, made me yearn for her. If we could talk, if I could just find the words . . .

I caught up to the redhead. 'Ma'am, can I speak to you?'

She fixed me with a look. She was short, not much over five feet, but the rage from inside of her was almost tangible. 'Have we met?'

I dangled the bait. 'My name's Charlie Yates. I'm a reporter.'

'I'm through with reporters, Mr Yates.' She said it stony-faced.

'I understand.' She tried to speak but I cut her off. 'I don't like Mr McGaffney either.'

Her lips moved, but no sound came. Her eyes narrowed, re-membering me now. 'You were outside his office before.'

I nodded. 'Sounded like you were giving him a pretty hard time. Mind if I ask what about?'

'I don't see what business it is of yours.'

'I didn't mean anything by it, ma'am. I'm new in town and it's my job to be curious, is all.'

'Your accent, where are you from?'

'New York City. Here on account of the killings.'

'You and everyone else, Mr Yates. I've got nothing else to say on the subject. Mr McGaffney will attest to that much at least.'

'I don't work for him. I'm from the *Examiner*. Maybe we do things a little differently where I come from. Would you con-sider talking to me about what's happening here? Seems like you'd give me a straight answer to a straight question.'

She looked up and down the street. 'I told you, I'm done with reporters.' She turned and walked.

In desperation, I asked, 'You look like Alice Anderson. Is she family to you, ma'am?'

She stopped, handbag dangling loose at her side.

'I want to help,' I said. It sounded small.

She turned and there were tears welling in her eyes. She looked at me for a long moment, as if she was reconsidering, or at least about to say something. Then she clamped her handbag under her arm and stormed off.

I was left stood there in the street, looking like the goose at the dance without a partner. I lifted my hat and flattened my hair, trying to figure my next move. The people here reminded me of Chicago, a place I'd learnt, first-hand, that no-one talks to outsiders. Everything I'd seen told me there was an undercurrent, something more going on than two random attacks. The problem was how to get through to that when nobody in the damn town would talk to me.

I decided the only way forward was to get back to the facts. Start there, then try to turn up some sources – even if that meant leaning on some parties who didn't want to talk.

CHAPTER FIVE

I set about the background work that afternoon. I called the *Chronicle* from a payphone, got a blank on Robinson. 'Haven't seen him all day, sir.' I checked for messages at the Mason: another blank.

The public library was four blocks east of the *Chronicle*. The building was new, looked no more than a dozen years old; since the New Deal, seemed like every town had built its own library, and they all looked the same. I passed the hospital on the way, the same image of Alice Anderson coming back to me, running in the dark, blood pouring from her stomach.

It stayed with me, getting more vivid as I read through the *Chronicle* reports on the two sets of attacks. They tallied with Robinson and McGaffney's versions; both were light on detail.

The first attack got two columns in the gutter of page four. There was a small picture of Alice Anderson, same as the one I'd picked up on the newswires, but no quotes. The driver who found her wasn't named. A follow-up article two days later noted that Dwight Breems had been taken to Pine Street Hospital, but, by morning, had been declared dead from his injuries – among them, a fractured skull and a gunshot wound to the side of his head. Doctors had said it was a miracle he survived as long as he did.

The Logan-Summerbell murders were real news and made the front page, underneath a story about the Russians plotting to steal A-bomb secrets. The two victims were pictured; Logan had short wavy hair and a face that never grew out of its puppy fat. The picture of Patty Summerbell was grainy, maybe a couple years out of date. It showed her sitting outside a house on a small set of steps, stroking a dog. She was smiling, looking right at the camera. She had long, curly dark hair and a bright face. There was no mention of the other attack in the article.

I checked the Dallas papers, got more of the same. Lieutenant Jack Sherman: doing a fine job of keeping everyone in line.

*

Friday night at the Hotel Mason: venue of choice for Texarkana's great and good. Men in suits and western shirts, women in pearls, swishing through on their way to one of the hotel's three restaurants. An unseen pianist played a grand piano in the far corner, the tune lost in the conversations echoing around the lobby.

I searched the bar for a friendly face. Peyton Reed from the *Dallas Bugle* was the closest thing to it, sitting at a table off to one side. I knew him from when we worked at the *Tribune* together in Chicago – two outsiders in a closed town. Me a California boy, using the Windy City as a stepping stone as I tried to claw my way up to New York and the big league; him a Texas native who'd moved around the country with Army parents, and stayed in the Midwest for journalism school. Reed was drinking a glass of beer with a man I didn't know. I ordered three whiskies at the bar, carried them over and set them in front of him. 'You quit drinking or something, Peyton?'

He looked up. 'Goddamn. Charlie Yates. I thought the

Examiner benched you for good.' He stood and shook my hand, gestured to the other man. 'You know Ron Gentry from the *Advocate*?'

I said no and shook his hand too, reeling a little from Reed's snipe. Sal had a line about there being three ways to spread a message quickly – '*Telephone, telegraph, tell a hack*'; even so, I was surprised that word of my disgrace had made it this far along the trenches already. 'How long you been in town?' I said to Reed, trying to keep my voice level.

'Couple days. Came over when them bodies fetched up last weekend. Ugly business.' He shook his head and lifted a whiskey, raised the glass to me and took a sip. 'What brings you to these parts?'

'"Roving National Correspondent",' I said. It was the made-up title Tom Walters had mockingly given me in his memorandum, now repeated like a justification. 'My beat's everywhere.' Reed opened his mouth but didn't say anything – wet lips hanging ajar like he was about to speak but thought better of it. Whatever he'd heard about me, he didn't want to ask. And that suited me just fine.

We sat down. 'Didn't see you at the Sheriff's briefing this morning,' I said. The ice in my drink rattled as I put it on the table.

'No need. They been saying the same things for three days now; they playing their cards real close to their chest.' Reed said. He took a drink, touching his throat as the whiskey slipped down. 'Sheriff's a piece of work though, ain't he?'

Gentry pulled his chair closer. 'You know the line on Bailey?' I shook my head. 'Story goes he was the only man from his company made it back from the first war. Took a bullet in the shoulder over there, didn't even drop his gun. Don't come no tougher than him.'

Reed dabbed his mouth with a napkin, picked up the story. 'They say he didn't want to come back. Had to drag him kicking and screaming onto the troop ship. He wanted to keep fighting – go kill him some Reds there in Russia.'

'Tell you that tale himself?'

'Naw,' Reed said. 'It's three bullets when he tells the story.' Gentry laughed, playing his part in the double act. Reed caught my frown. 'Don't discount him, Charlie. He's a showman, and he likes to run his mouth, but he's a damn fine investigator. Cracked the Trenton case back in forty-three.'

'Bailey talks a good game,' I said. 'He got a description of who he's looking for?'

Reed blew a breath out the corner of his mouth. 'Nothing that's gonna help much. Only person can speak to it is the girl that survived.'

'Alice Anderson.'

'Mmm-hmm.'

'You think they're looking for the same man for Logan and Summerbell then.'

He chewed the inside of his cheek, showing no expression. 'I'm doing like the Sheriff said and keeping an open mind.'

'You asked him about it?'

He shook his head. 'Not me, one of the boys out of Fort Worth. Couple of briefings back. When he kept pressing, Bailey took him to the woodshed for it – called him an amateur for "arriving at conclusions the evidence don't support". Threatened to bar him from the building.'

'So we're all supposed to just toe the line now?'

'You want in on the briefings, what else you gonna do?'

I scoffed, shaking my head. 'So what about the Anderson girl? I heard she wasn't talking.'

'Sheriff's office told us she wouldn't stop when they first got to her, at Pine Street Hospital – the shock I suppose. Didn't tell them nothing useful, though.' Reed focused on a spot above my head, like he was recounting verbatim. 'A tall man, taller than her fella, who was six foot himself; light shirt, dark pants – maybe blue, couldn't tell on account of it being night – and a hood over his head.'

'She say if he was white or black even?'

Reed hesitated, looked at Gentry. 'No . . .'

I looked at each of them in turn. 'What?'

'Just rumours,' Gentry said. He made a show of studying the crowd.

'Peyton?'

Reed lit a cigarette and pulled hard on it. Smoke billowed as he spoke. 'Word came out she thought the fella was white, but couldn't be sure. Sheriff's office scotched it in the last briefing – told us she never said no such thing.'

'Who spoke to her at the hospital? Took the description?'

Reed pointed at me. 'This turning into an interview now, Charlie?'

I grinned, held up empty hands – look, no notes. 'Just playing catch-up.'

'Don't shit me.'

'Come on, Peyton, spill . . .'

Reed finished his drink and set the tumbler down. Then he shrugged – the booze loosening his tongue. 'City cop got to her first, name of Jack—'

'Sherman?' I said.

Reed nodded. 'You meet him this morning too?'

'In a manner of speaking.'

Gentry whistled. 'Sherman's a hoss.'

'Tells me he's been in here some,' I said. 'You on terms with him?'

Reed shook his head. 'Jack is Bailey's enforcer.'

I noted he referred to him as 'Jack' instead of 'Sherman'. 'How's that work? They're different forces, right?'

Reed shook his head again. 'In name is all. Ward Mills is Chief of the Texas-side City Police, and him and Bailey go all the way back. Jack might as well work for Bailey.'

'You got a source inside the department?'

Reed played with the end of his tie, smirking. 'Settle down, Charlie. Think I'm gonna just give that up?'

The bluff was an easy read: no source. 'What about the Anderson girl – anyone talked to her yet?'

Reed dangled his empty glass in front of me. I signalled the barman for three more. 'Not yet,' Reed said. 'And you can bet the *Chronicle* boys will get the first go around anyhow.'

'Won't make no odds,' Gentry said. We both turned to him. 'Not if she's lost her mind for keeps.'

Reed pulled a face was like he'd smelled a backed-up sewer. 'Ron . . .'

'Can't discount the possibility. All I'm saying.' Gentry crossed his legs and angled himself away from the table.

The barman came over with a tray and placed a glass in front of each us. I took a slug, leaned in close. 'Look, Peyton, I know this is rough, but . . . was she violated?' A hunch on the part of the story that McGaffney left out.

43

Gentry put his glass down without taking a sip. I felt him watching the side of my face. Reed's eyes narrowed. 'Where'd you hear that?'

'Just reading between the lines. Seems like the whole town's talking about it without saying it.'

'Be careful listening to scuttlebutt, Charlie.'

'Second time I've heard that advice today.' Definitely closer to Jack Sherman than he'd let on.

'Lot of loose lips around here,' Reed said, 'but most of them don't know nothing. So they make it up, just to have something to say.'

'So you're saying she wasn't?'

'Don't be a fool. You want to write speculation and rumours, go ahead – but you ain't gonna hear it from me.' Reed sank the rest of his drink, looking at me over the rim of his glass. Cogs turning behind his eyes. Wondering if I was the lunatic he'd heard I was, about to spout off in print.

Gentry got up and muttered he was going to find a bathroom. He walked straight to the bar. I turned back to Reed. 'I just want to know what's going on here.'

'Look past your notepad, Charlie. There's bigger concerns at play.'

'I know that—'

'Police are getting calls every day from fools claiming to be the killer. They got to keep some details back to separate the crazies out from the real thing.'

'This isn't about what I write. You know I'd never put something like that in print.' Reed took a drag and blew smoke at the ceiling. It coalesced in the light from the chandelier high above. I pinched the bridge of my nose, tried

44

another tack. 'You speak to the families?'

Reed stabbed his cigarette out in the ashtray. His face was flush from the drink. 'Too many questions, Charlie. Go ask the Sheriff's office.'

I smiled and leaned back in my seat. 'I already tried.'

Reed ran his finger around the rim of his glass. 'And he told you to go hang, that about it?'

I swirled my drink, nodded. 'Not in so many words.'

'So do me a favour and leave me out of it, huh? Trust me when I say you don't want to screw with Bailey and his boys.'

He made to stand up. I put a hand on his arm. 'Why?'

He looked down at my hand, then brushed it off like he was flicking lint off his jacket. 'This ain't New York, Charlie. You're not protected down here, so think on that before you go off half-cocked again, right?'

'That a shot at me, Peyton?'

He leaned over the table towards me. 'Take it any way you like. But you can't go around smashing things up down here if you don't get your own way.'

I fumbled for some words but couldn't get anything out. He was telling me he knew the full scoop on me – or at least enough of the detail to embarrass me. Reed got to his feet, already scanning the room like he was checking who might have seen us together. 'Appreciate the drink. I'll see you around.'

I leaned back in my chair and rubbed my neck, watching Reed blend into the crowd. I was surprised he'd heard about my trouble, but he'd touched a nerve. It felt like everyone in town was talking about me. Jane would have just laughed at me, chastised me for the scale of my ego. She was good at keeping me level; when I was low when things had started to go south at the *Examiner* with Walters, she reminded me that most of the world didn't care a dime about Charlie Yates's business, and there was comfort in remembering those words now. I pushed the rest of my drink away, determined not to slip into feeling sorry for myself.

I took myself back to my room. It was almost eleven but I wasn't tired. I sat down at the desk in the corner and set about writing: names, dates, who I'd spoken to, what they said. My impressions – were they hiding something? Holding back? Flat-out lying to me?

I got it all down; it helped organise my thoughts. I filled up a dozen pages and kept going. I noted the facts I'd culled from the newspaper accounts, and the parts that were missing. The big question mark – Alice Anderson; what had she told police after the attack? Reed had supplied some gossip and quashed it just as fast, and the papers had no quotes from her. I remembered what I'd said earlier, wrote the words in capitals: GO BACK TO THE FACTS.

I kept writing until I was seeing double on the page. I passed out with my head on the desktop.

CHAPTER SIX

It was bright and cool again the next morning. Pine Street Hospital was a brilliant white in the low sun, the roof's gothic tower standing in stark relief against a perfect blue sky.

Alice Anderson's room wasn't hard to find – she was the only patient with a cop by her door. He had the same City Police uniform as Jack Sherman. I figured my press credentials wouldn't get me in, so I took a seat at the other end of the corridor and waited. An hour passed, but when the cop folded up his newspaper and walked off, I tapped on the door and slipped inside her room.

I stopped cold in the doorway. The redhead I'd seen at McGaffney's office and the diner was lying in the bed.

The air in the room was close and pungent with the scent of flowers, like a hothouse. The blinds were pulled, but it was light enough to see. I took a half-step closer and she turned her head and looked at me, showing no emotion. I realised it wasn't the same woman – but the two had to be sisters. The hair and eyes were the same, but Alice's face was rounder, softer. She looked tired and beat-up, but was beautiful nonetheless. I held my palms out in front of me to signal I meant no harm. 'Miss Anderson, I don't mean to alarm you.' I tried out a small lie. 'My name is Charlie Yates; I'm a friend of Lizzie's.' I stood still to make it clear I wasn't coming any closer.

She watched me, blank, like a child staring at the rain.

'I'm sorry to intrude, ma'am, but I just want to ask you a couple questions. Is there anything I can get you? Some water?'

She looked me up and down, only her eyes moving.

'I'm very sorry for what happened to you. I want to help find the man who did it.'

She moved her head again and stared at the ceiling. 'I know who you are.' Her voice was quiet but strong. 'Y'all look the same. Where's your star?'

'Ma'am?'

'You're just like all them others. Questions, questions. Always been questions, why you only asking them now?'

I stared at her, wondering if she was even talking to me. 'Which questions, ma'am?'

'Maybe I'm the one should be doing the asking. Who do you know and why did you go? What's your damn answer?' She ran her nails down her face, leaving red trails on her skin. Then she looked at me again. 'Tell us the truth, or by God you'll regret it, Alice Rose. What's his name?' She thrashed her arms about, tearing her sheet from the bed. 'What's his goddamn name?'

I didn't understand. I turned to go get a doctor, unsure what was happening to her. She slapped the bed with the flat of her hand. 'Where're you going?' Two strands of lank red hair were stuck to her face with sweat, laying across her eyes. She didn't do anything to move them. 'You the one with the star, tell me what it means.'

'Ma'am, I'm sorry to have distressed you. I wanted to speak to you about what happened that—'

'I already told you I don't know anything.'

'Please, Miss Anderson. I only came here to ask you one question.'

She looked at me and her breathing slowed. When she spoke again there was a new focus about her – like she was talking to me properly for the first time. 'So ask.'

I stared at the floor and took a breath before I spoke. 'Can you tell me anything about the man who attacked you? What he sounded like, how tall he was – anything at all?'

'I told you last time, I don't remember anything about him.'

'*Last time*' – I let it go. 'Can you tell me where his accent was from? Did he sound like he's from Texarkana?'

'I don't know him. I ain't never in my life seen him before; I swear to you, if I walked past him in the street I couldn't pick him out. On my Bible.'

'Could you tell if he was a white man?'

She covered her face and started to sob. She rolled away from me on the bed, gingerly, her legs barely shifting. Her body shook but no sounds came from her. A breeze somewhere moved the blinds, casting bars of light and shadow across her body. It felt like she was re-living a conversation we'd never had, and I wondered how much of Alice Anderson really survived the attack. I mumbled an apology and readied to leave. 'Ma'am, I'm sorry for having disturbed you. I won't do it again, but I want you to know I'm going to do everything to find the man who did this.'

She'd stopped shaking, and I figured she'd fallen asleep; but then she spoke again. 'You mean that?'

'Yes, ma'am.'

She was silent for a beat, then said, 'It's more than them other cops ever say. All they do is yell at me; they of a mind I brought this on myself. You think that's so?'

I wanted to put a hand on her back, some small gesture to

49

comfort her, but I didn't know how she'd react. I stayed where I was. 'No. And you mustn't think that way.'

'Maybe they's right. Momma always said not to park up with boys. Be back by curfew—'

'Miss Anderson, this isn't your fault. Nothing you did makes you deserve this.'

'You talk like Lizzie. She said that same thing, but it ain't change nothing, does it? Ain't bringing Dwight back.'

With everything she'd been through, I hadn't even thought about the sense of loss she must be enduring. 'Ma'am—'

'Name's Charlie Yates, you say?'

'That's right.'

'Did you fight in the war, Charlie Yates?'

I looked at the floor. Asking me the question I hated the most. The one I never had a satisfactory answer for. The one that made my insides burn with shame. 'No.'

'I met a soldier one time, and he told me he saw his best friend shot right there in front of him. Told me they rolled into this village in France that was supposed to be full of Nazis, but it was empty by the time they got there. He said they were standing outside this pile of rubble used to be a house; one second they were joking around, the next his friend was dead. He said the man must have died straightaway because he still had the smile on his face when he fell over. Didn't even have time to know what was happening to him. I thought he was telling me tales because we were on a date, and I knew he wanted to fool around with me some, later on. But I looked over at him, and he was crying. I didn't know what to say, so I went to find my friends, and after that he didn't say another word about it. I didn't know no better then, but now I do. He was seeing his friend get shot, over and over. Asleep and awake, didn't make no difference.' She rolled over and looked at me again, hair still plastered to her face. Her eyes were half closed and her voice was quieter. 'You think dying's the worst thing can happen to a man, Mr Yates. But you're wrong.' She held my stare a moment longer then closed her eyes.

I opened the door a crack and caught a break; the cop outside was talking to a nurse, his back to me. I slipped through the doorway and down the hall.

CHAPTER SEVEN

That afternoon was a bust. Mrs Summerbell hung up on me when I reached her at home on the telephone, so I drove to her house anyway to see if she might discuss what happened to her daughter with me. On the way, I noticed the same green Plymouth coupe in my rearview three times. I wondered if my mind was playing tricks on me, but the left end of the fender was mangled and pointed to the road – had to be the same car. I looked around for it again when I pulled up in front of the Summerbell house, but it was gone.

Mrs Summerbell opened the door when I knocked, but as soon as she got wind of who I was, she slammed it in my face. It was pretty much what I expected, so I'd already scribbled out a note with my contact details and a reassurance about my bona fides to leave behind. As I tucked it under her doormat, she leaned out of an upstairs window.

'I'm so tired of talking to journalists.' Her eyes were damp. I noticed she had the same curly dark hair as her daughter. 'Patty was my whole world, can't you understand that?'

I looked up at her, the sunlight like a flashlight beam pointed in my eyes. 'Ma'am, I'm sorry for your loss—'

'Don't say that. You didn't know her, please don't cheapen her memory with condolences.'

I looked away, the glare still in my vision as a green shadow. I started to say I was sorry again, thought better of it.

'Talking to you about all those horrible things isn't going to bring her back to me,' she said. 'Would you please just leave us alone?' She shut the window with a loud clap.

I stepped back from the house, down the three small steps leading up to the door. Looking again, I realised it was where Patty had been sitting, stroking her dog, in the photograph I'd seen in the paper. I looked around the small yard, saw it was overgrown in places.

I went back up the steps and picked up my note, crumpled it and put it in my pocket.

*

That night I took a drive out to Club Dallas. It was a week on from the night that Logan and Summerbell were killed, so I wanted to canvas the place, see if I could find anyone who'd been there the previous Saturday and jog their memory.

It was past ten when I pulled onto highway 82. A gentle rain fell as I drove, my headlamps illuminating the drops like lightning bugs in the night. The road was quiet, just one car a distance behind me all the way, visible only as a pair of high beams in my rearview.

Club Dallas was a low, blocky concrete building with a Roman-style carport over the front entrance and a small tower rising above it, the name wrapped around it in red letters. The hardscrabble parking lot was more than half full – Chryslers, Packards and Buicks, most sporting gleaming whitewall rims and freshly-buffed chrome; swell rides to impress a sweetheart.

I parked in the nearest spot to the entrance and went to go

inside. A Plymouth pulled in off the highway as I did, and I stopped and watched, struck by the fact it looked like the one I'd seen around town earlier on. It cruised to the far end of the lot, away from where everyone else was parked, and stopped there. At that distance in the dark, I couldn't be sure it was the same one. The car sat idling, the driver never climbing out. The rain was coming down harder now; I looked back one more time, then walked into the club.

The interior was dark and filled with cigarette smoke. There was a large wooden dance floor, tables set around the outside and booths along the walls. A band was arranged in two rows on the stage, brass players at the front behind black music-stands. They looked like they were fresh out of high school. A handful of couples were dancing, some kind of local variation on the Lindy Hop. Most of the men wore GI green.

I ordered a whiskey at the bar at the back. The bartender wore a black waistcoat and matching bowtie, but the cuffs of his shirt were frayed – a swing and a miss at adding a layer of class to the joint. The whiskey had been watered-down in the bottle. I sank it and put the glass on top of a dollar bill, then nodded for another. The bartender poured, looking at the money then at me. He reached for the note but stopped when I put a finger on it. 'You working here last week?'

He looked up from the money. 'Who's asking?'

'Come on. It's yours for answers to a couple questions.'

His eyes darted around the room. 'You ain't a cop.' A statement, not a question.

'Never said I was. I'm with the newspapers.'

'This is about them killings yonder, then.' He motioned be-hind him with his head as he said it, in the rough direction of the murder scene. 'I already spoke to the police, nothing more I can tell you.'

'How about you start with what you told them then?'

'Ain't nothing to tell.'

'The two that got murdered, they were in here that night?'

He slammed the whiskey bottle down on the bar, an acceptance he was going to have to work for the money. 'That's what the police was saying when they came by here. I saw their picture in the *Chronicle*, but if I seen them before, I couldn't speak to it. This place is full every Saturday, hundreds of young'uns come in and outta here.'

'You're sure about that? You didn't see them here that night?'

He wiped his nose with his knuckle. 'That's what I'm telling you.'

'How long have you worked here?'

'I only work weekends.'

I picked up the dollar, motioned to put it in my pocket. 'Wasn't what I asked . . .'

'What the hell difference's it make? Going on six months.'

'You get a regular crowd in here? Same people every week?'

He shrugged, eyes darting between mine and the floor. 'Sure, some. None I could put a name to.'

I nodded towards the booths. 'Anyone you see here now?'

He shrugged again. 'All them uniforms look the same to me.'

I dropped the dollar on the bar, picked up the whiskey. 'Keep these coming. You see anyone might have been here last Saturday, you point them out to me, understand?'

He stuffed the note in his waistcoat pocket. 'Sure thing, boss.'

I took a seat facing the dance floor. The first drink hadn't hit home – too much water. I sipped at the second and signalled for a third, but the alcohol only tightened the knot between my shoulder blades. It stirred memories of Jane. I watched the GIs moving with their partners, dancing the Balboa, then the Charleston, and thought about when we'd been happy. Those first months in Manhattan; the night we went to Harlem to see Bojangles Robinson at the Cotton Club – a California boy taking her to a part of her own city she'd never dreamed of going to. Riding the subway back downtown, then strolling along Broadway, lights and colour everywhere, the energy of the city carrying us like a fast-flowing river. I knew the memories were rose-tinted, but all I could hear was Jane, her arm looped through mine, giggling like a kid at some long-forgotten joke.

The whiskey left a bitter aftertaste, reminded me it wasn't always like that. I never had a problem with alcohol as such – I could go weeks without a drink and not even notice. The trouble was what it provoked in me in the wrong circumstance. Towards the end, liquor had been the catalyst for my temper. I drank more after the accident – at first to help with the pain, then to chase away the anger. It never worked.

The memory shifted and I saw Jane across a table. Chiaverini's in Midtown – a make-good dinner, latest in a line of them, another apology for a bout of rage at home. Seeing that look of distrust in her eyes – the one that said she'd heard the apologies before and knew they were empty, that it was going to happen again. Seeing the table, realising I was finishing my third glass of Chianti while she was still warming up to her first; the drink bringing on my self-righteous streak, making me forget it was on account of my behaviour we were there in the first place. Then seeing her face as it all went wrong; an argument with the waiter about bupkiss – no good cause, just a way to take out my frustration. Jane flushed with embarrassment as she stood up to leave, still poised enough to fold her napkin. Me asking her why she married me if she was so damn ashamed of me.

Her parting shot, a dagger: 'You're not the man I married.'

As the image of Jane's face receded, I realised she bore a resemblance to Alice Anderson – and the other woman, Lizzie. She had a similar shade of red hair, and the same porcelain skin. They weren't completely alike – Jane had a dusting of freckles over her face and arms – but the similarity was there, and I was surprised I hadn't registered it before. I thought about how much I wanted to help Alice Anderson, wondered if part of it was me trying to make it up to Jane by proxy.

I pushed the rest of the whiskey away from me, annoyed at slipping into a self-indulgent melancholy so close to where two people had lost their lives. I stood up to go back to the bar. The crowd parted and something stopped me – a face turning away from me a beat too fast; a watcher who knows he's been spotted. I looked again, noticed a man at a table in the opposite corner. He was sitting alone, now staring at something on the dance floor. A single stream of smoke floated up from a cigarette in the ashtray in front of him. Something about him was familiar, but I couldn't see him clearly. I walked to the bar and waved the bartender over. 'You recognise that guy in the corner?' I pointed, but the man had swivelled in his chair so he was facing away from us.

The bartender tapped the bar top, indicating for more money. 'Lemme see when he turns around.'

'Never mind.' Playing a hunch, I bustled through the crowd and out of the club. Just along from the entrance, a narrow alley ran between the building and a storage hut next to it. I slipped into the dark recess at its mouth and waited.

After thirty seconds, the man appeared, making for the parking lot. He walked past my car then stopped and looked all around, like he was lost. I stepped out of the alleyway. 'Looking for me?'

He jerked around. 'Say what?'

I circled around the other side of my car, stood in the gap between mine and the one next to it. 'You were watching me inside, and I've seen you before. What do you want?'

He made a show of looking around the lot. 'Can't remember where I parked my damn car.' He sniggered. 'Too much of the laughing juice, I guess.'

He was half a head shorter than me and skinny. I put a hand on his shoulder and turned him towards me. The glow from the Club Dallas sign lit him up; his face was lean, like there was no fat on his bones, and the skin taut. I took in the bruises and finally placed him. 'I saw you in the diner yesterday. You were at the counter, watching me. Why are you following me?'

The corners of both his eyes were red instead of white, filled with blood from whatever beating he'd taken. He shrugged my hand off. 'Get off of me. You got me confused, mister, I'm just looking for my damn car . . .'

'You drive the green Plymouth over there?'

He straightened up, face screwed into a confused scowl. 'The hell you know that's my car? Who's watching who, here?'

I backed him up against my car, crowded him. 'I saw you pull in behind me. You followed me all the way out from town.'

It came together in my head as I spoke. 'And I saw your car earlier today. You've been tailing me around town.'

He looked me in the eyes for the first time. His face was still screwed into a grimace, but it started to soften. 'Knew you was a smart one, Mr Yates.'

'Who are you?'

'Ain't matter who I am. Name's Davis. You want to call me something, my given name's Richard.'

He started to bring his weight forward, but I pushed him back. He was a featherweight at most, no resistance, like pushing a rocking chair. 'You want to tell me why you're following me?'

'What's New York City like, Mr Yates?'

'You're testing my patience.'

'Ain't never been further than Shreveport, but I always thought I'd like it up there in the big city. Figure anyone could fit right on in, just blend into the crowd.'

'I don't give a goddamn what you think. Tell me who you are.'

He shrunk away from me, like a dog that's been beaten. 'Take it easy, Mr Yates. I ain't for causing you no trouble.'

'Looks like you've caused someone trouble.'

He touched the purple welt on his forehead and smiled. 'This ain't nothing. Just some old friends of mine.'

I put my hand on the bonnet behind him and leaned in. 'Let's try this, Richard. You tell me why you're following me, or I take your ignition key and leave you to walk back to town.'

His mouth moved like he was chewing his tongue, and he looked down at the floor. 'You looking into these killings, right?'

I took a half-step back. 'What about it?'

He looked to one side, squinting, like he was deciding how much to say. 'I seen something. Last weekend.'

I stared at him, left the silence for him to fill.

'Seen the girl at a dance last Saturday night. You know the dancehall on Locust?' I shook my head. 'She was there, with her friends at first.'

'You just happened to notice her, out of everyone?'

'Patty was three years behind me at Texarkana High. But that ain't why I remembered.'

'So tell me.'

'I went outside about ten to sneak a drop.' He patted the pocket of his sport coat. 'Got me a hip flask.' He smiled, pleased with himself. Under the bruises, I saw he was just a kid, maybe no more than twenty. 'While I was out there, I seen Patty have at it with one of them GIs. Fella was wearing the green, right?'

I pulled my jacket back and put my hands on my hips. 'Go on.'

'They was tearing into each other, shouting, but it all stopped when she slapped him. Stormed off back inside. He just stood there, like he had his dick in his hand. Then he kicked hell out of a trash can and stomped off.'

'He didn't go after her?'

'No, sir, not so as I saw. Time I saw her inside again, Patty was dancing with the man she got killed with. I didn't know him then, but I seen his picture in the paper after. I remember his face 'cause I was thinking he was gonna take a whupping if the soldier came back.'

'You didn't see the GI again. That what you're telling me?'

'No, sir.'

'You get a good look at him?'

'Nope. Ain't no lights back there. All's I can say is he was a real big fella. Couple inches taller than you. And stocky. That's why I figured that Logan fella was going to have trouble on his hands.'

'Did you see the GI with Patty before, inside?'

'Not me. But I wasn't paying her no mind before. I knew her from school, but we wasn't friends. What you might call acquaintances, you know?'

I stepped back and took a deep breath. Davis fumbled a cigarette from his pocket and lit it, coughing smoke out. I looked up at the sky. A million stars pinpricked the night, brighter than in New York. 'Want to know what I think? I think this story is bunk. Otherwise you'd be telling the cops, not me.'

He took another drag. Bird calls echoed from the woods over the highway, followed by a high-pitched screeching – bats. 'I already told the police. Who you think put these hickeys on my face?'

'So they figured you for a liar too.'

'Like I said, me and Texarkana law's acquainted of old.'

'Which means your credibility is non-existent.'

'Because the police gave me a few licks? Ain't mean what I saw didn't happen.'

I ran my hand over my chin. 'Why come to me?'

He shuffled his feet. 'No-one else in town to tell it to. Cops ain't listen to me, and don't no-one want to believe it could be a GI behind these killings. You the only outsider here might give a man a hearing.'

I put my finger on his chest. 'You've got nothing, that's why no-one wants to hear it. You saw two lovebirds having a tiff, and a man you can't describe beyond a uniform that makes him the same as invisible.' I jabbed him harder. 'That's if you saw anything at all. So give me something I can use, or quit wasting my time.'

His lip quivered, and I thought he was going to start bawling. Then he spat on the ground next to me. 'You as bad as all the others.' He slipped around my hand and walked off towards his Plymouth.

Something niggled at me: Alice Anderson's words from earlier in the day, the story about going on a date with the traumatised soldier.

I walked a little way and called after him. 'Give me names, then. Friends. Who was Patty Summerbell at the dance with?'

He turned around and looked at me, the yellow lights of the Club Dallas sign dancing and flickering all over his face like he was standing in front of a bonfire. He spat again and walked off.

*

I drove back to town turning the kid's tale over in my head. It wasn't that far-fetched, but still I was circumspect. Even if there was something to it, finding a 'big' GI in Texarkana, with nothing more to go on, was damn near impossible – and that was assuming the man hadn't moved on in the past week. Then there was Alice Anderson's GI date; in a town full of soldiers, chances were slim it was the same man, if it had happened at all – so any link between the victims there was a long shot. I made a note to talk to Patty Summerbell's friends, find out if she really had gone to a dance in town that night, how she and Logan ended up at Club Dallas – and if she had something going on with a soldier on the side.

It was raining again, the streets quiet because of it. I stopped at a light on State Line. Two police cars raced past me in the opposite direction, sirens screaming, and I watched them in the rearview. The sound didn't fade though. I looked ahead again; four more black-and-whites were coming up the street. They sped by too, heading north in convoy, doing at least sixty. The skin on the back of my neck tingled, and my guts sank like I'd swallowed a quart of mud. I pulled a U-turn and set off after them.

CHAPTER EIGHT

I chased the sirens through the rain, up State Line and out of town. Past the limits, we hit roads that were like driving through a cornfield – trails turned to mud by the weather. I didn't know where we were, couldn't see anything – apart from the lights on the police cruisers. I focused on the red globe on top of the last car in the pack and jammed the accelerator.

We rounded a bend, and I saw beams of light moving in the distance. Flashlights. I knew then we were close – and what was waiting for us. The cops pulled up on the side of the road; car doors flew open before they even came to a stop, and policemen piled out.

I left my car behind theirs and jumped out into the downpour. The ground was soft underfoot, as slick as melting ice. Low bushes and dogwood trees fringed the road, towering pines behind them stretching into the darkness. A set of headlamps were aimed at a break in the tree line where a wooden picnic table and grill pit stood. A scattered group of officers were rooting through the undergrowth there, silhouettes in the light. Then someone shouted, 'HERE. OVER HERE.' All the cops ran towards the shout.

I scrambled after them, fighting to keep my footing. Two officers were on their knees in the dirt, a third standing behind holding two flashlights, pointing them at the base of a bush. He leaned forward, trying to see, as though he was on the edge of a hole and peering into it. Then he spun away and shouted, 'Aw, goddammit.'

The two on their knees yelled at him. One snatched a flashlight from his hand and turned back to his work. He shone the beam and pulled a low branch back with his free hand.

I saw a body. The face was covered in blood. It ran down the cheeks with the rain, like rusty tears. It was a woman. Her blouse was torn loose and her left breast had been hacked apart. She had cuts all over her chest and running down her torso, and her skirt was hiked up around her waist. Her legs were untouched; the pale skin glowed like alabaster in the harsh flashlight beam. Her panties were on the ground a few feet away, bloodstained also.

A cop pushed past me with a blanket and draped it over the woman. I closed my eyes and looked away. I pictured Patty Summerbell's face on the dead woman's body. The cop holding the flashlights was braced against a tree, saying, 'Goddammit,' over and over.

The rain was like a black waterfall. Little streams ran down from my soaking hair, into my eyes. The woods smelled of mould and rot, like a cabin that's been shut up through the winter. I could taste bile in my throat, hot saliva flooding my mouth. I heard more sirens in the distance.

Someone grabbed my arm. 'Who the hell are you, boy?'

I couldn't get the words out.

'You kill her, boy? Show me your hands.'

I looked at the cop; his face was like a broken-down bust of a real man – dented and craggy, but hard. I looked past him at the covered corpse, lifted my hands at the same time for him to see. He grabbed them and shone his light on them.

'I'm a reporter. I followed your men here.'

He jerked the flashlight so it was right in my eyes – a train coming at me in a tunnel. 'We'll see about that.' He slammed my shoulder with the palm of his hand. 'Go wait by the car over there. Try to run and I'll shoot you.'

'I'm not going any—'

A shout from behind cut me off. I knew what it was even before the words registered. 'HERE. WE FOUND ANOTHER ONE.'

*

The man's body was found face down, his head partially propped against a tree trunk. He was fully clothed and showed no signs of mutilation. Both his eyes were swollen, like he'd been punched. He'd taken a blow to the skull from a blunt object; could be the collision with the tree, could be from the butt of a gun – the same as Dwight Breems. He'd been shot in the back of the head. I heard a deputy in a black rain cowl say it looked like the man fought with the killer and maybe got free of him. I walked a wide arc around the body and stood next to him. 'You think he shot him trying to get away?'

The deputy kept looking at the body. 'Could be. Difficult to tell right now. We done trampled a million footprints into the mud, no way to know what belongs to who.'

'Put a name to either of them yet?'

Before he could speak, the city cop with the hard face appeared in front of me. 'I told you to wait by the car, boy.'

He marched me over to his car and bundled me inside, cracking my head against the doorframe as he did. He locked the door from the outside and tapped the window glass with his knuckle. 'I'll be back for you.'

I pulled out my notepad and scribbled what I'd seen. I was still writing when he came back and threw the door open again. Jack Sherman was standing behind him, raindrops splashing on the brim of his Stetson.

'This is him, Loot. Says he's with the newspaper. Checked his hands, ain't seen any blood.'

Sherman shone a flashlight into the car. 'What the hell are you doing here, Yates?'

I held a hand over my eyes to shield them. 'Saw your boys hauling ass up here. It's him, isn't it?'

Sherman turned to the other cop. 'Where'd you find him?'

'Saw him yonder when we found the girl. I told him to get lost, but—'

Sherman looked at me again, but addressed the other cop. 'Making a nuisance of himself, Walt?'

'Yessir, I'd say he was.'

'Sounds like obstructing an investigation.'

'Cut it out, Sherman,' I said. 'You know—'

'Means I can throw you in a cell. Bring you back to town in irons.'

'Lieutenant—' A shout in the distance. It came from where the girl's body lay. Sherman and the other cop looked around.

'It's got all the hallmarks,' I said. 'It's him. You see what that means, right?'

'Lieutenant!' Another shout from the same place, louder now.

Sherman put a hand on the roof of the car, muttered, 'God-dammit,' then looked straight at me. 'We're gonna speak on this, Yates. Bank on it. You don't print a goddamn thing without my say-so. Hear?' Before I could react, he snatched my notepad out of my hand; he tore a fistful of pages out and dropped them into the mud. He flung the rest of the pad into the distance, then walked off towards the dead girl.

Walt shouted after him. 'What you want me to do with him, Loot?'

Sherman looked back over his shoulder. 'The hell do I care? Get rid of him.'

Walt yanked me from the car with both hands. I tried to push him off, but he threw me to the ground, chest-first into the mud. I tasted grit and wet soil where the surface water splashed into my mouth. The car door slammed shut behind me. 'Go on, get. Goddamn jackal.'

Walt walked off after Sherman. The policemen were crowding around the girl's body, but their flashlights hung loose by their sides, like they couldn't bear to look any more.

*

It was two in the morning when I got back to the Mason. I washed and changed into a clean set of clothes, then ran across the street to the *Chronicle* building.

Word had hit the newsroom. It was half empty, but the people that were there worked in a frenzy. McGaffney was talking with two subs at the conference table, the flatplans laid out in front of them. I got the gist: the presses were rolling on Sunday's paper before the news hit, and now they were changing the front page.

I put a hand on McGaffney's shoulder. 'What have you got?'

He did a double take. 'Don't rag on me, Yates. Know you saw it, so you know what we got.'

'Names?'

He ignored me and barked for the man next to him to cut a story currently sitting on page three.

I put a hand on his shoulder. 'McGaffney?'

He shrugged it off. 'On your way, Yates. Plate change is costing me a hundred bucks a minute. You want what we got, buy a copy in the morning.'

'I'll trade you.'

'Got nothing I want.'

'So you see what's happening here?'

He wedged his stogie in the corner of his mouth. 'You making a joke of this?'

I took a deep breath to keep my composure. *Joke* was as far from what I was feeling as could be. I met his eyes again. 'I saw it, McGaffney, the goddamn bodies. There is damn sure nothing funny about what happened out there.' The newsroom had stopped, everyone looking at me or McGaffney. 'You're dealing with an animal here, but you're so busy taking shots at me, you can't see what's right in front of your eyes.'

McGaffney took the stogie from his mouth, pinched between his thumb and forefinger. He glared at me, grey eyes wide like a startled animal. He motioned to one of the subs he'd been standing with. 'Hansen, toss him on the street.'

The man looked unsure of how I'd react. He took a hold of my elbow. 'Let's go.'

I stood my ground, not resisting but not moving either. 'Seven days,' I said. 'That's what you've got to catch this man.' Hansen gripped harder, tried to lead me towards the door.

'McGaffney, do you want to hear me out or don't you?'

McGaffney signalled for him to wait. 'What did you say?'

'Once a week. He's hitting every Saturday night. Means you got seven days to stop this.'

'Don't even know it's the same killer.'

'I told you, I saw it. The victim had his head split open, just like Breems, plus he was shot, same as all the others. The girl was cut up all over. It's getting worse. Follow the logic: he stabbed Alice Anderson once, just to see if he had the stones to do it – he didn't plan it. Next time he stabbed Patty Summer-bell three times, and he liked it even more. So this time he went to town on the victim.' I glanced around, imploring someone there to hear what I was saying. 'McGaffney, it's the same man, goddammit, and he'll come again in one week.'

The room was quiet, the silence charged because it should have been filled with the sound of presses rolling.

McGaffney ruffled his moustache with his fingertips. Then he waved Hansen off. 'Let him go. And get me names, Christ's sake.'

*

Hansen ushered me to an empty desk and told me to stay there until McGaffney said otherwise. I started writing, longhand first, everything I'd seen. The details came easy, stamped into my memory: the sheen on the girl's wet legs from the rain; the man's hair stuck to his scalp, black and slick with blood and water.

Then I typed it up. My first-hand account, condensed to five hundred words for the National section, ready to call in to the *Examiner*. The specifics were too graphic to include, but the facts of the case were enough to give the piece juice. I referenced the first two attacks, but held back on explicitly linking them – or adding my theories about the killer.

The newsroom got busier as the night wore on, McGaffney rousing extra hands from their beds. The mood was somewhere between tension and fear, like waiting out a bomber raid. At some point the telephones started buzzing; then they never stopped. Desks overflowed with message slips, every telephone on the floor ringing again as soon as it hit the cradle. Rumours coursed around the room – a name for the male victim, then a different one, then a third. The same for the female. Overlaid on that, a different slew of calls: the terrified parents whose kids hadn't come home that night.

Jimmy Robinson walked in around four and went straight to McGaffney's office. I watched him cross the floor, leaving a trail of muddy footprints behind – guessing he'd come right from the scene at Spring Lake Park. I stared at the closed door, tapping a pen on the pad in front of me; after a second I got up and went over. I knocked once and went in.

Robinson had his head in his hands, elbows on his knees. He looked up when I entered, and ran his hand over his face, looking somewhere between exhausted and angry. His eyes were threaded with red veins, like he hadn't slept for a week. 'This a private meeting, New York. Get out.'

I pointed at the mud trail he'd left. 'You been out there?'

'Don't concern you, Yates,' McGaffney said. 'Lucky to even be in this building.'

I planted my feet. 'Police turned up anything yet?'

Robinson turned back to McGaffney before he spoke.

'They're briefing at ten this morning. Ask them your damn self. Can't say as they'll answer you, mind – nonsense you pulled.'

'You telling me you never bird-dogged the cops to get a story, Jimmy?'

Robinson ignored me, fishing a cigarette from his jacket pocket. He lit it and blew smoke at the floor, staring at it as it swirled against the boards and rolled back upward. I looked from him to McGaffney and back; the silence said they weren't going to say anything more with me there. A secretary knocked, slipped around the door, and dropped a copy of the paper on McGaffney's desk. The headline was block capitals: TEXARKANA COUPLE SLAIN IN SPRING LAKE PARK.

*

Dawn was breaking when I crossed the street to the Mason. Back in my room, I collapsed onto the bed fully-clothed, not even taking my tie off. Sleep wouldn't come though; each time my eyes closed, I heard rain falling, and the blackness behind my eyelids was streaked with rusty blood.

CHAPTER NINE

I must have passed out at some point because I woke with a start, and the sun was shining fiercely through the windows when I did. There was a racket coming from outside – car horns going crazy, sounding like River Avenue before a Yankee game. I smelled of stale sweat and my mouth was dry. I squinted looking out the window; State Line was packed, cars lined up nose to tail.

The clock showed just before eight. I went down to the lobby carrying my copy for the *Examiner* in hand. As I waited for a circuit to New York, a bellhop walked by and I hooked him over. 'What's going on out there?'

The man wrinkled his eyes and shook his head. 'There's been another murder, sir. In Spring Lake Park last night.'

'I know that part. What's with all the cars?'

'People been driving on up there all morning. Police are all over the radio telling folk to quit coming to the park because they can't work for gawkers.'

The bellman walked off and I turned back to the telephone. There was a stack of *Texarkana Chronicles* on a table at the end of the row of booths; I grabbed one and saw the same headline as the night before. At the bottom of the page, a single-column story caught my eye. It was headed *Survivor Speaks*. I flicked to the continuation a dozen pages in; it was an interview with Alice Anderson, conducted two days earlier. No name on the by-line. I skimmed the text. In it, she said, 'The man that attacked me is evil and I pray every day that the police catch him,' and, 'This man is still out there and I am sure he will kill again,' and, near the end, the line that made my pulse jump: 'I think the man that did this to me was a Negro. He had a hood and gloves on, but it was the way he spoke, and the curse words he used. I could just tell.'

A Negro killer: the opposite of what she was supposed to have said according to Peyton Reed's rumour. More than that, not one word of it sounded like the girl I'd met the day before; this person was lucid and controlled. Could be they'd ramped up the drugs by the time I saw her. Could be it was plain hinky.

The telephone rang behind me and I grabbed it. The operator said my call was ready.

'*Examiner*, this is Pecorino.'

'It's Charlie, Sal. You hear me?'

'Charlie, yeah, what's going on?'

'I'm filing. Keep Walters happy like you said. Ready?'

'Hold up, Charlie, you gotta whet my appetite you want me to sit at the table.'

'I got two more dead down here, Sal. That's five in three weeks. Stop kidding around and get your pen out.'

'Okay, okay. I saw something about that on the wires. Actually I thought about you when I saw the town—'

'Sal, you want this or not?'

'Give me what you got and I'll take it to Walters, see if he don't spike it.'

'Spike it? Sal, I'm looking out the window and every single person is on the street wanting a piece of this. He'll want to run it.'

74

Sal let out a long breath, then there was a rustling as he switched the receiver to his other hand. 'I'll do what I can, but . . .'

'What?'

'Lotta good stuff out there right now, Chuck. Walters says the "winning the peace" angle is selling good. And he ain't exactly chewing me out because you ain't filed, so . . .'

'Son of a bitch, he sent me here to get the story, so I'm giving it to him.' I leaned against the side of the booth. The silence dragged, Sal probably proofing another piece while he let me rattle my cage, knowing there was nothing I could do about it. 'This is important, Sal. Something's going on down here. The story's got legs.' There was a clacking sound down the line, harsh – Sal tapping his pen against his teeth as he churned it in his head. 'Come on. You'll get the by-line, and if I'm right, in a week's time this will be national.'

'Say that last part again?'

'You heard me.'

'What happens in a week?'

'Got that pen?'

I dictated my copy down the line, Sal abusing me periodically for my prose, making me pause as he edited it on the fly. The re-write boys called us legmen; from their perches in the newsroom they had us pegged as illiterate apes, only just worth the shoe leather we wore away scouring our beats. To Sal's mind, he was the great writer and I was just a conduit. When I finished reading my piece to him, I added my own theories about the killer.

Sal muttered for a moment, reading it back to himself. 'I'm telling you straight, this goes two hundred words, tops. If it don't get nixed altogether.'

'Tell Walters he can print it or go to hell, I don't give a damn which.'

*

The main office of the Sheriff's department was fit to burst. The briefing had been moved out of the squad room to accommodate the sheer number of reporters, with deputies posted at the doors to ensure only those with press credentials could get in. Hacks were everywhere, at least a hundred by my guess, everyone too hot in their raincoats.

Peyton Reed was near the front, talking. He made eye contact but didn't acknowledge me, went straight back to his conversation. I saw Jimmy Robinson on the edge of the crowd jawing with a couple policemen. He still had mud all over his shoes and halfway up his trousers. He saw me looking and raised his hat, lifting it by the crown, a stupid grin on his face. The cops turned to look; Robinson said something to them and all three smirked.

A grip on my arm. 'Take a walk with me.'

I turned my head. Jack Sherman marched me into a side office, pushed me against the wall and closed the door. He didn't say anything, just stared at me, nostrils flaring.

'How about we skip the posturing and whip right to the lecture, Sherman?'

His hands flexed. 'What the hell is wrong with you?'

'I was at the scene, so what? What I print in New York has no bearing. I've got no audience down here.'

When he spoke, it was faster than his usual drawl. 'Have you listened to a goddamn word I been saying to you? I told you we fixing to keep a lid on panic here.' He bent down so his face was just above mine. 'And now you been flapping your gums about a killer working to a schedule.'

I tilted my head. 'McGaffney or Robinson?'

'What?'

'Who's your stool pigeon?'

He pursed his lips so they were tight against his teeth. 'You one arrogant sum'bitch, know that? You been here two minutes and you throw that out there like an accusation. I speak to the *Chronicle* boys all day, every day. Know why? Because we all want to catch this animal. You fire out your little snipes like you Roy Rogers and we all men in black hats, but what the hell are you doing to help?'

I went to speak, but his question stopped me cold, struck the same nerve as the war posters that used to plague me – *What can you do to win the war at home?* Having to stare at them on subway platforms, on the walls of vacant lots, on utility poles – plastered all over the city. Every one another reminder of my shame.

It was more than that stopped me talking though. The information I was holding – the stabbing pattern theory, the GI links to at least two of the victims – was sketchy at best, but I wondered if that was my real motivation for keeping it close – or if I just wanted to find this bastard before the cops. Sherman let rip again before I could come up with the answer to that. 'You got a wife?'

Strike two, still no easy answer. Again Sherman didn't wait for one. 'I do,' he said, 'and she's scared clean outta her wits. When I work a night shift – which is every damn night right now – she goes to her mother's place to sleep, she's so scared.'

He took two steps backwards. 'I'm betting you want that, though, right? Suits you real good.'

'What?'

'Having the whole of Texarkana scared half to death. So you can write your stories about rubes chasing shadows—'

'No—'

'. . . and line the pockets of your Jew bosses on the back of our dead.'

'Go to hell.' I pushed him aside and tried to step around him, but he came back at me, stood directly in my path.

'Don't you ever walk away when I'm talking to you.'

The pressure in my skull rocketed like someone was piping steam into it. 'You keep coming at me, Sherman, it's like you want me to fire back. Give you an excuse, is that it?'

'That what you think?' He pointed to the badge on his chest. 'I'll take this off right now and we can get to it, partner.'

As mad as he'd made me, I wasn't stupid enough to try to fight him. I threw a curveball to slow him down. 'What did Alice Anderson say when you got to her at Pine Street Hospital?'

His face twitched, the question catching him off-guard. 'Ain't got a thing to do with you. That girl went through hell.'

'You think she knew the man who attacked her?'

'We'd have him by now if she did.'

'Not necessarily. Could be someone she knows, but not well; someone she dated once, maybe. He was under a mask, right?'

'What are you saying?'

I scratched my cheek. 'Most women that get attacked know their assailant. I learnt that much working the crime beat in Chicago.'

A voice rose above the crowd outside. 'Gentlemen, thank you for coming this morning.' Sheriff Bailey, getting the briefing under way.

'We're through here.' Sherman spun and started to walk off.

'Sherman? Answer my question.'

He stopped and faced me again. 'That girl was a wreck when I saw her. Couldn't hardly tell which way was up.'

'You asked her again since?'

'Who are you to tell me how to do police business?'

'Now who's twisting people's words?'

He put a hand on his gun. 'I ain't gonna tell you this again: write the facts, not rumours. Understand?' Then he turned and left.

My heart was beating like a jackhammer. Leaning against the brickwork behind me, I wondered if I should have told him straight out about the GI story.

My shirt was stuck to me with sweat by the time I stepped back into the main office. Bailey was in full flow addressing the mob. Sherman had joined the half dozen other cops arrayed behind the Sheriff. Next to them was an older man, noticeable because he was wearing a business suit, not a uniform. Something about him was familiar, but I couldn't say where from. I pulled out my notebook and jotted as the Sheriff spoke.

'. . . So I'd be obliged if you'd hold your questions till I'm done.' Bailey glanced down at a sheet of notes in his hand. 'First: the victims' names are Peter T. Hamilton, age twenty, of Texarkana, Texas; and Margaret Jane Langley, twenty-one, of Texarkana, Arkansas. Miss Langley's body was found on a spur road in Spring Lake Park, a little after midnight last night. She was spotted by a motorist who called it in. Deputies attending the scene discovered Mr Hamilton's body a little time after that.'

The crowd was almost silent, every man writing the same notes as me.

'Miss Langley suffered terrible injuries, which decency don't allow me to elaborate on, but we believe it was a gunshot that ultimately killed her. Mr Hamilton was shot as well, and also suffered separate injuries to his head, so right now we don't have a confirmed cause of death for you. Materials from the scene have been sent to the Department of Public Safety's lab in Austin, and we'll let you know what comes back when it's good and proper.

'This is what we know so far about their movements: Mr Hamilton collected Miss Langley from her home at eight o'clock, Saturday night; Miss Hamilton's father, Timothy Langley, was present at the time. At approximately eight-forty, they entered Texas Ranch Rib House at the bottom of Olive Street. By my reckoning it's a twenty-minute drive from the Langley house to there, so first thing we're appealing for is information on what else they did in that forty-minute time period. If anything.

'They remained at the restaurant until ten-thirty. Witnesses telling us they dined without company, and they didn't pay no mind to any other persons present in the restaurant. At that time, they paid the cheque and left in a hurry, Mr Hamilton remarking to a waitress that they wanted to get ice creams before the parlour closed up. The last sighting of them was at eleven that night, when a police cruiser passed a car fitting the description of Mr Hamilton's vehicle, heading north on Texas Boulevard – in the vicinity of Spring Lake Park.'

Bailey folded the paper he'd been reading from and looked out over the crowd. 'Now, listen to me carefully: at this time, we are pursuing all lines of enquiry as relates to the other attacks in recent weeks. We don't know yet whether this is linked, an imitator, or if this is something different altogether.' He unhooked his thumb from his belt. 'And that means you sure as hell don't either. So I don't want to see anything in print to the contrary, or any speculation. Our priority is catching the culprit or culprits. Our telephone circuits are fixing to melt as it is – folk are scared, and they want to know what we doing about this situation.' He took his hat off and pointed with it. 'So I'm ordering each man here to print that we will keep folk appraised of the investigation, and will release any pertinent information to them, via the press, just as soon as we able.'

Sherman was next to Bailey now, more deputies on either side, and each man was glaring out, daring someone to pull a 'freedom of the press' number. Murmurs went around but no-one spoke. 'Good.' Bailey put his hat back on his head. 'I'll field questions presently, but before I do, I'm gonna turn you over to Mr Winfield Callaway. For the benefit of folk from out of town, Mr Callaway is president of the Texarkana Chamber of Commerce. Mr Callaway.'

The old man in the business suit stepped forward. Some fool in the mob took the wrong cue and started to applaud, three lonely claps before he wised up. A movement to my left caught my eye; I turned in time to see Jimmy Robinson leaving the briefing. I didn't get his hurry; either he was clued in to what the old man was going to say, or he had somewhere better to be. Which made me want to know where.

Callaway was grey-haired and gaunt. He looked eighty at least, and his features were angular, but his eyes were bright and glistening – almost as if he'd been crying. I got a better look at his face, and it was then I placed him: the big shot from the photograph in my room, at the hotel opening ceremony. He'd aged, dropped some weight and a lot of hair, but the face was the same.

When he spoke, the voice didn't fit the man – it was strong and gruff, like he'd been chewing coal. 'Thank you, Sheriff, for affording me this forum. I think I speak for all of Texarkana – and I know I speak for the Chamber of Commerce – when I say that the attacks that have blighted our town in recent weeks have appalled us. Sheriff Bailey and Chief Mills have done a fine job leading the investigation to date . . .' Callaway glanced at Bailey and the man next to him, and both of them nodded. I remembered Peyton Reed's comment that Bailey and Mills, Chief of Police for Texarkana, Texas, were tight. 'But I want to go to bed at night knowing I've done everything in my power to stop this man.'

I scribbled *man, singular* on my pad and put a ring around the words. I wondered if Callaway was guessing, or if his clout gave him an inside track on the investigation. Smart money was on the latter – which meant Callaway just let slip that, in private, Bailey was talking out of the other side of his mouth.

Callaway continued. '. . . So I am today posting a reward of twenty thousand dollars for information that leads directly to solving these crimes.' There were gasps around the crowd as he said it. I was watching Sherman; he jerked his head up and stared at Callaway, then turned to look at Bailey, his expression saying the reward was news to him. Bailey made a point of not making eye contact. 'Please see to it that the public are made aware of this.'

Callaway watched the crowd, but he said nothing more. He

turned the dais back over to Bailey. Bailey took two questions, stonewalling both, then broke proceedings up, even as more rained in from all directions. As they walked off, I noticed Sherman make a beeline for Bailey. Bailey had his hands out, gesturing for Sherman to calm down.

*

I walked the two blocks back to the *Chronicle*. When I got to the newsroom, Jimmy Robinson was hunched over his desk, reading something on his typewriter. A cigarette was clenched between his teeth. I hadn't expected to find him there, but it canned my theory that he had a better lead to follow. I went over to him. 'You didn't stick around to hear Callaway's announcement?'

Robinson looked up at me then back to his reading. 'Nope.'

'You knew already? About the reward?'

'What is this, twenty questions?'

I shrugged. 'Can be. You got a beef with Callaway?'

Robinson put his coffee down, hard enough that some splashed out and onto the desk. 'In my official capacity: can I be of some assistance, New York? Or can I get the hell on with my work?'

I perched on the edge of his desk. 'I'm just impressed that you knew about it when Jack Sherman was in the dark.'

Robinson breathed out slowly. 'I don't even know what you're fishing for, New York. And I don't think you do either.'

'We're reporters. Our job is to ask questions, right?'

He stood up and stomped over to the coffee pot. The sub from the night before, Hansen, called to him as he went.

83

'Jimmy, thirty minutes till the two o'clock conference, you'll be finished, right? Gaffy's asking.' Robinson waved him away.

I snatched a copy of that day's paper from the desk and followed him. 'Hey, Jimmy, who did the interview with Alice Anderson?'

He filled his cup and turned back to me. 'I did.' His face was impassive.

'Got some nice quotes, huh?'

'She's been through one hell of a storm, but she's strong.'

'When did you talk to her? Friday?'

His eyes flicked towards McGaffney's office – as though he was looking for support. Then he chuckled, but it sounded forced. 'I ain't gotta run my movements through you. The hell you think you are?'

'Why so guarded?' He tried to pass me but I moved into his way. 'I told McGaffney I wanted to speak to her, but he said she was sedated and incoherent.'

'She was before. I guess she's feeling better.'

Now I knew he was lying. He'd spoken to her a day before I saw her – and there was no way in hell she was *feeling better*. 'Seems strange, don't it? McGaffney telling me that the day before you interviewed her?'

He looked me up and down. 'You know what bugs me most about you, Yates?' He pointed at me with his coffee cup. 'You ask your little questions like you got a god-given right to know anything you want. You can breeze on in here, Mr Big City, throw your weight around all you like. But you will sure as hell show me some respect while you do it.' He leaned close; I could smell the coffee on his breath. 'Hear me?'

My face flushed, knowing, in some ways, he had a point. I

glanced around the newsroom feeling adrift, suddenly aware of how isolated I was. There was a new sense of urgency about the place – folk running between the different desks, chairs scraping as people sprang out of them. Four hacks were hammering at their typewriters and it seemed like Hansen yelled at one of them about a deadline every couple minutes. Felt like this was the biggest story they'd ever dealt with, and the little operation was creaking.

Then I thought again about Jimmy's 'respect' line and realised it cut both ways. I went after him. 'Hey, Jimmy, were you showing me respect when you pulled that gun on me?' I was standing over him back at his desk now.

He glanced around, checking if anyone else heard me. If anyone did, they didn't react. Robinson concentrated on his typewriter again. 'I'm too busy for your foolishness, New York. Scram.'

Hansen yelled over again. 'Jimmy, what's going on? I need it now.'

I ducked down and spoke into Robinson's ear. 'Pull a gun on a newcomer – that how you do respect around here?'

'JIMMY?' Hansen had his arms spread wide.

Robinson pounded his palm onto his desk. Now the people around him jerked their heads up. He whipped around to face me, a vein bulging in his forehead. 'On Friday, Alice Anderson said she wanted to speak to us, to help stop what's going on. Warn people. So I went along and let her tell her story.' He stood up so we were eye to eye. 'Guess it didn't help none, and especially not the two got themselves killed last night.' He reached down and grabbed his hat without breaking eye contact. 'She asked the doctors to take her off sedatives long enough so she could talk with a clear head. It nearly killed her to tell me her story. But she did it anyway because she didn't want no-one else to suffer like she is.'

He shoved me to one side and walked out the door, shaking his head and muttering.

*

I stationed myself at an empty desk and tried to work. The chaos of the cramped newsroom was distracting; the telephone circuits buzzed incessantly. Scared people. Around midday, a rumour swept town that the police had taken a suspect in; that prompted a new flood of calls to the office looking for confirmation. It went on like that for half an hour, until McGaffney had to call the Sheriff's office for a denial.

I went back to the Mason to work, an update to the earlier piece, incorporating the details from that morning's briefing. When I finished, I stood by the window and read it through. There was a knock at the door. I opened it, and the bellhop was leaning against the frame on the other side. He was holding a folded piece of paper with both hands, like an offering.

'Message for you, sir.' He handed me the note.

It was handwritten: 'Mr Yates, I need to speak with you. I'll be waiting in the lobby for the next twenty minutes.'

'Who's this from?'

He shrugged. 'Reception told me to deliver it.'

I wasn't sure what to make of it. 'Mr Yates' wasn't the way most people in town would refer to me. Then I reminded myself it was my job to be curious. I reached for a notebook and took the elevator downstairs.

CHAPTER TEN

I sized up the lobby, looking for a sign of recognition. I saw a woman stand up and take two steps towards me. It was the redhead from the diner, Lizzie – Alice Anderson's double. She was wearing a grey woollen jacket and matching trousers, and she took another awkward step towards me. I didn't know what to expect from her; I wondered if Alice had told her I disturbed her at the hospital, and now it was my turn to get both barrels.

'Thank you for seeing me, Mr Yates.'

'Ma'am.' I nodded, half-expecting a slap. 'You didn't sign your note.'

'I was abrasive the last time I saw you. I wasn't sure you'd come if I did.'

'Put it out of your head.' I gestured for her to sit and pulled a chair over for myself. 'You wanted to speak with me?'

She crossed her legs and leaned towards me. 'May I ask why you approached me before? At the coffee shop?'

I looked off to the side as I figured out how to answer. 'A hunch.'

'I'm afraid I don't follow.'

'Like I told you, I thought you could help me figure out what's going on around here.'

'You didn't know who I was?'

'No, ma'am. You're family to Alice Anderson, I've worked that much out.'

She laced her fingers over one knee. 'You have to under-stand, Mr Yates, I've been hounded by reporters since . . .' She looked down at the floor, hiding her face.

'Ma'am, is Alice your sister?'

She nodded her head without looking up. I expected to see tears, but she dabbed the corner of her eyes with her knuckle, and when she eventually lifted her face, it was composed. 'People sometimes think we're twins. At least until they get to know us.'

'How's she faring?'

She chewed her lip. 'She has good and bad days. Most often bad.'

'Have the doctors said when she'll be able to go home?'

'It's too soon to say. She's . . . scarred. By what happened. She has terrible turns.'

Seemed like Alice Anderson hadn't told her sister I'd been to the hospital. Maybe she hadn't even remembered me being there. 'You have family around to help you?'

'Not really.' She picked at the red nail varnish on her thumb, looked like she was going to elaborate, but instead held her hand out to shake. 'Forgive my manners. My name is Elizabeth. Most everyone calls me Lizzie.'

I shook it, letting her change the subject behind the formal-ity. 'So what can I do for you, ma'am?'

She reached into her purse and rummaged. 'When we spoke before, you said you wanted to help. Was that a genuine offer?'

I nodded. 'I meant what I said.'

She pulled out a newspaper cutting and handed it to me. It was the interview with Alice Anderson. 'The *Chronicle* spoke with my sister a couple days ago. This is the result.'

I glanced at it. 'I saw this in the paper today. She wanted to speak out as a warning?'

Her mouth dropped open. 'That's what they told you?' She didn't wait for an answer, shaking her head in disgust. 'Alice didn't want to speak to them, she was too afraid. She was scared her attacker would come back for her if she spoke out.' She pointed to the piece. 'And besides, this is not Alice. She's not . . . she doesn't speak like this. The doctor said she's not present, right now. Meaning her mind.'

I almost blurted out that I'd had the same thought. It felt disingenuous not to tell her that I'd visited her sister, but it also felt like I'd let it run too long to drop it now. 'She's been sedated, from what I understand?'

'Yes, but it's not that. Since the attack, she's not . . .' Lizzie put her hand over her mouth and closed her eyes. 'It scrambled her brain, Mr Yates. That degenerate left her a wreck.' Now a tear came, streaking down her face from her left eye. 'He treated her worse than a dog, and she hasn't nearly recovered yet. I can't accept that she said these things.'

I had an urge to reach out, take her hand. 'Why would the *Chronicle* make it up?'

She'd pulled a handkerchief from her bag and was dabbing her eyes with it, leaving black kohl smears on the fabric and on her skin. 'That's why I came to ask for your help. I don't know, and I don't know what to do about it.'

I straightened in my chair, taking a second to draw breath. 'You have to understand, saying a reporter made something up is a serious accusation. The sort of thing gets a man blackballed for life.'

Lizzie scoffed. 'Perhaps in New York, Mr Yates, but not here.'

'You weren't there when they spoke to her?'

I put the question badly – she took it as an accusation. 'I didn't even know they were talking to her. As much as I'd like to, I can't be there all day every—'

'I didn't mean it like that,' I said. She folded her arms. 'I just wanted to know if you heard what she actually said.'

She shook her head. 'But I know this is wrong. She told me it was a white man.'

'What?' I set the cutting down and leaned forward in my chair. 'When did she tell you that?'

'I don't know exactly, I was in such a state of shock after the attack, and everything happened so quickly. The next day, maybe.'

'What else did she say about him?'

'I don't know. Nothing much.' She pushed her hair behind her ear. 'So much happened those first days. She said the man wore a hood, but she was sure he was white.'

'How could she be certain?' I wondered again if Alice Anderson knew her attacker.

'If you knew what he did to her . . .' Lizzie grimaced and closed her eyes. 'She knew, Mr Yates.'

I watched her face, saw that she knew the detail of what had happened, but decided not to press her on it. I let her compose herself, then said, 'Was your sister courting any other men aside from Dwight Breems?'

Her eyes snapped open. 'What are you saying?'

'I'm not saying anything, ma'am, just asking. A lot of times, when a woman gets attacked, it's someone known to her—'

She looked at me with wide eyes, shocked. She snatched up

the cutting and jumped to her feet. 'I should have known this was a mistake. So long, Mr Yates.'

I chased after her. 'Ma'am, where are you going?' I caught up and matched her pace.

'You're the same as the rest of them. I knew it, I should never—'

I stepped in front of her so she had to stop. 'What are you talking about?'

'That's exactly what the police said. "You know who he is, Alice, don't you?" That's all they said to her. Again and again.' She dug a fingernail into my chest. 'My sister is not some floozy who brought this on herself.'

'I never said that.'

'If she knew who did this to her, she'd say.'

'Call your dogs off, lady, I'm just looking for information. Anything to help find this man.' She went to speak again but I held my hands up. 'Did your sister say anything about going on a date with a GI?'

She thought about it for a second, her breathing still fast and shallow. 'No. She and Dwight were going steady. Why?'

'The other girl got killed, Patty Summerbell – there's a witness says she was arguing with a soldier the night she died.' The part of the story I could tell without giving myself away.

'My sister wouldn't have two-timed Dwight, she was crazy about him.' She pushed her bangs out of her eyes. 'Are you saying you think it's a soldier did this?'

The question caught me – what was I even saying? 'I'm just following every lead I can for now.' I put my hands in my pockets. 'Look, how about you let me go talk to your sister myself? It might help.'

She stuffed her purse under her arm. 'I don't know. How do I know you're not like the rest of them?' She waved the cutting. 'The ones that did this.'

'They're amateurs. At best. You can be there the whole time, just you, me and her.'

She stared at me, eyes roving over my face. 'I'll think about it.'

'How can I contact you?'

'I know where to find you.'

*

That afternoon, I figured every hack in town would be tracking down details on Hamilton and Langley, the victims from the night before, so I decided to take a different tack. A report in the Fort Worth *Telegraph* said Breems had lived with his mother in a subdivision for returning servicemen called Carson Courts. I drove there thinking about Lizzie Anderson. There was a fire in her temperament that made her seem stronger than she was; it was only when the anger subsided that her vulnerability showed through. I figured she used the hurt as fuel, converted it straight to anger to keep going – but she could only stoke that rage for so long before it exhausted her.

The whole situation stank. I would have doubted Lizzie's story if I hadn't seen Alice with my own eyes. Still, I couldn't discount the chance that one or both of them was lying. Alice was traumatised, drugged and confused; I could buy her saying one thing right after the attack, and changing her story two weeks later when the *Chronicle* interviewed her – but if the cops were insistent she knew her attacker, it raised the possibility that she was lying to protect someone. Which meant Lizzie was covering for her.

The other road was worse. If Robinson did alter what Alice had said to him, it opened up a slew of ugly possibilities. One was that he'd been forced to change what he wrote by someone else – Jack Sherman was the obvious candidate. Sherman flat denied to me that they were looking for someone known to the victim, but my sense was he'd lie to me soon as look at me.

But if Sherman didn't order it, there was only one other explanation: Robinson changed the story himself.

I thought about what I knew of Robinson. He was hostile and erratic, but I'd chalked it up to shock and cut him slack accordingly. His anger seemed righteous, and that shaped my impression of him. Rethinking it now, the man carried a gun and a temper, and wasn't slow with either. You only had to look at him to know he was on edge, and now I wondered if he'd already gone over it.

*

I parked out front of Breems's house and knocked on the door. I'd thought some about what I'd ask his mother if she answered, but part of me had already chalked it up as a fool's errand.

A woman opened the door. She looked about fifty, had a string of pearls around her neck, and hair that was black with grey roots. I told her my name and asked if I might speak with her about her son. She looked back, uncertain, and then at me again. After a pause, she said, 'You can come inside, I've made iced tea.'

She led me to a small living room and pointed to an armchair covered with floral fabric. There was a cabinet at one end of the room, running the length of the wall. On top was a Victrola player, and next to it a set of photographs, some framed, some loose – Dwight in uniform; Dwight as a child; Dwight posing by a car. Mrs Breems sat down on the davenport opposite; she took a Chesterfield from her pack, lit it and set it straight down in the silver smoking stand next to her, leaving it to burn. 'Dwight's daddy died six years back. Dwight's always looked after me since.'

'I'm very sorry for your loss, Mrs Breems.'

She nodded, said nothing, turned her head to look at the photographs of her son.

'Ma'am, I want to find who did this. Did Dwight have any enemies? Anyone you can think of who might have wanted to do him harm?'

'No.' She squinted, as if the sun was in her eyes, still staring at the pictures. 'Dwight only came home a few months ago, that's when we moved here. Before the war we lived in Lufkin.'

I took my notepad out. 'What about friends here in town? Who'd he pal around with?'

She tilted her head to one side, her eyes unfocused. 'I don't know.' She reached for her cigarettes and lit another one, placing it in the ashtray next to the first, still burning. 'Not that he told me about. Just the girl.'

'Alice Anderson?'

Her body language changed. She drew into herself, coiled, like a cat waiting to pounce on a bird. 'Yes.'

I inched forward in my seat. 'You didn't approve of them courting?'

94

She shrugged. 'Dwight knew his own mind, but he didn't know women and she was too wild for him.'

I scribbled the word down and underlined it. 'In what way wild?'

She flicked the ash off the end of one of the cigarettes and set it back down. 'Boys. She went with too many boys. She was the biggest tramp at Red River.'

'Red River?'

She looked at me, confused. 'How long did you say you've been in town?'

'Ma'am?'

'Red River Arsenal – the army depot. Half of Texarkana works there.'

I wrote the name down. 'You're saying Alice Anderson did too?'

She nodded. 'Dwight met her there. He worked on a munitions line there a couple months back.'

'And then he left?'

'That's right.'

'Mind telling me why?'

'That was the contract. It was only ever a makeshift deal.' She started to choke up, tears rolling down her cheeks. 'I'm sorry. I can't help thinking Dwight'd still be alive if he'd never taken that job. Two months . . . it's no time . . .' She covered her face with her hands and sobbed. I wanted to reach out to her, but in the quiet room, it felt like I'd be intruding on her grief.

I found a glass in the kitchen and poured some water into it, then went back and handed it to her. She wiped her eyes with the sleeve of her cardigan and took the glass, never looking at me or it. I crouched next to her but couldn't think of anything to say. I whispered a thank you and headed for the door.

*

I slipped into my car and followed the winding street out of Carson Courts. The effect the murders were having on the town was hard to stomach. Mrs Breems was another victim of the killer; a shell of a woman, almost as much as Alice Anderson. I remembered the way Alice looked in her hospital bed, and the line about her being better off dead than surviving; seeing what was left of Mrs Breems, I wondered if she'd feel the same way.

I came around onto the main drag, by the sign that marked the entrance to the development. A shout made me turn my head. I saw a flash of red hair and slowed without thinking. I knew it was her straightaway: Lizzie Anderson, coming down the path of the house across the street. There was a man with her; both of them were animated, but she was yelling. The man walked next to her, shaking his head at what she was saying. He dwarfed her, must have clocked six-six at least.

The car behind me sounded its horn. I pulled over to the side of the road, a little way down, and watched Lizzie and the man in my rearview. They stopped by a blue Oldsmobile parked in the street, and he pulled keys from his pocket. He went to open the door, but she tugged at his shirt and shouted something at him. He slapped the keys on the roof of the car and she flinched. He turned to face her, pointed a finger right in her face. His shirt was short-sleeved, and his biceps filled them like they might burst the seams.

I climbed out and crossed the road. Lizzie didn't see me

until I was close; when she spotted me, she did a double-take that made the man look around.

'Miss Anderson, are you alright?'

The man turned all the way around to face me. 'Get lost, buddy.'

Lizzie put a hand on his arm and half pulled him back. 'What are you doing here, Mr Yates?'

I ran my hand over my mouth. 'Just passing by.'

'So pass,' the man said.

'Randy, there's no call for that.'

I fixed the man with a look. 'I'm talking to the lady.'

The man took a step towards me, but Lizzie got in front of him and put a hand on his chest. 'Stop it, Randy.' She looked from me to him. 'Thank you for your concern, Mr Yates, but this is none of your business.'

'Who is this guy?' the man asked.

'It's not important. There's no need to cause a scene here.'

The man never took his eyes off me, but he seemed to take note of her words, and he took a step backwards.

I held his stare, balling my fists in my pockets. 'If you're sure, ma'am . . .'

'I'm sure. Thank you.'

I backed up slowly, still watching the man, only turning away when Lizzie opened the passenger door of the Oldsmobile and climbed inside, not waiting for him to close it for her. I had a flash impulse to tail them, but by the time I reached my car, they'd already taken off. The man bothered me, and not just because of his size. Seeing him up close, I noticed that his hair was much shorter on the sides and back of his head than on top. Like a military cut that was growing out.

CHAPTER ELEVEN

I drove over to the police building, determined to get some answers. I felt as though I'd collected ten pieces of a puzzle, only to find they all belonged to different jigsaws. All the while, the clock was ticking down to Saturday night.

That made the waiting worse. I parked out front and watched the entrance for Sheriff Bailey. I knew I couldn't go inside; Jack Sherman didn't need another invitation to send me packing, and Bailey wouldn't see me anyway.

Time dragged. An hour in, I'd thought about Lizzie Anderson a half dozen times. She played it tough, in a way that didn't come across as an act, even though there was a vulnerability to her that she only barely displayed. I wanted to help her, and her sister, but couldn't figure if that was as far as it went. The fact it was her creeping into my head, not Alice, suggested maybe not.

Cops came and went, but no sign of Bailey; more and more it seemed like a bad move to be waiting for him blindly. I turned the story over in my head. If Alice Anderson did know her attacker, what did that mean for the other victims? The crimes looked like the work of an opportunist, picking couples at random – but what if he wasn't?

I snapped to when Bailey appeared at the top of the steps. He crossed the street and went into Annie's diner, opposite. I followed him inside and found him in a booth by the far wall. He looked up when I got to his table, his expression blank. He stared at me for a moment without speaking, then broke the silence: 'Unless you intending on taking my order, take a walk.'

I slid into the seat opposite him. He had dark circles under his eyes. A waitress came by, poured Bailey a coffee and took his order. She asked what she could get me, but I passed. Bailey put his hands on the table, glanced at his watch. 'Lunch at six in the evening is about normal right now,' he said. 'It's days like today, when it's the first damn thing I eat, that I get a little cranky.' He took a drink of his coffee. 'Your reason for interrupting me, Mr Yates?'

'I wanted to ask you about the case.'

'That's what the briefings are for.'

'Off the record, then.'

Bailey picked up his fork and examined the tines. 'In my experience, ain't no such thing.'

'What do you know about Langley and Hamilton so far?'

He placed his hands on the table, one on top of the other, still holding the fork. He looked off to one side. 'Nothing much. Looks like they's on a date, they had dinner, they took themselves up to Spring Lake Park. And you saw how that turned out.' He looked at me out of the corner of his eyes.

'Backgrounds?'

'We're working on it.'

The waitress came back and placed a plate of ham and eggs in front of Bailey. He scooped up a heap of egg from the centre of the plate. The smell made my stomach growl, and I couldn't remember the last time I'd eaten. 'What's the connection between the victims?' I asked him.

'That a trick question?' He eyeballed me. 'They was all on a date when it happened.'

'Apart from that. Is he choosing people at random?'

Bailey stopped with the fork halfway to his mouth. 'You asking me, or about to tell me something?' He put the egg in his mouth and chewed, eyes flicking back to his plate.

'Asking.' Thinking. GIs. Robinson.

'You're trying to get me to tell you the murders are all one case, but like I already said this morning, we don't know that yet.' He cut off a piece of ham and pointed at me with his knife. 'And I believe Lieutenant Sherman made it clear to you how we feel about rumours.' He locked his eyes on mine.

'I got the message.' I slouched down in my seat. 'I told you, we're off the record here. Speculate for me.'

Bailey laughed, a hand over his mouth to cover the food he was chewing. He took a sip of coffee to wash it down before he spoke again. 'You something else, Mr Yates. My men spending half their days chasing dead ends because all people doing is speculating. I had to send a car to Dallas yesterday on account of a call about a nigger was heard saying he went crazy and killed some white girls over the county line. Turns out he was a drunk, running his mouth – but we got to follow up on every little thing comes our way. You think I can afford to lose a two-man car for a whole day like that?' He shook his head. 'So I'll decline your offer, thank you.'

The unspoken line, evident in his tone of voice: *We still ain't got through to you, have we, boy?*

'Alice Anderson said she thinks the killer's a Negro. In the *Chronicle* interview.'

'Don't mean it's this dumb nigger in Dallas—'

'That's not what I meant. I've got a source who says Anderson told you her attacker was white.'

He shrugged. 'Girl's a mess.'

'So she never told you it was a white man?'

Bailey closed his eyes and breathed out through his nose, the question hanging there. At last, he said, 'She told Jack Sherman it was a white man, correct.' He pushed some ham around his plate. 'Also told him he was black, and one time, a Red Indian. If she'd have said it was President Roosevelt attacked her it wouldn't have been no shock to me. Poor girl's a wreck.'

'So you don't give it any credence?'

'That's a ten-dollar word, Mr Yates. We deal in quarters around here.'

'The country rube act is beneath you, Sheriff.'

'And playing cop is above you.'

'Maybe I'll go ask Alice Anderson exactly what she said.'

'Again?' He looked at me, the hint of a grin on his face. 'Ain't you gonna give that girl any peace at all?'

I willed myself not to show surprise. I should have figured he'd find out I'd been to the hospital. I held his stare, determined not to give him the satisfaction of trying to explain myself. I put my hands on the table, one on top of the other, mimicking him. He went back to his food. I picked up the salt shaker and turned it in my hands. 'What about soldiers?'

He looked up at me through his eyebrows. 'What about them?'

'Town's full of GIs. Means a lot of young men who've killed before. You looking at any of them as the murderer?'

He set his fork down, a clanging sound as the metal met the plate. 'You fight in the war, Mr Yates?'

Again and again and again . . .

No answer that satisfied, no reason that could explain it. An image of my father came to me, the way I always imagined his final seconds in the first war. Face down on a French hillside, cut down by German machine guns. Calling out my mother's name. The fear he must have felt. The fear it had always inspired in me. 'No.'

'Y'know, somehow I knew you didn't.' Bailey was leaning over the table on his elbows now; the booth felt smaller, claustrophobic. 'You like one of them little dogs that's always yapping, always looking for a fight. Until he finds one.'

I slipped back in time – the accident, the old picture show in my mind. No memory of what happened on that road, just an impression, my brain recreating those last seconds anyway. It came back to me in dreams I could never remember afterwards, and I always woke up at the point of impact – the sound as loud as a bomb blast, the forces acting on my body as real to me as they were on that day. 'I got injured before—'

He cut me off. 'I bet you were a regular warmonger when you was behind your typewriter, huh? Real brave, till it came time to ship out. Then I bet you went looking to someone else to do the fighting for you.' I slid along the seat to get out of the booth, not wanting to hear it, but he stabbed the table with his finger. 'SIT your ass down, boy.' His voice was forceful enough to stop me in my tracks. 'I fought for this country, son.' He touched his shoulder. 'I'm still carrying the lead to prove it.' His voice was a low hiss now. 'I killed men so the likes of Patty Summerbell and Margaret Langley could live they lives in peace. I seen my brothers die fighting for the same thing. So it offends me when a pissant coward like you says you think it could be a soldier doing this killing. You ever picked up a gun, you'd know killing's the last thing on your mind if you lucky enough to make it home. More likely to eat your gun than turn it on a civilian.'

My head started spinning, all the old doubts flooding back.

Bailey pointed at me. 'You a coward, son. You got a coward's heart. It's all over your face, it's in the way you walk, it's in the way you sitting there now.' He put his finger on my forehead. 'And it's how I knew you never fought no-one in your damn sissy life.'

The half-full diner was silent. The waitresses and customers were staring at us. Bailey was watching me, his eyes and mouth motionless, his finger still pressed against my skin. I felt real fear at the power of the man, as if whatever he decided to do next, I couldn't stop it.

'Like I said, you a coward.' He stood up, stepped around to the front of the booth. 'Gun or no gun, a man said what I just said to you, you bet your ass I'd hit him.' He took two paper napkins from the dispenser on the table and wiped his mouth. 'I could throw you in jail, but you ain't worth the paperwork.' He dropped the napkins on his plate. 'Pay the ladies when you done, hear?' He walked to the door, tipping his hat to the waitresses as he passed.

CHAPTER TWELVE

Driving back to the hotel, I made my mind up that I was leaving in the morning. If it was weak of me to let Bailey do more with a few words than Jack Sherman had managed with his threats, I didn't give a damn. All I could feel was shame and anger, the same demons that had shredded my soul for three years. Worst of all was the knowledge that Bailey was right about me being a coward. I knew it, and so did everyone in New York. My first day back on the job when I'd got out of hospital, I'd got to my desk and found my chair painted yellow, and a small white flag draped over it – the *Examiner* boys making damn sure I knew what they thought about me.

I went to my room and called room service to order a whiskey, but before they answered I thought better of it and hung up. A few months ago, I would have sunk a quart of whatever hooch I could lay my hands on and trashed the room. I was determined not to fall back into that.

Instead, I threw my belongings into a bag, turning the implications over in my head. If I left now, Walters would castigate me for going back to New York early and use it as his excuse to fire me for sure. I thought about what was waiting for me at home – no Jane, a job I'd disgraced myself at, a reputation as a coward. Add quitter to the list if I ditched out on the story. The prospect of going back to all that was too much to take.

I dwelled on it, not wanting to, but my mind refusing to

contemplate anything else. At length, I found a glimmer of hope in the idea that maybe it wouldn't be so bad. That I could bite the bullet at the *Examiner* and make a fresh start someplace else. Walters had all the power; he'd find a way to force me out eventually anyway, so why keep fighting to save my job? Better to get out clean.

I was grasping at straws and I knew it. I stood by the window, watching the last of the light fade away as twilight descended. Maybe I'd known it was over at the *Examiner* since the minute I'd been sent to Texarkana, and unconsciously, I'd already accepted it. The thought of telling Jane crushed me. Then the kicker: she wouldn't give a damn anyway. I was old news to her.

After that, I couldn't get thoughts of Jane from my mind. I came to another conclusion – that if I could talk her into coming with me, into trying again someplace new, then maybe I could salvage something from the wreckage. I remembered her face on the day she'd told to leave; the way she'd been so dispassionate about it all – 'Charlie, I want you to please go. It will be better for both of us in the end.' Me trying to argue it, her quelling that by saying she'd be moving her things out if I didn't. Precise, like always; all the eventualities covered off.

Remembering that day hurt worse than anything Bailey had said.

Still, I had to try.

*

I slumped against the booth waiting for a circuit. I thought about what I would say; Chicago was an option. Maybe back to

California even. Jane had been fascinated, at one time, by the idea of Los Angeles. She just needed to know that I was different now—

'Hello?'

Her voice jolted me straight. 'It's me.'

A pause. 'Charlie? What do you want?'

'I'm . . . Nothing. I'm coming home tomorrow and—'

'Have you been drinking?'

'No, I haven't.'

There was a nervous pause, neither of us knowing what to say. She broke it. 'Care to tell me why you're calling?'

When I started talking, the words came in a jumble. 'Jane, listen, I see it now. I know I was the problem, and I want . . .' I leaned my forehead against the booth, not sure what to say – where to start even. I blurted it out. 'Come away with me—'

'Where are you?'

'I'm in Texas, but that doesn't matter. I'm coming back to make it right. I thought we could go away. California maybe, someplace by the sea.'

'What are you talking about?'

'You and me. Like it used to be. We just need to get away from New York. Start over.'

She took a deep breath. 'You're not making any sense, Charlie. You need some help. Is there someone there who can help you?'

'No.' I looked around the lobby, almost laughing at the notion. 'There's no-one here can help me.'

'It's getting late, Charlie. You should go to bed—'

'Don't do that, don't dismiss me.'

She sighed. 'Sounds like your temper's still the same.'

'I'm sorry.' I closed my eyes to calm myself down. 'I'm sorry. I didn't mean to shout, I just hate when you brush me off.' I pushed my hair back. 'I need you.'

'We've been through this. Whatever you need, it's not me. I'm done picking up the pieces every time you lose your head.' The choice of words was a deliberate swipe.

'I've changed. I'm not like that now.'

'We haven't spoken in weeks and now you're calling out of the blue to tell me we should run away together. When I tell you no, are you going to smash up the telephone booth you're in?'

Strike three. I opened my mouth but no words came.

The operator spoke to tell me I was almost out of credit. I talked over her. 'Just know that I'm sorry and . . . that we can make it work.'

'We spoke about this, over and over. You need to get on with your life.'

'Just see me. I'll be back in a few days, and if we talk—'

'I'm going now, Charlie. Goodnight.' There was a crack in her voice. And then another noise, this time in the background; sounded like a man's voice.

'Jane? Is there someone—'

'Please don't call here again.' She said it and the line went dead.

I dropped the receiver and it clattered against the wall, dangling from its cord. I planted my hands against the sides of the booth. A bellhop looked over, saw my face and backed off.

I went back to my room. The stack of scribbled notes on the writing desk caught my eye. I thought of Alice and Lizzie, and then the others, and suddenly they felt like evidence of a betrayal.

CHAPTER THIRTEEN

I woke early, still in my clothes, my case next to me with my belongings spilling out of it. I walked to the window, recalling snatches of the conversation with Jane. At first it wasn't her words that came back to me, just the weariness, the resignation – hearing a tale she'd heard too many times before.

Then I remembered the worst part: the man's voice in the background, not certain that was what I heard, but somehow knowing it was. I'd never imagined Jane with another man, but what did I expect? She was a beautiful young woman with no attachments – the divorce papers were in process, filed at her father's behest, his attorney having assured her my behaviour would make proceedings a formality and ensure her a sympathetic hearing. Someone was always going to sweep her off her feet. I pictured the man, standing in our apartment, holding her after she finished talking to me, telling her it would all be okay, he'd look after her now and she'd never have to worry about me again. Strange: in my mind, the man looked like the meathead I'd seen with Lizzie Anderson.

There was Lizzie in my head again. The thought of running out on her provoked the same streak of guilt I'd felt the night before. I picked up the stack of notes and leafed through them absently – some of the pages barely legible where I'd been writing so fast. I remembered the zeal I'd felt when I wrote them and tried to suppress it, the feeling only adding to the guilt. I stowed them in my case and fastened it closed.

*

I stopped at a coffee shop at the bottom of State Line on my way out of town. I laboured over a cup of straight black, Bailey's words playing on my mind. Charlie Yates: coward. I couldn't blame Jane for wanting nothing more to do with me – right then, I didn't even want to be in my own skin.

Glancing around, I noticed every man in the diner was reading a copy of the *Chronicle*. The front page was impossible to miss: PHANTOM KILLER STALKS TEXARKANA. The alarmist headline struck me as strange; I couldn't figure why McGaffney would needle at Sherman and Bailey like that.

I left my coffee and went to buy a copy of the paper. Under the headline, yearbook-style pictures of Peter Hamilton and Margaret Jane Langley took up most of the rest of the front cover. The report on their murders was spread across the first six pages; it felt like it happened a week ago, but it was only thirty hours since I'd seen their corpses in Spring Lake Park. Even with all that copy, the detail was light. McGaffney left out the mutilation suffered by the girl, the facts too gruesome for publication.

I skimmed the assorted articles, the paper resting on the hood of my car. A train whistle sounded somewhere behind me, barely registering. I kept glancing back at the pictures on the front page of the paper, couldn't reconcile what I'd witnessed at the scene with the beautiful woman in the photograph. It showed Margaret Langley in profile; she had raven-black hair and eyebrows, with full lips painted red or dark pink with lipstick. Her skin was as pale as I remembered, but her features were almost Mexican. She was looking right at the camera and smiling, a confident smile that belied the brutal way her life would be taken from her.

Without realising, I'd taken my notepad out and was writing. Peter Hamilton was a twenty-year-old carpenter. He and Langley had known each other since junior school. One line that stood out: friends of Langley said they weren't dating, and that she thought of him like a brother. The same friends said they didn't know why the pair would have been in Spring Lake Park, at what was known as a popular make-out spot. I looked at the picture of Hamilton; he wore a sport coat and tie, had buckteeth showing in his grin, and hair that was combed across in a neat side parting. He had the kind of face that couldn't sustain a lie without breaking into a giggle. He was a child next to Langley, and I believed the friends who said there was no way they were involved romantically; she would eat him up.

I flipped back to the front page. There was another splash that detailed Winfield Callaway's announcement of the reward money. It described him as the town's most prominent citizen. The end of the piece urged Texarkanians to contact the police if they had information of value. It also cautioned that they should not spread rumours or gossip, and only to come forward with facts of which they had personal knowledge.

I looked up from the paper and leaned on the car, thinking through it all. Something nagged at me; I looked back at the notes I'd written. The sun had climbed higher into the sky and I was starting to sweat, so I sloughed the story off and climbed into the car. I headed along Front Street and onto highway 67, east towards Memphis. Even though I was dreading going back to New York, I expected to feel relief at leaving town. And yet I didn't.

A mile along the blacktop I came to a junction with highway 82; the marker said 'Red River Arsenal, 20'. I swerved over to the side of the road and reached across the bench seat to where I'd flung the copy of the *Chronicle*. I snatched it up and scanned the pages again; it was on page three: 'Margaret Jane Langley, of Texarkana, Arkansas, graduated from high school three years ago, finding work as a checker at Red River Arsenal.' The same place Alice Anderson met Dwight Breems. Breems's mother said half the town worked there, but it was still a link between three of the victims. I sat for a moment, rubbing the back of my neck, not liking the urge I was getting, but knowing from years of chasing stories that I couldn't fight it. Part of me wanted to keep going, put as many miles between me and Texarkana as I could. But the stronger instinct was to go take a look at this place, just to see it. Sal told me once he didn't believe in coincidences; his words were in my head as I pulled back into traffic and turned onto highway 82.

*

I passed Club Dallas, quiet and empty in the early-day light, and pressed on along the highway. The Texas-Pacific tracks paced me to my left, visible in the intermittent breaks in the pines. I wasn't sure what I was looking for at Red River, but the name had come up too many times to just ignore. I felt a surge of excitement at having a lead to run down.

Suddenly the trees cleared and there was a turn-off. The

road crossed the train tracks but was then blocked by a barrier attached to a gatehouse, a chain-link fence stretching from either side of it as far as I could see. A sign over the entrance said *Red River Arsenal*.

I stopped on the shoulder. I left the car running, and the door open, and climbed out. The road beyond the gate ran all the way to the horizon, but there were factory buildings visible in the distance now, fronted by rows of parked tanks and Jeeps; the facility stretched for miles.

A soldier stepped from the gatehouse, a rifle strung over his shoulder. He watched me, not saying anything at first. I walked towards him, slowly, keeping my hands in plain sight. He stepped fully out now, and then called to me. 'Help you, sir?'

'Name's Yates. I'm a reporter working on the killings back in town.' I motioned vaguely behind me with my thumb. 'You hear about them?'

'Yes, sir.'

I kept ten yards between us. 'Three of the victims worked here. Dwight Breems, Alice Anderson—'

'I don't know anything about that, sir.'

'Margaret Jane Langley? Any of those names familiar to you?'

'Sir, there's twenty-sum' thousand people work here.'

'This is a base? Why so many civilian workers?'

'This is a production facility, sir. And depot.'

'Who's in charge here?'

The soldier looked behind him, down the access road into the base. A vehicle was moving towards us, a low swirl of dust kicking up in its wake. As it drew closer I saw it was a Jeep. The soldier turned back to me. 'Sir, you can't be here. This is Army

112

property, you're going to have to move on.' He brought his rifle off his shoulder and held it across his body.

I looked around, tugging at my shirt to get some air moving. It felt ten degrees hotter out of town, but I wondered if that was a psychological effect of being in the Texas backcountry. 'Who's in charge of Personnel here? I'm looking to conduct an interview for the paper, on the record.'

'You really need to go now, sir.'

The Jeep came to a stop on the far side of the barrier and two more soldiers jumped out of the back and jogged over to join the guard. An officer sat in the front passenger seat, a peaked cap shielding his eyes. He stared in my direction. I was suddenly acutely aware of my vulnerability; of the fact that I could be made to disappear real easy out here in the boondocks, and no-one would come looking for me. I called to the officer in the Jeep. 'You in charge here?'

The man nodded. 'Right now I am.'

'Then you're the man I need. I'm with the *New York Examiner*. I want to speak to someone about the murders in town. Some of the victims used to work here.'

He looked over at the troops by the guard post and gave a very slight nod. The first soldier moved his rifle so it was trained on me, shouted, 'Sir, you constitute a threat to this facility. If you don't leave now you will be detained.'

I held up my notepad and tried to laugh, my insides fluttering. 'I've got a pen and a notepad, soldier. I'm not a threat.'

The other two guards moved towards me; the third motionless, his finger on the trigger. I looked back at the officer, a look that said *Can you believe this baloney?* hoping he'd do something. But he just watched, his expression hard.

I climbed into the car and turned it around. Stopping on the shoulder of the highway, I noticed a small memorial set under the Red River sign. The plaque across its base read, *Of your charity, pray for the souls of the men of this county who gave their lives that we may live free.*

The engine ticked over and I sat there, uncertain now in my decision to leave town. I glanced in the rearview; the Jeep was heading back down the access road, but the soldiers outside the gatehouse were still watching me, gesturing to each other like they couldn't believe the jerk they just sent packing. I rested my head on the wheel and thought about my reasons for going home. I'd told myself I wasn't running away from a fight, but as those soldiers stood there, it felt like that was exactly what I was doing.

Exactly what Jane would have expected me to do.

I felt sick to my stomach at the thought. The same knock on me as back in New York: *Did you do your part?*

The soldiers wanted me gone, same as Bailey. If I left now, I'd be backing down – and that alone made me mad enough to want to stay. But there was more to it; I thought about Lizzie and Alice, promising them both that I wanted to help. And now I was going to turn tail and run? What kind of man did that make me – driving away and saying the hell with honour and justice?

I knew the answer to that: it made me the kind of man I'd been trying to believe I wasn't for the last three years.

There was nothing left for me in New York, only bad memories and battles I'd already lost. A marriage that was over. Texarkana wasn't the beaches at Normandy, but it was where I could make a difference.

Where I could make a stand.

CHAPTER FOURTEEN

The houses in Carson Courts looked as if nothing had moved since my visit there the day before. I thought about the servicemen that came to live here, how they could come straight off a troop ship crammed with GIs, all they'd seen, and be expected to adjust to picket fences and perfect yards. It made a mockery of Bailey's certainty that a soldier couldn't be committing the killings; this place could make anyone crazy.

I retraced my path and found the house I'd seen Lizzie Anderson in front of, giving it to the oversized meathead – Randy, as she called him. His place was a pristine redbrick, with a low, pitched roof and the uniform rectangular yard out front. The Olds I'd seen him leave in the day before was in the driveway; I edged around it and thumped on his door. It opened after a short pause and the man stood there, as tall and solid as a redwood, a look on his face like I just interrupted his favourite meal. 'You types are usually more clean cut. Whatever you're selling, I'm not buying, buddy.'

'I'm not selling anything. I saw you with Lizzie Anderson yesterday.'

Irritation morphed to recognition, and the man bristled. He reared up to his full height. I got a whiff of his cologne. 'You got some front.' He looked past me in both directions. 'Ain't no cooze around to stop me popping you in the eye today.'

'Don't get cute, pal, I didn't come here for trouble. The

name Patty Summerbell mean anything to you?'

He took a step through the doorway, and I backpedalled. 'Who the hell are you, *pal*, come to my house asking questions?'

'I'm a reporter. I do it to everyone.'

'You the one Lizzie's always complaining about?'

For a second I didn't know what to say, surprised I was even a topic of conversation. Then it hit me – Robinson's interview with Alice, him thinking that was me. Made me crack a half-smile. 'No, I'm not with that outfit.'

'One reporter's the same as another. Y'all been bugging her since her sister got herself attacked. Why don't you take a hike?'

'What did you say? About her sister?'

'Move on, buddy. This conversation was boring five minutes ago.'

'Go back to the part about how she brought it on herself.'

He ran a hand over his face and sniffed. 'I shoulda known y'all would try to get to her through me. I should've ditched Lizzie when it happened.'

The confirmation that they were an item stirred a weird set of emotions – a pang of jealousy, or something close, mingled with anger. It was stupid, feelings borne of nothing about a woman I barely knew.

Randy clicked his finger in my face. 'Hey, buddy, am I getting through to you? Get the hell off my porch.' He stepped towards me again.

The promise I made myself at Red River: no more backing down. I held my ground. 'Answer the question. Patty Summerbell.'

The muscles in his neck tightened. 'I read the papers

and I ain't a fool. Course I know who she is.'

'What about before she died? You ever meet her then?'

'Who the hell knows? I got here five months ago, and the cooze in this place straight threw themselves at me. Never bothered much with names.'

'What about a dancehall on Locust Street, ever been there? Weekend before last?'

He came even closer, loomed over me. 'I don't answer to you, boy.' His face changed, the penny dropping. 'Say, that the weekend she got killed? What the hell?'

I stared at a spot in the middle of his forehead, focused on it so as not to lose my nerve. 'The dancehall. On Locust. Yes or no?'

'No, goddamn you.' His eyelids twitched when he said it.

'You're lying.'

'I look the type to dance the goddamn Jitterbug to you?'

'Plenty of *cooze* in a place like that, though, huh?'

'I told you, I ain't been there. Now you gonna take my word on that? Because I'm itching to work you over if not.'

I took a long, even breath, a chance for him to cool off. I watched his hands. 'What's your name?'

'Randall Johnson.'

'You wear your uniform when you're picking up girls, Randall?'

His giant frame slackened a touch – a sign he was simmering down. 'Sometimes. Cooze love me either way.'

'How long have you been seeing Lizzie?' I blinked, surprising myself with the question, not sure what made me ask it.

He laughed. 'Forget it, buddy. She wakes up every day dreaming of finding me down on one knee.'

'Why do you say her sister deserved what happened to her?'

He shrugged. 'Play with fire . . .'

I looked around, but the street was quiet, no movement I could see. 'What's that supposed to mean?'

He wiped his lips with the back of his hand. 'It means she liked to toy with fellas. Two, three at a time, keep them all hopping.'

It chimed with what Breems's mother had said about Alice. Seemed like Lizzie either didn't know about her sister, or was pretending she didn't. Either way, it was clear I needed to talk to Alice again to see if someone she'd dated could fit as a suspect. But how the hell did I broach it with her without sounding like an insensitive jerk? I cottoned now to why the police were insisting she knew her attacker. 'Doesn't mean she deserved that. Not one iota.' I started back to the car, sick of his attitude and not sure what else I could accomplish here.

He called after me and I glanced back. 'You don't know the broad.' He scratched his chest. 'Now get off my property. I see you again, you and me are gonna have trouble.'

'That a fact?' I tipped my hat to him. 'I'm staying at the Mason anytime you feel a need to discuss it.'

*

I drove back to the hotel, my head swimming with possibilities, connections. A stroke of luck: they hadn't given my room away when I got there. I slipped the maid a five spot to get my key back and went inside.

I stashed my case and set about rearranging the furniture, clearing as much floor space as I could. My notes next to me,

118

I pulled a sheaf of paper from the desk and started writing – one sheet for each victim: name, date of attack, place of work. I made a timeline along the floor, with Breems and Anderson at one end, Red River under both their names, Hamilton and Langley at the other, Red River under her name only. Logan and Summerbell were in the middle, a question mark under both for work; the first thing to check. Robinson said Logan got out of the army two months ago – could be something there. Summerbell was still in school when she died. The Red River angle felt like it could turn out to be a dead end real easy – but it needed checking anyway.

From Alice, a branched line to a blank sheet of paper – her alleged suitors, including the GI she mentioned. Another line from Alice, this one to Lizzie, and then a branch from her, connected to a sheet for Randall Johnson. From him, a dotted line to Richard Davis, the kid with the bruised face and the story about Summerbell arguing with the giant GI the night she died. I thought about putting a line between Johnson and Summerbell, but the connection suddenly felt tenuous. That weird jealousy jolt I'd got when he talked about Lizzie, and me asking him how long they'd been together – the question coming straight out of leftfield: it dawned on me that I'd made a huge leap when I first saw him, on some thin circumstantial evidence. I didn't like the way he'd talked to Lizzie in the street, but worse than that, I saw his face now every time I thought about her. It was ridiculous, and yet I couldn't shake the image. It made me doubt my own agenda where he was concerned. I reminded myself my purpose here was to see justice served – for the dead and the living.

I rubbed my eyes and stood, the floor half-covered with

paper. I looked again at the sheet for Richard Davis, decided he was next in line. Could have been my conscience making the decision – looking for a way to prove to myself that Randall Johnson really was involved somehow. Davis could help with that. If I could find him.

CHAPTER FIFTEEN

I passed the bank of telephones, felt another pang of embarrassment as more of the conversation came back to me: *Please don't call here again* – Jane's voice steady and calm, no trace of emotion, just certainty. Her face swirled around my head, joined by Lizzie, then Randall Johnson. I thought about the man's voice I could have sworn I heard in the background, not sure now if it was even real, and wondered if it was a product of my imagination; my own mind's way of forcing me to accept what was clear as day: we were through for good. I felt dizzy, as if the room was spinning around me. I closed my eyes and steadied myself against a wall, deep breaths to tamp it all back down.

'You decided to stay then, sir?'

I opened my eyes; the bellhop who'd first shown me to my room was standing in front of me. 'What?'

'Y'all hightailed it this morning. We thought you'd left.'

'Just some time out to collect my thoughts.'

'Mr Kempton was about to sell your room. We packed tight right now.'

I pulled a five spot from my pocket and held it out. 'Lucky you didn't.' The bellhop reached to take it; I held onto it. 'There's another five with your name on it, if you want it.' He inclined his head. 'I'm looking for someone. Name of Richard Davis. Skinny as a rake, got a bunch of bruises on his face.'

He shrugged. 'Don't know him, but I'll ask around.'

I let go of the money. 'Thanks.'

*

I crossed to the *Chronicle* and walked into the newsroom. The floor was rammed again, the same commotion as the day before, maybe even ratcheted up a notch. Every desk was occupied, and the hacks, copy-editors and subs looked like they hadn't slept.

I went towards McGaffney's office, people cutting across my path from all angles as they weaved around each other. I looked around for Robinson and couldn't see him, but when I got to McGaffney's doorway, they were both inside. McGaffney was chewing on a stogie and listening to Robinson talk, no expression on his face. They both looked up when I rapped on the stencilled glass.

Robinson swivelled to fully face me and leaned back in his chair, face stretched in an exaggerated grin. 'Well, now, who's a lucky boy, New York?'

It was the first time I'd seen him since Lizzie had come to find me at the hotel; the question screamed through my head: *Did you change Alice Anderson's story?* I iced it for now. 'What are you talking about, Robinson?'

McGaffney watched me through narrow eyes, as though he could read my thoughts.

Robinson raised his eyebrows. 'The coon almost got himself killed last night?'

'What?'

'Out by Bringle Lake. I thought you knew everything happens round here now?'

'Pretend I don't.'

'Well, this posse of farmers up there got liquored up and went after a fella name of Otis Washington, on account of the fact he raped a white girl over in Boyd a couple years back. Course, they ain't think twice of marrying they cousins in Boyd, so who knows what the truth is. Anyways, these old boys saying Otis's kin been talking about him being out of the pocket last Saturday night when Langley and Hamilton were killed. Maybe he was, maybe he wasn't, but these good old boys seen the paper saying it's a black man doing these killings, and I guess they put the rest together themselves.' Robinson put his hands behind his head and kept grinning, but his face was strained. His eyes were wet, like he was on the verge of tears.

'Doesn't bother you at all?' I asked.

'Bother me? Why—' he stood up and looked at McGaffney, then at the ceiling, 'Why in the hell should it bother me?' His voice rose as he said it, so he was almost shouting by the end of the sentence. 'I just wrote what the girl said when I saw her. Ain't me picked up a noose and went looking for a scapegoat.' He was staring at McGaffney now.

I wanted to tear into Robinson, go at him until he told me what Alice Anderson really said – but I needed information out of him still, so I had to let it slide – for now. The tension in the room was electric; McGaffney didn't show any reaction, but something unspoken passed between them. Then Robinson let his arms flop down to his sides and crashed back into his chair. The room fell quiet; the atmosphere was like a dinner table after a family argument. 'Did they kill him?' I said.

Robinson ignored me, his eyes glazed and unfocused, fixed on the wall. McGaffney peeled his eyes away from Robinson and turned to me. He took the stogie from his mouth, said, 'Beat him half to death. Police got there in time to save him from the rope.'

'Took Jack Sherman to do it, though.' Robinson was looking at me now, his eyes still vacant. 'Sheriff had to send Jack all the way out there – local boys couldn't handle it. Otis'll be in Pine Street a spell. Be sure and send him some fruit.'

I folded my arms. 'What's this got to do with me?'

Robinson bit a hangnail off and spat it onto the floor. 'Seems to me he saved you from a visit. If Jack hadn't been off dealing with that, figure he'd have been at your door about that dressing down you took off the Sheriff yesterday.' I looked away, felt my face redden. 'The hell did you say to fire Bailey up like that?'

I tried to change the subject. 'It's not important what I said. They've got five days to stop another murder.'

McGaffney shook his head. 'Can't be sure of that. If the man's smart, he'll vary his movements.'

'You got kids, McGaffney?'

He frowned at me, then nodded once. 'Two girls.'

'Old enough to be out on Saturday night?'

He nodded again.

'Would you gamble on letting them out this Saturday night?'

Robinson whistled derisively. 'No wonder the Sheriff got so riled at you.'

McGaffney held up a hand to silence him. 'What're you driving at?'

'That Bailey and Sherman need to focus on finding this lunatic, not me.'

Robinson yukked. 'Ain't one or the other. You a bug they can squash anytime they want.'

I wouldn't admit it, but I knew it was the truth, and the thought scared me. I shoved one hand into my pocket and walked over to the desk. McGaffney had a stack of that morning's papers in front of him, the pictures of Langley and Hamilton plastered over the cover; I picked up a copy. 'Got a motive for these two yet?'

'Ain't no motive for this,' Robinson said. 'Man's a maniac. An opportunist.'

'You got insight into the way he thinks now, Jimmy?'

'The hell has insight got to do with it? Pretty damn obvious, ain't it?'

'So there are no links between the victims,' I said. It was a statement, not a question, daring him to challenge it.

'You're fishing again, New York.'

I shrugged. 'Edward Logan. He got out of the Navy two months ago, right?' Robinson nodded. I glanced at McGaffney; he was watching me through hooded eyes. 'So what's he been doing since then?' I wasn't going to say the words *Red River* until I knew if it meant anything.

Robinson lit a cigarette and hollowed his cheeks sucking on it. He let it dangle from his lips as he spoke. 'He was bagging and carrying at a grocery store on State Line. What about it?'

Dead end looming. 'He work anywhere else?'

'You try working a real job, see if one ain't enough for you.'

'What about Patty Summerbell? She was still in school, right?'

'I've had enough of this.' Robinson stood up and brushed past me. 'I can't listen to his guff any more.' He walked out and went to his desk, bellowing something at a sub as he did.

I turned to McGaffney. He looked up at me but didn't speak. I pointed in Robinson's direction. 'Is he up to this?'

'Jimmy cares. You could learn that from him.'

'I'd be gone by now if I didn't.'

'Back to New York? Not the way I see it.' He looked me up and down as he said it, like a butcher examining a cattle carcass on a hook.

'You don't know anything about me, McGaffney.'

He dropped the stogie into the ashtray on his desk, still smouldering. 'Edited this newspaper twenty-two years. Think I don't know how to read a situation?'

'Meaning?'

'Saying they didn't send you all the way here because you a hotshot. No-one offered me no explanations, but my estimation is they putting you out to pasture down here for some reason. Right or wrong, they don't want you in New York, do they?' He puffed on his stogie. 'Best you think on that before you start in on Jimmy.'

I rubbed my eyes with my thumb and index finger, searching for a defence, finding none. I sat down in the chair Robinson had been sitting in. 'How did Logan and Summerbell meet? I mean he was ten years older than her and she was still at school, didn't that raise eyebrows?'

'He was a war hero, Christ's sake. Good kid with it, by reckonings. Who's going to mind?'

I set the newspaper back down on the desk; as I did, a secretary burst through the office door. 'Mr Yates, there's a lady trying to reach you on the telephone. She says it's important.'

'Who is it?'

'A Miss Anderson, sir.'

My first thought was Alice – foolish, borne out of my need to talk to her. I jumped up and followed the secretary to a desk; she passed me the receiver. 'Charlie Yates.'

'Mr Yates – please, you've got to help.' Lizzie's voice, panicked.

'What's—'

'It's Alice. She's gone. I called the hospital to enquire about her and they told me she must have left during the night.' Her voice cracked as she spoke, but she wrestled it under control, fighting to keep composed.

'What?'

'She hasn't been home and I don't know where else she'd go. She can't look after herself on her own.'

I glanced around the room, thinking. 'Have you spoken with the police?'

'Yes. They said they'll look for her but how can they? They're tied up searching for the man that . . .' She stopped, had the same thought I did. 'What if he finds her first?'

'Take it easy. There are hundreds of cops and one of him. And you don't know she's out there – she might be holed up somewhere.'

'Where? Where would she go? She's got no money, there's nowhere—'

'Where are you? I'll come by and pick you up.'

'I'm at home. 225 East 12th Street. Please hurry.' She hung up.

I dropped the receiver and turned to see McGaffney watching from his doorway. I flicked a glance at Robinson, hunched over his typewriter, hammering the keys like a carpenter

127

banging nails into a two by four. Telling them would get the word out faster, but I didn't trust either man. If Robinson was mixed up in this somehow, he was the last person I wanted searching for Alice. My mind jumped around. I reasoned it out: tell them, they'll hear soon enough anyway. Then another jump: maybe they know already – McGaffney and his 'sources'. If that was so, telling them was just showing my cards, and giving up my only advantage. Better to see what Lizzie and I could find before word got out.

I headed for the exit. Robinson followed me with a glare as I crossed the floor, so I called out to him: 'I'm going for lunch. Want something?'

I couldn't tell if the look on his face was shock or amazement.

CHAPTER SIXTEEN

Lizzie's place was a two-storey white clapboard house with a gabled roof and a small porch out front – the type I'd seen all around town. Her street came to an abrupt end a couple of houses down where Highway 67 cut north across it. On the far side of the highway, a freight train was rumbling slowly along the tracks.

Lizzie ran down her driveway as I pulled up. 'Mr Yates, thank God.' She popped the passenger door and jumped in. 'I've been trying to find you all day.'

'I had leads to chase down. Where to?'

'I don't know. I don't know where to start.'

'Any word from the police?'

'Nothing.' She put her hand on the dash, and I saw it was shaking. 'They don't know anything.'

'What time did she leave the hospital?'

'I don't know. They said no-one saw her go. They won't tell me a damn thing.'

I dropped the clutch and headed back towards Pine Street.

*

That afternoon was a blur. Pine Street Hospital: Lizzie on the attack, all that anger fuelling her again, steaming ahead at a hundred miles an hour. We found the administrator in charge of Alice's care, a man named Penrose, and Lizzie reeled off question after question. An orderly checked on Alice around two in the morning, saw her sleeping. Around three, the cop posted to her door went for a bathroom break. He didn't check on her when he got back – but she must have left in that time period; when the nurses came in with breakfast at six, Alice was gone. She'd taken a small bag of clothes and whatever money she had. A note was found in a drawer next to her bed, saying only: *No-one can help me in this place.*

Penrose said he'd canvassed the staff on duty, but no-one had seen Alice leave. Not a shock, he said – they ran a skeleton staff overnight, 'And besides, it's a big hospital.' I had to step in front of Lizzie to stop her slapping him in the face.

It was past three when we left Pine Street – thirteen hours since anyone had seen Alice. Time enough for her to be almost anywhere – including, I didn't say, on her way to some other town. We cruised State Line twice, eyes glued to the street, looking for her in crowds and diner windows. We passed police every now and then; Lizzie made me stop so she could grill them to know what they were doing to help. She showed a recent photograph of Alice to each man, willing them to re-member the face. The futility dawned on me: she doesn't look like this any more; this is Alice from before.

At five, I convinced Lizzie we should check the trains, in case Alice was running. She just nodded. We drove the short distance down State Line to Texarkana Union Station. The building was an ugly brownstone that looked more like a pris-on. Like the Federal Building, the state line ran through the middle of it. Inside, there were GIs everywhere, sitting or lying on the floor, using their tote bags as makeshift pillows. The air was thick with the smell of foreign cigarettes. I jogged the length of the concourse, checking benches, walking the platforms in the vain hope that she might still be there somewhere. I knew it would be fruitless, but I needed to keep moving, show Lizzie that someone was doing something. Lizzie showed Alice's picture to every station official she could find, the dead ends she kept hitting making her blood boil. No-one had seen anything.

Dusk was falling by the time we got out. We sat in the car outside the station, the adrenaline that had kept us going ebbing now, and my spirits dragged lower by the sense that there was no happy ending coming. I thought back to the Alice I'd seen, what seemed like a lifetime ago; a broken girl, just lucid enough to recognise the army of demons that were going to live in her head from now on. I remembered the way she was just before I left her room, strands of lank hair plastered across her face like knife-slashes, and the words she'd spoken, about death not being the worst thing can happen to a person. Sitting in that dark parking lot outside the station, it felt as if she was already gone.

Lizzie was holding the picture of Alice, now crumpled at the corners, but she was gazing straight ahead through the windshield. I let out a long breath before I spoke. 'Let me take you home. I'll come by at first light and we'll start again.'

Her eyes moved, darting from point to point like she was thinking. Finally she said, 'Not yet. I want to go to the police building.' She looked at me now, said softly, 'Please.'

CHAPTER SEVENTEEN

The atmosphere was jittery in town after dark. State Line was quiet, but not empty. The cops had cars or men stationed every few blocks after nightfall – an attempt to reassure people. It wasn't working. Some places still attracted a crowd; the Saenger Theatre had a line outside, people seeking safety in numbers. But most of the restaurants and diners were dead, empty tables visible in the lit-up windows.

Parking outside the police building, I felt like I had crows pulling at my intestines. I didn't know what reaction to expect from Bailey and Sherman when I walked into their place, but I knew it wouldn't be good. We climbed the stairs to the Sheriff's floor. There was a staging area at the top – just a collection of mismatched chairs around two walls, and a battered chipboard counter at one end. Lizzie threw open the door leading to the main offices. I followed; there were rooms either side of the corridor, some lit, some dark. Ten feet short of Bailey's office, I glanced into an open doorway as I passed. It was an interview room, two men inside. I stopped dead in my tracks: slumped in a chair in the corner was Richard Davis, looking like a runaway kid. He had a fresh welt on his cheek. An old cop with thin arms was grilling him from behind a table, a pack of Lucky Strikes and a dented metal ashtray in front of him.

Lizzie was at Bailey's door, knocking hard. I glanced back at Davis; he had his knees pulled up to his chest and his head buried between them. He was barefoot, his feet the colour of coal dust, and he wore a dirty white vest. I wanted to say something, but when I looked again, Lizzie had just pushed Bailey's door open; I hesitated, then ran after her.

I caught the end of her opening line. '. . . Apologise for the intrusion, Sheriff, but I'm about going out of my mind.' The pitch of her voice had jumped higher, and her accent was more pronounced. 'Please, I need to know what's going on. Anything.'

I stopped in the doorway, as if I was defying him somehow by not going in. He looked up when he saw me, and I met his stare. My hands were sweating; I hid them in my pockets. The office was rectangular, wider than it was deep. The wall behind Bailey showcased a number of plaques and framed certificates, centred around a snap of Bailey in military uniform, arm in a sling, having a medal pinned to his chest by military brass. I remembered his line about taking a bullet in the first war.

Bailey turned his gaze back to Lizzie and half uncurled one finger in my direction. 'You keep poor company, Miss Anderson. Take a seat.' He offered the chair opposite him.

Lizzie shook her head. 'Sheriff? My sister?'

Bailey laid his palms flat on his desk, fingers splayed. 'Right now, I don't have much of anything for you.'

Lizzie set her handbag on the edge of his desk. 'But you're looking?'

'We're looking. Much as we can.'

'What does that—'

'I've spoken to any kind of law you care to name. Chief Mills has got men looking for her, and Bobby Landell over in Miller County is detaching three deputies to my command – I'll send them right out. The State Troopers are briefed. We've talked to Lafayette Sheriff's, Little River Sheriff's – every county within ten miles. If your sister's for finding, we'll find her.' Echoes of the line he used talking about the killer at the first briefing, less convincing each time he trotted it out.

'She has no call to be anywhere else,' she said. 'You ought to be looking for her here in town.'

'Of course we doing that. But you can't ignore the possibility she's running. If she's scared—'

'If she's scared, it's because your men did nothing to allay her fears. The way they spoke to her was atrocious.'

'Miss Anderson, I can appreciate this is a time of deep distress for you, so I'll let that comment pass – but be aware the men you referring to are the same men working double and triple shifts trying to find her.'

'Dedicated? Is that what you're saying?' I could tell she was fighting hard not to raise her voice. 'Then let me ask you this: where was the officer posted to her room on the night she disappeared?'

Bailey tilted his head, the corners of his mouth turned down. 'The gentleman in question was on a comfort break—'

'Is that so? Because the number of times I've been there and there's been no-one by her door—' She breathed out sharply, frustrated. 'How do you know she even left of her own accord? What if . . . What if someone took her? If your man had been where he was supposed to be . . .' Lizzie picked at the red nail varnish on her left hand, making it fleck off like tiny blood spots. She opened her mouth but nothing came, and she looked down at the floor. All the anger was gone and her vulnerability was showing.

I took over. 'Have you got any idea where she could be headed, Sheriff?' I said it in an even tone, but he took it as a question to his competence.

'We've got nothing to go on, Mr Yates. She was gone a long time before anyone knew it, so there's a heap of ground to cover.' His lips hung apart slightly, a tiny strand of saliva stretched across the gap, and I knew what was coming. 'You being a reporter and all, I imagine you got some insight into these things. You saw her in the hospital, what's your feeling on where she's at?'

Lizzie turned towards me slowly, Bailey watching on. She closed her eyes, simmering, and it felt worse than if she'd had right at me. 'I don't understand – you saw Alice?'

'I needed to speak to her,' I said.

'When was this?'

Before I could answer, a deputy stepped around me and into the office, holding a wad of papers – callout sheets. 'Sheriff, all hell's breaking loose out there.' Lizzie's gaze bored into me as the man spoke. 'We had another seven calls from folk saying the killer's outside their house, we got a report that three Negroes been stomped near Spring Lake Park, and Walt Mosier just called to say he found two kids in a car off New Boston Road, saying they was decoys, trying to draw the killer out. We flush out of men to send, and the phones won't quit ringing.'

Bailey exhaled, then stood up, reaching for his hat. 'You can see our problem, Miss Anderson. Milton – get my car, I'll take care of the Negroes in the park. Where's Jack?'

The deputy pushed his hat back. 'The Lieutenant? Don't know, sir.'

Bailey put a hand on Lizzie's shoulder. 'I'm sorry about your sister, Miss Anderson. We'll do everything we can, and for now I suggest you get on home and get some rest. I venture Mr Yates will drive you.' He ushered us out of his office.

I backed into the hall, but Lizzie stood in the doorway so she was blocking his exit. 'You'll call me as soon as you know something, Sheriff.' Her voice dropped to a whisper. 'Please?'

Bailey nodded and pulled his door closed behind him. Lizzie glared at me again and stormed off down the corridor. Bailey walked past me like I was a ghost.

I rubbed my right temple, the start of a headache breaking. I thought about going after Lizzie, but figured there was no point while she was so hot at me. I waited until Bailey had cleared the corridor, then went back down the hall. The room I'd seen Davis in was still open, only the older cop in it now. I stepped inside and he looked up from his report. 'I'm looking for Richard Davis.'

He screwed his face up. 'He ain't here. Who're you?'

'I'm his attorney. Where is he?'

'Attorney? That's a first, never known him to call one of them before.'

I took a step closer, figured the bolder the lie, the better chance it had. 'What's your name, deputy?'

'What's it to you?'

'If you're obstructing access to my client, I'm going to need your name. In New York I wouldn't have to ask twice.'

His face came over serious. He pushed his glasses over the bridge of his nose, then shrugged. 'Hey, you want him, he's all yours. He's in holding – end of the corridor on the left.'

The holding pen was right where he said. I walked in and

almost gagged; the room was windowless and hot, the smell of urine and body odour overpowering. There were three cells on each side, but only one was occupied; I wondered how bad it got when it was full. And where all the suspects were.

Davis was sitting on the bunk with his head hung low. He looked up when I called out, squinting at me as if he thought he might be seeing things. 'Mr Yates?'

'What are you doing in there, Richard?'

He ambled over to the bars, then slouched against the cinder block wall. 'Feels like I ought to be asking you that.'

'I had business with the Sheriff.' I glanced around his cell, taking in bare walls and the cracked toilet in the corner. 'What did you do?'

'Texarkana law didn't trouble to tell me what they arresting me for.'

I cocked my head to one side. 'Everyone in jail's innocent, right?'

One side of his mouth curled up. 'Me and innocent ain't been on terms in a while now. But I ain't know what I'm here for.'

'Police must have a reason for hauling you in.'

'Drinking. Indecent behaviour. They'll come up with something later.'

'This is a regular thing then?'

'Wouldn't go so far as to say regular, but this ain't my first time, no.'

'When do you get out?'

He shrugged. 'Day or two maybe. At a guess, depends how charitable the Sheriff's feeling.'

His demeanour was startling. I doubted he was locked up

for nothing, and it was clear he was no stranger to trouble, and yet he talked like it was a game. I gripped the cell bars. 'Listen, the GI you saw with Patty Summerbell the night she died – you remember what he looked like?'

Davis smiled. '"Quit wasting my time," that's what you said. Changed your mind?'

'Let's call it an open mind.'

'I told you all I know about him – big fella, uniform.' He rubbed the side of his head.

'What if you saw him again?'

Davis pushed off the wall and stood straight. 'Mr Yates, are you saying you seen him?'

I shook my head. 'I saw someone fits the description. But if you got a look at him . . .'

He took a deep breath, his skinny chest blowing up like a balloon and hiking the bottom of his vest. 'I mean, I could look. If you think it would help?'

I searched his eyes for sarcasm, but there was no hint of it. 'I'm staying at the Mason – call me there when you get out, I'll come pick you up. Reverse the charges.'

His hands dropped to his sides. 'A ride when I get out? Gosh, you a regular Santa Claus.' I didn't need to look for the sarcasm this time.

'I thought you wanted to help?'

'I can help sooner if you get me outta here.'

'And how would you suggest I do that?'

'You the hotshot reporter from the big city. Telling me you can't pull no strings?'

I cupped my face and rubbed my eyes. 'Okay, okay. I'll see what I can do.' The lie left a dirty taste on my tongue.

'Much obliged.'

'In exchange for the names of who Patty Summerbell was at the dancehall with that night. Her friends.'

His shoulders shook gently with a resigned laugh. 'You a sly one, Mr Yates. Always working the angles.'

'You want out? Give me names.'

'Alright, but I only know two and a half.'

I was reaching for my notepad but I stopped midway. 'Two and a half – are you razzing me?'

He looked surprised at my reaction. 'No. Two and a half. The one girl, Darla, I only know her given name.'

I held his gaze, not sure if I was dealing with a child, or a brilliant actor. I scribbled the name down anyway. 'Know where she lives?'

He scratched the side of his nose. 'Nope. Only her name.'

'What about the other two?'

'Well, there was Marcy Pettinger – she was there. Making a spectacle of herself, like always.'

I wrote as he spoke. 'And the other one?'

He paced across his cell, parallel to the bars. 'You really think this man could be the killer?'

I lifted my pencil from the paper again and looked up at him. 'No way to know. But if your story's true, he's worth a proper look.'

He pointed at me, wagging his finger. 'Still don't believe me, Mr Yates, huh? Ain't it strange that you want me to give this fella the once over when you don't even believe I seen him like I said I did?'

I stared at his face, feeling like I'd underestimated the kid's smarts.

'Who is he, anyway?' he said.

I thought about it for a second, not sure how to answer. Someone's boyfriend. A veteran. A self-proclaimed ladies man. None of them seemed to fit the bill. 'Just a real big guy, ex-army. Can't be too many his size in town.'

He raised his eyebrows, nodding agreement.

'So, the name?'

'Anna Mendoza. I known her from school, her and Patty in the same class—' His eyes dropped to the floor and his shoulders sagged. 'Was.'

The names recorded, I closed my notepad. The room hummed with the noise of a working building in the background. The kid was all bravado, but I almost preferred it when his mask was up; when it slipped, there was a desperate sadness about him. 'Look, let me see what I can do, okay?'

He nodded, still looking at the floor. Seemed like he was choking up. 'Mr Yates, you really wanna help me, maybe you could write about me. I got a story to tell.'

Every second person I met said the same thing. 'You tell me it when you get out.'

I stepped into the hallway reinvigorated, the reckoning I had coming with Lizzie temporarily forgotten. The names swirled in my head – *Marcy, Darla, Anna*. Girls who were with Patty Summerbell the night she died, maybe got a look at her killer. Friends. Witnesses.

Leads.

CHAPTER EIGHTEEN

I decided against going to Lizzie's house, thinking to give her time to calm down. But when I made it outside, she was standing by my car, her hair a dull adobe colour in the streetlight. 'You shouldn't be out here on your own, it's not safe.'

'Why didn't you tell me?' There was no anger in her voice, just disappointment.

'Never seemed to be a good time.'

'That's a cheap line. Is that the best you've got to offer?'

I unbuttoned my collar and loosened my tie. 'Look, I want to help, but I barely even know you. I'm not about to start explaining myself.'

'I came to you because I thought I could trust you.' She shook her head. 'Seems I was wrong.'

'Look, so you know, I went to see your sister before I had any idea who you were. I'd seen you in the diner and that was all. You can't hold it against me.'

'It's not that you went to see her – I just don't understand why you kept it a secret. When I came speak with you at the Mason, you never mentioned a thing.'

'I didn't want to scare you off. You were just starting to open up.'

She turned away from me and put her hand over her mouth. There was the sound of sirens in the distance and then the flashing red lights of a cop car zipping across the empty intersection a few blocks down. 'May I ask how she was when you saw her?'

'I wasn't there a long time. She wasn't making too much sense, and I could tell she was in bad shape. But she seemed like a fighter.' I stepped around her so I was facing her again. 'Would you let me drive you home?'

She shook her head. 'I can't face it. I'm scared to be there on my own.'

'Where are your family?'

'I don't have any. Apart from Alice.'

I wanted to ask what happened to their parents, but her tone said not to press it. 'There someplace else you can stay?'

I waited for Randall Johnson's name to come out of her mouth; instead, she shook her head. A tear ran down each cheek. I opened the passenger door for her. 'What do you say I sleep on your couch then? Just for tonight.'

She climbed into the car without saying a word, and I wasn't even sure she'd heard me.

*

I drove us back to her house, Lizzie barely saying a word. She pressed her head against the window and gazed at the road, exhaustion apparently catching up with her.

I parked on the street and followed her to the door. If she was concerned about the neighbours seeing me, or what they thought, she didn't show it; seemed like she was too preoccupied with Alice.

My footsteps clacked on the buffed hallway inside. She led me into the lounge, and when she flicked the lights on, I saw

there were photographs everywhere. Posed shots on the wall –
a happy family, Mr and Mrs Anderson standing behind their
daughters; silver-framed snaps on the mantelpiece – Alice,
Lizzie, together and apart, as children and as adults. There were
two sofas, both upholstered in pea-green fabric, separated by a
wooden corner table that held a Philco wireless. Behind it, an
array of white and purple roses and hydrangeas had wilted in
their vase.

Lizzie poured two glasses of brandy, handed me one, then
folded herself into the wingback leather armchair facing me.
'The thing I hate most is hearing it from that . . . mealy-
mouthed fool.'

'Bailey?'

She nodded. 'That's why I ran off back there, I couldn't bear
giving him the satisfaction. He's done nothing to help me since
it happened.'

The insistence Alice knew the man who attacked her. Their
suspicion about her story. The police had been heavy-handed
for sure, but I still shared some of their doubts; Lizzie couldn't
– or wouldn't – acknowledge the other side of her sister that
apparently existed. 'What does your gut tell you? Who's behind this?'

'I just . . .' She took a sip of brandy from the heavy tumbler in
her hand. 'I can't think. Truly. When it first happened, everyone said it had to be a boxcar Joe – someone passing through
who'd moved on.'

I'd seen the same thing with other murder cases – a certainty
that it had to be an out-of-towner. 'It's easier that way. If it's a
stranger, not someone close to home.'

'But it keeps happening. I just can't see how it could be.'

'Alice and Dwight have any enemies?'

'No, none.'

'Don't take this the wrong way, but is there anyone else Alice would have confided in? Family, a cousin?'

She rested her head against the armchair. 'If you want to know about our family, you should have the guts to ask me straight.'

'You don't say much about them.'

She hesitated, and I thought she was halting that line of conversation there. But then she said, 'Our parents died three years ago.' Her eyes were closed, as though she were seeing their faces as she spoke. 'They were in a car wreck travelling back from Shreveport.'

I shifted in my seat at hearing her say it – the words calling my own memories to mind.

'A farm truck, the Highway Patrol told us later. The driver passed out drunk behind the wheel. They told me that they would have been killed instantly – as if that was a measure of comfort. We were supposed to go with them that day, but Alice convinced them to let us stay home because she wanted to sneak out to a dance.' She covered her face. 'Doesn't seem fair. We survived and they didn't. And now I'm alive, and Alice . . .' Her eyes popped open as she spoke, realising what she almost said.

'I'm sorry.' I handed her my handkerchief.

She dried her eyes. 'I couldn't bear being here at first – this is their house and it was so empty without them. Alice made things easier – she would make out like we would be just fine, the two of us against the world. I still miss them terribly though. I don't know how I'd cope without her.'

I listened without saying anything, letting her tell it at her own pace, evident that she wanted to air her feelings.

'Alice was closer to them. Being the younger sister, I suppose. When they died, I resented her for such a long time. I suppose I blamed her somehow; sounds awful when I say it now.' She pulled at the edge of the handkerchief. 'But it passed and we were closer for it. The only good thing.'

'You told me people think you're twins.'

She nodded, a fleeting smile crossing her lips. 'Sometimes. Only because we look so alike. People that know us can tell we're apples and oranges.'

'How?'

'Alice has a way of . . . getting on with the world. People always like her. Immediately. She's scatty with it, unreliable, but folk just accept her.'

'That doesn't sound like you.'

'The good or the bad?'

I smiled. 'Both.'

She turned her eyes to the floor, her cheeks reddening a little. 'I'm the older sister. Sensible, confident, driven. That's what people say, anyways; I never saw it. Someone told me once I never seem comfortable in my own skin; it stuck with me, sounds about right.'

'I don't know. You seem plenty confident to me.'

She took another sip of her drink; the liquor was compounding her tiredness; her pupils had dilated and given her that tell-tale hazy look. 'What's that supposed to mean?'

'It means I've seen you go toe-to-toe with Bailey, McGaffney, the counterman in the diner, and none of them backed you down.'

She rested one finger on the rim of her glass, tapping it gently. 'Well, it worked, didn't it?'

'What did?'

'The diner. I caught your attention.'

I kept quiet and straightened in my chair, unsure where she was taking the conversation now.

'I wanted to see what you were made of,' she said. 'I'd heard Mr McGaffney talking about a reporter coming down from New York, and I thought maybe you could help us – but I had to see you first.'

'Wait, are you saying you followed me from the *Chronicle* to the diner that day? After I saw you outside McGaffney's?'

Her face was impassive. 'Don't be dramatic, Mr Yates, it wasn't as underhand as you make it sound.'

Mr Yates was starting to sound like a teacher was scolding me. 'I'd be obliged if you'd call me Charlie.'

She nodded. 'Charlie, then. And before you get a big head, I'd have done the same with any reporter from the big city. Anything to get the story out there.'

'So I passed your little test?'

She shrugged. 'You could say that. I was impressed that you came after me – that took intuition. And some guts, after the scene I made.'

I smiled, shaking my head at myself for not seeing it before now. My old editor in Chicago used to say when you can't see what the angle is, it means you're the mark.

She finished her drink and put it down. I offered to fix her another but she declined. 'I'm not a drinker, it makes me say stupid things. I don't know why I just told you that. About the diner.' Her eyes were glazed now, and she was staring into the distance.

I excused myself to go to the bathroom, Lizzie directing me to the end of the hallway. When I came back, she was asleep in the armchair, one leg tucked underneath her. I called her name to wake her, and gave her my hand to help her up. She weighed almost nothing. I asked which was her bedroom, opening the door for her when we got there.

'Thank you, Charlie.' She went to make for her bed, but then she turned back and kissed me on the lips. She held it, lingering, and I was too shocked to react. Then she stepped away again, coy now, wished me goodnight, and shut the door.

I went back to the front room, extinguished the lights and stretched out on the sofa. I lay awake in the gloom, eyes open, a hot sensation in my chest – almost a glow. I wondered, again, if I was being honest with myself about why I'd stayed in Texarkana.

CHAPTER NINETEEN

I woke early, the first milky light of the dawn creeping through the windows. I was stiff and my legs ached from sleeping on the cramped sofa, same way they did in cold weather. Weak bones get that way.

I slipped into the shower, not wanting to wake Lizzie, but she was coming down the stairs by the time I got out. She was dressed, wearing a round-necked eggshell-blue blouse and tweed trousers. She'd fixed her face, ready to leave the house. Without her saying a word, I sensed shame or embarrassment coming off her, a regret for something that never happened. I started to wonder if I'd imagined the kiss.

'You were shouting. In the night.' She was sheepish as she said it, answering a question I hadn't asked.

'I was? Sorry. I hope I didn't disturb you too much.'

'You can't have slept a wink on that sofa.'

'I've slept in worse places. It was warm at least.'

She didn't say anything to that, instead rummaging through her purse. It was clear she was uncomfortable and I figured there could only be one thing making her feel that way. I wanted to say forget about it, that it was nothing, but I could tell she didn't want to bring it up.

I stuffed my feet into my shoes. 'Where are you headed?'

She looked uncertain, like she hadn't thought about it until that second. 'I want to go back through town. I'll do everything we did yesterday again if I have to.'

'You think that's wise? Seems to me like retracing your steps is a waste of time. Maybe you should stay at here for a while – in case Alice tries to call.'

She chewed on the corner of her lip. 'I can't sit at home; I have to do something.'

I nodded. 'Come on, then, I'll drive you.'

'There's one other place I want to try.'

'Name it.'

'I have to go to where it happened.'

*

We walked to the car and I noticed Lizzie stealing a look in the direction of her neighbours as we went. Didn't take a mind reader to know what was troubling her – the presence of a strange man at the Anderson place big news on the quiet street. I didn't give a damn, but I felt bad for her, knowing what conclusions folk might jump to. Most of all, though, I was puzzled – Lizzie was different that morning, quiet, distracted. I figured the strain she was under was enough to make anyone unpredictable.

Lizzie directed me along New Boston Road. When she guided me onto the dirt track where her sister and Breems were attacked, my mood darkened, mind racing with sounds and faces – Alice, bloody and alone in the night, running from the killer; Randall Johnson talking about cooze; Bailey and Sherman; Richard Davis; Jimmy Robinson. By the time Lizzie said to pull over, I felt lightheaded and short-fused, as though I'd drunk too much black coffee on an empty stomach.

We stepped out of the car. Lizzie stood behind her open door, grasping it like a shield. It was a bright morning, overcast without being cold, but the feeling I got standing on the edge of the woods was like standing at the top of a staircase to a dark cellar. Lizzie took several faltering paces into the undergrowth, eyes fixed somewhere in the distance. I followed behind.

She moved through the trees, head turning from side to side; occasionally she looked back to check I was still there. Then she stopped, still, and her whole body sagged. 'It was here. The deputies showed me.'

I drew up next to her. 'What are we doing out here, Lizzie? You're torturing yourself.'

'I had to be sure.'

'Of what?'

'That she wasn't here.' She toed a small dirt pile on the ground. 'I had a dream last night, that she'd come back here. She looked at me and told me she had to go to where she died.'

I reached out and put a hand on her shoulder. An insignificant gesture that meant nothing, but was as much as I could do.

'She's dead, isn't she, Charlie?'

I took a breath before I answered, considered what to say. My gut told me she was right, but why confirm her worst fears on the strength of nothing more than my instinct? 'You can't give up on her.'

'I can't stop from thinking about what he did to her. I see it in my nightmares.'

I closed my eyes, thought about ways to get her away from there. The place was dragging her down into a dark abyss. 'Being here serves no purpose.'

She scraped her fingers down her face. She had paled, her

jaw trembling. 'What would drive a man to do such terrible things?'

'We oughtta leave.' I reached for her hand, but she withdrew it.

She stared through the trees. 'I've searched my conscience. Every day since it happened, trying to think of what we might have done to bring this on us. At first I was sure God was punishing us for something – but then I considered it some more and realised Alice never did anything to deserve this.' She covered her face with her hands. 'So I thought it must be because of something I did. That I'm the reason this happened to her.'

I put my arms around her, feeling her hair against my face, the scent of Ivory Soap. 'This is the work of a man, and he's the only one responsible. Don't ever think otherwise.'

'Alice told me she wished he'd killed her. So she wouldn't have to live with it all.'

Echoes of the waitress in the coffee shop on the day I arrived: '*There's folk say she's better off dead . . .*' The dirty truth they couldn't have known: the victim agrees with them. I grabbed Lizzie's hand, not letting her pull away this time. It was cold as sheet metal in winter. 'We're leaving. She's not here and we can't help her standing around this place.'

She let me lead her but stopped after a couple of steps. 'How could they ever think she would know someone as evil as that?'

'Bailey?'

She gave a little nod. 'And Sherman. They were so determined Alice knew the man.'

'They've got their own agenda. I don't know what it is, but I don't think it's about helping your sister. That's down to us.'

I set off again, almost dragging Lizzie behind me. The undergrowth was mulch under my feet. To my left, I noticed an elm that had *tXk* carved into its trunk, just under eye level. I stopped and ran my fingers over the letters, rough edges splintering as I did. *tXk* – shorthand for Texarkana? I glanced at Lizzie, but she was staring at the ground. Trudging back to the car, I saw three more trees with the same carving. Dead soldiers got memorial plaques and prayers for their souls; Alice got three letters hacked into rotting bark by persons unknown.

CHAPTER TWENTY

We ran the same loops through town, State Line north to south and back again, and showed Alice's picture in every coffee shop, diner and restaurant that we could find. In most it was the same waitresses and hostesses as the day before, and the looks of pity they afforded Lizzie were impossible to miss. No-one had any information about Alice, no-one had seen her. Part of me clung to the hope that she'd split, got as far away from Texarkana as possible, but with every shake of the head, I grew more certain she was dead. I tried to hide it, but I sensed Lizzie felt it too. At seven that evening, she asked me to take her home. She looked tired, but I could tell it was the despair setting in that had beat her down.

I dropped her at the end of her driveway. I offered to sleep on her sofa again if she wanted, but she shook her head, said thanks anyway. 'I'll pick you up in the morning,' I said. 'We'll lean on the police again, see what they've got.'

She nodded once, but her heart wasn't in it. She shut the car door, then leaned in through the open window. 'I know you had a run-in with Randy, and I want you to know I don't care. I hope it wasn't on my account, though.'

I rested my hands on top of the steering wheel, surprised she hadn't mentioned it before. 'Your sweetheart's some piece of work.'

'I wouldn't call him that. Not really.' She backed away from the car. 'You might have taken the opinion he's overbearing from when you saw us together, but he's not always like that. He's a good man.' She took another step back, the feeling like she was distancing herself from me. 'Thank you for all your help, I'm in your debt.' With that, she was gone.

*

I drove back to the Mason trying to work up a list of priorities in my head – the leads I was working on before Alice's disappearance. I was distracted, though, my mind turning to thoughts of Lizzie every time my concentration slipped an inch.

I wasn't even certain what I felt for her. Compassion, sympathy? No question. A need to help her? For certain. Attraction, desire? Call that a maybe – moving on yes; the jealousy I felt when she was telling me what a swell fella Randall was seemed to confirm that much. I thought again about the kiss – so fleeting as to be inconsequential, and yet it'd sparked an excitement in me that I hadn't felt in years, not since those early days with Jane.

Memories from the time came back to me: the nickel-ride on the Staten Island Ferry, her so excited for me to see Liberty up close for the first time. Bicycling over the Brooklyn Bridge so we could picnic next to the river, taking in the view of the city. Eating Cannoli from Arturo's deli.

Thinking about those times made me realise the memories were just that, and that in truth, it had been a long time since things were good between us. Dredging up the past served no purpose; all that mattered now was finding the killer and getting justice for Lizzie and Alice.

I parked behind the Mason and went to check my messages. Richard Davis was my priority; I wanted him to get an eye on Randall Johnson as soon as he was out of his cell. But the clerk said they had nothing for me, so I crossed to the telephones and called the sheriff's office. The deputy that answered told me they'd kicked Davis loose at lunchtime. He declined to give me an address for him.

I set it aside temporarily. Three more nickels and a story about being an insurance assessor with claim money to dole out got me numbers and addresses for Patty Summerbell's friends Anna Mendoza and Marcy Pettinger – the girls Davis claimed were with her the night she died. I put a call in to Mendoza's house first but no-one picked up. Her address was West 6th Street – Texas side; I circled her details in my notebook and figured to try again later.

Marcy Pettinger answered straightaway. Her voice was nasal and she sounded anxious when I told her I was a reporter. Worried she'd hang up at any moment, I came right to the point and asked her if Patty Summerbell had an argument with a man the night she died.

'Mister, I wasn't the only one there that night, I barely even talked to Patty.'

'Miss Pettinger, you're not in any trouble. I just need to know what happened.'

A pause, then: 'I only know the parts Anna told me.'

I glanced at my pad, checking the surname. 'Anna Mendoza?'

'Y'already spoke with her?'

I let it ride. 'Some. Give me your version anyway. Fill in the gaps for me.'

'Look, this is all I know, on my life.' She sighed. 'Patty went outside early on and when she came back she was steaming mad. She was tight-lipped, so I asked Anna what went on and she told me Patty had a fight with someone. I don't know who, and I don't know what about. Then, right when we were talking, this sailor asked me if I'd care to dance the Lindy with him, and I plain forgot about it after that.'

Bingo: confirmation of Davis's story. 'You didn't see the man? Get his name?'

'No, sir, I'm sorry.'

I thanked her and broke the connection, put another ring around Anna Mendoza's name in my book.

Last nickel, last call – this time the *Chronicle*, certain they'd have heard about Alice's disappearance by now. It took four tries, the circuits still jammed. I finally got through to Robinson, who cussed when he heard my voice.

'You heard about Alice Anderson?' I said.

'Yeah. What about it?'

'Got a line on her yet?'

He growled something I didn't catch, but when he spoke again, his tone was defensive. 'There's nothing out there. I've shaken down about every fool in the book and no-one knows a damn thing.'

'How hard you shake?'

'Plenty hard. That girl shouldn't be out there on her own.'

Real defensive now. And a nervous silence when he finished speaking – not Robinson's style at all. 'There something you're not telling me, Jimmy?'

A crackling noise came down the line, like he was scratching the mousey-blonde stubble on his chin. 'For instance?'

I gripped the cord of the payphone, overtaken by urgency now. 'If you know something, Jimmy, now's the time to get it off your chest.'

'When'd you start caring so much, New York? This is just a story, right; "Murder sells" – ain't that your line?'

He gave me pause with the question, one I'd been wrestling with myself. Lizzie Anderson was at the heart of it – I could admit that to myself now. I had to find the killer to do right by her. Whatever attraction existed was too vague to put a name to, but undeniable all the same. I told myself to put the kiss aside, that it was a traumatised woman's cry for help. Didn't stop the memory of that flickering excitement from coming to mind every time I thought about her. But there was more to it. I recalled the soldiers at Red River, Jack Sherman trying to scare me off, Bailey excoriating me, and knew for sure now that the biggest reason was the one I couldn't put into words. The one that said I had to do this, just so I could look at myself in the mirror again without hearing people calling me a goddamn coward. 'I didn't know anything back then. Now I do. So give.'

He let out a long breath. 'It's loose talk, is all.' He sounded shaky when he said it.

'Try me.'

He spoke in a near whisper, newsroom shouts almost drowning him out. 'I spoke to a nurse at Pine Street, says she saw a stranger hanging around the place the day Alice disappeared.'

'Hanging around?'

'I told you it was loose.'

157

I took my hat off and ran a hand through my hair. 'Why's the nurse connecting this party with Alice? She see them together?'

His breathing was shallow down the line. 'No, no. Way she tells it, she saw him all that day, but not before or after.'

'Pretty damn thin.'

'S'what I already told you. I knew I shouldn't have said noth—'

'You get a description?'

'Ain't much of a one. Brown hair, had on grey pants and a green check shirt. Said she only saw him sitting down, so she can't say how tall.'

It felt like I was being fed a line of hooey. 'Sounds like every other man in Texarkana.' I couldn't see what angle Robinson was playing, but my guess was he was trying to send me on a wild goose chase. His nervousness came off as an act, and with every conversation, I got more certain he was mixed up in it all. And more angry at him. 'Why would she even notice him then?'

'They hell do I know? You work a ten-hour shift, I guess you'd remember a fresh face sitting around your place of business all day.'

I weighed it up for a moment. 'There's nothing to this, Robinson. It's all hot air. Call me when you get something solid.' I went to hang up.

'There's more.'

I froze with the receiver halfway to the cradle. I hesitated, then put the handset back to my ear.

'Yates? You hear me?'

'I'm listening,' I said.

'My source says she's sure the man was a cop.'

CHAPTER TWENTY-ONE

My head felt like it was full of helium gas as I ran to my room to change my shirt, and I couldn't concentrate for any length of time. Robinson was stringing me, no doubt about it – but he knew how to bait the hook. When I'd pressed him on why this nurse thought the man was a cop, he clammed up, said he couldn't say any more.

I opened the door expecting to see my case diagram spread across the floor, but was greeted by a pristine carpet. The papers I'd arranged were gone, and the furniture had been replaced in its original position. I stood in the doorway, unnerved. Could have been an over-zealous maid. Or it could have been someone else entirely, trying to make it look like that. I examined the lock on the door, and the bolt, but it was futile; whoever had been in had entered with a key. I ran my fingers over the door handle, the feeling like I wasn't alone in the room. I pulled the door shut behind me, locked it, and propped myself against the wood.

I went to go to the closet, determined to press on, but something on the floor stopped me. I rubbed my eyes. There was a piece of paper – but it wasn't mine. It was a small note, swept to one side when I'd opened the door.

I glanced around the room, checked the bathroom too, but it was empty – the note slipped under the door sometime when I was out. I picked it up. It was typewritten in block capitals.

RED RIVER IS THE KEY. PULL THE THREAD
AND IT ALL UNRAVELS. WATCH YOURSELF.

A shiver ran through me. The atmosphere in the room was electric, like the air before a summer thunderstorm. I read it again, looking for meaning beyond the words. Lightheaded to woozy, the letters blurring on the page. I checked both sides twice, held it up to the light, but there was nothing else to it – just black ink on clean white paper.

Somehow it felt authentic – the opposite of Robinson's big act. And it meant there was more to this than a killer picking couples at random; there was a motive here, and that meant there was a method to it all.

More than that, someone knew what was happening – and why.

CHAPTER TWENTY-TWO

Wednesday morning. Only three and a half days to stop the killer.

I rose early after a fitful sleep, eager to get moving. The night before, when I finally stopped re-reading the note, I'd collared every bellhop in the building, dropping five spots and asking if they'd seen anyone go by my room, or walking around on my floor. Thirty bucks-worth got me bupkiss. I greased the receptionists, the bartender, even the duty manager, but got goose-egg from them too.

So the note remained anonymous. I kept running through candidates as I drove across town that morning, but no-one fit the picture. When I got to the public library, it wasn't due to open for another hour. I sat in a diner around the corner and passed the time drinking coffee, feeling my nerves jangle with adrenaline. The note was in my jacket pocket, as heavy as a moon rock and almost as unknowable.

When the library opened at nine, I was the first person through the door. I made for the newspaper archives.

Three hours of hit-and-miss searching got me this much: Red River Army Depot opened in 1941 as an ammunition storage facility. In the same year, on a neighbouring site six miles east, the Lone Star Ammunition Plant was opened, churning out every type of bomb, shell and bullet the army could use. When the war ramped up, RRAD was converted to a general supply depot and tank repair facility. Then in forty-four, RRAD and Lone Star merged to form the sprawling Red River Arsenal. Until that point, the plant had been GOCO – Government Owned, Contractor Operated, and the contract to operate the plant was held by a company called the Texas Defence Corporation, owned by Mr Winfield Henderson Callaway. When the two sites merged, the army took over running of the plant directly.

There were newspapers scattered all over the tables in front of me, and my notepad was covered in inky fingerprints. I set the typewritten note on the tabletop and read it for the hundredth time, then let my head loll back.

Every move I had was compromised. I wanted a list of employees from the Red River plant, to see if any familiar names jumped out – but the army had near as hell shot me just for going to the front gate; there was no chance they'd give me the information I wanted. The other tack was to cross-check the police list of suspects for names that worked at Red River. If a name did cross over, it didn't make for solid evidence, but it was a starting point – another lead to run down. But again, Bailey and Sherman were more likely to cuss me out than to help me.

And then there was the question of trust. I hadn't told the police about the Red River connection I was putting together, and as much as I was sure Robinson was playing me, if there was anything to his tipoff about the 'cop' hanging around Alice's room the day she disappeared, it confirmed I'd made the right decision by keeping quiet.

I checked my watch – midday. I hadn't thought about Alice all day and I hadn't spoken to Lizzie since the night before.

The bright sunshine made me blink when I stepped outside.

I jogged to a telephone booth across the street, fishing nickels from my pocket. Two calls to Lizzie's house went unanswered; I dialled again, this time connecting to the Mason.

'Charlie Yates, room 316. Any messages from Elizabeth Anderson for me?'

'Hold please.' The line crackled, and then, 'I'm afraid not, sir. I do have another message for you though.'

'Shoot.'

'From a Mr Davis – requests that you call him. Would you like the number he left?' I said yes and scribbled it on my hand as she read it out. I thanked her and hung up as soon as I got the last digit down, then dialled again.

Davis picked up on the first ring, sounded pleased when he heard my voice. 'How goes the hunt, Mr Yates?'

'I told you to call me when you got out of jail.'

He scoffed. 'Oh don't pay that no mind. Turns out I knew the way back home just fine.'

'That's not what I meant. We had a deal.'

'I knowed what you meant. Didn't get me out of the joint no faster, though, did it?'

I dipped my head, embarrassed. 'I got caught up; I was helping to look for Alice Anderson. She's missing.'

'That right?' He whistled in mock admiration. 'Guess we're copacetic then, huh?'

Every now and then he used a word that didn't fit with the rest of his vocabulary. I wondered where he had picked them up. 'Did you ask me to call just to rag on me?'

He laughed softly. 'Okay, okay. You right.' He cleared his throat. 'Look I still want to help. I can't promise nothing, but you put your man in front of me and I'll take a good look at him.'

A little spark travelled up my chest. 'Good. I'll come collect you. Give me your address.'

'I'm at 225 Beech Street. Go to Fifth and Beech.'

'Stay right there.'

'Hey, Mr Yates, you find the Anderson girl?'

I glanced around the cramped telephone booth, guilt, frustration, anger, futility all crowded in there with me. 'Not yet.'

*

Beech Street was on the edge of town to the east; the homes were dotted at irregular intervals, closer to shacks than houses. The air smelled of wood smoke and there were weeds sprouting out between the sidewalk slabs. It was the poor relation to the pristine order of Carson Courts, just across town.

Davis was waiting on his stoop when I arrived. I swung the passenger door open before I even stopped. 'Hop in.' He had on a worn pair of brown slacks and a purple shirt with the sleeves turned up. There was one window at the front of his house, cracked and stained, a pair of flimsy drapes barely visible through it. I'd assumed he lived alone, and the look of the place seemed to confirm it – no sign of anyone else that I could see.

He slid along the bench seat next to me. 'Where to?'

I pulled away from the kerb. 'Carson Courts. You know it?'

'Sure. Mean to say I heard of it, ain't never been there.'

We rode in silence at first. Davis was a hard read. I watched him out of the corner of my eye; if he was nervous, he didn't show it. 'Tell me your story again,' I said.

He fussed with the widow handle. 'You forget it? Or you still testing me out?'

The kid was razor sharp at times. His version of events was clear in my head, so I wanted to see if it was in his too. Keen as I was to hang something on Randy Johnson, I had no reason to trust Davis; it only made sense to see if a detail would change or slip with another telling. And now he'd called my tune, there was no sense in trying to hoodwink him. 'You're damn right. Let's not forget, the two times I've seen you, the first was when you tailed me, and the second time you were in jail.' I glanced at him. 'Far as I'm concerned, your credibility is still in question.'

He lit a cigarette and blew smoke at the roof of the car. 'Have it your way . . .' He told his tale again – Patty Summerbell slipping out from the dance and slapping the big GI she was arguing with. The hazy description of the man. It all chimed with what he'd given me before. Saying that, it was so light on detail, there wasn't much to check.

'You remember anything else about the man?'

He clamped his smoke between his front teeth and shook his head.

'What about Summerbell? What can you tell me about her?'

'Speaking plain, not a lot. Ain't like we ever talked at school; I knew her on account of her being on the cheerleading team. All the boys knew those girls – dreaming about marrying one of them someday. Got to be on the football team for that kind of thing, though.'

'You ever know her to court any boys?'

'Couldn't tell you. Likesay, we kept different company.'

'Figures. I can't see you making the football team.'

'Why not?'

'You can't weigh a hundred-fifty pounds soaking wet.'

He dangled his smoke out the window. 'Speed's the thing; I always been quick. And I can take a knock or two.'

I glanced at his face, the new swelling on his cheek on top of the fading ones I'd first seen him with. 'The police put that one on you too?'

He touched the welt with his little finger. 'This? Naw, not this one.'

I expected he'd want to tell the story – proud of himself – but he just kept looking ahead.

'So who did?' I pressed.

'This just a disagreement. Over a girl.'

'You win or lose?'

'You should see the other fella.'

I stifled a laugh at his line of baloney – the far-fetched notion of him winning a bar fight. We passed the Carson Courts entrance sign and I slowed down. I circled around Johnson's block, coming onto it from the opposite direction this time. I parked at the end of his street, across from his house, giving us a clear view of his front door, but from far enough away not to be seen.

'Now what?' Davis asked.

I slouched down low, rested my head on the seat. Johnson's Olds was in his driveway, so I figured to wait him out. I pointed. 'Watch that house, and when he comes out, you make the call.' It dawned on me then that I'd missed a trick: I should have put a fake or two in front of Davis first; if his story was just a cry for attention, then he was likely to pick out anyone I showed him – keep the train on the tracks. I reprimanded myself for being sloppy.

'What if he's not home? How long do we wait?'

'His car's there, he's got to go someplace eventually.'

We sat in silence. The temperature rose as the sun beat down, enough cloud in the sky to trap the heat, not enough to provide shade. We lowered the windows all the way down, and the car filled with the smell of lantana flowers from the freshly-planted yards. Davis got fidgety, like a kid, started futzing with the radio; he jumped around the dial, flipping between four country stations, and ending up on a newsreader criticising the draft holiday Congress had just passed. My legs were starting to ache, so I stretched to work out some kinks. 'What do you know about Red River?'

'As in RRAD?'

I nodded, eyes trained on Johnson's house.

'Why you asking?'

'Passing the time.'

Davis stretched, mimicking my movements. 'Not too much. The one benefit to being blackballed I guess.'

More drama. 'Care to elaborate on that?'

'They wouldn't take me on.' He picked a piece of lint off his shirt. 'Kid like me, coming outta high school with nothing to his name, got three choices for work around here: he can join the Army, he can go south to the oilfields, or he can go work at RRAD. Chances of dying on the job's about the same for the first two, so most folk go for RRAD. Lucky for me, Old Man Callaway's next thing to a Nazi, so he wouldn't look twice at a bum like me. Callaway's this local bigwig, used to run the place.'

'I've seen him. He put up the reward for information on the murders; didn't seem so bad that day.'

Davis screwed up his face. 'He's a good ol' boy, pride of the south, a gentleman to the bottom of his boots. Do anything for anyone – so long as you ain't a Jew. Or a nigger. Or a woman, or—'

'Why was it lucky he didn't take you on?'

'Who the hell wants to work a munitions line all day?'

I could feel sweat soaking through my shirt under my armpits. I was twitchy and I wanted to be on the go. 'Let me put the question another way: who can I talk to for information about the place?'

Davis chuckled and opened his mouth to say something. As he did, Randall Johnson's front door opened. We both bolted upright in our seats. Then Lizzie walked out, and for some reason my heart dropped into my guts. The envy I'd felt the day before, when she'd talked him up, came back tenfold at seeing him with her. Worse, my pride was wounded at the fact that she'd gone running back to him for protection after sending me home. Suddenly it felt like finding Alice had been my chance to prove myself to her – and I'd blown it. So far.

She stopped on the driveway, turned and said something in the direction of the open door, Johnson out of sight. Then she walked off. I fought an urge to go after her, check she was alright.

I looked at Davis, his face almost pressed to the windshield. His mouth was drooping open and his complexion had gone several shades whiter, like he'd seen a ghost. He saw me watching him, glanced at me and looked away again, like he didn't want me to see his reaction.

He went to speak, but before he could, the door opened again and Randy Johnson appeared. Son of a bitch was wearing a hat – impossible to get a good look at him. He strode down the driveway and jumped into his car in a hurry; the Olds rocked on it springs when he hefted himself into it.

Davis was hunched forward, squinting, but I could tell by his face he hadn't got a look. I started the engine. 'I'll get us closer.'

'Good, because I can't see a damn thing from here.'

I swerved into traffic just as the Olds pulled away. There were two cars between us, so I stayed wide in my lane and watched Johnson's wing mirror. Carson Courts was strictly low-speed, so I made no attempt to overtake the middle cars. Johnson was driving like he was on a Sunday cruise anyway, so it wasn't hard to keep up.

We followed him back towards State Line Avenue. Before we got there, though, Johnson turned off onto New Boston Road, and I started to get a bad feeling. The cars between us thinned out, so I kept my distance; chances were Johnson wouldn't recognise my ride, but I didn't want to risk it. We cruised a mile along the road, then Johnson turned onto a dirt track.

My pulse thundered through my body. It was the same dirt track Lizzie had taken me down when she showed me where her sister was attacked.

I followed Johnson down the lane, his Olds only just visible through the cloud of dust it was kicking up. The dust was good, gave us cover, but I still didn't want to get too close. The car shook and rattled as we bounced through potholes along the way.

'Where the hell are you taking us?' Davis said.

I didn't answer.

'Mr Yates?'

I pushed us on, determined to keep Johnson in sight, even though I had a good idea where he was headed.

Johnson disappeared around a bend. I slowed as we approached it, knowing we were close now, and when I saw he'd pulled the Olds over, I backed up until we were just out of sight. I jumped out of the car and jogged a little way, hugging the verge for cover, until I had him in sight again. I saw him fling his door open and step out into the afternoon haze. He looked around, but not like he was checking for anyone else – more like a man who's lost, trying to get his bearings. Then he took off into the woods. It was right by the spot Lizzie had taken me to.

Davis caught up to me. 'Mr Yates, what's going on?'

The words registered like something from a dream, distant. I was too focused on deciding what to do to respond. Reason it out: Johnson being there was proof of absolutely nothing; but then again, what good reason could he have? I stood there, indecision gripping me.

I heard him move before I saw it. The noise snapped me to attention; Davis stormed past me and off down the dirt road. 'I'm done waiting around, I'll go look the sum'bitch in the face, and we'll get this straightened out.'

'Richard . . .' I crept forward a step and called him again, but he didn't answer. I chased after him.

Just then Johnson reappeared between the trees. Everyone froze. Johnson spotted Davis immediately, now only twenty yards away; he looked at him the way a lion looks at a wounded zebra. Then he saw me over Davis's shoulder, and it was like Davis wasn't there – Johnson staring past him, peering at me.

Davis glanced back at me, his bravado faltering, then faced front again. I started towards them both, hands in my pockets, casual. There was a tense silence, the only sound the intermittent crunch of stones under my feet.

Davis called back to me. 'I think it's him, Mr Yates.' His voice wavered.

Johnson pointed at me. 'What the hell are you doing here?'

I kept moving, passed by Davis and then stopped so I was between him and Johnson. Over my shoulder, I murmured for Davis to keep quiet. Then, to Johnson: 'Could ask you the same thing, Randall.'

'Are you following me?'

'Answer the question.'

'The hell with you. I told you before I don't answer to you. And I told you what would happen if I saw you again.'

'Threats don't carry much weight with me.'

'Your smart mouth is gonna talk you into real trouble.'

My hands were still in my pockets, but balled into fists now. I felt sweat running down my back; if it came to a fight, he'd break me in two. 'Tell me what you're doing out here and we can all go home.'

Davis piped up. 'You best answer him, boy.'

'Boy' – in another situation it would have been funny.

Johnson pointed at Davis. 'Who's this little string bean? What's going on?'

Davis pushed past me, chest puffed out; his skinny frame was like a metal coat hanger, bent out of shape inside his clothes. I grabbed him and pulled him back.

Johnson bent down and picked up a handful of rocks. He reared back and pitched one at us, like a fast ball; it sailed just wide of me. 'Get outta here, you shitbirds.' I'd started backing up, but he threw another one, on target this time; I sidestepped just before it hit me. 'Go.'

I scrambled for the car. Davis was behind me, walking slowly backwards, still facing Johnson. He beat his own chest with both hands. 'I know about you, mister. I seen you.'

Johnson launched another stone, taking a two-step run up now for extra power. I jumped in and started the car and shouted over the engine for Davis to get the hell in. Davis took longer strides now, still facing down the onslaught, then whirled around and ran the last few paces. A rock hit his door just as he ducked behind it. Johnson scooped up another handful and kept throwing, the sound like heavy hailstones on the roof. One hit the windscreen; I flinched, expecting it to shatter. It held, but a crack split the middle of the glass.

The car lurched forward. I skidded through a U-turn and sped off. Johnson receded from sight in the rearview; I took a deep breath and rubbed the sweat out of my eyes with one hand. We flew along the dirt track, my breathing short until we made it back to New Boston Road. In my mind I saw Johnson's face as he'd hurled those rocks, the mask of hatred and aggression that descended so quickly, and more and more I could imagine him capable of terrible acts of violence – exactly the manner of man I was hunting. Then another thought came, one that scared me to the core: Lizzie alone with him. Trusting him as her protector.

CHAPTER TWENTY-THREE

Davis babbled as we drove. 'I didn't know whether to laugh or wind my wristwatch. He damn near took your head off.' He was giddy, his adrenaline running high. 'I thought he was gonna kill us. That big sum'bitch coulda pulled up one of them trees.'

I kept one eye on the mirror, checking Johnson wasn't tailing us – but the road behind was clear.

'We shoulda fought him, Mr Yates. He'd have had a problem with both of us—'

I couldn't put it together in my head. Johnson reacted like he'd been caught doing something he shouldn't – and it made me even more suspicious. But when I stepped back, I knew I couldn't trust my instincts where he was concerned; I disliked the man, and I disliked him being around Lizzie – and that was clouding my thinking. 'What you said back there – how certain are you?'

'I think it was him, Mr Yates.'

'"Think" isn't good enough.'

'Well, I mean, it was dark that night and all, and I didn't see him for long, but . . .'

'But you think it was him?'

'I'm pretty sure. That fella had the size and the build.'

I clenched my teeth, my head fuzzy with it all. What if I was in so deep on Johnson, I'd lost perspective? The killer could be anyone in Texarkana. If the trail I was following went cold, people were going to die because of my failure.

'What do you think he was doing all the way out there?'

'You ever read a newspaper, Davis?' The name sounded strange and I couldn't figure it at first. Then I cottoned on – I'd been calling him Richard until now. The mask had slipped pretty fast now I didn't need him any more.

'I don't read so good.'

'Figure of speech,' I said, waving it off. 'That was where Alice Anderson was attacked.'

His face went white and his lips parted and shut twice without a sound coming out. He rubbed his eyes with his palms. 'Don't that just about prove it? He got no business being out there.'

'It doesn't prove anything.' I said it to myself as much as to him.

*

Ten minutes later, we pulled up outside Davis's place, a shaft of sunlight breaking through the clouds and strafing the patched-up roof. I set the brake and held out my hand. 'Thank you.'

Davis took it like it was the first time he'd ever shook one. 'You wanna come in for a lemonade?'

'Thanks, but no. I got work to do.'

He got out and rested a hand on the open door. 'Hey, you know you was asking me about Red River earlier?'

I leaned across the seat so I could see his face better. 'What about it?'

'Well, I was thinking you could try asking Winfield

Callaway about it. Ain't nothing goes on there without his say-so.'

I righted myself, deflated. 'He's the old news on Red River. I need someone with access—'

'Old news?' He chuckled to himself. 'Ain't you ever read a paper, Mr Yates?'

'What are you talking about?'

'Contract's up to run the plant again. Ain't no-one but Callaway gonna get it. I mean, I wouldn't roll him over if he was passed out in a puddle, but you need information, he's your man. If he'll talk to you.' Davis shut the door and walked off, one hand held up as a goodbye.

I shook my head, more worried than ever that I was losing my touch.

CHAPTER TWENTY-FOUR

Weighing up what I had, it was incomplete going on light-weight. I could put Randall Johnson in a fight with Patty Summerbell the night she died. I saw him visit the place Alice Anderson was attacked – for reasons unknown. I could link three of the victims to Red River, which was key according to the anonymous note. A note which, for all I knew, could be bunk. I had an alleged cop hanging around Alice's room the day she disappeared – and not the smallest clue where she might be.

Lizzie didn't answer when I telephoned, so I called at her house, but she wasn't home. It was quiet and still, only the white swing seat on the porch swaying gently in the breeze. There was a sadness to the place, so much loss. It was too big even for the two young women; I could see why rattling around in it on her own would have been so hard for Lizzie – the empty quiet a constant reminder of what used to fill it.

The *Chronicle* building was next. I figured to write a piece to call in to Sal in New York, and then see what I could pry out of McGaffney about Winfield Callaway. But when I pulled up outside the building, Robinson and two others, one a photographer, were exiting in a hurry. I called out through my window. 'What's going on?'

'Sheriff's briefing, right now. Some kind of announcement too.'

'They got a suspect?'

Robinson shrugged, lifting his hands in an exaggerated fashion, aping like it was all a big joke. The man was as unpredictable as a rattlesnake.

*

Bailey was already behind the lectern when I got to the briefing, looking like a politician making a speech at a rally. The mob of reporters pressed as close as they could, the crowd moving like a wave as men jostled and surged forward. I spotted Robinson working his way through it, elbows getting him almost to the front. Jack Sherman stood on Bailey's left, arms crossed; he was flanked by five assorted deputies and city cops.

Bailey cleared his throat and a hush descended, the hacks at the back calling for quiet. 'Thank you for coming, gentlemen. Y'all know we're stretched right now, so I'm gonna keep this brief. First order of business, some bulletins for you. One: I can now confirm that Peter Hamilton's death Sunday last, in Spring Lake Park, was as a result of the bullet wound to his head. Mr Hamilton was beaten extensively before and after he died . . .'

The noise level jumped at that, even cynical hacks shocked to hear he was beaten post-mortem. Bailey paused to let it die down again.

'. . . and so it has taken some time to rightly ascertain what done for him. Two: the DPS lab in Austin is done with the ballistics work, and the gun used to shoot both Mr Hamilton and Margaret Langley, is the same weapon was used in the murder of Edward Logan and Patty Summerbell, seven days previous. The gun in question—'

From the crowd: 'What about Dwight Breems and Alice Anderson?'

Bailey's face changed, his lips turning down like he'd just eaten something that had gone bad. 'The ballistics in that case are inconclusive, so y'all know I can't comment to that.'

The crowd made its own conclusion. Two different voices shouted out at the same time, the louder one saying, 'It has to be the same man, surely? Come on, Sheriff.' That drew a hard look from Sherman.

'We can't put together a case based on assumptions. We go as the facts go, and right now, they ain't telling us either way. So we keeping an open mind.' Bailey ran a finger along the brim of his hat. 'Item three: analysis of the bullets found in Spring Lake Park indicate they were fired from a weapon with a barrel having six lands and grooves with a left hand twist. That would indicate a Colt .22 automatic pistol or similar.' Bailey lifted his hat by the crown and straightened it. 'Texarkana authorities turning over every stone on that front. We talking to gun shops, pawn shops – anyone might've sold that type of weapon – and to anyone with a Colt .22 registered in their name. What we need, is for citizens to supplement our efforts. So get this message out there: if you know someone who recently got a hold of one of these guns, or if you had one stolen in the last six months, or you just seen someone waving one around, you need to holler. We providing stock images of the type of firearm we talking about, so make sure you print the damn pictures; I ain't gonna ask twice on this.'

Bailey took a breath, and the questions from the crowd cranked up again. 'Have you got any suspects yet, Sheriff?'

Bailey signalled for quiet; it took almost a minute for the

crowd to settle. 'I'll take questions presently. Second order of business. Due to the current circumstances, the decision has been taken to impose a curfew within the greater Texarkana area, from ten till sun-up, for the protection of all citizens. Anyone found on the streets in violation of this curfew will be subject to arrest.'

A new voice from the crowd: 'That mean you're expecting more murders, Sheriff?'

'It's a sensible precaution, that's all.'

Another crescendo of noise, each man deciding to speak his opinion aloud, as if it was a town hall meeting.

I waited for it to die down, raised my hand and shouted over the residual din. 'Sheriff, have you got any leads on the whereabouts of Alice Anderson?'

I noticed Robinson shoot me a look as I said it, a hint of nervousness on his face – likely worried I was going to ask the cops straight out if they'd had a man hanging around her room the day she disappeared.

Bailey glared at me a moment before he spoke, and I felt a little judder of fear. 'Not at present. Our working theory is that she done left town.'

Bailey looked away as soon as he answered, and I realised then that Sherman had been glaring at me the whole time too. We were long past any pretence at a working relationship now; I stuck my hand up again just to rattle them some more. 'Why haven't you brought in any suspects yet, Sheriff?' I held a notepad up as I said it, my most innocent *just-doing-my-job* expression on my face.

Before either could speak, another hack shouted out. 'Yeah, what about it, Sheriff? It's been three weeks nearly.'

Bailey glanced at Sherman, who looked ready to start knocking heads together. 'Settle down, son. We've questioned more than two hundred men – some we eliminated, some we still looking at. We requisitioned new premises to work out of because there ain't room enough in our building.' Bailey's face was red now, a controlled fury in his voice. 'We don't tell you about suspects because they's just that. Don't mean we ain't making progress.' Shouts were coming from all directions now, cutting over him, all on the same theme – *Who are your suspects?*

'We . . .' Bailey held a finger to his lips to demand quiet, but the briefing had slipped out of control. Looking around, it seemed like every man was yelling. The hack next to me had a fat vein throbbing in his neck as he shouted something, his words lost in the noise.

I fought my way out the back of the crowd, relieved to escape. I made for the door, glancing back at Bailey. He'd stepped away from the lectern. His hand hung down by his holster, and his face was the colour of badly sunburned skin. He was staring right at me.

CHAPTER TWENTY-FIVE

I'd just reached McGaffney's office when a shout ripped through the newsroom. I turned and saw Robinson sauntering to his desk, his tie hanging loose around his collar.

McGaffney pushed past me and onto the main floor. 'Something happened?'

Robinson had picked up a pen, pointed at me with it. 'New York lit the touch paper.'

People at their desks were watching him now, some turning to me when he gestured.

McGaffney jerked his head. 'My office.'

Robinson put the pen behind his ear and came over. I wheeled around, maintaining my position in McGaffney's doorway – no way was I taking orders. Robinson gave me a sideways look as he passed.

McGaffney stationed himself behind his desk, arms folded across his chest. 'Tell it.'

Robinson looked at his thumb. 'New York decided he'd go ahead and ask the Sheriff why he ain't got no suspects yet. That bunch of half-brains out there took it as they cue to do likewise. Bailey was plenty mad when all was said and done.'

McGaffney was shaking his head. His face was grey and he'd shed weight, even in the few days I'd known him. 'Why'd you antagonise him like that?'

'The question was appropriate.'

Robinson looked to the ceiling. 'When are you gonna get it in your head? Just 'cause some folk here don't want you touched, you reckon Bailey or Sherman would think twice about working you over?'

I shook my head. 'You're like a child, Jimmy. You're so desperate for attention you'll say anything to make the big boys notice you.'

Robinson squared up to me. 'Answer my question.'

Every part of me tingled, as if my heart was pumping blood so fast my skin couldn't hold it all in. 'I'll be deep in the ground before I explain myself to a lowlife like you.'

Robinson took hold of my tie, smoothed it down gingerly. 'And I'll be standing over you, throwing on the dirt.'

I saw red and felt all the old urges overtaking me. I closed my eyes and stepped back, determined not to hit him. When I opened them again, the question I'd wanted to ask him for days came off my lips without having even thought about it. 'Why did you change her story?'

A quizzical look came over his face.

'Alice Anderson. The interview you did – she never told you it was a Negro. Why'd you change it?'

There was silence for a long moment. Then Robinson flipped my tie in my face and turned away. 'I don't know what you're talking about.'

McGaffney stepped between us. 'That's enough.'

I ignored him, still looking at Robinson. 'Yes, you do.' I was tense, unsure if Robinson was going to come at me. 'Why'd you do it, Jimmy? You covering for someone? Yourself?'

Robinson looked at McGaffney, a worried expression. Then the last thing I expected: his eyes welled up. He choked back a sob and backed away, gripping his face like he wanted to pull his eyes out. He took a second, then dragged his jacket sleeve across his eyes.

McGaffney grabbed him by the arm and manhandled him out of the office, Robinson kicking a chair as he went. McGaffney marched him across the newsroom, hissed something into his ear that looked like *get a hold of yourself*, and sent him out of the building with a gentle shove.

When McGaffney came back, I was sitting in his chair, still turning it all over. 'What did he mean when he said I can't be touched?'

'Get up.'

'Who gave that order?'

'Just a figure of speech. You still a guest here, even if you an unwelcome one.'

'Tell it to the birds, McGaffney.'

His voice stayed level, no trace of emotion in it. 'You can leave my office now.'

'Did you know he changed her story?'

He gripped the chair on the other side of his desk. 'You smart, Yates, I'll grant you that, but you only know part of it. You ever think he was trying to protect her?'

I sat up in my seat, hardly believing what I was hearing. 'What does that mean?'

'It means you look somewhere else and leave Jimmy alone.'

I stood up. 'You knew he changed the story, and you let him? You're a goddamn disgrace.'

He bristled. 'Who the hell you think you are lecturing me in my own office?'

'Why'd he do it?'

He worked his forehead with his fingers. 'When this is done, you'll be on the first train north. Rest of us gotta live here.' His eyes flickered and something stirred behind them, like he was reliving a bad dream. 'Best you give Jimmy a wide berth.'

I looked him square in the eyes. 'Not if he's as dirty as I think he is.'

CHAPTER TWENTY-SIX

I drove to Lizzie's again, wanting to know what she made of McGaffney's line about protecting Alice. His and Robinson's words were ringing in my ears; I couldn't tell yet how deep they went in what was happening, but with McGaffney as good as admitting Robinson changed the story – and that he knew about it – they had to be caught up in it somehow.

That wasn't all of it, though. I had to know Lizzie was okay after my run-in with Randall earlier. If he was the man I thought he was, it wasn't beyond him to take his anger out on her. Her cream Chevy was parked in the driveway, and I felt my heartbeat quicken at the prospect of seeing her. I rapped the door knocker; she looked surprised to see me when she opened up.

'I need to talk to you. Can I come in?'

She invited me inside.

'I'm sorry for showing up unannounced. I called earlier but you weren't home.'

She perched on the armchair. 'I've been tearing my hair out looking for Alice. She's nowhere; it's like she disappeared into the wind.' She looked at the floor as she said it, and it was obviously she'd given up hope.

'There's still a chance she's running.'

She searched my face but said nothing. I hoped she couldn't tell from my expression that I thought it a long shot. 'You said you wanted to speak with me?' she finally said.

I took a breath before I started, knowing it would be painful for her to hear. 'I was just at the *Chronicle*. McGaffney as good as admitted to me that Jimmy Robinson changed the story when he did the interview with your sister—'

'He said that? That shameless—'

'There's more. He implied they did it to protect her. Does that add up to you?'

She was standing now, taking hesitant steps towards the mantelpiece. 'No.' She thought about it, then said it again, her face reddening. 'No, I can't understand what he means by that. Cajoling maybe. Or intimidating – but not protecting.'

I thought out loud. 'You said Alice was afraid her attacker would come back for her if she told anyone about it. Could that be a part of it?'

She pulled at her earlobe absently. 'No, that doesn't make any sense. She didn't want to speak to that reporter at all. If they were that understanding, they wouldn't have sent him to talk to her in the first place.'

Dead end. I paced, frustration making me antsy.

'I told you they were no good,' she said. 'That's why I went to give Mr McGaffney a piece of my mind. When you saw me at his office.'

I realised I'd let McGaffney off too lightly this time – and that I'd go at him again next chance I got. I thought about the other leads I had, the anonymous note at the forefront; I toyed with the notion of telling Lizzie about it, eventually deciding not to until I could verify it. 'How long did Alice work at Red River?'

'Red River? Why do you ask?'

I told her part of the truth. 'I'm looking for a way to link the

186

victims. She first met Dwight there, right?'

She nodded, her fingers on her bottom lip as she thought it over. 'A year, almost.'

'Did she ever have trouble there? An argument with a co-worker, anything of that sort?'

'Not that she ever told me about. She seemed happy working there, especially once Dwight showed up.'

All the dope on Red River so far was insubstantial; I had to get to the heart of it. I stood up and stationed myself along the mantel from Lizzie. 'You should get some rest. You can't keep running after her forever.'

'It feels like I ought to try. I owe her that much.'

I put my hand on her shoulder. 'No-one could have done more than you have.'

'Thank you, Charlie.' She raised her hand and placed it on top of mine, meeting my eyes in the mirror, and then looking away again. 'You've been a rock. It's a comfort knowing you're still chasing this.'

I felt my cheeks flush, at the same time wondering if I'd really done all I could. 'If you'd like me to sleep on your couch again, it's no trouble.' The line was a surprise to me, not something I'd planned to say.

'You're sweet, but I'll be fine, thank you. Randy is coming to take me to dinner in a while.'

A little slash of disappointment cut through me, but I was determined not to show it. He was like a malign presence in the background at every turn. I wanted to lay out my suspicions about him, warn her off – but I knew I'd just sound like a crazy. 'I'll come by tomorrow, check you're okay.'

I drove back to the Mason, night having fallen and a huge, almost-full moon still climbing in the sky. I passed the Federal Building, the white-grey lunar light giving it a look of abandonment. Three GIs were stumbling along the sidewalk, arms around each other's necks, singing Perry Como's 'Till The End Of Time', and missing the low note every try.

My mind was restless, all the unanswered questions plaguing me. I couldn't stop fretting about Lizzie being alone with Johnson. On top of that, ever since the kiss, it felt like she was giving me the blow-off; even earlier, it was like she was pulling away from me when she wouldn't meet my eyes. I felt a fool for letting emotions cloud my thinking. I crossed the hotel lobby and determined to put it out of my thoughts. The Red River note was the best lead I had – that should be my focus.

'Sir?' The bellhop came up to me, a slip of paper in his hand. 'The man you asked me to find out about – Davis?' I stared, the request half-forgotten. 'I've got an address for you.'

'You're too late. I found him myself.'

He slipped the paper in my pocket. 'You promised me another five bucks if I found him for you. Didn't say nothing about finding him first.'

I grinned, impressed with his moxie. 'Tell you what: I'll give you the other five for what you know about Winfield Callaway – starting with where he lives.'

He stepped back. 'Not here. Order room service.' With that he was gone.

I glanced around the lobby, dazed by his sudden exit. Then I

caught a whiff of Robinson on my clothes again, made me want
to take a bath in ammonia.

*

Room service was a world record: ninety seconds from when I
called to arrival. Two bottles of soda and a shortstack of blue-
berry pancakes. When the bellhop wheeled it in, the smell
made my stomach flip – another stretch of not eating suddenly
registered. He set the tray down. 'Don't forget the tip.'

I tore off a piece of pancake and wolfed it down. 'What's
with all the secrecy?'

'Mr Callaway's as big a wheel as they come.'

'You're afraid of him?'

He shook his head but I didn't buy it. 'He's got points in
this place,' he said. 'Don't pay to be dishing on the boss. So you
can't tell no-one you got this from me.'

'I don't know what I've got yet.'

He fretted the white cloth that dangled from the silver
platter. 'I'm serious, Mr Yates.'

I made a motion of zipping my lips. 'Shoot. What's his
address?'

He shook his head. 'Don't have an address – he's practically
got his own county. Lives out past the country club. You take
highway 71 to Blackman Ferry Road, then follow it till you see
the lake. Can't miss the house from there.'

No slip of paper this time, I noticed: nothing in writing.
'How'd he make his money?'

'You mean is it legit?'

'Same question.'

He pointed to the sodas. 'You mind?' He cracked the top off one and took a drink; kid was more brazen than the Statue of Liberty in a tutu. 'Story goes he took over his daddy's lumber business and built it up from there.'

'You don't believe that?'

'It's before my time, but you speak to some of the old timers, they'll tell you ain't no way he made the kind of coin he's got just by cutting down trees.'

'So . . .'

He took another pull from the bottle. 'The rumour goes that he took the money from his sawmills and used it to move liquor up outta Mexico when Volstead was still going. Say he ran mule trains across the border far as Laredo, then loaded it onto trucks and drove it on up by way of San Antone. Even paid the Texas Rangers to run shotgun on his loads so they wouldn't be hijacked.' His eyes were wide now, Callaway the bootlegger as some kind of local hero. 'You believe it? Talk about brass balls.' He gave a little whistle to underline the excitement of it all.

'If he made his money bootlegging, how'd he get to run Red River?'

'I don't know about that. Maybe he knew who to pay off? But once he got the contract – hell, he might as well have started printing money in the place.'

'You know anyone that worked for him?'

'Apart from me?'

'I mean at Red River.'

His bottom lip jutted out. 'Well, I mean sure, but they would've seen him about as many times as I have. It ain't like he comes in to count his money.'

I ran my hands through my hair, not sure any of this was useful. 'What about family?'

He shook his head now. 'What's this about, sir? I mean, an address is one thing, family's another.'

I held my notepad up. 'Just prep. I want to interview him for my story.' The story – what the hell did that mean any more? I hadn't written a word in days, and the line between personal and professional was so blurred as not to mean a damn at this point.

'You swear you'll keep my name out of it?'

I nodded.

'Well, he's got one son, Jefferson. Don't know him myself, but people say he's strange.'

'Strange how?'

'For one thing, he went to school at Patty Hill – that's where all the rich kids go. But he used to try to be buddies with kids from Texarkana High.'

'That's strange?'

'You bet that's strange. I went to Texarkana High, weren't no-one from no mansions went to that school.' He drank the last of his soda and eyed the other bottle. 'Folk I know said no-one wanted nothing to do with him, though. He's supposed to be . . . awkward. Around people.'

'Be specific.'

'Just passing on what I heard. Awkward, that's it. To talk to, you know?'

'Any other family? Callaway got a wife?'

'Used to, but she died, I heard. Don't know more than that. Mr Callaway's real private about his personal life, family, that kind of thing.' He checked his watch like he had somewhere to be and then held out his hand, clearing his throat.

I forked over a bill. 'Last question: anyone holding a grudge against Callaway?'

He pocketed the money and made for the door. 'No-one I know about, but who knows? My daddy always said the only thing a rich man can't buy is friends.' He saluted me with one finger to his temple, and left.

I walked to the window and looked out over town. My mind drifted to Lizzie, the same place it went every time I stopped to draw breath, wondering if she was safe, if one of the yellow dots of light below was a restaurant she was dining in. It occurred to me that if Randall did something to her, I'd never forgive myself. Or him. I thought about Alice too, looked at the dark streets and wondered if she was out there somewhere – dead or alive.

But some part of me was already thinking about my next move. Speeding down highway 71, out past the country club.

*

Thursday. Driving out to Callaway's – the weekend looming like a maw, time slipping through my fingers.

I'd called his house from the Mason and got through to his personal secretary, Mrs Cornette. I name-checked the *Examiner* immediately; that kept her from hanging up, but when she said she'd speak with Mr Callaway, and to call back in an hour, I figured that was the last I'd hear. My alternate plan was to head out anyway and doorstep him, but she surprised me by calling me back to say Callaway would give me fifteen minutes if I could get there at eleven the next morning, and on the condition that we were off the record.

Blackman Ferry Road was a single lane stretch of asphalt, branching off the highway twenty minutes outside of town. I passed the occasional house dotted along it, all of them long, low-slung single-storey buildings – no shacks around here. Only other structures were churches – seemed like the Baptists had the area overrun. There were small bodies of standing water visible through the trees, marshy country that was water-logged on account of the spring rains.

The lake the bellhop mentioned was hidden by a stand of loblolly pines, and the house was on the far side of it. Set on a low rise, it was fronted by five huge Roman columns and topped with a gabled roof the length of a football field.

The air was crisp with the scent of pine needles when I parked outside. Somewhere behind the house, a horse was whinnying against a stable door, the bolt rattling in its notch. A black man in a wide-brimmed straw hat was pruning a hedgerow. Across the porch, a butler in a penguin-suit was waiting for me in the entranceway; he nodded when I approached, said, 'Follow me', and led me through to a large study.

The room smelled of leather and polished wood – three burgundy chairs and a bookcase that lined one entire wall the source of the former; the latter from the gleaming walnut desk sat at one end of the room. I walked over to the desk and trailed my finger along the surface. A strange coincidence: there was an address book on one corner, open, turned to the 'M' listings; the third name down was *McGaffney, S.J.*

Behind the desk was a huge picture window overlooking the grounds and the lake. I carried on over to it and looked out. A short way down the slope stood a small summer house, with whitewashed walls and a square deck looking out over the water. I noticed a man sitting on a bench out front of it, shaded by a cypress tree. I thought he was reading a book, but then I saw he had a pen in his hand and was writing with it. A gardener in a white overall was working near him, pulling a rake across the already pristine lawn.

'My son, Jefferson.'

Callaway was standing in the doorway; I hadn't heard him come in. He had a little more colour in his face than when I'd seen him announce the reward, but he still looked like he'd blow over in a strong breeze. The *son* line threw me – the man under the tree looked about twenty, and I was thinking grandson. 'Charlie Yates, Mr Callaway. Thank you for your time.'

My thoughts must have been written on my face because he jutted his chin towards the man, said, 'Mrs Callaway was much younger than me.' He circled around the desk, keeping me at more than arm's length. 'Take a seat, Mr Yates.' He tapped the back of one of the chairs, indicating it was mine. He moved with surprising ease, no hint of his age in the way he walked. He stopped at a small drinks tray next to the window and picked up a crystal decanter. 'Drink?'

I shook my head.

'We're agreed on the rules?' He waited with the stopper over the decanter, as if my answer would determine whether he'd pour or not.

'Yes.'

'I don't mean to be unwelcoming, Mr Yates, but you understand, in my position . . .' He took a sip of his drink and let the sentence trail off.

'Everything's off the record.'

He set his glass down on a black leather coaster and turned

to the window. 'He wants to be a writer, you know.'

'Your son?'

He nodded slowly, still gazing through the glass. 'Books this week – a novelist. But it changes with the wind. It was poetry before; I'm sure journalism will have its turn too.'

'You don't approve?'

He turned to face me. 'I mean no disrespect when I say this, sir, but are you acquainted with many wealthy journalists?'

I sat down in the chair and crossed my legs. 'I guess it depends on how you define wealthy.'

'What are you, a Red?' A hint of a smile played on his lips. His eyes moved around the room, lingering on the trappings on display, as if to say, *This is how I define wealthy.*

'Mr Callaway, I came today to ask you—'

'Yes, quite right; I've managed to use up five minutes of your allotted time already. You're here to talk about these damn attacks, I presume?'

It was obvious he wanted to dictate the conversation, keep it on his terms. It was a trait I'd seen time and again in men of power; the mayor of L.A. did it the one time I spoke with him, in thirty-six, and so did half the editors I'd worked for. 'That's part of it—'

'The other part?' He arched his eyebrows.

He already had me on the run; I wanted to warm him up before we got to Red River, but he was determined to make me show my cards before I'd even stacked my chips. 'Let's start with the reward money.'

He lowered himself into the chair behind the desk and drummed his fingers on the leather armrests. 'What about it?'

'It's a generous amount. What made you offer it?'

He looked up at the ceiling. 'I felt I had to do something.' His face softened. 'And I'm a little old to be hiding in bushes trying to catch this degenerate.'

'You feel a responsibility to the town?'

'I've lived here a long time. There's little point in having the means if I'm just going to sit on my hands.'

'So it wasn't because the police have been ineffectual to date?'

He looked at his watch. 'I thought an *Examiner* man would be better than asking asinine, leading questions.'

I smiled my best *you-got-me* smile. 'I'm sorry to disappoint. What about—'

He held up a hand to stop me. 'Mr Yates, you're going to think me rude, and for that I ask you to excuse me. I promise I'm not – I just don't have time for banality. Do you know why I granted you this visit?'

I hesitated, took a second to switch gears. 'To be honest, I was curious about that myself.'

A single drop of liquor sat on the rim of his glass; he touched it with the tip of his finger and then sucked it off. 'Truth of it is I was intrigued. Big city newspaperman here covering this case, and now he wants to talk to me.' He held the finger up as if silencing a room. 'Don't misunderstand me, I'm not star-struck. I mean I wanted to be impressed.' I laced my fingers together, waiting for the payoff line. He went on. 'You didn't come here to ask me about the reward, you came here because you need something and you think I can help you somehow.'

I inclined my head, then nodded. 'Fair enough. I can appreciate when a man wants to get down to brass tacks. Let's talk straight.'

'Do you have a lead?'

'Yes.' No way was I going to tell him about the note. 'Three of the victims worked at your plant.'

'My plant?'

'Red River Arsenal.'

'You're misinformed – I don't run that any more.'

I arched my eyebrows now. 'I thought we were talking straight?'

He rocked back in his chair, grinning. Then he stood up and went back to the drinks tray, poured another glass and came over and shoved it in my hand. 'That's more like it.' He stood in front of me, leaning against the desk. 'Alright. But it's not my plant at present – that much is true.'

'Let's say the contract's in the mail.' I pretended to take a sip of the booze for the sake of appearances. 'Can you get me a list of employees? Last three years or so?'

He swilled his drink in silence for a moment, then said, 'To what end? You pick any six people in Texarkana, at least two will have worked at Red River. What you have is a coincidence, not a lead.'

'Maybe so. But that's why I want a list of everyone the police have questioned too. I want to crosscheck one with the other. I know I'm looking for a needle in a haystack, but this is the only link I can see between the victims.' I swallowed, my throat dry because I knew I was pushing my luck. 'And I'd like to see copies of the case files too.'

He frowned. 'I don't follow. You're suggesting someone is hunting Red River employees? That's ridiculous.'

'That's not what I'm saying. I'm saying I think the killer is picking his targets for a reason. People that are known to him.'

'This man is an opportunist and he's striking at random,' he said. 'I've seen no evidence to the contrary.'

Seen no evidence – a tacit admission that he had access to police material. At a guess, no accident that he'd dropped that into the conversation either. 'It's rare, Mr Callaway. I've worked crime beats for years, in Chicago and Los Angeles before New York, and the numbers show that in the region of eighty per cent of all murders are committed by someone known to the victim.' I sat forward, arms on my knees. 'I'm not saying they have to be friends. Think about it – a man develops a fixation on a girl at work, tries to talk to her in the break room, she ignores him because she's never even noticed him, and there's your motive. It sounds crazy, but we're dealing with a maniac, and sometimes that's all the provocation they need.'

'You can't honestly believe that to be the case here.'

'That's just a for instance. Could be anything, but believe me, it happens. In L.A., I wrote about a man killed a broad because he didn't like the red lipstick she wore. Told the cops it made her look a tramp. Turned out he'd never so much as spoken to her. She was a girl he saw on the street and developed a liking for. He followed her for two weeks straight, then strangled her outside The Moonlight Lounge one night.'

Callaway stabbed the desktop with one finger, some fire showing now in his eyes. 'But this is not Los Angeles, Mr Yates. We don't get those kind of mental defectives here.'

'What harm can it do to give me the names then? I'm only wasting my own time.'

He looked at me as if I was a kid that just asked why he couldn't play with matches. 'How will it look when it emerges that the *New York Examiner* is investigating my plant in connection with the murders?'

'It's not your plant yet, remember?'

He bent low so his face was almost in mine. 'My patience has limits, Mr Yates.' He tapped his watch without looking at it. 'Your time here's about played out.'

'If I find anything I'll make sure your name is kept out of it.'

'Even if that were true, every newspaper here will have my name, picture and pant size next to any story with a mention of Red River in it. And I can't afford that.'

I pushed myself out of the chair and set my tumbler down on the silver platter; the tap of glass on metal seemed to ring out around the room. 'I thought you wanted to know you'd done something to help? All that money . . .'

I meant the reward cash, but the way he blanched when I said it told me he took it as an indictment of his riches. I put my hat on, tipped the brim to him and headed for the door. The thick pile carpet muffled my footsteps so they didn't make a sound – explained why I hadn't heard Callaway when he came in.

He sighed, sounded like a man whose head was fighting his heart. One of the two must have won out. 'The police files are out of the question.'

I stopped but didn't turn.

'Even I don't have that kind of influence,' he said. 'Especially the way the authorities are in this town.' I thought back to the deference Bailey had shown to him at the briefing, wondered if Callaway was soaping me. 'The employee names I can get you. It will cost me a favour with the military brass that are still running Red River, but I'll wear it and sleep well knowing that the man from the *Examiner* has sanctified my efforts to help.' The words dripped with sarcasm. He slurped the last of his bourbon, almost as though he was scouring his mouth out. 'Mrs Cornette will make the arrangements and deliver the list to you – and only to you. Where are you staying?'

I told him, and we agreed Mrs Cornette would call me to arrange a drop-off time once everything was set. I thanked him and offered my hand, but he just stared at it, then at me – the same wet eyes I'd noticed when I first saw him; not tears, just eyes that had seen great sadness and couldn't hide it any more. His line about his wife came back to me, and I remembered the bellhop saying she'd died; figure that was part of it.

'Remember our agreement,' he told me. 'It won't profit you to have my name anywhere near this story.' He glanced over his shoulder towards his son outside, then took a faltering step towards me. I thought at first he was going to hug me, but then he gripped my face with his hand, the skin cold and dry like a desert night. 'And there's a price.'

Should have seen that coming. 'Take your hand off my face and maybe I'll listen.'

He removed it slowly, then held it out for me to shake instead. 'If you find this man first, you bring him to me. No police.'

I looked at the hand, then back at his eyes. His eyebrows were bushy and wild. 'What do you mean? So you can do what?'

His eyes were distant now, like a veil had dropped over them. He placed his hands on the desktop, hung his head. 'I lost my wife and daughter on the same day in 1927. My daughter would have been nineteen years old now if she'd lived.

There's not a day gone by when I haven't thought about her in that time.' He grabbed a paperweight and wrapped his fingers around it, gripping it like a skull he meant to crush. 'I mourn her still, and I didn't even know her. Can you understand that?' Turning to me again now. 'The thought of this animal ripping away someone's daughter – a daughter they've loved and cherished in a way I was denied – it . . . it makes me question the existence of a merciful god.'

He fell silent and stared through the window, seeing a past he couldn't touch. I ran my hand over my face, at last seeing this meeting for what it really was; me thinking I was in control, but really part of his agenda all along. 'So you want to drop the killer yourself?'

He stood in front of me, the paperweight still in his hand, a fleeting thought that he intended to hit me with it. 'Let's act like adults here, Mr Yates. Neither of us wants me to answer that question out loud.'

I took a deep breath, my chest tightening at what he was asking of me. I'd never got as far as thinking what I'd do if I did find the killer. In many ways, delivering him to Callaway was the smart play. What alternatives did I have? Turning him over to Bailey or Sherman didn't sit right – and I didn't trust them. I could try Chief Mills, but that was the same as handing him to Bailey direct.

Which left option B.

I'd stayed in Texarkana to prove the Baileys of this world wrong. To prove to myself that I could do the right thing this one damn time. And for Lizzie; to ensure justice for her and Alice. I realised now, the thought forming in that moment, that it could mean having to put the killer down myself.

Problem was, every veteran I ever interviewed said pulling the trigger on their first kill was the hardest thing they ever did. A handful of soldiers told me they'd seen men die because they couldn't bring themselves to do it, even though they knew it would cost them their own lives – kill or be killed. I'd never fired a single bullet. When the call came, I didn't have guts enough to get on that boat to Europe. If men of bravery couldn't pull the trigger to kill another man, then I was just deluding myself if I thought I could.

And yet turning him over to Callaway was just as bad. Could be some misguided sense of justice – but I doubted it; the son of a bitch that was killing these kids deserved no mercy. When I boiled it all down, maybe I just couldn't stomach the idea that power gets you whatever justice you want; that Callaway could decide for himself whether another man lives or dies – make himself judge, jury and executioner. After all, didn't that make him the same as the killer? 'I can't do that.'

Callaway closed his eyes, grinding his jaw. 'You can and you should.' He turned the paperweight over in his hands like Rosary Beads, as if I'd betrayed him. Then his eyes flicked open and he stared at me, drilled into my face. 'Bring him to me and I'll give you fifty thousand dollars.'

CHAPTER TWENTY-SEVEN

I went back to the Mason and left instructions to contact me as soon as Mrs Cornette called, along with a list of places to try if I wasn't in my room. Then I made for the street, heading to the *Chronicle*. Callaway's offer was still bouncing around my head; I'd taken his hand and nodded my assent, not able to bring myself to say the words.

I agreed to take his money just to get out of there, buy myself some space to think. I tried to square it with myself: I was playing the smart game – string him along until he delivers the list of names and then all bets are off. Use him like he's trying to use me. If that meant double-crossing the old man, what of it? But even when I settled on that, I couldn't shake the feeling that I was just plain afraid to say no to him. Another capitulation in the face of power.

A voice called my name. At first I didn't register it, lost in my thoughts; then Richard Davis's face was right in front of mine.

'Mr Yates, I been waiting on you.' His eyes were bulging and his cheeks burning. 'We gotta talk.'

I blinked, trying to focus, feeling sweat on my temples. 'What's—'

He grabbed my arm, bundled me into the corner next to the revolving doors. 'The big fella, I saw him again. He went to where Patty Summerbell got killed. Out by Club Dallas. '

I yanked my arm free. 'Slow down. Start from the top.'

He looked around, jumpy. 'I saw him there, in the middle of nowhere. Just like when we trailed him.'

'Johnson?'

'Right, the monster. You never told me his name.'

'Start at the beginning, dammit.'

He was out of breath, almost panting. 'I went back to get another look at him—'

'What? What the hell for?'

He curled in on himself, like a scolded dog. 'This here's serious business, Mr Yates. It was on my mind all last night. I couldn't sleep, thinking I could've picked this fella out wrong. He goes to the chair on my say so – I mean, I need to be sure.'

It was typical of the kid's flair for melodrama: the thought that his word alone could put the man on death row – wrongly or otherwise.

'So I went by his house, to get a better look. I waited outside some, but when he came out, it was him and the redhead and they was going at each other again. I mean really yelling this time.'

'What's this got to do with—'

'Then he pushed her.'

I felt the blood drain from my face.

'She shouted something at him, had this look like she couldn't stand to even see him, and then he shoved her. Both hands. She landed on her behind on the grass.'

That old feeling. Bile climbing my throat like lava. An urge to drive my fist through the glass in the door next to me.

'She looked real shocked,' he continued. 'Just sat there for a minute, staring up at him.'

I pictured her fighting tears, way too tough to let him see she was upset.

'I thought he was gonna backhand her for a second, but he charged over to his car and took off.'

'He didn't hit her?' I looked down, realising I was gripping Davis's forearm.

'No. He split. But I was mad at him, on account of what he done, and on account of the fact I seen him properly now – and I was sure this time. So I went after him. I ain't know what I was thinking to do, but I wasn't thinking real clear at the time.'

'Then?'

'He took the highway out the Texas side. I cooled off while we went, and I was thinking about turning back to town seeing as he coulda been driving to Mexico all I know. But then I saw Club Dallas, and he turned off onto this little track into the woods. So now I'm starting to get hinky, 'cause I know Patty got killed out there, and 'cause it's the same kinda track we seen him take. I left my car at the turnoff and walked down there behind him. I thought I was gonna fill my britches – I was sure he'd seen me and was waiting on me. But then I see this clearing, and he's just standing there.'

'Doing what?'

'Just standing. I hid behind a tree, a ways back, figured I'd see what he was up to. But he ain't do nothing, far as I could tell.'

Some piece of evidence he was hoping to retrieve from the murder scene? Or guilt? A surge of regret that he had to try and alleviate. But why go back there? It was a huge risk to take with the cops patrolling all the lovers' lanes. Then I realised they weren't – not at that time of day. 'Did you say anything to him?'

'No, hell no.' He had tremors in his voice as he said it, the adrenaline coming back to him. 'If he saw me, he mighta punched my ticket – one way, you know what I mean? Very least he'd have given me a hiding.'

'You came straight here?'

He nodded.

My hands were clenched so tight, my fingernails cut into my palms. No man had the right to do that to a woman, and especially one as big as him; the fact that it was Lizzie just made it worse. It confirmed all my fears about him, and I was mad at myself for not voicing them to her; it felt like I'd let this happen. I couldn't understand what she saw in the man – and the sentiment wasn't coming from jealousy any longer.

Through the anger, enough clarity remained to realise that this was new information, another connecting line on my diagram – albeit between Johnson and Summerbell, two people I had already linked. Like everything else in this case, apparently significant, but maybe just so much static, obscuring the true signal.

'What're we gonna do, Mr Yates?'

I blinked, suddenly aware I'd fallen silent. 'We? We don't do anything. You go home and stay the hell away from him.'

He made his disappointment obvious. 'That ain't right. I given you the skinny, you gotta let me in on the get-back.'

I turned him around and pointed him towards the street. 'Go home, Davis. I'll deal with this.'

He twisted free and threw his arms towards the floor, like a kid having a tantrum. 'To hell with that. I know how to fight, I can help you.'

I stepped around him, shaken by a realisation: the way I felt in that moment, if Johnson was the killer, I'd take Callaway's money in a heartbeat.

*

I left Davis standing outside the Mason, a look on his face like he couldn't believe I wasn't taking him along. No doubt he'd imagined some movie scene where we kicked in Johnson's door and wailed on him together. Damn silver screen had taught a generation of kids that if your anger was righteous enough, you'd win in the end, overcome any odds. The kind of thinking that allowed men to charge fortified machine gun nests on French beaches. Realising the lie too late.

And besides, wasn't that exactly what the killer was thinking? That no matter what the rest of the world said, he was in the right? We can't all be on the side of the angels – but we can all think we are.

Turned out Davis would have been disappointed anyway: there was no sign of Johnson at his place. I hammered on the door hard enough to bring his neighbour out, checking what the commotion was. I banged the door one more time in frustration, ignoring the neighbour as I stormed back down the path.

Something told me to check his mailbox. I found two final demand notices inside. A surprise that shouldn't have been: Randall lied to me about his last name; both letters were addressed to Randall Schulz.

Different explanations sailed through my head. Could be he did it through force of habit – a reflex to ditch the Germanic surname for something as American as Johnson – but that was the sucker's bet. The explanation that felt right: he was trying to put distance between himself and Patty Summerbell, and whatever caused them to be arguing just hours before she died.

*

The anger in my gut had subsided some by the time I reached Lizzie's. She opened the door with red, puffy eyes, but her makeup was all in place; she'd been crying, but damned if she'd let the world know it.

'Charlie? What are you doing here?'

'Where is he?'

'Who?'

'Your sweetheart. Schulz.'

'What's this about?'

'Did he put his hands on you?'

She looked over my shoulders, nervous, checking the street. 'Step inside.'

I followed her into the lounge. The drapes were pulled more than halfway, the photographs on the walls only just visible in the dull light, as if the house was frozen in perpetual dusk. I spread my arms. 'So?'

She looked at me, a hard stare. 'I'll thank you not to take that tone with me. You're barking.'

'Just tell me if he pushed you.'

'What do you . . .' A look of confusion. 'Are you spying on me?'

'Don't talk crazy. Someone saw what happened and told me about it.'

'Well, may I at least ask who?' Her hands were on her hips now, standing her ground.

I didn't know where to start. So I didn't try. 'Alright.' I made to leave. 'I'll sit on his doorstep until he crawls out of his hole, then I'll ask him myself.'

She followed me as far as the hallway. 'You'd walk out of here and not even ask about Alice?'

Her voice broke as she said it. It stopped me in my tracks. My first thought was that they'd found a body – a smack around the head that reminded me the torment she was enduring. And made me realise I was taking my anger out on the wrong person. I faced her and softened my voice. 'What happened?'

'The police.' She folded her arms across her chest, one hand to her mouth. 'They're not going to search for her any more.'

I took a short step towards her and stopped, unsure what to say, feeling every inch the heel I was.

'Lieutenant Sherman telephoned me to say they can't spare the manpower, not with Saturday coming and all.'

'They can't just stop.'

'It's already done. They keep telling me she's most likely left town.'

I put a hand on the wall. 'It's possible.'

'I'm not a fool, Charlie.' She chewed on a knuckle and I noticed it was already red raw. 'They think she's dead.'

'It doesn't mean—'

'Yes it does. It's the only reason they'd give up like this.'

Another version of events came together in my mind, and I wasn't so sure she was right. I recalled Robinson's rumour about a cop hanging around the day Alice disappeared, and made a jump – a big jump – to another reason might have made them quit: the cops knew where she went from the start. 'I told you before, they've got their own agenda. What if they don't want her to be found?'

'That doesn't make any sense.'

'Not to you or me. Maybe to them.'

'What are you getting at?'

I dipped my head, shaking it, concerned now that I'd got her hopes up. 'I don't know. I don't know anything. Except I don't think you can trust anyone in this town.'

She took her hand away from her mouth, an irritated movement, like she suddenly realised she'd slipped back into a bad habit. She straightened her dress and went back into the lounge. 'It's not what you think,' she said. I went after her, found her propped on the edge of the sofa. 'I mean with Randy. It's not what you think.'

'You don't want to know what I think about him. And now you're gonna stand up for him, is that it? *"It wasn't his fault, I made him do it."* That the idea?'

'Don't be absurd.'

'So tell me how it is.'

A shadow crossed her face, the memory uncomfortable. 'I was trying to stop him.'

I felt a twitch in my neck, not knowing where this was about to lead. 'From what?'

'When I told him about the police giving up on Alice, he lost his mind. He was going to go down there and raise hell. He'd have got himself arrested. Or worse.'

'What do you mean?'

'You've seen what he's like. He's got a temper; I was afraid. He'll just get himself in trouble if he goes to the Sheriff's.'

'So he pushed you instead of them?'

Her eyes met mine now. 'So quick to judge, Charlie. You've never lost your temper?'

A ripple of shame coursed through me, the memory carried with it, and suddenly I was back in our apartment in New York, standing in the kitchen surveying the damage, having trashed it in a fit of rage – the fifth time in four months. I saw Jane running out the door because she was so scared. A snatched vision of endless broken plates and cups, thrown around our dinette because I was so damn mad at the world.

At myself, in truth.

Then the scene shifted and I was back at the *Examiner*, hurling that typewriter through Walters's window. The final blow-up. The one that put me on ice and made me see I was hurtling out of control. Too late, as it turned out. I blinked, focusing on Lizzie's face to bring myself back to the present. 'Whatever I've done, I've never put my hands on a woman.'

'Randy was just trying to move me out of his way. My shoe got stuck in the grass and I landed on my behind.' She stood up, the colour coming back to her face. 'What of it?'

I held my hands up, mock surrender. 'Like I said, it was your fault, I suppose.'

'Who even came to you about this?' She said, pointing her finger at me. 'Sometimes it's as if you know everything that goes on in this town and it makes you so superior.'

'Hold on, don't forget who came to who, right? You needed my help and you got it. No strings attached.'

'Maybe so, but you jumped at the chance to get involved because it got you your story, isn't that so? I told you, Charlie, I'm not a fool. You're just using me to get your next scoop.'

Any other time in my life it probably would have been true,

but this time, I was on the level. It hadn't once occurred to me to manipulate Lizzie for the sake of the story; I thought too much of her for that. The conflict of interest wasn't lost on me, but as desperate as I was to nail it – and keep alive any glimmer of hope I had of saving my career – there was no question where my priority lay. Lizzie, Alice, justice won out every time. And still it wasn't doing me any good. 'You know where he went when he left?'

She moved as if to stand up, but then dropped back into her seat. 'I haven't seen him since.'

I walked over to the window and pulled one of the drapes back. Dust motes caught in the light and floated between us, like all the unspoken words. 'The weekend before last, were you with him?'

'What are you asking me?'

I looked at my shoes. 'The night Patty Summerbell and Edward Logan were murdered. Did you spend any time with him?'

Her face twisted as if she didn't comprehend. 'I don't . . . What are you saying?'

'I'm asking if you can account for his movements that evening. Where he went.'

Her bottom lip dropped open, maybe the most I'd ever seen her give away with her expression. 'You can't seriously think—'

'How well do you know him? You told me he's not really your sweetheart.'

'I can't believe what you're suggesting. Are you . . . I don't even know the word. Are you investigating Randy?'

'I've got two sources that put him with Patty Summerbell a few hours before she died.'

She let out a small laugh, incredulous now. 'And that makes him a killer?'

'They were arguing, something private. He ever tell you he knew her?'

This time she shot out of her seat. 'No, he didn't. And I'll tell you something else. When I said he's not my sweetheart, I meant because we've only just started courting. And I know there were other girls before, he was never shy about it—'

'Sounds like a real prince.'

'I don't see how any of this adds up to anything.' She crossed the room and closed the drape. 'You have no idea what it's like. Losing the only family you've got left. Not just losing them; like this, never knowing.'

I flinched when she said it, Jane in the room with me again now, remembering the day she told me we were finished. Shutting herself in the bedroom until I left the apartment, not even able to look at me any more. Knowing I'd brought it on myself. A sickening sense that I was driving Lizzie away in the same fashion, the last thing I intended. 'I've lost people, alright. Not the way you have, but I've made mistakes and I'm still paying for them.'

'What's that supposed to mean?'

'It means I'm an expert on losing the things that matter. But I'm sorry for the mistakes I made. How about Schulz?'

'Randy's not perfect but there's a side to him he doesn't show to just anyone. Besides, he makes me feel safe,' she said. 'You can understand that, surely.'

I laced my fingers together. In a very soft voice: 'What about the night Alice was attacked?'

The room went quiet, the atmosphere like a funeral

interrupted by a metal cigarette case clattering to a flagstone floor. She stared at me in disbelief. 'Are you asking—'

'Do you know where he was?'

She snatched her purse off the coffee table and lobbed it at my head. I caught it, reflex. 'Get out.'

'There's more, I just need to know—'

'Get out. Now.'

I held out her purse for her to take. She slapped it away, so I set it back on the table.

'My God – I trusted you . . .'

I started for the door. 'I'm not accusing, I'm just asking questions. Think about it for me.'

CHAPTER TWENTY-EIGHT

The Mason had nothing for me from Callaway's secretary. It had only been half a day, but somehow I thought the list would be waiting – Callaway's down payment on my loyalty, sent express. Maybe I was just desperate for something to take my mind off of Lizzie. I felt lousy about how things had gone; riding in there like I was a white knight there to save her, coming out the bad guy, leaving her feeling even worse. It bugged me to think of her madder at me than at Schulz; I couldn't understand why she was making excuses for him.

I sensed something as I crossed the lobby – a pair of eyes looking away in a hurry. I glanced around but saw nothing. I looked one more time, to be certain, then joined the line of people waiting for an elevator.

The doors opened and we filed in. As they slid shut, a latecomer slipped inside, made eye contact with me for just a second, then faced front. He wore a light brown topcoat, and his black fedora had crease lines around the crown, like it'd been crushed sometime. I hadn't caught his face, now wished I had: his clothes and posture said cop.

We stopped at two floors before mine, the elevator half-empty by the time I got out. I stepped around the man and into the hallway, feeling his eyes on my back. I reached for my room key, listening for the elevator doors closing. When they did, I glanced back and knew what I'd see. The man was walking slowly behind me, hands hidden in the pockets of his coat, his head pitched forward to obscure his face. My mind raced, my instincts telling me everything was wrong with this scene.

Thirty feet from my door, I sped up. The man kept in step with me. I thought about stopping dead, calling his bluff – but if he was coming for me, that was playing into his hands. I decided it was best to get into my room, get a deadbolt between us, and work it out from there.

My hand slipped as I stabbed the key in the lock, my eyes on him. He stopped just short of me and lifted his head. I expected him to say something, but he was silent. I turned the key . . .

A smell from inside, out of place. Cigarette smoke.

The door swung open, yanked from the inside. Jack Sherman was sitting on my bed, looking up at me, his elbows resting on his knees. The man in the corridor sidled up behind me.

I took in the room, realised Sherman wasn't alone. Three other policemen were in the there – two sheriff's deputies, standing on the far side of the bed, and a city cop lounging on the windowsill, a cigarette burning between his fingers. I looked down the hall one more time.

Of your charity . . .

Wondering if I'd live to see it again. Realising my folly too late.

Pray for the souls of these men . . .

Thinking it was a game to go up against the cops. A misplaced belief in justice. Understanding now that they're playing for keeps.

Pray . . .

I felt the room swirl around me, and I wondered if any of it had been worth it.

'In,' Sherman said, a flick of his head to beckon me inside. His tone was bored, going on resigned.

'So this is how it goes, Sherman?' The sound of my voice surprised me – strong, level. No hint of the panic overtaking my insides, the sensation like a swarm of spiders scurrying up my windpipe.

'You knew this was coming. You been warned, Yates.'

The man behind shoved me, just hard enough to get me into the room. He stepped in after me and shut and locked the door.

I nodded towards the other men, my eyes trained on Sherman. 'Couldn't do it on your own?'

Sherman looked puzzled, glancing at the man by the window before it dawned on him. 'These boys?' He shook his head. 'They here for you.' He stood up, flexed his right hand. 'Stop me from killing you.'

I took my coat off, let it drop to the floor. 'Well, I suppose that's something.' The man by the window flicked his cigarette away outside and slipped off the sill. My eyes flitted from him to the two deputies and back to Sherman. 'Still not a fair fight, though, is it? They ready to stand aside if I put you down?'

The man by the windowsill looked at the two deputies and all three smirked.

'Ain't gonna happen,' Sherman said.

He came towards me, rearing back with his fist as he did. I saw half an opening, knew it was the only one I'd get. I jinked to his right, stepping inside his punch. I got my elbow up, covered the left side of my head so it took the blow. Then I twisted the other way, uncoiling, bringing my fist up – a short uppercut. I caught his chin flush and his head snapped back.

I followed in, connecting with a left then a right as I tried to press. He staggered backwards, found his legs and stepped outside my range. Then he came back at me. He feinted with his right, enough to make me juke the other way – and walk head-on into his straight left.

Something in my cheek cracked. My guard sagged, enough for him to come over the top of my fists with a right hand that put me on the floor and made my vision go black. I tried to sit up, but someone kicked me in the head. From the side, not Sherman – the others getting in on the act after all. The floorboards vibrated against my cheek as they all moved towards me, jackals to a carcass. I had enough left in me to pull myself into a ball and protect my head as the blows hammered down.

The pain was so intense, all-encompassing, I almost couldn't feel it. I tried to block it out by thinking of Lizzie.

It stopped as fast as it started. A gush of hot blood ran down my throat, the iron taste unmistakable. The bathroom door opened and I heard footsteps coming towards me. The other cops filed out of the room. A man crouched by me and lifted my head with a finger under my chin. The extra pressure on my ribs made me cry out in pain.

Bailey.

'Yeah, that'll hurt a few days,' he said.

I closed my eyes and tried to get some air into my lungs.

'Nu-uh. You look at me, boy.' He rolled me onto my back and put his boot on my throat until I opened them again. 'You remember my face when I tell you this.'

I lifted my arm and tried to push his foot away, but didn't have the strength. Bailey rubbed his nose with his knuckle, looking at the wall, as untroubled as a man waiting for a train.

'You understand, now, ain't no more warnings. Right?'

I let my head topple sideways, and spat a broken piece of tooth onto the floor. It came out red.

He reached into his pocket; I expected a gun, but he pulled out a small envelope. He dropped it onto my chest. 'Train ticket. One way. Yours.'

I swallowed, trying to clear the blood and bile out of my airway. I managed a single word. 'Or?' My voice came out cracked.

He locked his eyes on mine. 'Or I kill you.' No hesitation. He nodded as he said it, emphasising he meant it. 'Understand, you're done here. I even see you again in Texarkana, I'll kill you myself. And don't make the mistake of thinking this is another warning.' He reached into his other pocket, pulled out a photograph. 'This here's the last man couldn't tell the difference between a warning and a death sentence.' He held the picture in front of my face. My insides were already jelly, now it felt like they were about to come out of my mouth. The picture showed a man lying next to a shallow pit; his eyes were open but his face was battered and the sand around his head was black with blood. The real sickener: there was a shovel sticking out of his chest, sagging at an acute angle, like the mast on a sinking ship just before it dips below the water.

He put the picture away, pointed to the envelope on my chest. 'By morning, hear?'

I touched my face, fingers probing my cheekbones and nose, everything burning and throbbing. He watched me, detached – the way a chemist watches an experiment in a lab. I tried to sit up, couldn't get off the floor. I slumped back down and figured I had nothing left to lose by throwing Robinson's rumour in his face. 'Where's Alice Anderson?'

No change in his expression. 'She done vanished, you know that.'

'Bullshit. There was a cop watch-dogging her that day.' The words came slowly, each one an effort, slurred. 'You did it. Or you know . . .' My voice trailed off. 'One or the other.' Almost a whisper now, not even the strength to speak.

He looked at me closer now, like he was seeing me in focus for the first time. 'What did you say?'

'You had a man there.' I swallowed, tasting blood again. 'Tell me.'

His hands twitched, an involuntary movement, his eyes focused on me but something turning behind them. 'Who's saying that?'

'A source.' A wave of pain jagged under my liver and I grimaced, waiting for it to pass before I spoke again. 'Mean to kill him too?'

He cocked his head to one side, then the other, stretching his neck. He walked to the door and opened it, looking back at me. He pointed at my chest again. 'By morning.'

I lay motionless when he left, waiting for the pain to ebb. I thought about Bailey's reaction, wondered if it meant anything at all. My head was fuzzy, thoughts coming slow, and I couldn't concentrate. I got this far: his first response wasn't a denial, but a question, *Who's saying that?* Should have expected that from him; whatever the truth, he saw it meant someone was talking out of turn, out of his control. It seemed ridiculous – inconceivable, even here – that the cops had disappeared the only survivor of this killing spree. But was it?

I tried again to get to my feet, but only made my knees. The room was spinning, and my left eye was swollen half-shut. I dragged myself so the envelope he'd left was in reach. I tore it open and pulled the ticket out. The depths of Bailey's spite almost made me laugh, the man so bent on punishing me. The ticket was stamped to Santa Fe, New Mexico.

*

Sometime later I made it into the corridor, groping along the wall, trying to make the elevator. Halfway there, my legs gave out and I crumpled to the floor.

A bellhop came around the corner and saw me collapsing in instalments. He came running over and tried to prop me up. Confused, I tried to push his hands away, fight him off, no strength to do it. His face came in range so I clawed at his eyes; that was enough to make him back up.

'Take it easy, sir, I'll get you to a doctor.'

'No doctor.' It still hurt to speak.

'Don't worry, we'll get you taken care of.'

'No doctor. No hospital. He'll kill me.'

'Sir?'

I tried to get up again. There were four guests by the elevator, watching me like I was a drunk.

'Sir, please, you should stay still.'

I made it upright, stooped and bracing myself against the wall. 'Help me get to my car.'

The bellhop started to protest, but stopped mid-sentence to catch me when I buckled again. 'You can't drive, sir. I'll take you downstairs, get you seen to.' He draped my arm over his shoulder. The wall and the bellhop kept me upright. We made it into the elevator, the group waiting there parting to usher me through. Inside, the bellhop, sweating, leaned me against the wall. The sound of the car sliding down the shaft; a rush straight to hell. 'Sir, someone should take a look at you.'

'No hospitals.' I winced as I said it. The bellhop watched, his face wrinkled in horror as he looked me over, and I got scared about just how bad a shape I was in. Stumbling out into the lobby, he tried to guide me, but I pointed in the direction of the back exit. He told me to stop, relented when he saw I was going with or without him.

We came out into the night, and the air was like a cold blade touching my skin. I was short of a plan beyond getting myself away from the Mason, buying myself some time to regroup. I thought back to the previous day's briefing, Bailey's face when it all dissolved, him staring at me across the crowd, and realised he'd made up his mind in that moment. The question worrying me most was would he really let me go? Dropping the line about a cop watch-dogging Alice Anderson was already starting to feel like a mistake – calling a raise when the man with the gun is telling me to fold. Then the rest dawned on me: he might lean on Lizzie next. Bailey had seen us together at his office; if he did know what'd happened to Alice, and got the idea that Lizzie was my source, then it stood to reason she'd be next in his sights. I'd put her in danger with my big mouth, and that notion hurt worse than the beating.

We rounded the corner and I stopped, trying to get my bearings, thinking I'd come to the wrong place. My head was muddled, but I reached for one clear thought, got it, and was sure I'd left the car there.

And now it was gone.

CHAPTER TWENTY-NINE

I opened my eyes and saw lights passing by at regular intervals through a window. At first I thought I was on the Subway in New York. A crazy thought: I'd been airlifted back to Manhattan, the glorious homecoming I'd always wanted.

My head cleared, and I realised I was lying across the backseat of a car, seeing the streetlamps pass by. I tried to sit up. A shadow moved in the front passenger seat, and then Jack Sherman turned around and looked at me, his eyes replaced by two red hot coals. I kicked with my feet, trying to get away—

'Charlie?' A woman's voice, desperate.

The pain hit again, startled me close to lucid. Lizzie's voice, coming from the driver's seat.

'Can you hear me?'

'They took my goddamn car,' I said. Through the pain, a wave of relief came over me that she was safe. For now at least.

'What?'

I coughed. 'Where are we?'

'I'm taking you to Pine Street. Who did—'

'No hospitals.'

We stopped at a traffic signal and she craned around to look at me, her face lit red in the stoplight's glow. 'What? Why not?'

'Please. Just take me to a motel.'

'Don't be absurd, you're hurt. I couldn't live with myself leaving you like this.' She looked at me like I was one of those

GIs who came back missing an eye, or half their face. She paused, like she was afraid to ask. 'What happened?'

I ignored the question. We started moving again. 'Where did you come from?'

She glanced in the rearview, her eyes just about visible to me. 'A man telephoned me at home, didn't even give his name. He told me you were passed out in the street outside the Mason and he thought you were dying.'

A man – the bellhop?

'I drove straight over as soon as I got the call. There was a bellman waiting with you, he managed to carry you into the car. I was so worried.'

I touched my mouth, feeling split lips, a flashback to a blurred fist coming at my face, one of the cops wearing a class ring. 'Thank you. Really.'

'You have to see a doctor.'

'Tomorrow. I just need to rest.'

She sighed, and for a moment we drove in silence. Then: 'What happened, Charlie?'

'Cops didn't like the questions I was asking.'

'The police did this?'

'Bailey. And his lapdog. They came to run me out of town. Said to be gone by morning. So no hospitals.'

'They can't do that . . .' She trailed off, realising they could do any damn thing they pleased. 'Is this to do with Alice?'

A wave of tiredness came over me and her voice sounded far off. 'Maybe. Some. Can't . . .' My eyes started to close. 'Can't see all the pieces.'

*

224

When she woke me we were outside her house, the car all the way up the driveway, as close to the door as it could get. She reached under my head and helped sit me up.

'This is a bad move,' I said.

I grabbed the roof of the car and pried myself out, Lizzie gripping me by my jacket. We made it across the driveway and into the house, the front door already open. She took me into the lounge and helped me collapse onto the sofa.

At the sideboard behind me I heard her toss ice into two glasses, then pour something on top. She came back and handed it to me, set her one on the table. Scotch. I took a sip and let the burn work its way down my throat. She handed me four aspirin and I took them, a gulp of Scotch to wash each down. She left the room without saying a word, then reappeared a minute later holding a bowl and a pouch of ice. She pressed the ice to my head. 'Hold this here. We're too late for the swelling, but it might numb it some.'

'You don't have to do that.'

'I'm not just going to leave you like this.' She tilted my head towards the light. 'Hold still.' She took a flannel from the bowl and started gently cleaning my face. When she wrung it out, the water in the bowl turned light red, reminded me of Margaret Langley's bloody face in the rain.

Lizzie leaned close; I was startled, for a second thinking she meant to kiss me, but instead she dabbed a spot above my eye. Her perfume flooded my nose and the effect was like smelling salts – everything just a little sharper now. Then I tensed, struck by a thought I should have had sooner, a tremor rattling through me. I tried to get up.

'Where are you going?'

I made it to my feet, stooped like a cripple. 'Did they tail you?'

'Charlie?'

I staggered to the window and parted the drapes a crack. 'When we drove here. Was anyone behind us?'

'What are you talking about?'

I looked both ways down the street. There was nothing moving, but it was too dark to see inside the parked cars. 'The cops, they'll be watching. I shouldn't have come here.' I started for the door.

'Charlie . . .' She overtook me and stood in the doorway, blocking the way. 'Would you sit down?'

'I've put you in danger—'

'There was no-one behind me. I'd have seen.' She looked me over, recoiled at the state of my face. 'Sit down. Please.'

Everything was telling me to run. Everything except her.

She put a hand on my chest. 'Please.'

I backed off. She put her arm around my waist and helped me to the sofa. She picked up the flannel and started dabbing my cuts again. 'You were shouting. In the car. You sounded in pain.'

'Seeing things. Stupid. Spooked me.'

'What are you going to do now?'

I stared at the ceiling. I thought I heard a trace of nervousness in her voice, but couldn't tell. 'I don't know.' I took another slug of Scotch, the alcohol working its way through my system. 'You think any more about what I said?'

'About what?' She pressed down with the flannel, knew exactly what I was talking about.

'About Randall.'

226

'We haven't spoken.' A glare as she said it. 'And I don't want to talk about it. I can't believe you're even thinking about that now.'

I took the ice bag away from my forehead, put it on my neck. The alcohol was dulling the pain a little. 'He went to the place you took me . . . Where Alice . . .'

She dumped the flannel in the bowl, water splashing out over the sides. She didn't notice the drop that landed on her cream blouse, staining it red. 'What?'

'I saw him. What was he doing out there, Lizzie?'

'That's enough, Charlie.'

'He lied to me about his name. Told me it was Johnson. I think he did that because he got spooked when I asked him if he knew Patty Summerbell. Why would he lie if he was clean?'

'What do you mean you saw him? Just what were you doing there?'

'I was following him. I needed him to straighten some things out for me.'

'Following him? Is that all you do, follow people?'

I dumped the ice pack on the sofa, adrenaline and Scotch reviving me now. 'That's right. The same way you followed me to the coffee shop that day.'

She blushed. 'That was different.'

'Hear me out. I've got him arguing with Patty Summerbell right before she died. I've got him at two of the scenes after the fact. He lied about his name. And he's a grade-A lowlife where women are concerned.' I lifted my head so I could look at her straight now. 'He's at least got some goddamn questions to answer.'

She laughed, incredulous. 'It doesn't amount to anything.'

She stood up but looked lost, not sure which way to turn in the room. 'You're obsessed with him. Every time I see you, all you talk about is Randy.'

There was something in her face, the passion in her anger; it reminded me of the kiss. I could almost feel her lips on mine again. 'All we've got is other people.' I pointed at her, then at myself, indicating our connection. 'Randy. Alice. That's all that's between us. Right?'

She turned side-on to me. 'I don't know what you mean.'

'You came to me when Alice disappeared. You didn't go to him.'

'And what of it? I want to find my sister, Charlie. I'll do anything.'

I lifted the bowl off the sofa and put it on the table, the flannel draped half out of it. 'You might think to tell me this then: why did you kiss me the other day? Then make a point of telling me he wasn't your sweetheart.'

She stared blankly at the wall. 'I don't remember.'

'Kissing me?'

She shook her head. 'Why.'

Bursting my balloon, just like that. A kiss I knew meant nothing, from a woman only just holding herself together – and still I'd managed to attach a significance to it that was never there. Hell, it'd been enough to get me thinking that maybe life could go on after Jane – a notion too painful to let see the light of day before then. Realising, now, that I'd been building that idea on quicksand made Lizzie's words that much harder to swallow. 'Fine. You love Schulz, he makes you feel safe, I understand. But at least let me ask him the questions. He owes you an explanation—'

'Do you hear yourself? Are you honestly that jealous of him?'

'Jealous? Jealous has got squat to do with this lady. I want to stop a killer before—'

'I sent him there. Okay? Alice, the place – I asked him to go.'

'What?'

'I sent him there, the same reason I took you there. I just thought . . . I had this feeling she was there. That she'd go back to where it happened.'

I looked down at my glass, the last of the ice bobbing in the Scotch. I felt like I'd been caught cashing a bad cheque.

'The dream I had . . . it was so vivid. I couldn't forget it, but I couldn't face going back there either. So I asked Randy to go for me.'

I kept quiet.

'You don't have to say it. I know it's absurd. He thought so too; that's what we were arguing about. But you don't know what it's like.' She touched her temple with a chipped red nail. 'In here. In this house.' She gestured to the pictures of Alice on the wall and wrapped her arms around herself. 'Everywhere. Going out of my mind. I had to know for sure.'

I hesitated, thinking about what she said. 'It's alright.' I got to my feet, leaning heavily on the table to push myself up. I handed her drink to her. 'Come on, take a seat.'

She accepted the Scotch, clutching the glass to her chest with both hands. 'You know what's worse?' Her eyes were wet with tears now. 'I was lying awake last night, and I had this thought that at least if she was dead, I'd know. I could bury her, take flowers to her grave.' Her lip trembled. 'Isn't that the most wicked thing you ever heard?'

Better off dead; everyone seemed to have the same thought about Alice Anderson. No matter how misplaced. 'Your mind's not your own right now. You're not to blame.'

She sat down in the armchair, white as a sheet. The tumbler looked huge in her small hands; she took a sip from it and made a face like she'd drunk bad milk, the Scotch too harsh. Her eyes glazed over; she put the glass down and let her gaze drift to the floor. 'Do you honestly think Randy could be involved in this?'

I studied her face, not sure what answer she wanted me to give. Maybe not sure myself any more. Then I saw there was one question glaring at me. My hand moved to the inside pocket of my jacket, and I was relieved to feel the typewritten note still there. 'Did he ever work at Red River?'

'Red River? What's the relevance?'

'We can keep going question for question here, but one of us has got to answer one eventually.' It sounded more sarcastic than I meant it to – liquor and tiredness making me sloppy.

She gave me a hard look. 'That wasn't called for.'

'Sorry. I didn't mean to come off sharp.'

She tutted, but then let it pass. 'I'm not sure.' The tip of her tongue poked out between her lips, thinking about my question. 'I don't think so.' She looked worried now, like she was reconsidering him for the first time. 'Does that mean something? What are you driving at?'

I rested my head on the sofa again and closed my eyes, the throbbing pain coming back. 'It doesn't matter.' Tiredness overcame me, and then I wondered if I should be trying to stay awake – if Sherman had beaten a concussion into me; if I'd fall asleep and never wake up. Slipping away in the night, unconscious and unawares; maybe not the worst way to go.

'It does matter, Charlie.' An insistence in her voice – my eyes flicked open again. 'Randy got a medal for bravery in the war. He saved four men from a burning Jeep in France, nearly died doing it. That's the kind of man he is. Not what you say.'

'Maybe he did, but it doesn't mean anything when it comes to what's happening here. I've seen enough vets couldn't adjust when they got back. It's tough to go from burning Jeeps, right back to paying bills and working a job without doing something cockeyed.'

Her eyes flared, as if she couldn't believe what she was hearing. 'How can you say that? I suppose you showed up with the press corps right when the fighting was done to take pictures?' She leaned forward in her chair, pointed at me. 'Wait, you've never said – were you even there?'

I covered my face with my hands and rubbed my eyes. Saw the train coming down the track, same as always. 'No. I was in the States.'

She threw her hands up in the air. 'So you sat the war out in New York City, making your judgments on the men that did go? Sounds a little unfair, don't you think?'

'I volunteered.' Loud, almost a shout. Too defensive. 'In forty-three. I never got to go.'

She looked off to one side, folding her hands in her lap. 'Oh. I didn't . . .' She glanced around, embarrassed. She picked up her glass, raised it to her lips, but put it back down when the smell of the liquor hit her nose. 'Why not?'

My turn to pick up my drink now – but I drained half of it. I thought about telling one of the old lies – bad eyes, a bum heart. Somehow it didn't seem right to mislead her. 'I broke my legs in training. Smashed them like breadsticks. I couldn't walk for a year.'

She studied me, a vacant smile forming on her lips until she realised I wasn't joking. 'What? That's awful. Charlie, I'm sorry—'

I scoffed, a rueful laugh. 'Don't be.'

'No, I mean it. I was out of line.'

I swirled my drink, staring at it, the fumes catching in the back of my throat. 'You should hear the rest of it before you make any apologies.'

She sat back a fraction – the feeling like she was pulling away from me already. 'Why, what's the rest of it?'

A phantom ache ran through my legs as the memories came back to me, as clear as a newsreel in my mind. 'I hit the side of an underpass doing forty miles per hour in a Jeep.'

'You crashed?'

I stared at the floor, shaking my head – disbelief more than denial. 'I don't remember anything about it. First thing I know is waking up in the military hospital in traction.'

'I don't understand. You had an accident. It's embarrassing but there's no shame in it.'

A deep breath. Drain the rest of the drink. 'If it wasn't an accident?'

She searched my face, and as she did, I read every emotion I'd ever felt about myself in her expression. 'What are you trying to tell me, Charlie?'

'Two officers were a couple cars back and saw me do it, said it was intentional. Said they saw me accelerate, and that I swerved off the road on purpose.'

She screwed her eyes up, frowning at me. 'Why would you do that?'

'We were two weeks from shipping out. The state I was in after the crash meant no way they could deploy me. When the Army heard what happened they figured one thing had led to the other. And my CO agreed with them.'

'You . . . you crippled yourself to get out of fighting?' A look of horror on her face now.

'No . . .' I stopped. 'I don't know.' Already admitting more to her than I ever had to anyone else apart from Jane. And getting a similar reaction. When I'd told Jane about the Army's suspicions, she'd flat walked out of my hospital room. It was another twenty-four hours before I saw her again; when she came back, she stood at the foot of my bed and asked, '*How can it be that you can't remember?*' Doubt. The word that would define our relationship from then on.

'My memory is a blank,' I said to Lizzie. 'I can't remember anything in the week before it happened.'

'Doesn't mean you can't remember how you felt. Were you afraid? Before?'

'Sure I was. Everyone was. Any man said otherwise was lying or drunk.'

She wrapped her arms around herself. 'Then why did you volunteer in the first place?'

I shrugged. 'Duty. There's a line that goes something like, "All evil needs to triumph is for good men to do nothing."' The rest of it was right there, about to come rushing out of my mouth. Part of me was desperate to confess; what I'd wanted all along – to have someone tell me it was all ok. The way Jane was supposed to. The way she never did. But even I wasn't selfish

233

enough to use Lizzie as a substitute for her. And besides, I knew damn well that nothing anyone else could say would take the guilt away; that it would always be there.

Truth was, I didn't even know if I did it on purpose – my memory of it was gone. Docs said severe trauma can do that. It was wet that day, someone told me later; could be I skidded. But I'd been looking for a way out, I know that much. I pulled every string I could at the *Examiner* to get reassigned to the press corps, but I didn't have enough stroke, and the Army blocked me all the way. They used that as evidence against me after the accident.

Afraid wasn't the word; those last weeks before we were due to ship out, I was terrified. I barely slept; when I did, oftentimes I woke up covered in sweat. My father fought with the Lost Battalion; he died in the Argonne Forest in the first war, and I was scared as hell it was my fate to go the same way. A German bullet cutting me down, dying with a mouthful of foreign mud. Even so, it wasn't the getting killed scared me most; it was what I stood to lose. I had the girl, the career, the apartment – everything I ever wanted. Far as I was concerned, I was the prince of New York City. The irony of it all wasn't lost on me: I was scared of dying because I had so much to lose. So I dodged the war – and lost it all anyway. 'Seems like I came up short on that one.'

She stared at me a moment, then stood up, shaking her head. 'It doesn't make any sense. I've seen you, Charlie, I thought you were a brave man.'

'Being brave and being scared can look the same sometimes.' I touched my chest. 'Depends what's going on inside.'

'What does that mean?'

I dipped my head and held it in my hands, already feeling an idiot. 'It means I'm full of baloney and you shouldn't listen to a damn word I say.'

'I hate when you do that to me, Charlie.'

'Hate when I do what?'

'You push me away and treat me like I'm a stupid little girl who wouldn't understand what the grownups are talking about.'

'You got plenty on your plate as it is.'

'Don't you dare. Don't hide behind Alice.'

I spread my palms without looking at her, my energy about spent. I checked my watch: after midnight. 'I've got to get some shuteye. Can I sleep on your floor for a couple hours?'

She went to the window again and looked out, her back to me. Her reaction was no surprise – desperate to find somewhere else to focus so she didn't have to look at me. 'I don't know what to say. I can't believe what you're telling me.'

'I'll be gone by morning, make sure you're not dragged into this. You won't have to worry about me then.'

Her gaze fell to the floor, her fingers tugging at the sides of her blouse. Then she turned to me again, studying me as if someone new had taken my place in her living room.

'Please,' I said.

She dropped her arms to her sides. 'You can't go anywhere like that. I'll make up the spare bed for tonight.'

I nodded. 'Tonight is plenty. Thank you.' She went out into the hallway and I heard her footsteps on the staircase. I closed my eyes and felt like I was falling. In that instant, I was back in the bed at Lennox Hill Hospital, the smells coming back to me – Lysol and boiled cabbage. Six months I spent there, my muscles wasting to nothing as they put my legs back together. Sal, Walters and a few others from the *Examiner* came by every couple weeks. They paid lip service to my bravery, to how unlucky I'd been. But they'd heard the story and the doubt was written all over their faces. No-one asked me outright – easier all around to let me talk like the war hero denied. I played my part too: '*The pain's nothing – not compared to knowing I won't get to fight.*' To hear me tell it, I was ready to swim across the Atlantic just to get my shot at the Nazis.

Afterward, Sal never said a word about it to me; he'd played up a punctured eardrum to get his 4F and skip the fighting. In some ways we were closer as a result. Walters was a different story. Too much of a coward to say anything to my face, he took up against me from then on – ending up with me on a flight to Texarkana.

The only one I cared about was Jane. She came to the hospital most every day, bringing her own doubt – unspoken, after that first time, but there all the same. It took me a time to notice, but once I recognised the shadow that crossed her face when she sat by my bed, it was always between us. It was another two years and a thousand quarrels before she finally threw me out, but I knew it was coming from the first time she looked at me and wondered if I was a coward. Sometimes I think I was trying to force the issue with her through violence – breaking into rages at the drop of a hat. The only thing I clung to was that I never hit her. As I thought about that now, it seemed a pretty hollow victory to be holding on to.

With hindsight, the real problem was that I knew damn well what I was, and I hated myself for it. I saw it every time I looked in the mirror. Because no matter how many times I told people how desperate I was to do my duty, it couldn't change one fact: every morning I woke up in that hospital, I thanked God I was there – in that bed – and not at the front.

*

Lizzie woke me at seven the next morning, stepping into the room with a mug of coffee in hand. She barely spoke, but it didn't feel like silent treatment borne of anger – more like we were strangers again.

It ached when I sat up. Lizzie set the coffee on the bedside table, pulled the drapes and winced when she saw my face in the light.

'I look that bad?'

She started to shake her head, then quit. 'It's bad.'

I ran my tongue over two newly chipped teeth, my own mouth feeling alien to me. 'What day is it? Friday?' She nodded. Her eyes landed on mine, and the same thought passed between us: one more day until another attack. 'Any news?'

'You mean Alice?'

I nodded.

'No. There won't be now.'

I wanted to say something to reassure her, but even in my head the words sounded empty. I chased four aspirins with coffee, then edged my way out of bed and started dressing.

'You're leaving?'

I paused, shirt in hand. I reached for the train ticket Bailey gave me, tossed it onto the bed. 'This is what he left me with. Said he'd kill me if I didn't get on the train by now.'

She picked it up and looked at it. 'They can't do that. It's just scare talk.'

I took the ticket back from her. 'I don't think so. I get the feeling Bailey was one of those crazies enjoyed being at war. I think I'd be just another notch on his gun belt.'

'They're lawmen. A beating's one thing, but killing you?'

I pointed at my face. 'What the hell do I owe this town, Lizzie?'

She gathered her hair over one shoulder and stroked at it, like a comforter. 'I've been thinking. What if I agreed to speak to Randy?'

I pulled my shirt on one arm at a time, gingerly. 'What for?'

'That's a heck of a thing to say. You wanted me to ask him all those questions, so—'

'Don't use Schulz as your excuse.'

'As my excuse for what?'

'For keeping me here.'

She stepped around me and went to straighten the bed sheets, busying herself. 'I don't know what you're talking about.'

I put a hand on her shoulder and pulled her towards me. 'I mean tell me that you want me to stay.'

We stood there, eyes locked on each other. My hand was still on her shoulder, and I thought about pulling her towards me. I wanted to kiss her but was afraid to make a move, too many emotions clouding my judgement; uppermost among them, the fear that she'd shoot me down – and for good this time. She was the first woman to make me forget about Jane – the first woman I'd even noticed since; the idea of her slamming that door in my face, now, was enough to freeze me on the spot.

She searched my face, the emerald eyes catching in the light from the window. 'Who's Jane?'

Hearing the name from her lips made me pull my hand back, involuntary, like I'd touched a hot oven.

'You were shouting again last night. In your sleep. The same as the other night. *Jane* – that was the name I heard.'

I didn't know where to begin. 'She's my wife. Was.'

'You're estranged?'

I rolled my head to ease the throbbing in my neck. 'Yes. She left me.'

'Because of what you did? The crash?'

I turned away, reaching for my shoes my excuse. 'That was the start of it. But more than that. It's a long story.'

'And yet you never mentioned her once.'

'Why would I?'

'That's my point. You don't want to talk about her, which tells me it still hurts.'

I looked around at her, stunned, wondering how long she'd been thinking about this. 'It's . . . It's complicated.'

She stepped to me and straightened my collar. 'I told you before I'm not a child, Charlie. I know what you want me to say, but I'm courting Randall, and you've got a wife. And I don't know what to think of you any more.' She put her hand on my cheek and leaned over to peck me on the other. Then she picked up my cup and slipped out of the room.

I tried to say she was as good as my ex-wife, but I stopped mid-sentence – Lizzie already gone, and me sounding so pathetic I wanted to slap myself out of it. I sat down on the edge of the bed and fumbled trying to tie my laces, my head feeling like it was going to rupture. Downstairs a telephone rang and Lizzie answered it. As I finished tying the knot, I heard a cup smash on the floor and Lizzie scream.

I stumbled down the staircase, adrenaline carrying me. Lizzie was sobbing, the telephone cradled in both hands and pressed against her forehead. The coffee mug was in a dozen pieces on the hallway floor. One look at her and I got a sinking feeling like all the blood in my body was draining into my feet.

I took the receiver from her. 'Hello?'

A voice I didn't recognise came back at me. 'Who's speaking?'

'I'm a friend of Miss Anderson's. What's going on?'

Lizzie had crumpled to the floor, her legs folding under her. Her cries were coming in long bursts, punctuated by desperate gasps for air.

'This is Deputy Bagwell of Bowie County Sheriff's. I'm afraid I've just had to deliver some bad news to Miss Anderson.'

'You've found her? Alice?'

The man grunted. 'Sir, are you fixing to stay with Miss Anderson today? She gonna need someone.'

'Where is she? Her sister?'

'Sir, I'm real sorry but we've found a body matching Alice Anderson's description. Sheriff Bailey is at the scene, and he's informally identified it as her. We'll need Miss Anderson to confirm it, of course.'

The call I prayed wouldn't come. I said nothing as the words sunk in.

'Sir?'

I glanced at Lizzie, then turned away from her, trying to keep her from hearing. 'How did she die?'

The cop hesitated. 'We can't say for sure just now, but it's our belief that this woman took her own life.'

I cursed under my breath. 'Where did you find her?'

'Sir, who did you say you were?'

'I told you, a friend.'

The man made a disapproving sound, but relented anyway. 'A railroad worker found her on the tracks by Rose Hill Cemetery. About an hour and a half ago.'

'Where is she now?'

'Still at the tracks. We got enquiries to complete before we can move her. She . . . she was hit by a train so the body's in pretty bad shape.'

'Meaning?'

'The train was going full speed, so . . . I mean, ain't right discussing this over the telephone. Sometime soon, we gonna need Miss Anderson to come down to the morgue and identify her for the record. Y'all should wait by the phone. I'll call again just as soon as we can get that fixed up.'

I hung up. Lizzie had folded over double, her face cupped in her hands on the floor, shaking. The sobs had retreated to irregular whimpers. I kneeled next to her, put my arm around her shoulders and the two of us stayed like that, mourners at our own private memorial.

CHAPTER THIRTY

After ten minutes, I made a cup of strong black coffee and put it in her hand, but she didn't seem to even notice it. She'd cried herself dry, her face and eyes red and swollen, and now she was gazing vacantly through the doorway at the pictures in the living room.

'You should lie down.' I reached out for her.

'No.' She put the coffee on the floor and stood. 'I've got to see her.' I tried to guide her into the living room, but she pushed my arm away. 'I mean it, Charlie. I can't just sit here.'

'Did they tell you about where they found her?'

'Yes.'

'You don't want to see her that way.'

'Will you come with me?'

The deputy said Bailey was at the scene. A safe bet Sherman wouldn't be far away either. Bailey's words came back to me: '*Don't mistake this for another warning.*'

'I can't.'

'Can't?'

I touched my bottom lip, one of the cuts cracked, now seeping blood again. 'After yesterday. Bailey's there.'

'Fine. I'll go myself.' She hurried past me, out the front door.

I called after her. 'Lizzie—'

She whirled around and fixed me with a look that stopped me dead. Her face was flush with fury and despair; a woman

242

who'd lost everything. I watched her turn towards the car again, five foot-nothing of her charging towards her own personal hell because she knew no fear. Suddenly I was more afraid of letting her go; of leaving her to deal with the worst day of her life alone, monsters like Bailey her only protector. I pulled the front door shut and went after her. 'Give me the keys.'

*

The railroad crossing was on the south edge of town; Lizzie reeled off directions and we were there in minutes. There were five police cruisers parked either side of the tracks, deputies and city police dotted around the scene. They'd closed both crossing barriers; a hundred yards down, short of where the body was, a freight train had been stopped, the driver out of his cab and talking to a cop. On the south side of the tracks, a low brick wall marked the perimeter of the cemetery. The sun was still low in the early morning sky, so the headstones cast long shadows over the grass.

I pulled up beside the first black-and-white. I looked around for Bailey, but as soon as we stopped moving, Lizzie threw her door open and jumped out, sprinting off across the ground. I thumped the steering wheel and hauled myself out. Standing up, I saw what she'd seen and where she was headed: a white sheet covering a body a little way from the side of the tracks. I took off after her, but she had too much of a head start and my broken body wouldn't carry me fast enough. The closest officer to the corpse was thirty feet away; he whipped around and ran to intercept her, but it was too late. She dropped to her knees next to the corpse and pulled the sheet back, then gripped her sister in a fierce embrace, her sobs echoing off the tarmac.

The two cops got there before me. They grabbed Lizzie and dragged her away. She was screaming and fighting them, clawing to hold her sister a moment longer. I ran up and took her from the cop's arms.

'What're you doing, mister?'

'It's okay,' I said. 'I've got her.' I spun Lizzie away so I was between her and the body.

The cop called after me to stop.

Lizzie was limp now, a deadweight in my arms. I noticed a smear of blood on her neck from the body – dark red and sticky. Old blood. I glanced over my shoulder and got a last glimpse of Alice before the deputy covered her again. Her hair was plastered over her face, just as I remembered her from the hospital; her skin was pale underneath the bruising, her head at an awkward angle, her neck probably broken by the impact. Her left leg was missing from the thigh down. I gripped Lizzie tighter and walked her gently away from where Alice lay.

The cop put his hand on my shoulder. 'I said stop. Turn around—'

'This is her sister.' I didn't look back.

The cop stopped in his tracks. I kept moving, Lizzie walking awkwardly, like a rag doll in my arms. We staggered a few more steps; I looked up, saw Bailey standing a few feet away from Lizzie's car, shaking his head.

I paused, struggling to keep Lizzie upright now. I was terrified my legs wouldn't hold. Sweat ran down my back and my forehead. Bailey stared at me from behind dark glasses, chewing on a matchstick. A standoff.

'Sheriff?'

It was Lizzie's voice. Startled me, and Bailey too by the look of him.

'Miss Anderson.' He took his hat off, held it against his chest. 'My sincere condolences.'

She straightened now, supporting her own weight. Bailey looked from her to me and back again, suddenly unsettled. Lizzie spoke again. 'What happened?'

Bailey took his glasses off and came closer. 'It's too early to say for sure, but it looks like she threw herself in front of a train.'

Lizzie glanced back at the freight train behind us, confusion on her face. 'What do you mean looks like?'

'Miss Anderson, maybe you should—'

'Tell me.' Lizzie's voice had a new steel in it now.

Bailey shifted his weight like he was deciding what to tell. 'The Sunshine Special came through here at five this morning, we thinking that's the one hit her. Train's been stopped outside of Sulphur Springs – Hopkins County Sheriff's got a car going out to speak to the driver. But it was dark, so chances are he never even saw her.'

'Where . . .' Lizzie was searching his face, still clinging to hope for answers, any kind of explanation. 'Where's she been?'

'We don't know anything yet, Miss Anderson.'

'Her leg... I can't bury her like that. I have to . . .' Her legs went bandy and I took her weight. She was sobbing violently again.

I looked at Bailey. 'Open the car for me.'

He stepped backwards slowly, eyes on mine. He opened the car door and held it. I scooped Lizzie up and carried her over. Bailey stayed where he was; when I ducked down to put her on the front seat, he leaned close and whispered in my ear. 'This don't change nothing.'

I set her down and shut the door, then pushed past him and

walked around the car. I pointed at him across the roof. 'This is your fault.'

Bailey's eyes wrinkled. 'You had a deadline, Yates.'

I snatched a look at Lizzie, face down on the bench seat. Her body convulsed with each sob. 'To hell with your deadline.'

Bailey cocked his head. 'Say that again.'

'I'm not leaving her like this.'

He ran his hand over his face. 'All the things I pegged you as, dumb wasn't one of them. You know what happens now. I gave you the choice.'

'That girl would still be alive if she never left the hospital.' I threw my door open and climbed in. I jammed the car into reverse and turned it around fast. As I drove away, I saw Bailey in the rearview, still watching me. As if he had a gun sight on my head.

*

I raced back to Lizzie's place, watching for a tail car all the way, sure Bailey wouldn't waste any time following through on his promise. Lizzie stopped crying a couple minutes out, lost in her thoughts. I ran a red coming off State Line, thinking to shake anyone trailing me, and she didn't even react.

When she finally spoke, I almost didn't hear her over the engine noise. 'I should have guessed.'

I stole a sideways glance. 'What?'

'Rose Hill.' Her voice was distant, hollow. 'The cemetery. That's where she'd go.'

I gripped the wheel tighter. 'There's no way you could've known.'

'Yes I could. It's where they're buried.'

'Who?' I was concentrating on the road, a half step behind

what she was saying. I cottoned too late.

'Our parents.'

I glanced again, the corner of my eye. 'No one could have done more than you did.'

She was staring ahead, her face a void. She'd never looked more like Alice.

*

I stopped at the far end of Lizzie's block, scanning for police watching her place. Waiting for me.

'Charlie, what are you doing?'

I looked along the street. There, outside her house – an unmarked black Ford, two men in the front. 'Bailey must have radioed in.'

She looked at me, then followed my line of sight, trying to see what I could see. She sounded scared. 'What are you talking about?'

I put my arm over the back of the seat and craned my neck to look as I reversed. I pulled around the corner, out of sight. 'They know I'm with you, I've got to go. You have to get out here. And I need your car.'

'You're frightening me, Charlie.'

'Go. I'll call you. I'll bring the car back as soon as I can.'

'I don't care about the car,' she said. 'You can't leave. I need you—'

'I'll find somewhere. A motel. I'll be in touch as soon as I do.' I reached across her and opened her door. 'But you have to go. Now. It's not safe with me.'

She slid out, catching her shoe in the foot well as she did,

247

all her energy sapped. Standing on the kerb, the tears came in earnest again, her head bowed into her chest. I felt like the world's biggest heel as I drove away.

*

I drove for an hour. I checked in at two motels outside of town – one at the northern end of State Line and one outside the city limits on the road to Little Rock. I paid for two nights at both and used my driver's license for identification, making sure they got all my details. Both times, I walked out and drove away immediately.

The Sulphur River Inn was south of town. I paid three nights up front, negating any talk of producing identification, and checked in under the name of Tennison. I made sure to stash the car out back, out of sight from the road.

The room was bare but clean – a big drop from the Mason, but better than dozens of motels I'd stayed in chasing stories around the country. There was a wooden desk and chair, both peppered with black cigarette burns, and a bed with two mismatched pillows. All I had with me were the clothes on my back and the contents of my pockets, everything else still in the room at the Mason – assuming Bailey and Sherman hadn't had it cleaned out. Either way, it was all lost to me now. I tossed my jacket on the bed and sat on the chair, head in my hands.

I felt as if the answers were all there, but just out of reach. Maybe I was kidding myself. Alice Anderson was dead, apparently suicide – but I couldn't shake the feeling that the town wanted her that way; better a dead martyr than a living reminder. Could be something worse than that: she was the only person who'd seen the killer and lived; convenient for some, then, that she took her secrets to the grave with her. The mystery cop that was watch dogging her the day she disappeared troubled me; Bailey's reaction when I'd asked him about it convinced me the story had credence, but I couldn't figure where it fit in. Between that and his determination to be rid of me, I had a bad feeling about how deep into this he went. I'd dealt with cops of every stripe over the years, but I'd never seen anything like Bailey and Sherman. Texarkana was rotten to the core, and they were the maggots making it that way.

Then there was Randy Schulz, a.k.a. Johnson. The burning question: did I make him as the killer? I could place him at two scenes; there was apparently an explanation for why he went to Alice Anderson's, but no good reason for him to be at Patty Summerbell's. The argument he had with her the night she died made it even more troubling. Odds on: his casual brush-off when I dropped Patty's name was pure front, meaning he was determined to keep whatever was between them from me. Same went for lying about his name – something to hide there too. Still, the case against him was thin, and the closer I got to Lizzie, the less I trusted my instincts where he was concerned.

And now I had a death sentence hanging over me. The un-marked waiting for me outside of Lizzie's nixed any chance that Bailey was bluffing. I couldn't even move around town without the threat of being spotted, and the night-time curfew made it twice as difficult. I reached into my pocket and pulled out the note about Red River Arsenal. Still anonymous, the sender was as important as the contents, but both still a mystery. What I needed was an ally. And there was only one person with the clout.

One person that wanted the killer as badly as me.

CHAPTER THIRTY-ONE

I called the Mason first, to see if Callaway's assistant had come through with the list of names from Red River.

'I've got no-one by the name Yates registered as staying here, sir.'

The call booth at the motel was out front of the reception office, the telephone an old wind-up model with a permanent bad line. I looked out from the booth across the road to a scatter of dark pines, the brown water of the Sulphur River visible behind them, flowing slowly. 'I was a guest there till a couple days ago.'

'You're not in the book.'

It had to be Bailey. Covering his tracks by erasing mine. 'Room 316. I left some things there.'

The clerk sighed down the line, a note in his voice that hinted he remembered me just fine. 'I'm sorry, but I don't have any record of you.'

'What about messages?'

'We only take messages for guests.'

I pounded the side of the booth and hung up. 'Goddammit.'

*

Lizzie's Chevy topped out at sixty-five, so I kept the pedal to the floor all the way to Callaway's place, watching for cops as I went – a traffic stop the last thing I needed. I didn't have the time or patience to negotiate a spot in Callaway's diary, so I settled on the direct approach. Coming up the main drive, I saw a truck parked by the house and workmen coming out of a side entrance carrying a chest towards it. I parked a little way off to the left and went to the front door.

The same butler as last time opened it but he showed no recognition. I marched past him, demanding to see Callaway. When he chased after me, I brushed him off. 'It's urgent.'

'I'm sure you think it is. Nonetheless, Mr Callaway—'

I spun on my heel. 'Owes me fifty thousand bucks.' I jabbed him in the chest. 'So you can pony up, or he can.'

The man stopped, too shocked to react. I heard raised voices coming from the direction of the study where I'd met Callaway last time; before the butler could move, I was gone again, almost running towards it. As I drew close, I caught a fragment of what was being said. It was Callaway's voice: '. . . and it's for your benefit.'

The door was open when I got there. Callaway was inside, behind his desk; his son was the other side of it. Odd: he was flanked by two of the gardeners I'd seen before, both wearing the same white overalls. The son was pointing at his pops, the veins in his neck throbbing. 'My benefit? You're deluded, old man. How on earth can it be to my benefit?'

'What else would you have me—' Callaway stopped mid-sentence when he saw me. His son registered the change in his demeanour and snapped around to see what he was looking at. The gardeners did the same.

I focused on Callaway senior. 'This a bad time?'

The butler had come up behind me now, but Callaway waved

him away. 'Yates?' Callaway planted his fingertips on the desk. He looked me over. 'What the hell happened to your face?'

The son eyeballed me. He was skinny, the slacks and striped shirt he wore hanging off him; the burly gardeners made for an even bigger contrast with his wiry frame. He had a mop of straw hair, little tufts shooting out in different directions. 'Who are you supposed to be?'

Callaway held up his hand, trying to take control of the room. 'This is the reporter from New York. I told you about him.' He was addressing his son but looking at me. 'And he's got a damn good reason for why's he's intruding. Correct?'

The two gardeners looked awkwardly at Callaway; he gave a very slight shake of the head. Both seemed to be on edge; I couldn't read the dynamic in the room, what I'd walked in on.

'I need to talk to you,' I said.

The son laughed, surprised. 'Who does this fellow take himself for?'

Callaway ignored him. 'Then you make an appointment with my secretary.'

'I don't have time to stand on ceremony. Either you help me, or I breeze.'

Callaway tilted his head slightly. 'I sincerely doubt that.'

The son was flicking his gaze from me to Callaway, like he was watching a tennis match. He settled on his father. 'You're going to let him talk to you like that?'

Callaway dismissed the gardeners with a tiny flick of his finger. Then he addressed the boy. 'Jefferson, you can go.'

Jefferson rolled his tongue around his mouth, bulging his cheeks. Then he sat down in the chair facing his father. 'To hell with you. I want to hear this.'

Callaway twitched like he was about to explode at him, eyes bulging. 'Jefferson.' He took a slow breath, the sound heavy in the room. Then he spoke again, voice back at a normal level. 'Go.'

Jefferson picked a silver fountain pen off the desk and poked the end in his ear, like he was trying to get at some wax. 'You send your only son away but let this lowlife hack stay? Is that the size of it?'

'This is neither the time nor—'

Jefferson cut him off, pulled the pen out of his ear and pointed at me with the dirty end. 'Say, why don't you ask my old man about his precious Red River?' He shifted to look at his father. 'Is that what you want to talk to him about, Pa?'

Callaway moved fast, rounding the desk in a hurry. He backhanded Jefferson across the face, rocking him back in his chair. The old man stood over him, right arm cocked to hit him again, breathing hard. The two stared at each other, Jefferson's face still angled away from the old man by the force of the blow. The air in the room almost crackled.

Then Jefferson jumped to his feet. He made a grab for Callaway. I moved at the same time and managed to get between them, my arms around Jefferson's chest, bundling him away. Suddenly the gardeners were back, grabbing at me. I got my elbows up, tried to protect my injured face, but realised that they were going for the boy. I let go of him and they shoved me aside. The two men seized Jefferson under the arms and manhandled him to the door.

He struggled like a man being taken to the gas chamber, screaming at the old man as he fought them. 'GODDAMN YOU.' As they wrestled Jefferson through the door, he arched his whole body back. He strained, managed to turn his head just enough to be able to lock eyes with his father. 'It's a mercy mother died and got away from you.'

The men lifted him clear of the floor and carried him down the hallway, Jefferson shouting and cursing all the way.

Callaway was trembling, the muscles in his jaw pulsing. The pen Jefferson had cleaned his ear with was lying on the carpet, like a spent bullet casing. I hadn't the first idea what I'd just witnessed, whether it was an argument that had escalated suddenly, viciously, or the culmination of something else. Seeing him backhand his son reminded me of what Richard Davis had said about Callaway, badmouthing him and calling him a Nazi.

Callaway gripped the edge of his desk and hung his head. 'Get out.' There was no force behind it, the old man depleted by the scene before.

I stepped inside the room and shut the door behind me. 'What was that?'

He looked up. 'You've got a damn cheek coming here like this.' He glared at me, and for a second I thought he was going to come at me the same way he did to Jefferson. Instead, he turned around to his drinks tray and poured himself a large measure of whisky, drinking off two large gulps right away. He stared at the lake in silence. When he spoke again, he said, 'It's a family matter.' He was calmer, the liquor soothing him somewhat.

I stood behind the chair Jefferson had sat in. 'I need your help.'

He remained by the double doors behind his desk. 'You've found our man?'

'Not yet.'

He swirled his drink, thinking. 'Then you want money. An advance on the reward.'

'No.'

Callaway turned at that. 'Then what?'

'The police.' I pointed to the bruises on my face. 'This was my last warning. I can't do what you need if I can't even walk the streets.'

'Your problems don't concern me, Yates.'

'My problems are your problems. You know what happens tomorrow night if we don't do something.'

He finished off his drink and slammed it down on the desk. 'What progress have you made?'

I felt my face flush, his words like an admonishment. 'I need the Red River employee list. They had me kicked out of the Mason before your woman could deliver it.'

'This again.' He pulled back from the desk, eyes closed and shaking his head. He fidgeted with the class ring on his finger, turning it, distracted. 'I told you when we spoke at the outset that it's a wild goose chase. I expected more of you.'

Angry now, I pulled the note from my pocket, unfolded it and slapped it on the desk. 'Read this, then tell me it's a wild goose chase.'

He picked it up, his eyes moving slowly over the words. Then he let it fall away, like it was a candy wrapper. 'What is this?'

I snatched it up again. 'It was put under my door. Someone knows what's happening, and it's tied to your plant.'

'How do you know it's genuine?'

'Instinct.'

'Instinct? What is that? Who sent this?'

I walked around the desk so we were face to face. 'That's the point: I don't know.'

He looked incredulous. 'What?'

'I've been doing this fifteen years. I've had plenty tips like this before, and it's always followed by more notes, or a telephone call, or someone coming up to me. You know why?'

'Enlighten me.'

'Because they're always lunatics looking for attention. With this one, I've had nothing. Which means what they're saying has something to it, and that's what they want me to focus on.'

He rolled his eyes. 'Do you have any notion how many enemies I have, Yates? This is an attack on me, nothing more. There are people that do not want me to run Red River again.'

'No.' I tapped the tabletop to make my point. 'They'd put your name in it if that's what they wanted. Make it easy for me.'

Callaway poured another drink for himself and sat in his chair. I suddenly felt like I was back in Tom Walters's office, arguing to get a story into print. Callaway sighed. 'Alright.' He extended the hand with the drink in, pointing at me. 'Assuming it is real, what do you propose to do?'

'The names. That's the starting point.' I held the note up. 'Unless this means something to you?' I watched his face, looking for a reaction, evasiveness, anything. But he was a blank slate, nothing there to read.

'Fine. Mrs Cornette is working on it; she will deliver them to you as agreed. Where can she contact you?'

I hesitated, some little alarm sounding in my head. I thought about what I knew of the man, whether I really trusted him. I remembered the address book I'd seen on his desk the first time I came, opened to a page with McGaffney's name on it; it wouldn't take much for my hideaway to get out, even inadvertently. I took a scrap of paper off the desk and scribbled down Lizzie's telephone number. 'Leave a message for me here.

I'll call you back to set up a meeting.'

Callaway shook his head. 'Not me. Mrs Cornette.'

'When can I expect the list? Time's against us.'

He bristled, not used to direct questions. 'Tomorrow.'

'That's too late.'

'Sooner is impossible.'

I put my hands on my hips, exhaling a long breath, already hearing the minutes tick away as I waited for the morning. The frustration was bubbling, but I could tell from his face there was no discussion. 'Alright. Tomorrow then.'

'See that you keep your side of our deal. My name is nowhere near anything you write.'

'Agreed. One more thing—'

'Your line of credit is stretched as it is.'

'The police. Lean on them. Get them to leave me alone.'

He put his glass down and laced his fingers in front of him. 'Out of the question. I told you, even I can't—'

'Yes, you can.' Callaway looked shocked. 'I was there when you offered the reward money at the press briefing. Bailey deferred to you like you were holding him by the short hairs.'

'You're out of line, now, Yates. You don't know what you're talking about.'

I leaned against the wall, arms folded. 'Cut it out. You walked on that stage like you owned him. All I'm asking is you get him to back off.'

'No.'

'No?'

'I can't and I won't.'

There was a determination to the way he said it – a note in his voice, if not fear then at least trepidation. I wondered if Bailey had something on the old man; some dirt that made even Callaway wary of crossing him. I thought back to the story about Callaway bootlegging to make his money, wondered if it tied in somehow.

'Keep a low profile and you'll be fine.' Callaway opened his top drawer. 'If they arrest you, call this number.' He handed me a business card – Gene Kofax, Attorney-at-Law. He reached back into the drawer and pulled out a bundle of cash, tossed it onto my side of the desk. 'And here. Some walking around money.'

I took the card, almost laughing at the thought of being arrested – so far past that now. I picked up the money and lobbed it back to him. 'I don't need money. My expense account is generous.'

He shrugged. 'As you will.' He stood up, his eyes dropping to the pen still lying on the floor. 'But now I'd like you to leave. And don't come here without an appointment again.'

I took three paces towards the door and stopped. 'What do you think the note means?'

He reached for the stack of bills, still on the desktop, riffling one corner like a card dealer. 'I think it means someone is using you.'

'The same way you are?'

A thin smile. 'That's different. We both want the same thing.'

I thought about that. I thought about everything he'd said. His determination to keep the spotlight off Red River, even as he courted publicity for his reward money. His insistence on keeping his name away from any investigation of the plant. His refusal to back Bailey down on my behalf. And I wasn't certain, any more, that we did.

CHAPTER THIRTY-TWO

The sun was low by the time I got back to the motel, the Sulphur River now a slate grey colour in the shadows. I raced to my room and ripped a dozen pieces of paper from the crumpled notepad in the desk drawer and pinned them to the wall – names, dates, connections; a recreation of the diagram I made at the Mason. I had no notes to work from this time, but it didn't matter, it was all in my head, nagging at me, willing me on.

I put the victims' names across the top, images of each one clear in my mind now. Alice Anderson was the sharpest, her life's tragic arc played out in a series of snapshots in my mind: the photograph of her I brought from New York, the hopeful optimism of youth burning bright in her eyes; the picture Lizzie had showed of her around town when she disappeared, almost a woman, strikingly beautiful; the broken shell I saw in Pine Street Hospital, haunted and scared; and the corpse on the railroad tracks, finding peace at the cost of her own life.

It wasn't just Alice, though; I could picture Edward Logan's puppy-fat face; Patty Summerbell on her porch – overgrown when I'd seen it – stroking her dog; Margaret Langley's raven-black hair. I felt like they were all in the room with me.

My eyes roved across the sheets of paper. The same problem still lingered: Logan and Summerbell, no links to Red River that I could see. I stared at the words, thinking, the feeling of something missed. I racked my brains and at first drew a blank, but then I saw Richard Davis's sheet again, and it came to me: Anna Mendoza, the name of Patty Summerbell's other friend that Davis had given me. I'd called her house but got no answer. I couldn't remember her number and she wasn't in the directory, but her address had stayed with me – West 6th Street. I made a note to cruise by and try to track her down.

I looked at the dotted line from Randall Schulz to Patty Summerbell. I drew another one, from Schulz to Alice, via Lizzie. Randy the womaniser; a new thought – could he have been messing around with Alice behind Lizzie's back? He said Alice deserved to get attacked, that she toyed with men – what if she had toyed with him? That would explain his attitude – the hound-dog who got a taste of his own medicine and didn't like it. It was something close to a motive. Alice's description of her attacker was vague, but could be she was too afraid of Schulz to give him up. Or maybe she wasn't certain. Whatever it was, if she gave herself away somehow when the cops were interviewing her, it would explain why they were certain it was someone she knew.

I told myself to slow down. This was a real stretch, pure guesswork now – my determination to get Schulz creating connections out of thin air. Even if it was true, it still left questions. I grabbed a blank sheet and scribbled them down. First, the weapon: did Schulz own or have access to a Colt .22? I thought about ways I could get inside his pad to search it, see if I could turn anything up. Second, Schulz and Red River; there had to be a link there if the anonymous note was real – and correct. I pulled it from my pocket, the edges tattered now, and pinned it on the wall. Lizzie said she didn't think he'd worked there, but she couldn't be sure. It was too important to let it lie; the list from Callaway would hold the answer.

The last question: Schulz and Margaret Langley and Peter Hamilton, the Spring Lake Park victims – was there a connection there? The obvious one: if Langley had stepped out with Schulz at some point, he was halfway to the electric chair. That was the next thing to check on.

I stood back from the chart and stared at it, looking for holes, oversights, implications. Nothing more came. I locked the room up and went to find a telephone directory. Margaret Langley's father lived on the north side of Texarkana, ten minutes from Spring Lake Park. Timothy Langley answered on the second ring when I called. Despite fielding my questions with one-word answers, when I told him I wanted to find his daughter's killer more than writing some damned story, he agreed to see me that afternoon.

He was watching out the window when I got there, eyes hard but empty. He opened the front door before I could knock. 'You Yates?'

I nodded and shook his hand. 'Appreciate you seeing me, Mr Langley. I'm so sorry about your daughter.'

'Name's Tim.' He pointed for me to come in. The door opened straight into the living room; it was clean and neat, but the armchairs were threadbare and the table in the corner of the room was chipped and scratched. A comfortable life fallen on hard times.

'What paper you say you're with?'

'The *Examiner*, in New York.'

If he was curious about what I was doing in Texarkana, like everyone else, he didn't show it. He sat down in the armchair by the window, his posture rigid, and looked up at me. 'What do you know that the police don't?'

I squinted at him. 'I'm not sure I understand.'

He drummed his fingers once on the armrest. 'You want me to go through it all again, you best have something for me because otherwise you just wasting my time.' He said it in a matter of fact way.

'Alright. Let's start with Red River Arsenal.'

'What about it?'

'Margaret worked there?'

He nodded.

'How long for?'

'Couple years. Three.'

'She like working there?'

He looked away, then back at me. 'Maybe. Job's a job. She didn't talk much about it. Not to me anyways.'

'What did she do there?'

'She was a stock checker in the warehouse. Kept the inventory ledger. What's this got to do—'

'Did she ever court anyone from the plant?'

His face twitched, the first reaction he'd given to anything. 'No. Not that I know of.'

I pushed gently, getting the feeling that something had crossed his mind. 'Not even a friend, anyone she talked about?'

'No.' He stared at me, mulling it. 'But I'm her daddy and she was a grown woman. She ain't tell me everything.'

There was something there, but he wanted me to tease it out of him. 'Have the Texarkana police or Sheriff's ever asked you about Red River at all?'

His face went blank again. 'No. So why are you?'

I went with a half-truth. 'I'm looking for something that links the victims. Alice Anderson and Dwight Breems both worked there.'

He screwed his face up at that. 'And what's that worth? Everyone worked there one time or another. Even the women once the war started up.'

I sensed him withdrawing again, so I changed tack. 'Did your daughter have a sweetheart that you know of?'

He shook his head. 'Not for a year or so. Had one coming through school, they courted for a while, but he moved to Plano or somewhere.'

'What was his name?'

He looked at his nails. 'Don't remember. Byron, something like that.'

I noted down the name to follow up later. As I scribbled, Langley went to a small bookcase across the room. 'Wait now, I'll tell you.' He searched the middle shelf, came back holding a high school yearbook. He sat down again and set it down on his lap. It fell open about halfway through. He stared down at the page and his eyes softened, a distant smile flickering on his lips, him suddenly transported to another time and place. A place that only existed in his memory now. I glanced at where he was looking and saw Margaret's entry, her photograph sitting above a block of text. Tim Langley stared at it a little longer, savouring it, then turned the page over. He leafed through the book, stopping when he found what he was looking for. He put his finger on it. 'There. Myron Cantrell. Good kid, far as I know.'

He passed it to me. I looked at the face smiling up from the page, suddenly feeling adrift – every lead branching off into more questions, more possible suspects. No reason to suspect this kid, but another name to chase down anyway – and no time to do it. I held up the book to give back to him; as I did a photograph slipped from between the pages, fell to the floor. I picked it up but Langley snatched it from me. He met my eyes and looked sheepish. He showed me the picture. 'That was her when she was sixteen. She was the sweetest girl in the world.'

I took the photograph from him, holding it carefully as if it was an artefact. It showed a class standing in front of the school building. Even at sixteen, Margaret Langley had taken on the features that she'd carry into womanhood – the long dark hair and playful smile. I was about to hand it back, but my eye caught another face in the crowd, standing in the row behind her. Richard Davis. Shorter than the man I knew, and looking less put-upon, but definitely him. I held the picture up and pointed to him. 'You know this kid at all?'

Langley brought it closer to examine, the pushed my hand away. 'Him? What you want to know about him for?'

'He never told me he knew her.' I said what I was thinking before I could catch myself.

'What?'

'He . . .' I took a breath to organise my thoughts. 'He's a fellow I met, is all. He never mentioned he was in the same class as your daughter.'

Langley motioned to have the picture back, so I passed it to him. 'He wasn't for long. They ran him out of there – boy was a born troublemaker.'

'In what way?'

He looked at the photograph one more time and put it back in the book. 'Any way you care to mention. Fighting.

Sassing the faculty. Starting fires . . .' He saw the surprise on my face. 'You heard me, a regular firebug. Set his home room desk ablaze one time, I heard.'

It sounded like hearsay from the way he said it, and I wondered how much the story had been exaggerated over time. Still, I couldn't draw a bead on Davis – the meek kid with the big mouth who talked dumb at times but was quick as a whip others; the skinny wretch who liked lemonade and fighting and starting fires. At times it seemed as though everyone in Texarkana was two people in one, same as the town.

Langley put the yearbook down on the coffee table. 'Anyway, you ain't come here to talk about that, did you?'

I shook my head, still thinking it over. 'Margaret's boyfriend – Cantrell? Was he still in touch with her?'

'No. Far as I know, they lost touch when he went to Plano.'

I glanced at the list of questions I'd written down before I came. 'Mr Langley, is the name Randall Schulz familiar to you at all? Sometimes goes by Johnson?'

His face was blank. 'Don't know the man.'

'Margaret never mentioned the name?'

'Not to my recollection. Who is he?'

I played it down. 'A possible witness is all. What about Peter Hamilton – what can you tell me about him? I read that he and Margaret were childhood friends, not a couple. There a chance they were courting in secret?'

He was shaking his head before I even finished the question. 'No. Peter was like kin to her.'

'You said yourself she didn't tell you everything . . .'

He leaned forward in his chair. 'I got eyes. I didn't need her to tell me that.'

I nodded, conceding it because it led into my next question. 'So why do you think they went to Spring Lake Park together that night?'

His face twitched again and there was a new alertness about him. 'Well that's the question, ain't it?'

'You have a theory.'

He nodded. 'I do.' He stood up and paced back and forth. 'She told me she was going to dinner with Peter that night. I trusted Margaret because she earned it. Only reason she'd lie to me is so I wouldn't worry. Which means she was doing something dumb that I wouldn't have let her.' He kicked the wall, his frustration pouring out. 'Like meeting someone in Spring Lake Park at night when all this trouble's going on.'

I saw where his train of thought ran. 'So she took Hamilton . . . as a chaperone?'

He pointed at me. 'Right. Hold her hand. That's what I reckon at least.'

'Because . . .' The pieces fell into place even as I spoke. 'Because she was nervous about who she was meeting there.'

He nodded. His voice came out hollow now, despondent. 'You figure out who she went to meet, you got the sum'bitch that killed her.'

'You've got no ideas?'

His eyes were focused on a faraway point now. He shook his head.

I stood up and stepped closer to him. 'She might have told someone. A diary? Her friends?'

'I thought of all that. She never kept a diary and her friends ain't none the wiser.'

'What about Hamilton's family?'

He shook his head again. 'This is why I got you here, Yates. I told the police all this and they said they was looking into it but they ain't come up with a single damn thing. You a reporter, maybe you can figure it out. Find the man who done this.'

'Go back to Red River. When I first mentioned it, you thought of something.'

He looked up at me again. 'That was all of it – Red River. Never thought about it but could be she was courting someone from there. It's somewhere to start.'

I picked up my papers. 'I'll call again if I think of any more questions.'

He shut his eyes and nodded that was fine. He seemed exhausted, the strain of talking about it writ large on his face. But his theory had set wheels spinning in my head; I thanked him again and hurried back to the car.

CHAPTER THIRTY-THREE

I drove back out of town as fast as I could. If Tim Langley was right, Margaret had arranged to meet her killer – so it had to be someone she knew. Someone she was nervous enough about to take a chaperone with her – but not so much that she didn't go. It narrowed the field some, but still left me the problem of where to start. I needed to check where her old beau, Myron Cantrell, was at these days.

Just outside the limits, I stopped at a gas station and called Lizzie from the telephone booth. She sounded groggy, like I'd woken her up, but insisted I hadn't.

'Have you spoken to the police?' I asked.

'Not really. They want me to identify her officially. I can't bring myself to.'

'Is there someone can sit with you? You shouldn't be alone.'

A silence. Then: 'Randy's coming over.'

'What?' Nasty pictures appeared in my mind: Lizzie beaten and mutilated, left on that sofa in her living room, blood staining everything. 'Darn it, anyone but him.'

'I've got no-one else, Charlie. You ran off like a thief.'

I dipped my head. 'I had to.' I scanned the highway in both directions, watching for police, suddenly feeling exposed. 'Are the cops still outside your place?'

'I don't think so.' She sounded dazed, halfway through a bad dream. 'Where are you?'

'Right now I'm nowhere. Look, I don't think you should see him. Schulz. At least until I can figure this out.'

'Why not? What's the worst that can happen, Charlie? I've lost everyone.' She took a breath, almost sounded like she was going to laugh. 'Besides, you wanted me to talk to him, so I thought I'd do it today.'

I couldn't think of anything to say, no words that could make her feel any better. I wanted to go to her, hold her – anything to ease her pain and make sure she was safe. I leaned against the side of the booth and fed another nickel into the slot. 'Listen, someone's going to telephone you tomorrow, looking for me. When they do, I need you to call me at my motel and leave a message. The message needs to be for Mr Tennison – got that?'

'You're making me your secretary? After what's just—'

'That's not how it is. But this is the only way. It's important; I wouldn't ask otherwise.'

She went quiet and I could tell she was reluctant. Eventually she said, 'Why the alias? What are you mixed up with?'

'Nothing. I can't let the cops find me is all.'

'Are you going to tell me what this is about?'

'It's to do with Red River. You don't want to know any more than that.'

'False names and strangers calling me. Who's putting me in danger now, Charlie?'

'Please. You're the only person I can trust.'

There was a rustling sound like she was running her hand through her hair. She sighed and said, 'What's the number for your motel?'

I gave it to her, thanking her as I did. 'I'm trying to stop this, Lizzie. I'm getting closer.'

There was a pause, but then she said, 'I believe you.'

'Look, about Schulz . . .'

'I know what you want me to ask him—'

'It's not that. I just wanted to say, be careful. If you have to meet him, do it somewhere public. Don't be alone with him.'

'I haven't told him about Alice yet. He called to apologise for what happened between us. He said he'll bring me flowers to make good.'

'That doesn't mean—'

'I know.' There was a hard edge to her voice, a hint at the fire in her character that had drawn me to her from the day we met. Vulnerable as she was, she was a fighter, and it was a measure of reassurance.

The longleaf pines along the opposite side of the road moved in the breeze, the smell of engine oil coming from the ramshackle workshop behind me. 'I'm sorry it has to be this way, but I swear I'll get this man for you. For you and for Alice.'

CHAPTER THIRTY-FOUR

Saturday. Out of time.

West 6th Street ran for more than a dozen blocks on the Texas side, bisected by a branch of the railroad line. I weaved along side streets to the end furthest from the centre of town – and the most police – and started looking for Anna Mendoza there.

The houses were timber frame buildings, set way back from the sidewalk on both sides of the street and separated by un-fenced yards of scrub grass – not a rich neighbourhood, but not poor either. I walked down the south side checking mailboxes, my hat pulled low over my face. I was jumpy, sure people were watching me from behind curtains – a stranger on the street might be reason enough to call the law.

On the third block, I lucked out, found a mailbox labelled Mendoza. I knocked on the front door. A dog barked inside. A light-skinned Mexican with a patchy moustache opened up, did a double take when he saw my face, and then looked me up and down. 'Yes?'

I gauged his age, pegged him as too young to be the dad, must be her brother. 'Is Anna at home, son?'

He shifted his stance, looking at my cuts, moving to fill the doorway. 'No.'

From inside: 'Miguel, who is it?' A girl came up behind him. Her hands flew to her mouth when she saw the state of me.

'No-one. Go back inside.'

I looked over the man's shoulder. 'Anna?'

The man moved so he was in my line of sight again. 'You with the police?'

'No.'

'Then get lost.' The man tried to shut the door. I jammed it with my foot and he shouted in my face. 'What are you doing?'

I stepped to one side so I could see the girl again. 'Anna, my name's Yates, I want to ask you about Patty Summerbell.'

The girl locked eyes with me, a look of anguish at hearing the name.

The man tried to push me backwards, so I let him, holding my hands up to show I wasn't resisting. He called back over his shoulder. 'Go into the kitchen.'

I stepped off the porch and backed off, still holding my hands up. 'I just want to ask some questions. I think Anna can help me find the man who killed Patty.' I was looking at the brother but speaking to her.

He turned around and went back inside, tugging the girl's sleeve to bring her with him. She hesitated, then said something quietly in Spanish to him, sounded like she was pleading. Whatever she said made him relent; he held her stare, looked at me one more time then disappeared inside. She came out and stood on the porch. 'My brother thinks he has to protect me. Everything that's going on.'

'He's doing the right thing.' I kept my distance, not wanting to spook her. I held up my press card. 'These are my credentials. Is there somewhere we can talk? Your brother can come too.'

She stared at me, chewing the inside of her cheek. Then she pointed to her right. 'There's a church down the block. I'll meet you in there in ten minutes.'

*

The church was called St Edward's and it was more like twenty-five minutes by the time she arrived. I was sitting at the end of a pew near the back, looking up at the soaring roof above. The church was empty apart from us. A kaleidoscope of colours patterned the floor to my left, the watery sunlight turned red, blue and yellow by the stained-glass windows.

Anna had changed into her church best – a long green dress with a matching pillbox hat. She genuflected and crossed herself, then slipped into the pew behind mine. 'My brother knows where I am.' She said it as a warning.

'Good.'

'And Father Murphy knows we're here. So—'

'Anna, I'm not here to cause you trouble. I want to help.'

She relaxed a little at that. 'What happened to your face?'

'I had an accident.'

'Looks like more than an accident.'

'It's nothing. I want to ask you some questions about Patty. About the night she died.'

'I already spoke to the police three times.'

'Then it won't hurt to tell me.'

She touched the corner of her mouth. 'How did you find me?'

I rested my elbow on the back of the pew, turning to face her. 'You were with Patty the night it happened. At the dancehall.'

'Who told you that?'

'It's not important. But you were, right?'

She looked around, unsure, as if she was about to get herself in trouble. Then she nodded slowly.

273

'That's ok. I want to know about who else was there that night.'

She was perched on the edge of the pew, still eyeing my face as if deciding whether the cuts and bruises had a bearing on whether she should trust me or not. 'Me, Marcy, Patty . . .' Her bottom lip trembled and she looked away, a struggle just saying the name. 'Darla. Sarah was there for a time but she left because her date was being a . . .' She looked at the altar and crossed herself. 'A fool.'

'What about boys? Patty was with Edward Logan all night?'

She shook her head. 'No. Ted came later on. He had to work, I think.'

'What time was that?'

'I can't remember, sorry.'

'Who was she with before Logan came? Did she dance with anyone?'

Her eyes darted around the church. 'Not really. She was just talking to us, you know? Waiting for Ted.'

I tapped the back of the pew with my finger, letting her dwell on her own words for a minute. 'One of your friends told me she went outside to speak to another man. A soldier.'

She flushed and looked down at the floor.

'Anna, it's alright to tell me about it. I just want to know what happened.'

She fiddled with the button on her dress. 'Marcy told you that?'

I nodded, left Davis out of the story for ease. 'Was Patty stepping out with someone else besides Edward Logan?' Her hands were in her lap and she couldn't keep them still, tugging and kneading them. 'It doesn't matter now if she was, but it's important to tell the truth.'

She covered her face with her hands, retreating into herself. 'You can't write about this. Ted's family . . . it's not fair on them.'

I touched her shoulder. 'This isn't for the newspaper. This is about finding out what happened. I promise.'

She took her hands away and sat on them. 'Patty always had a liking for older men.' She closed her eyes and carried on. 'She was crazy about Ted too, but about a month before . . . before it happened, she met this other soldier. She didn't even tell me about it at first, or Darla, and she tells us everything.'

I nodded once. 'Keep going.'

'She didn't talk too much about him at the start; I think she felt guilty because of Ted and all, so she kept it quiet. But after a while it was as if they were courting. She spent a lot of time with him.'

'What was his name?'

'She never told me. She always called him RS. First time she said it, I thought she said Boris – like a Russian or something.' She smiled. 'That was our nickname for him after that, Boris.'

'You ever meet him?'

She hesitated. 'Yes. Only one time, in passing.'

'Can you describe him to me?'

'He was a big man. Really big. That was one of the things she liked about him. And she thought he was handsome.'

I turned it over in my mind, still more questions than answers. 'So what was the idea agreeing to see him that night at the dance? Sounds like a big risk to take with Logan there too.'

Anna put her hands on her knees. 'Patty didn't know he was coming. He just showed up.'

'By chance?'

She shook her head – short, stilted movements. 'Patty broke it off with him that day. Earlier on. She told me she thought he was . . .' She fell silent and looked down again.

'Was what?'

She covered her mouth, half her face hidden. The words came out muffled. 'She found out that she wasn't the only one he was with, and she couldn't stand it. So she told him to go swing.' She crossed herself again.

Randy the Womaniser, given the flick by a kid. Not the way the script was supposed to go. The timing set off alarm bells in my mind; more than just an argument – Randy fired up at getting ditched by a broad. 'Did Patty tell you the name of the other woman?'

'No. I don't think she knew. She just knew there was someone.'

I scratched my neck. 'Kinda hypocritical for Patty to be sore at RS for two-timing her when she was doing the same to Logan, wouldn't you say?'

She straightened her skirt. 'I suppose so.' She looked guilty now. 'We told her what she was doing was wrong, but she always said it wasn't that way—'

I raised my hand. 'It's alright. You did what you could. Don't get the notion this is your fault. Or Patty's.' I took a deep breath and tried to keep it all straight in my head, seeing Randall Schulz's fingerprints all over the case, wondering if the other woman was Lizzie, or someone else again. Margaret Langley? Alice, even? 'Why did he come to the dancehall that night, if she'd told him they were through?'

She looked at me like I was naive. 'To talk her round, of course. But Patty told him to get lost.'

'This was outside?'

'Yeah. He showed up in the foyer at first, but she got him to go outside because she didn't want anyone to see.'

'And they argued? Patty and RS?'

'I think so. She was shook up after – and that's not like Patty, she was . . . I mean, nothing ever troubled her.'

'Do you know what happened?'

She nodded. 'He called her a curse word. So she slapped him.'

'Did you see him again after that?'

Another shake of the head. 'Ted arrived a little while after. That was the end of it.'

I checked my watch, wondered again when Callaway's secretary would call Lizzie. If she'd called already. 'Did Patty and Logan leave together that night?'

She thought about it a moment, and nodded.

'Did anyone go with them?'

She giggled, embarrassed. 'No, of course not.'

'So why did they drive all the way out of town to Club Dallas?'

'Ted's buddies go there sometimes, and Patty liked it because she knew they'd serve her drinks.'

A motive and an opportunity. The means still a question mark. It fit and it didn't. I checked my watch again and decided time was up. 'Is there anything else you can tell me? Was Patty scared of RS?'

She tugged at her lip. 'I don't think so. I think she figured she had him wrapped around her little finger.'

I picked my hat up off the pew and went to stand up. 'Thank you.'

She put her hand on my forearm to stop me. 'There was one thing. I told the police this, but I don't know if it meant anything.'

'What?'

'Patty thought she was being followed. She said she kept seeing the same car tailing her home.'

I dropped my hat. 'When was this?'

'Couple weeks ago. And before.'

'Where?'

'When she was coming back from work.'

'I thought Patty was at school?'

'She was, but she had a Saturday job, in the cafeteria.'

A little shiver ran up my spine, knowing what was coming. Say it: 'Where?'

'At Red River Arsenal.'

Anna sensed something had changed. Her eyes scoured mine, worried. 'Did I say something wrong?'

'This is important, Anna. Tell me exactly what she said about being followed.'

She spoke quickly, words tumbling out on top of each other. 'Just what I told you. She wasn't certain at first but then she kept seeing it, the same car.'

'What kind of car?'

'I don't know.'

'Who was driving?'

'I don't . . .' She creased her face, frustrated. 'She never said. I don't think she ever saw the driver.'

I gripped the back of the pew. 'Give me something here, Anna.'

'You're scaring me—'

'Dang it . . .' I bit my tongue and took a deep breath, raised my hand as an apology. 'I'm sorry. I need you to be sure. Please – this is important.'

She protested. 'I told the police about this, Mr Yates. They said they'd take care of it.'

I got up out of my seat. The police knew. So either they ignored the possible Red River link, or were too incompetent to put it all together. 'You did good, Anna. I just need you to think real hard: did Patty say anything else about it?'

'I can ask Darla. She might know more.'

'Okay good, please do. Could you speak to her today?'

'I'll try.'

'Thank you. I'll call you later to check in.' I put my hat on.

'Mr Yates?' I stopped, standing in the centre aisle of the church. 'You think this is the man that killed her, don't you?' she said. The look in her eyes was a mix of fear and hope, like she was desperate for me to put her out of her misery.

'Could be.'

CHAPTER THIRTY-FIVE

The call came at six that evening. The receptionist from check-in knocked and said he had a lady on the line for me. I barged past him and down the stairs to the office. The receiver was on the counter, the line connected.

'Hello?'

'Charlie, it's me.' Lizzie's voice.

'They called?'

'Yes, they called. A woman – a Mrs Cornette. She asked you to telephone her at the house. Who is she?' Lizzie's tone was angry, almost accusing.

'I promise I'll explain when this is done.' I looked at the clock on the wall behind the desk, time ticking down, only a few hours until another killing. 'Lizzie, I'm sorry, I've got to go—'

'Charlie, wait. I'm afraid; I don't want to be alone in this house. Not tonight.'

Frustration boiled inside me. I wanted to tell her to come to me, keep her safe myself, but I couldn't risk the cops tailing her. 'Check yourself into a motel. Leave me a message here to tell me where you are. I'll pay.'

'I have my own money, that's not what I'm asking—'

'I know that. I just want you to be someplace safe. Until I can come get you.'

She was quiet for a beat, the way a person is when they know what they're about to say will draw a reaction. 'I asked Randall about the night Patty Summerbell was killed, like you wanted. He flew off the handle at me.'

I held the phone tighter. 'What did he say?'

'He wouldn't talk about it. He yelled at me, said I was trying to make trouble for him. He said you'd poisoned my mind.'

The blood in my face ran hot. 'If he laid a finger on you—'

'He didn't. He didn't, I swear it. He stormed out.'

I felt a rush of emotions – anger and relief at the same time. Anger that he'd lose his temper at Lizzie again, relief that he wasn't around her. I felt a pull in my gut, an urge to go to her, and I hated Bailey even more for the bind he had me in. I gripped the counter, the wood's grain rough to the touch. 'Has he bothered you since?'

'No, but—'

'Stay away from him, whatever happens. He's dangerous, Lizzie.' I looked down, realised my hand was shaking from being clenched so tight.

'Charlie, listen to me. When he left here, he said he was going to find you. I don't know what he's capable of any more.'

I felt the hairs on my neck stand – not fear, anticipation. The idea that we could settle this once and for all. 'Good. It'll save me having to look for him. Don't worry about me.' I snatched another look at the clock. 'Will you do like I said and go to a motel someplace? Please?'

She let out a long breath down the line, exasperated. 'I don't know. I don't want to be alone, but I don't like the idea of being chased from my own house.'

'It's just for now. I'll make sure this is over soon.' I felt bad saying the words, not sure if it was an empty promise – but determined to see it through.

'Please be careful, Charlie. I couldn't stand it if something happened to you too.'

I felt a surge of hope – a light at the end of the tunnel that maybe I'd given up on too quickly. 'I will.'

*

Mrs Cornette instructed me to collect the list from Callaway's house. It meant driving through the south edge of town, but I had no time, and no choice – those were the terms.

Heading into Texarkana, I passed over the same railroad crossing where Alice's body was found. On the other side of the tracks I saw black-and-whites right away, two posted outside Union Station. Every cop from miles around would be on the streets tonight, trying to stop the killer. My stomach flipped; jittery lawmen with itchy trigger fingers was a bad situation for me, especially as the streets were empty otherwise. The only good thing was they wouldn't be looking for me so hard.

I made it onto the highway heading out of town and picked up speed. Two yellow dots appeared in the rearview, snagged my attention – maybe a hundred yards behind me. I tried to make out what kind of car it was, but all I could see was a silhouette. No sirens that I could tell. It looked like there was just one man in the front seat. I kept going, the sense of urgency willing me on, even as a creeping dread pooled in my stomach.

It was pitch dark on Blackman Ferry Road, only the tarmac under my beams visible in front of me. Another look in the rearview: the headlamps were still behind me. Definitely the same car. They'd been there a couple minutes now. I pushed the accelerator harder. The speedometer needle shook just under seventy, like it was afraid to go further around the dial. The headlamps behind stayed with me, maintaining the distance between us. My knuckles were white gripping the wheel. I tried to think, remember where the road went and if I could get back to the highway somehow, but my mind was overloaded, my thoughts like radio static. I checked the road, checked the mirror, nearly swerved when I saw the headlamps were right behind me, riding my bumper; dazzling, no need to look at the rearview to see them now. A line of cold sweat ran down my face. I thought about trying to spin around, make it back to town, dismissed it; no point – no safety there anyway.

Then the tailing car rammed me. I slammed the brakes with both feet. The tires screeched and my hands came off the wheel. My car spun ninety degrees and lifted on one side. I was thrown against the door. I thought I was going to flip, and time froze.

Then the car fell, slamming back down to the road like a mortar shell. I opened my eyes, dizzy. My car had come to a stop sideways on, across the blacktop. Smoke shrouded it, and the smell of burnt rubber filled my nostrils. I looked out but couldn't see anything.

I tried the ignition. The engine shuddered but didn't catch; there was smoke coming from under the hood. Suddenly the car was lit up as if it was caught in a spotter beam. I shielded my eyes and turned towards the source.

The chase car was idling twenty yards away, pointed right at me, brights on full. Its driver's door was open.

I tried the ignition again – nothing. A silhouette appeared in the light. A figure, five yards away, moving towards me. I twisted the ignition key one more time, a guttural shout filling the car as I cried out. I gave up and reached for the door handle just as the figure got close enough to fill my window and block out the light.

The window exploded. Glass hit me like a shower of sparks. I put my guard up but something hit me hard. A rag covered my face.

CHAPTER THIRTY-SIX

Music was playing in my head. A nursery rhyme. Children singing. I had the sensation of having been asleep for days.

I snapped to and the music stopped. There was deafening silence and blackness – crushing me, suffocating me. Consciousness torqued up another notch, and the pain registered. It raced up my spine and jagged outwards, along my shoulders and neck. My head pounded with a headache worse than any hangover; my face felt like it was on fire, and then I remembered the window shattering all over it.

I couldn't move. I was seated, my hands behind my back and tied to the chair. My left eye was swollen over, and it was too dark to see anything with the other. There was a smell like gasoline, and for a moment I thought I was back in my car. It was cold, but the air was still against my face – indoors.

'Hello?' My voice was small and rough, like my throat was full of gravel. I took a couple of breaths, mustered some will. 'Is someone there?' The shout was discordant in the silence, like a gunshot in a church. The words bounced around the walls but didn't echo, sounded like a normal size room in a house.

I pulled at my restraints, wrists burning against the rope. I tried to stand but my ankles were tied as well, knotted against the chair legs. Anger overtook pain, and I struggled violently, trying to move my limbs. My shoulders ached, but I got some movement in my right foot. A frustrated growl escaped from my throat.

The chair was rickety but the ropes held. My chin dropped to my chest and I was out of breath, panting; the pain came back like the tide coming in, smashing into me. Drool ran from my mouth, and the silence settled again.

Not quite silence.

I was motionless. The wind had picked up outside and there was a creaking noise, wooden beams bending under the strain. Another noise too. Closer. I listened hard.

Breathing. Someone in the room.

Fear gripped me. The breathing was shallow and muffled and it was coming from behind me. 'Who's there?'

It stopped. There was a scuffing noise, a boot scraping a floorboard.

'Show yourself, you goddamn coward.' My mouth was bone dry; my lips stuck to my teeth. 'People will be looking for me.' I pulled against the ropes, got more movement in my right foot, but my breath ran short again. 'Son of a bitch.'

'You through whining?'

I sat dead still. It was a man's voice, deep and hard. 'What do you want?'

The room was silent again and I wasn't sure if he was still there. My heart was beating hard enough that I could hear it.

Then he spoke again: 'Ain't said I want anything, have I?'

I turned my head, looking over one shoulder then the other, trying to catch a glimpse but getting nothing. 'Then what am I here for?'

The man sniffed. 'Because we got business to take care of, partner.'

'Kill me or let me go. I don't care which.'

Three footsteps. Moving behind me. 'Ain't no choice to

make there,' he told me. 'You already a dead man. But you gonna tell me just what it is you know before you check out.' The voice was closer now. I thought I could smell rotting meat on his breath. 'Who's feeding you your information?' he said.

I tried to laugh, making any noise I could to cover the sound of another kick with my right foot. It sounded more like choking. The rope gave a little more. My head drooped, a sense of helplessness smothering me. Suddenly it felt like I was back on that high ledge, my fingertips slipping, my grip all but gone. A voice in my head saying, *let go, it's harder holding on.*

I thought about everything that had happened to me in the three years since I crashed the Jeep. Everything I'd lost, every false step, every humiliation – all of it brought on myself in one way or another. Tied to that chair, I wondered how things would have turned out if I'd just gone to the war. Maybe died a hero's death like my father. A plaque on a wall bearing my name somewhere, etched into history in some small way. *Of your charity . . .*

Couldn't have been worse than this, butchered in an abandoned farmhouse in the middle of nowhere, my body dumped in a ditch or an unmarked grave. No-one ever knowing. No glory. I thought about Lizzie, her words on the telephone, the glimmer of hope for the future that I'd felt swell in my chest. Everything that might have been. The regret made me angry, gave me a last surge. 'A girl told me not long ago that dying isn't the worst thing can happen to a man. I thought she was crazy, but she was right.' I lifted my head up. 'So get to it, because I won't tell you a damn thing.'

The footsteps moved to a spot in front of me, across the room. The man pulled a drape aside, let the weak moonlight in. He was standing side on to me, and he was holding a small handgun. He had a white hood on, two holes to see through.

The killer.

My guts dipped. I clawed at the chair, my fingernails catching and tearing. He grunted and pulled the drape closed. The room went black again and there were more footsteps, circling around behind me now. Then there was a hand at my belt, and he stuffed the gun down my pants.

He pulled the trigger.

The flash burned white on the back of my eyes and the noise was like a thunderclap next to my head. My groin burned. I thought he'd shot me. I shook violently, yelling my lungs out.

Time stretched, seconds passing like hours. When my ears stopped ringing, the first thing that registered was him laughing, coupled with hacking coughs. There was no pain in my groin, no blood gushing from me. I realised it was a warning shot, the bastard missing me on purpose, firing through the crotch of my pants.

He clamped his hand on my shoulder, and his mouth was next to my ear. 'You scared now, Charlie?' His breath was on my neck. 'Because you sure as hell look it.' I jerked as the gun barrel touched my skull, hot metal burning my scalp, and then the voice was in my other ear. 'So tell me what you know, and who you've run your mouth to, or next time I won't miss.'

It was too soon, but I had to do it anyway. No second chances.

I snapped my head back. I heard a crack, felt a stabbing in my skull and knew I'd connected with his teeth. All the scars and bruises on my face were burning and pounding, adrenaline keeping me moving. I planted my right foot, just enough slack in the rope now, and pushed off it with all my strength, smashing backward into the man's body. We collided with a wall. Metal clattered on wood – the gun hitting the floor.

I heard him slump down. I mustered everything I had left. The chair still tied to me, I rocked forward and pushed off my right leg again, launching myself up and back.

I crashed down on top of him. The chair broke apart. I was still tender from the beating at the Mason, and the pain shooting through me was almost enough to keep me on the floor. Then I felt him buck underneath me; the jolt sent me rolling away, holding my aching ribs. Lizzie flashing through my mind again, finding an untapped reserve, not ready to give up on the hope she represented. I came to a stop and scrambled to my feet. I heard him moving. He spluttered, then smacked the floor. 'Where you at?'

I backed away from the sound of his voice, coming up against a clapboard wall.

'I hear you, boy.'

I shuffled sideways in the dark, groping for a door. The man clicked a flashlight on and the beam moved over the bare floorboards. I moved faster along the wall. My hands came to a gap behind me – a doorway. The flashlight beam found the gun and the man grabbed it. Then the light moved again, landed on me this time. He aimed; I rolled through the doorway and out of the room. I heard a crack, and something fizzed past me, a dull thud when the bullet hit the wall.

I was in a hallway, a door at the end of it. I ran to it and turned the handle. It was unlocked; my bladder almost blew with relief. The flashlight beam strafed the hall just as I pushed through the door and tumbled out into the night.

289

I scrambled away from the entrance. I was outside, darkness all around me. The wind blew hard against my face, and I could smell pig muck. I stumbled off a low porch and took off across the ground as fast as I could. There was a barn next to the house, and I ran to it, using it as cover. Coming around the far side, I saw a dark-coloured Pontiac parked next to the house, back where I'd just come from. I scanned the ground; nothing moved, and there were no sounds except the wind and my breathing.

There were no lights in any direction. I flattened myself against the barn and listened hard. It felt like my heart was coming out of my chest. I edged closer to where the car was parked, expecting the killer to appear around the barn at any second. I reached the corner closest to the car, thirty feet of open ground separating it from me. I looked around one more time, then set off in a running crouch.

I heard a shout behind me, muffled by the wind. I made it to the car and flung the passenger door open, diving across the front seat as a shot rang out – a metallic ding as the bullet punched through the bodywork someplace. My hunch paid off: the keys were in the ignition. I righted myself behind the wheel and gunned it down the dirt track, ducking low as I went, never slowing down as the car bucked and jumped, sure an axle would snap.

The track led to a road. At the junction I snatched a look, couldn't see the killer anywhere. I didn't stop, took off down the blacktop.

CHAPTER THIRTY-SEVEN

I sped down the road not knowing where I was or where I was going. I checked the rearview every few seconds, but there was nothing behind me. I didn't pass any houses or lights, just rows of dark trees stretching into the black sky.

It took ten minutes for my heart to slow down. After another five, I decided I'd put enough distance between me and the killer to risk stopping, and pulled over onto the verge. When I set the parking brake, it all caught up with me. I opened the door and vomited into a grassy ditch.

I searched the inside of the Pontiac for some kind of identification, but it was bare. The glove compartment was empty and there was nothing on or under the seats. I lifted myself out and opened the trunk, even that simple motion a hardship for my stricken body, but the only item inside was a dented crowbar. I shut the lid and looked over the rest of the chassis, keeping one eye on the road. The licence plate had been smeared with mud, making sure it couldn't be read by other drivers. It was an old trick used by thieves moving hot cars across state lines; I wiped some away, revealing a Louisiana plate underneath. Figure it was recently stolen.

I got back behind the wheel and tried to remember what I could about the killer, surprised to find how little I'd retained. I sorted through it in my head – his height, his accent, the way he smelled – but it was all hazy. I thought back to Alice

Anderson, her statements vague and contradictory, and suddenly felt a surge of empathy – understanding now what the terror must have done to her mind.

*

I drove blindly for another ten minutes until I came to a highway. A sign marked it as the 71 so I followed it west, back towards town. A mile along, I recognised the turnoff for Blackman Ferry Road; without thinking, I swerved onto it and retraced my route from earlier. Just being on the same stretch of road made my heartbeat rocket. I had no idea of the time, only the inky blackness of the night telling me it wasn't near dawn yet.

I drove another minute or two, my nerves stretched like piano wire, at first not finding any sign of Lizzie's Chevy. Then the headlights picked up tyre tracks – burnt rubber scarring the road. I pulled over and lumbered out, my beams lighting up the marks on the tarmac. They stretched for a hundred yards or more, had to be mine. There was no sign of the car.

I expected to see it burnt-out or pushed to the side of the road, but there was nothing. For a second I was more worried about what Lizzie would say when she found out her car was gone. Then I got to thinking about what it meant. I climbed back into the killer's Pontiac, more confused than ever. Could be he'd moved my car at some point between when he ran me off the road and now.

Or could be he had help.

*

There was a siren wailing in the distance as I followed a country road around the back of Union Station, towards Sulphur River Inn. The sound echoed like a cat wailing in an empty alley, and in my mind I saw the town locked down, the streets deserted apart from the cops, trying to stop the inevitable.

I made it back to the motel, stashed the car behind the office and went to my room. I flicked the light on and collapsed onto the bed, shaking and wracked with pain, the effects of adrenaline all but gone. The clock showed one in the morning. I lay staring at the ceiling, wondering if this is what all those GIs felt like, men who'd seen friends take bullets and wondered why they themselves managed to survive. The thought didn't sit right, no heroism in what I'd done. A chance to stop him, to avenge Alice and all the others; maybe to save lives. A chance I'd let slip by me.

I felt hollow inside, the reality of another defeat settling in my head; the killer out there now, about to make the next move in his own personal war, fuelled by some hate that only he understood. I wanted to call Lizzie, but I couldn't get off the bed – the weight of failure pinning me down. At some point I drifted, never quite asleep, but enough to let my mind run riot. I saw horrors: Lizzie's throat a bloody mush, broken glass tumbling out of it. The image warped and became Randall Schulz standing over her, stabbing at her face with a broken bottle, his own hands dissolving in a bloody mess on the jagged glass.

I stirred slowly, disoriented, unsure at first where I was. It was three in the morning. Outside there was another lonely siren in the distance. I got up and poured water from the bathroom faucet into a dirty glass, walked to the window to drink it. My face seared, the cuts on it opening again as I drank. It was still dark outside, the night so complete that I couldn't even see the river over the road.

The siren outside grew louder, and was joined by another. Then another, and suddenly it was a cacophony, a rush of police cars, somewhere close by. I pressed up to the glass to see, but they were passing the other side, behind the motel. I barrelled outside and down the stairs, circled around to the back of the property. There were dark pine woods beyond the gravel parking lot, and somewhere beyond that, another road. I could just make out a faint red glow flashing through the gaps in the trees as the police raced south, away from town.

I ran around to the front again and snatched up the payphone. I dialled the *Chronicle*, but the line just rang out, noone picking up. Another nickel, another try – but now the line was busy. Whatever was happening, word had reached them. I looked up at the sky, no light visible, the moon and stars now hidden by a blanket of black clouds. The cops would all be going to the scene, so there was a chance I could get into town without being spotted. Going to the *Chronicle* was still a risk – but one worth taking.

CHAPTER THIRTY-EIGHT

The newsroom was less than half full when I got there. I expected to find bedlam, but it was verging on silent. People looked at me as I walked in, quickly recoiling when they saw the state of my face, but they just stared, no-one acknowledging me. It was like I'd disturbed a funeral.

A hack in the corner was talking into a telephone, his voice the only sound, not much above a murmur. Two women huddled together along the wall next to me, both sobbing. I looked around, noticed the telephones had been taken off their receivers – explained the busy signals when I tried to call. Robinson was nowhere to be seen. McGaffney's door was shut; I went towards it, not sure what was going on, my stomach doing flips. The sub-editor, Hansen, was at the flatplanning table; as I got close, he darted over and pulled me back violently.

'Where the hell you think you're going?'

I backed away, shocked by the man's aggression. 'I need to talk to McGaffney.'

Hansen stared at me, his face lined and drawn like he hadn't slept in a week. Then he let me go and seemed to fall apart, slumping against the wall. 'He's dead.'

I bundled him into McGaffney's office and sat him down. He was trembling, his head in his hands. I found a bottle of bourbon in McGaffney's bottom drawer, poured a measure and handed it to him. 'Tell me.'

He guzzled half the glass. 'He's dead. Sum'bitch killed Gaffy.'

I grabbed a wooden chair and sat down facing him, gripped his shoulders. 'What happened?'

'Bobby Landell's men called it in an hour ago. We was just finishing up the last plates and . . .' He grabbed the glass and drained the rest.

'Who?'

He looked up and met my eyes. 'The killer.' He shouted it, bourbon fumes in my face. 'Same bastard as all the rest of them.' He threw the glass across the office and it smashed against the wall.

I stood and gripped my hands together, feeling like a bomb about to go off. 'It doesn't make sense. He kills couples. Why change now?'

The question was rhetorical, but Hansen snapped his head around and answered. 'Killed Gaffy's wife too. Killed them in they own damn house—'

'What? Goddammit, no.'

Why McGaffney and me? Two attacks that didn't fit the pattern. I walked across the room and planted my hands on the wall, trying to make it add up. 'It still doesn't fit.'

He stood and pointed at me. 'That's all you got to say? You think you know better than the Sheriff, you go tell him.'

I kicked the shattered glass to the side, the shards rattling against the wainscoting. 'Wait, Bailey told you it was the same killer?'

He nodded once. 'Just before you got here.'

'But . . .' I stopped, the thoughts still coalescing. After weeks of denials that the killings were linked, why suddenly chalk this one up to the killer immediately? 'It's too quick.'

'The hell are you talking about? Gaffy and his wife's dead and you're talking in riddles.'

I waved my hands, signalling for him to ignore me. 'What about his children? McGaffney had daughters, right?'

He shook his head and I thought he meant they were dead too. 'They weren't at home. Gaffy sent them to stay with his sister in Frederick last week.'

I nodded, relief welling inside me even though I'd never met them. 'Where's Robinson at?'

He closed his eyes and slumped into the chair again. 'Jimmy drove out there soon as he heard. He finds the sum'bitch that done this, he'll kill him with his bare hands.'

'Where's McGaffney's house?'

'Line Ferry Road, outside of town.' The name sounded familiar. 'But you can't go there. Police don't want no horde of people showing up like what happened with Spring Lake Park.'

I didn't tell him that as long as the cops were there, it was the last place on earth I could go. Wouldn't have mattered anyway; Hansen had slipped off into his own world. He reached across the desk and picked up the bourbon. He tipped it back and drank off the rest of the bottle.

*

The rest of that day was pure frustration, pacing the room at Sulphur River and waiting for nightfall so I could take a run out to McGaffney's place.

I'd slept two hours when I got back from the *Chronicle*, waking around seven that morning. First thing I did was switch the radio on. The news of the murder was the only story they were covering. The basics came quickly: McGaffney and his wife had been found shot to death in their farmhouse in Miller County, Arkansas. A neighbour had raised the alarm at approximately two-forty that morning, when he saw flashes and heard loud bangs coming from McGaffney's property, a quarter mile to the west of his own. Miller County Sheriff's arrived twenty minutes later, Deputy Terry Hardin being first on scene and finding McGaffney dead in his lounge, shot in the head from behind. McGaffney's wife was on the porch out front, apparently killed while trying to flee, presumably roused from her sleep by the gunfire. A screen door in the kitchen had been torn away and was believed to be the killer's means of entry.

I thought about the sequence of events. I'd made it back to Sulphur River around one that morning, making it around midnight when I'd escaped the killer. That left him two-odd hours to pick, or move onto, his next target, and travel to McGaffney's house. It was possible, but didn't seem to fit the mind of the man as I imagined him. Too many moving parts. And especially as I'd taken his car. I wondered again if I was dealing with more than one party.

The newsreader on the wireless went on: Sheriff Landell of Miller County was leading the investigation, in conjunction with Sheriff Bailey of Bowie County; Bailey was given co-command when initial findings indicated the double murder was linked to the Bowie County killings of the previous three weekends. Texarkana City Police and Arkansas State Troopers had also been brought in to help. The radio newsman peddled a quote from Bailey: 'We are deeply saddened by the loss of a great public servant in Saul James McGaffney, along with his wife Barbara, a loss that the whole of Texarkana will mourn. Law officers of all stripes have been working around the clock to catch his killer, and we will not rest until we do so. We appeal to anyone with any genuine information to come forward immediately.'

When the radio chatter had turned to straight retread, I'd started making telephone calls. I tried Lizzie first, my fears for her safety allayed when she answered almost immediately.

'Charlie? I'm so relieved it's you. Have you heard?'

'I heard. I went to the *Chronicle* last night.'

'I'm so scared, it's like this whole town is damned. We've got to get out of here.'

'You make it to a motel like I told you?'

'No.' She hesitated. 'The police came by last night, after we talked. They said they were stationing a car outside, as a precaution. To watch out for me.'

Not even taking the trouble to hide it any more. At best a watch-dog waiting for me to break cover; at worst, shades of the cop hanging around Alice right before she disappeared. A snatch car. 'Are they still there?'

'Yes.'

I pinched the bridge of my nose. 'What about Schulz?'

'I've not heard a word. If I know him, he'll still be tearing the streets up looking for you. Unless – what happened last night, do you think . . .'

'No.' The word came out before I had a chance to consider. The certainty behind it was borne of a truth that was hard for me to admit: the hooded man in the farmhouse wasn't Randall Schulz. 'I don't know.' I'd already decided not to tell Lizzie about the attack on me – no sense worrying her even more.

'This is unbearable, Charlie. I can't believe what's happening here.'

I held a deep breath, the pressure too much to take. 'Lizzie, please, get out of town today. Now. Just go. Go to a motel anywhere else and call me. I'll find you in a couple days, as soon as this is done; we'll straighten everything out.'

'I can't just go, Charlie. There's Alice's funeral, and the house—'

'Please, Lizzie. No-one's safe now. No-one. You have to go. Make sure you slip away so the cops don't see.'

She said nothing, her sobs rippling down the line.

I raked my nails over my scalp. 'Pack a bag and go. I'm calling back in two hours, make sure you're set by then.'

I cut the line and dialled again. Two tries to Callaway's house went unanswered; I tried a half-dozen more times throughout the day, but no response. Between attempts, I called Sal in New York. It was eight-thirty in the morning on the east coast, an hour ahead, and Sal had already picked up the story on the wires. 'Jesus, Chuck, you nailed it. This thing is going national. You know *Life* magazine are flying a crew down your way this morning?'

'That mean Walters will give me some column inches now?'

Sal hesitated.

'What is it?' I said.

'Well . . . problem is *Life* ain't the only one sending a crew down.'

'What does that mean?' But I didn't wait for Sal to speak, the answer coming to me. 'Wait, Sal, no—'

'Charlie, I'm just the messenger—'

'Over my dead body.'

He sighed. 'It's done already. Walters sent Maloney and McGill to the airport first thing. It's their story now, you're off.'

I slammed my hand against the telephone, rattling it. 'It's my goddamn story, he can't just take me off.'

'He can and he has. The boys arrive at four o'clock your time. Walters wants you to pick them up from Dallas airport, brief them, then get yourself back here. By land.'

I rubbed my temple with my free hand. Then I had a realisation; Walters couldn't touch me down here. 'What if I say no?'

'No? What's no?'

'No. I can't stop them taking the story, but he can't make me leave. I'm staying here and I'm working it for myself.'

'Have you lost your head? Walters will fire you. Don't make it easy for him.'

Getting fired – with Jane already gone, it was the thing that worried me most when I left for Texarkana. It seemed insignificant now, didn't even rate on my list of fears. Fears like staying alive. 'This son of a bitch tried to kill me, Sal. No way I'm walking away from that.'

'What? Are you alright?'

'Yeah, I'm aces. I got away by the skin of my teeth. Tell Walters that.'

'You get a look at him? Was it the same man?'

'I don't know. He had the mask on, all the right traits.'

Sal sounded shocked. 'Look, I'll tell Walters alright, but you know he'll say it's all the more reason for you to get back here now.'

Tom Walters looking out for my wellbeing – priceless. 'I'll live,' I said. 'But it doesn't add up, Sal.'

'What?'

'Me, McGaffney, it doesn't fit the pattern of the other attacks.'

'So what? The guy wised up, decided to take a shot at you two. Ain't the first time a nut's gone after the gentlemen of the press. You got lucky, the old timer didn't.'

'There's more,' I went on. 'I had a real good suspect.' I told him about Randall Schulz, ran him through the evidence, the case I'd been piecing together against him. I left Lizzie's name out of it. 'Problem is, it wasn't him under the hood in that farmhouse. So then I got to thinking, what if there's more than one killer?'

Sal sniffed. 'I don't know what to tell you, Chuck, but it sounds kinda flimsy to me. I mean, you got a lot of circumstantial there, but not a lot of substance. It wouldn't stand up in an editorial meeting, let alone a court.'

I unbuttoned my collar, deflated. 'I know.'

He took a deep breath. 'So what am I supposed to tell Walters?'

I was picturing the farmhouse the night before, the killer's outline visible in the moonlight, willing it to be Schulz. The memory sent a shiver down my spine 'Tell him anything you like.'

Sal whistled, drawing it out, and then was silent a moment. Then he coughed, snapping himself out of his thoughts. 'Can you believe he shot the editor? Got to be your killer's a hack. You imagine if someone put a bullet in Walters? They'd have five hundred suspects right here in the building.' He started to laugh, but clammed up when he realised I wasn't joining him. He waited a beat and said, 'Just look out for yourself, Chuck, okay?'

CHAPTER THIRTY-NINE

I rode out to McGaffney's at eleven that night. I slowed as I drew near, scoping the place for cops or gawkers, ready to re-evaluate my plan, but there was no-one around.

The house was two hundred yards back from Line Ferry Road, its own dirt track leading up there. A glance at the roadmap before I set out told me why the name was familiar: it was an isolated back lane running off Blackman Ferry Road – Callaway's road. The proximity was another tentative link between the two men, right there with the address book I'd seen in Callaway's office.

I skirted around the edge of the dark house, echoes of the night before making my legs tremble; stumbling around another bleak farmhouse, unsure where I was and what I was doing there, the killer's presence so real I could almost smell him. I found the screen door the killer had used, the slashed bug netting flapping in the wind; I pulled on a pair of gloves I'd taken from the lost-and-found at Sulphur River and reached through the tear to let myself in. It felt like a slap in the face to McGaffney, coming into his house the same way as his killer, but there was nothing I could do about it.

With no moonlight, I could barely see across the room when I got inside. I clicked on a flashlight – more swag from Sulphur River – cupping the end with my hand to shade the beam. A spooked neighbour seeing it and calling the cops was the last thing I needed.

The kitchen was long and thin. There were plates and pans still on the drying rack next to the sink. Normal life, ripped away in an instant. I stepped towards the doorway at the far end. A snapping sound underfoot froze me on the spot, my breathing fast; I pointed the flashlight at the floor: broken glass, a trail leading to a smashed beaker in the corner of the room. More collateral damage.

I picked my way around the shards and stepped into the hallway. The front door was at the far end, and two rooms led off on the right. A staircase ran alongside me to the left, panelled with dark wood. I moved through the closest door, found myself in a dining room. There was a small table in the middle, four chairs tucked neatly underneath it – giving no clue to the way everything had went to hell the night before. I glanced around one more time and went out into the hall again. Even in the cool night, my shirt was stuck to my back with sweat.

Next door was the family room. As I stepped inside, I stopped and backed up. It was the colour that did it, vivid even in the dim glow from the flashlight. There was an armchair right in front of me, facing away from the door; the top of it was covered with blood. I traced the path of its spray with the flashlight beam, found it splattered up the wall next to the chair as well, almost black in colour. McGaffney had never had a chance; standing there, I could almost see it happen, the killer stepping into the room and blowing the back of his head away before he even had time to turn.

More blood had pooled on the floor at the base of the chair, and some had made it as far as the wireless in the corner, specks visible on the dial, but the rest of the room appeared untouched by the madness. There were books everywhere – bookcases against both walls were overflowing, more volumes stacked on the floor in front of each of them, waiting to be put away. Aside from the blood-soaked chair, it looked like a room you'd find in any house in America, waiting for its occupants to return. I don't know what I'd expected, but somehow, finding such normalcy in direct counterpoint to the blood made the killings seem that much more brutal – the invasion savage and complete. I couldn't stomach being there any longer. I checked the soles of my shoes to make sure I hadn't stepped in the blood, and went out of the room to the staircase.

As I climbed, I asked myself what I was doing there – what I was looking for. I came up blank, nothing I could put into words. The truth was, I just had to see the house with my own eyes. Too much about the McGaffney slaying didn't make sense. The choice of victims, the location, the shift in MO – all wrong. Bailey had immediately told the *Chronicle* it was the work of the Phantom Killer, and I wondered what evidence they had that made them jump to that conclusion. And if there was no evidence, what the hell were they playing at?

The landing at the top of the stairs was L-shaped, four doors coming off it. I went into each room in turn, getting more flash-light glimpses of lives cut short. The first three were bedrooms – the room McGaffney and his wife shared first, then one each for his girls. I searched the main bedroom, finding nothing un-toward, but stopped short of going into the girls' rooms. I saw no sense in it, and already felt wretched enough without in-truding on them any more than I already had.

The last room was different, a small office. Inside was a desk with a typewriter on it. An ashtray next to the typewriter held a stogie butt that had been smoked right down to a nub, as wide as it was long. There were piles of newspapers all over the floor – old editions of the *Chronicle*. There was one drawer in the desk; it had a lock, no key, but when I pulled the handle it slid open. I pointed the flashlight at the contents: the usual flotsam of a newspaperman's desk – pens, paperclips, handwritten notes, receipts. Underneath all that, another newspaper.

I moved the flashlight beam so it shone on the typewriter. There was a sheet of paper loaded, a half-dozen paragraphs typed on it. I skim-read the text, an unfinished piece on a political spat between the Mayor's office and the Chamber of Commerce over the sale of a parcel of land adjacent to Red River. As I read it, something nagged at me and I felt the hair on my neck stand. I read the piece again, more slowly this time, not sure what it was; the local politics it was talking about were unknown to me, irrelevant. I didn't know any of the names it referenced. And the story was the sort of standard fare you'd find in any newspaper, anywhere in the country.

I looked one more time and was about to turn away when it came to me. It wasn't the content, it was the type: Red River. The capital R – a flaw in the typewriter key that meant the top of the letter on the left hand side was missing, didn't join with the rest of it. I'd seen it before, recently: the anonymous note back in my hotel room.

The flashlight crashed to the floor, the noise making me jump. I crouched to pick it up, staying low as if I suddenly needed to be out of sight. The implications swirled through my head, and I couldn't take it all in. I thought about McGaffney's wife, his daughters – the only other people that had access to his typewriter – but dismissed the idea as quick as it formed. The note had come from McGaffney. Had to have. And that threw everything out of kilter.

I stood up to leave, but I stopped in the doorway; the idea of McGaffney as some kind of secret ally was already putting matters in a new light. I looked around again – the piles of newspapers all over the room. I rifled through the nearest one; they were all different editions – no order to the dates, no theme among the headlines. Had to be five hundred copies in the room. I went back to the desk drawer. What was different about the newspaper it held? Why pick one out in particular, hide it away?

I plucked it out of the drawer. The paper had hardened and yellowed, the way newsprint does with age. It was dated 11 March 1943. The lead was President Roosevelt ratifying the bill to extend the Lend-Lease program for another year. I opened it up and placed it on the desk, reading by flashlight. I read the first spread, found nothing, turned over and skimmed every page. Nothing jumped out. I rifled through again, going from back to front, still seeing nothing. I went through one more time, scouring each column. This time, a story on page four made me take notice.

10 March 1943: the body of eighteen year old Vivian DeWitt, of Texarkana, Texas, is found in a car in a drainage ditch off Tri-State Road, near the eastern perimeter of the Lone Star Ammunition Plant. Miss DeWitt had been shot in the head with a small calibre pistol, and police were treating her death as murder. The article didn't say it directly, but mention of 'further injuries to the body, inflicted in the course of her slaying', was a re-write man's way of saying she was stabbed,

cut or beaten – and maybe worse. It went on to say that the car belonged to Miss DeWitt's beau, Mr Lawrence Suter, 25, also of Texarkana, Texas, but that Mr Suter's whereabouts were presently unknown; Bowie County Sheriff's were seeking to speak with him urgently. A two-column story, nothing more than that.

Underneath where the paper had been, I found two sheets of handwritten notes. I pored over them; it was a handwritten copy of a police report. There was no victim name or date, but it had to be related to the woman in the story, Vivian DeWitt. The details read familiar – mention of cuts and punc-ture wounds to the abdomen, consistent with a sharp object, but not a knife.

I stepped back from the desk feeling short of breath. Anoth-er young woman, killed in her car. Cut and brutalised in the course of her murder. The man was an unknown, but the sim-ilarities were too glaring for me to make him the killer; odds were he turned up dead himself some time after. And besides that, there was the date.

10 March 1943: exactly three years prior to the day that Alice Anderson and Dwight Breems were attacked in their car.

CHAPTER FORTY

I thought it over as I sped back towards town.

McGaffney was trying to help me. He did so on the QT because . . . why? Work it back: he couldn't help me overtly because he was afraid of someone finding out. It followed, then, that he'd have to be hostile to me in public – hence his attitude. He was afraid of someone because, three years prior to Anderson and Breems, the same killer had struck, and McGaffney knew this. Put the two together: McGaffney was afraid because he knew who the killer was. And the killer knew this.

So he killed McGaffney to make sure he couldn't talk.

It left more questions – why'd the killer let McGaffney live in the first place? Why didn't McGaffney do something three years ago? Nonetheless, it felt solid. I needed a day to go through the old newspapers and see where the story went after that first report, but it could only be that the killer was never found. What I needed was someone who could fill me in on the rest of the details – where the investigation got to, if anywhere. And someone who knew McGaffney well enough to cover that angle too.

*

I tracked Robinson down in a bar on 16th street. I had to ask four different people at the *Chronicle* before I got a lead on his whereabouts, and even that only got me to Finnigan's on Hickory Street, that Robinson had left an hour before. The bartender: 'Jimmy'll be at Hamblyn's by now. Watch yourself if you gonna trifle with him.'

At Hamblyn's, I found Robinson on a stool at the end of the bar. He was sitting alone, head bowed, a half-full bottle of whiskey and four glasses in front of him; he was muttering something into the only glass that still contained liquor. His tie was pulled loose and his hair was lank with sweat, but he seemed calm. The one upside of finding him in a dive like that: no other patrons, and no cops present. I couldn't even see a bartender.

I called to him from fifteen feet away. 'Jimmy.'

He looked up, and at first it seemed like he didn't recognise me. Then I realised it was the state of my face had thrown him. 'Boy, someone did a number on you good.'

I let it pass. 'I heard about McGaffney. I'm sorry. He was a good man.'

Robinson stuck a finger in his drink and swirled it. 'Yee-haw.' He slurred it quietly, loaded with sarcasm.

I was on a knife-edge; I had no idea if I could trust Robinson, how much to tell him. But for everything that he was, he wore his emotions openly, and it was evident he was broken up about McGaffney. Chances were at least even that he was on McGaffney's side. Either way, I needed what he knew, so had no choice but to show him some cards. 'I mean it. I found some things out. I was wrong about him.'

He pointed his finger at me, liquor dripping from the end. 'I'll tell you what you know, New York: you know nothing.' He hiked his jacket and reached for the back of his waistband, pulled out a revolver. He slammed it down on the bar top and looked at me again. 'Stick around, maybe we can fix that right up. It's loaded this time.' He opened the bottle and refilled all the glasses, one continuous pour that splashed booze all over the counter.

'I'm going to find the man who killed him, Jimmy. I want your help.'

He threw back half a glass and rubbed his eyes, ignoring me.

'You said I couldn't be touched, remember? In McGaffney's office?' He didn't look up. 'Well, I figured out it was McGaffney gave you that order.' I took one step towards him and perched on a stool. 'Am I right?'

Now he looked up at me, his head bobbing gently as he tried to hold it level.

'You hear me, Jimmy?'

He belched, blew it in my direction. 'I hear you. You say something interesting, I'll let you know.'

'Who was he protecting me from? Who was he afraid of?'

He lurched up, sending his stool flying, drink spilling from the glass still in his hand. He staggered forward two steps then slumped his weight against the bar. 'Fourteen years I worked with Gaffy. He's ain't been dead twenty-four hours, and you got the gall to breeze in here and tell me he was a good man?' He bared his teeth; they were wet with saliva, like an animal about to feed. 'He was the best man this town ever knew, but that ain't saying much. You ain't fit to speak his goddamn name.'

'Vivian DeWitt.'

It was a split second, but it was there – in his face, in the slight hesitation before he spoke: instant recognition.

'Who's that?' he said.

'The girl who was killed three years ago. *Chronicle* covered it. McGaffney remembered her. So do you.'

He turned away, waving me off like he always did, but there was too much pantomime in it this time.

'What happened to her, Jimmy?'

'I ain't know who—'

'Dammit, Jimmy, it's the same killer. Tell me what happened and we can stop this.'

He'd planted both hands on the bar. His head dropped against his chest, and he grimaced like he'd stamped on a nail. 'Leave it alone—'

'No.' I stepped towards him. 'Tell me.'

He snatched the gun up and pointed it at my face. 'LEAVE IT.' His arm shook, but at that range he couldn't miss. 'Please.'

He almost sounded like he was begging. In that second, with that one small word, I realised I'd had Jimmy Robinson wrong the whole time. He was angry and frustrated, no doubt about it; but most of all, he was scared. I stood still, hands up, and met his eyes. 'Is that what you're going to do? Just let this slide?'

'No.'

'That right?' I shifted my weight from one foot to the other. 'So what do you propose then?'

'Don't concern you.'

'That's a hell of a thing to say.' I lowered my hands and cracked my thumbs. 'It was McGaffney made you change Alice Anderson's story, wasn't it?' My eyes flicked to the gun and back. 'Who was he protecting?'

He was shaking his head now, tears welling in his eyes, his breathing shallow and rapid. He pushed his hair back off his forehead, the sweat making it stand at awkward angles. 'Look, I know we ain't seen eye to eye, but listen to me when I say you need to get out of Texarkana. Go back to New York and forget you was ever here, 'cause they'll kill you same as they killed Gaffy. Only reason I'm telling you this is 'cause they'll kill me anyway, so it ain't matter any more.'

'Who? Give me a name.'

He threw his head back and every muscle in his neck contorted. I thought about moving for the gun, but wasn't sure I'd make it. He spoke to the ceiling. 'I don't know who exactly. Gaffy never told me.'

'So how do you know—'

'Because Gaffy was plain terrified of them, and now I know he was right to be.'

'How much did he tell you? Who killed Vivian DeWitt?'

He looked back at me, blinked as if he'd only just realised I was standing there, then cocked the gun. 'Just go, Yates.' He shifted his aim slightly and fired.

I flinched and ducked to the floor before I realised he'd fired at the wall. I scrambled to my feet, using the bar to pull myself up, and backed away. He watched me the whole time, the look on his face unmistakable: despair.

CHAPTER FORTY-ONE

It was two in the morning when I left Hamblyn's. I drove straight out of town, praying not to run into any cops. The stolen car I was driving was an advantage – not the car they were on the lookout for. Also on my side was the fact that every man would have been pulled off patrol and detailed to the McGaffney investigation. Even so, being on the deserted streets made me conspicuous – but with nowhere else to go, I had to get back to Sulphur River.

When I came close, panic set in: a police cruiser was parked out front of reception. I had a split second to make a decision, decided to drive on instead of doubling back. As I passed, I saw the outline of a cop through the office door. The Stetson on his head said he was Bowie County Sheriff's – Bailey's men.

I carried on straight, driving into the night. Could be the cops were canvassing every place of lodging in the area on the back of the McGaffney killings, could be they were on to me. Whatever the reason, I couldn't go back. McGaffney's note was still pinned to the wall in the room, but there was nothing more it could tell me now.

*

I kept moving through the night. With nowhere to stay and not wanting to risk hanging around town, I decided to regroup.

I drove twenty-five miles east before I felt safe enough to stop; out there, in the middle of nowhere, I found an all-night truck stop and hunkered down, six cups of coffee to keep me awake until morning. I called Lizzie's house but got no answer. I hoped that meant she'd shipped out like I told her to.

Exhaustion was gaining on me by the time I drove back to Texarkana; a dirty mix of coffee and nervous tension kept me running on fumes, but had me feeling hollow and strung out. I went direct to the public library, enough morning traffic on the roads now to risk breaking cover.

In the end it was a wasted trip: apart from the original *Chronicle* article, I couldn't find any further mention of Vivian DeWitt's murder. A trawl of every edition in the eight weeks after she was killed turned up nothing. Ditto Lawrence Suter; if he was found – dead or alive – it wasn't mentioned in that two-month period. I thought about widening the search to three, four months after it happened, but I could have been there all day and not even got through all of 1943. And I was already feeling exposed, staying in such a public place so long.

The telephone directory was a bust too. There were two listings for DeWitt in Texarkana. The first number had been disconnected; when I called the second, a man named Albert DeWitt answered, but said he'd never heard of a Vivian; even mention of the news story drew a blank.

I slumped to the side and kicked my heels against the call booth. But then a thought struck me; Vivian DeWitt was eighteen when she died in 1943, which would have made her the same age as Margaret Langley. It was a long shot, but worth a nickel.

Tim Langley answered with the same toneless voice as when

I'd visited him at his house. I apologised for bothering him, and asked if Vivian DeWitt was in his daughter's yearbook.

'I don't need to look, I know the name. She was killed a few years back.' He came on indignant. 'And she was at Texarkana High with my daughter. Figure you already knew that.'

'No, sir, I didn't. That's what I wanted to find out.'

'What's the relevance of this?'

'Do you remember much about the case?'

'Are you suggesting it's linked to Margaret's death?'

'It's only just come to my attention, but I'm looking into the possibility, yes.'

He sighed. 'Then you're wasting your time. The knuckle-head she was seeing killed her and disappeared, what I understand.'

I looped the telephone cord around my fist. 'Care to tell what makes you so sure? No-one was ever arrested.'

'It was common knowledge at the time. The police said as much.'

Muddy waters getting muddier; what if Lawrence Suter did kill his girl? If he was never found, there was the possibility he'd drifted back to Texarkana hoping time enough had passed – and now was picking up where he'd left off. Then I realised I hadn't even seen a picture of the man; he could be walking around with a new name, new identify. I thanked Langley and rang off, hurried back to the car.

CHAPTER FORTY-TWO

I idled at the end of Richard Davis's street, not wanting to risk driving up to his house if he wasn't there, in case the cops were watching for me at his place. But his Plymouth was parked out front of his house, so I took that as a sign he was home. When I pulled up outside, Davis was at the kitchen window, barely visible through the grime on the glass.

He opened the door before I got to it, and folded his arms. 'Howdy, Mr Yates. Didn't think I'd be seeing you again.'

'Keeping out of trouble, Richard?'

He shrugged, smirking. 'Much as I can.' He blocked the doorway, taking in my face. 'Could ask you the same thing, but I can see trouble been finding you.'

'Couple scratches is all.' I looked to the side, shying away from his gaze. 'I need your help with something. Can I come in?'

He cocked his head. 'Last time I saw you, you didn't want no help from me.'

I resisted rolling my eyes, sidestepping his hissy fit instead. 'Well now I do.'

He stood for a second longer, then moved aside. 'Hell, ain't like I've got anything better to do.'

The front door opened into a cramped, dark living room. The couch was made up as a makeshift bed; he flopped onto it and pointed at a stool in the corner, gestured for me to sit. 'You want a drink or something, kitchen's through the curtain. Help yourself.'

'You live by yourself, Richard?'

He laughed, staring at the ceiling. 'That's right. All this space, just for me.'

'Where are your folks?'

He stiffened. 'Gone.' He picked at a hole in the sofa upholstery, staring blankly. 'My momma died a few years back. And my daddy never wanted to know us in the first place. What's it to you?'

'Just asking.'

'That what you came here to talk with me about? I'll get the family Bible out if you like . . .'

Still sullen like a child; I ignored it. 'I came to ask you about a girl from your school. Vivian DeWitt.'

He got up and walked into the kitchen. 'I was only kidding about making you help yourself. What you want to drink?'

I could see the whole kitchen from my seat, so I watched as he went to the sink and washed out a glass. 'Nothing, thank you.' I waited for him to come back but he pulled out a loaf of bread and started making a sandwich. I stood up and stationed myself in the doorway behind him. 'Richard? You recognise the name?'

'What about her?'

'She was murdered, right?'

He spun around, a knife smeared with peanut butter in one hand. 'So what?'

I couldn't understand his change in demeanour, but it was no big surprise – seemed like he was always a hair-trigger away from a temper tantrum; I wondered if that was part of his troubles with the law. 'I'm seeing another dead girl in similar circumstances, and I'm trying to join the dots. You want to help me out or don't you?'

He tossed the knife into the sink, metal clattering on metal, his sandwich abandoned on the side only half-made. 'I already gave you your man. Put him on a plate for you. What more can I do?'

I flexed my neck, fatigue and his attitude stretching my patience. 'I appreciate your help so far, but I need solid evidence to get this man. Whoever it is. Until I've got it, I have to chase up every angle.'

He moved past me into the main room. He fished a butt out of an ashtray on the table and lit it, double dragging before he exhaled. 'So you fixing to look at everyone ever got killed in Texarkana? That your plan?'

I tried to railroad him back to the point. 'Did you know her? Wasn't she in your year?'

'I knew her some, but only to say howdy to. No more'n that.'

'What was it like at school when she was killed?'

He shrugged. 'Well ain't nobody was smiling. What you think?'

I looked at the floor, feeling like I was banging my head against a brick wall. 'Did anyone know her man – Lawrence Suter was his name?'

His eyes flicked to one side and back. 'Not me.'

'What does that mean?'

He pulled hard on his cigarette, then went to the window and tossed the butt outside. 'Nothing.'

I pulled him round to face me. 'Don't talk sideways at me, Richard. You're a bad liar.'

He looked at my hand on his shoulder then back at me. 'You ever speak to someone when you don't want something from them? You remember what that's like?'

I threw my hands up. 'I should've known it was a mistake to come here.' I backed away from him.

'Ain't as if I invited you over.'

I turned the knob and opened the door to go, but he toed it closed again.

'No, hold up now. What I know about it ain't worth a Confederate dollar. But I don't tell you, you'll be back here tomorrow, or the next day, and tell the truth I don't never want to see you again.' He wiped his nose with the back of his hand. 'All I was thinking was that there was a rumour she was carrying on with Jefferson Callaway about the time she got killed. And that's it. Two parts of nothing.' His face was red and he was breathing hard. 'Now tell me, was it worth it?'

*

I parked at the end of a residential street, next to the train line, figuring it was secluded enough to avoid attention from the cops. Jefferson Callaway's name being linked to Vivian DeWitt probably meant nothing, but it was another line and another intersection point on a chart that was becoming so crowded with them that the truth was more obscured than ever.

I reached for the copy of that day's *Chronicle* that I'd picked up earlier. McGaffney's murder was the only story in town. Page two covered the police briefing from the day before, reporting that a death threat had been found among McGaffney's personal effects. Whoever penned the story was smart enough not to relay the contents verbatim, but the gist was that the killer had threatened McGaffney because of the *Chronicle*'s coverage of the previous murders, warning him to bring 'balance' to the reporting. The newspaper quoted Sheriff Bailey as saying they were treating the note as genuine.

Means, motive and opportunity. The holy trinity of criminal investigation according to just about every lawman I'd ever encountered. With McGaffney's killing, the means and opportunity were obvious from the get-go; it was the motive that had me stumped. Now it seemed the cops had their motive, and it wrapped the murders up in a convenient package with the other killings, the change in M.O. explained away in a sentence. It was neat as hell – and it stank.

*

I called Sulphur River late that afternoon, checking for word from Lizzie. The man at the desk said he had nothing for me. He was guarded, asked me if I still wanted my room and when I'd be back. It wasn't subtle, and I wondered if he was even trying to tip me off that the cops who'd been there last night would be waiting for me when I did return. I told him I'd be there late that night and rang off. I already knew I was never going back again; may as well keep Bailey and Sherman chasing a ghost.

I called the *Chronicle* and got hold of Hansen. I started to ask him about the reported death threat, but suddenly he was gone, the receiver snatched from him, and a new voice came on the line.

Robinson.

'Where you at, New York? Been trying to find you.'

'I'm all out of patience with you sticking guns in my face, Jimmy.'

'Forget about that. Meet me.'

'What for?'

'Because I'm sober right now, but I ain't fixing to be for long.'

My scalp prickled. 'You got something to make it worth my while?'

'Not over the telephone.'

*

Robinson pulled up ten minutes late. The drive-in was his suggestion, and with all the other movie-goers around, it had merit as a place to hide in plain sight. Also meant there was less of a chance he was setting me up.

He parked next to me and climbed in my passenger side. The smell of liquor preceded him, and it looked as though he hadn't changed his suit since I'd seen him the night before.

'You look terrible, New York. When'd you last take a bath?'

In other circumstances, the line might've made me laugh. As it was, I was more concerned with making sure he wasn't coming after me. 'Where's your gun, Jimmy?'

He pulled his jacket open and showed me the bulge in the inside pocket. 'And it's staying there, before you ask.'

I shook my head and opened the glove compartment. 'In there.'

He stared at me, incredulous. 'You think I came here to plug you? Hell, I'd have done you through the window.' He watched my face and relented when he saw I was serious, taking the revolver out slowly and putting it in the compartment. 'Satisfied?'

'What do you want?'

'Your face like that last night?' he said. He examined me in the flickering light from the screen. 'Wait now, that wasn't me, was it?'

I watched his expression. 'No. You just took a shot at me.'

He shrugged. 'I remember that part. I was shooting at the wall, you ain't none the worse for it.'

I glared at him, wanting to kick him to the kerb, determined to play this out first.

He produced a hip flask and took a gulp. 'You a hard man to find these days,' he said. 'Where you staying?'

'Here and there.'

He guzzled at the flask again then replaced the cap. 'Look, I ain't here to cross you. Truth of it . . . let's say you hit a nerve last night.'

'You even remember what we talked about? Smells like you haven't stopped drinking since.'

'You were in my shoes, you wouldn't have neither.'

'Meaning?'

He rubbed his eyes with his thumb and forefinger. 'I'll be damned if I can figure you out, New York. You shoulda walked away from this mess a long time ago. I would have. You ain't invested here, you got no stake, you can go back to New York and everything is right in your world. Instead, you're still here and you just keep digging, and they're gonna kill you for it and you don't even care.' He looked up, eyes bleary. 'I guess what I'm saying is that you were right. Gaffy deserved better from me. So

I'll tell you what I know, and . . . hell, ain't got nothing to lose now, anyway.'

I stared at him, my skin tingling, a thousand questions forming in my mind, but not daring to interrupt and risk him losing his nerve.

'It was me caught the story when the DeWitt girl got murdered.' He leaned back in his seat and closed his eyes. 'Got the call at seven in the morning, so I drove straight out to RRAD, got there while the cops was still working the scene. They'd taken the body away by then, so was just the car to look at. There was blood on the inside of the windscreen, all over the dash, the wheel, the seat. Bad as any I seen. Could still smell her perfume when I got close; they reckon she'd sprayed some on not long before she died. Bowie Sheriff's were running it, so I talked to the deputies; they'd got so far as identifying the victim, and the owner of the car. Registered to a Lawrence Suter – her man as it turned out.

At first there weren't much to say, in story terms at least. Girl was dead, killed – looks like – by her fella, who's taken off for parts unknown. Only fingerprints in the car are his and hers. I gave Gaffy five hundred words for the next day's paper and started working it properly after that. Talked to the girl's momma, her friends, usual routine. They's all in shock; she was a pair of wings short of being an angel according to the folk I spoke with – honour student, played in the school band, headed to the University of Arkansas up in Fayetteville – all of it.

Now Suter's a different character. Got himself a chequered past, best I can tell; he's a west Texas boy so he ain't got no family to speak up for him in Texarkana, but what I dug up speaking to his acquaintances, he was an auto mechanic who swept her off her feet when they met through common friends. He's got a short police file: burglary, couple bar fights – nothing serious, but a different kind of character all the same, and now nowhere to be found. So two, three days along, it looks for all the world like a lovers' tiff gone bad – he's shot her and gone on the lam.'

His face was bloated with alcohol, his lips barely moving as he recounted the story. Now his eyes popped open and he lurched forward.

'But then I get a call from a source at the DPS lab in Austin. They've tested the blood in the car, come up with two different blood groups: B and O. Vivian DeWitt belonged to group O. In other words, not all the blood was hers. And there was plenty of it too. I managed to get a look at Suter's medical records, turns out he was group B.'

I saw where he was going. 'Doesn't mean it was Suter's blood.'

He nodded along as I spoke. 'No, it don't. But when I talked with the lab, they told me it's rare to find type B; only about ten per cent of folk fall into that group. So I get to thinking, what if Lawrence Suter ain't the killer, but was actually a victim too? What if his body's out there, ain't been found – in the woods maybe?' He reached for his flask and flipped the cap, then seemed to forget about it, holding it halfway to his mouth as he started talking again. 'So I figure to call the Sheriff's, see what-all they know. And they fob me off with a no comment – what I expected.' Now he raised the liquor to his lips. 'Not an hour later, Jack Sherman marches into the newsroom, giving me the fish eye as he goes to Gaffy's office. After he's done, Gaffy comes right over to me and tells me to drop the story;

Sheriff Bailey don't want it looked at while Suter's still *at large* – their words.' He was animated now, jabbing the air with his finger. 'Gaffy knew about the blood types, and so did Bailey and Sherman, because I told them myself. So this is garbage, right? Gaffy's white as a sheet, says, "*No discussions, Jimmy, it's dropped.*" And that was the end of it.'

The air in the car seemed to fizz. McGaffney covering for Bailey and Sherman: the implications of what he was saying were too big to comprehend. 'So you let it alone after that?'

He thumped the dash. 'You listening, New York? I had no choice. You still ain't figured out that you don't go against the law here. Especially if it meant going against Gaffy too.' I could tell by the way he said it, almost an admonishment, that it was himself he was angry at.

He rubbed both eyes with his knuckles and started talking again. 'Turn the calendar forward three years. Alice Anderson and Dwight Breems. Not exactly the same, but too close to chalk up to coincidence. Same date, same type of gun, cut up both girls similar. Only difference was the girl got away this time, and the man's dead at the scene.' He took a breath, the words tumbling out now. 'The day it happened, Gaffy looked like he'd just walked over his own grave. I went into his office and he shushed me before I could say a word. Told me to say nothing for both our sakes. I swear I ain't never seen him look like that before. Scared the life outta me.'

'I kept quiet like I was supposed to, convinced myself could be it was just coincidence. Then a week later Logan and Summerbell got killed, and that was it. I told Gaffy I was working the story no matter what, and if he didn't like it he could fire me and go with god. You know what he says to me? He says,

'*Don't be a fool. You work this story, ain't me you gotta worry about. There's things I can't tell you for your own good, but if you stick your nose into this, we both end up dead. I'm doing what I can, so trust me.*" Word for word. Ain't never forgot it.'

Doing what I can – referring to me. The note. McGaffney selects Charlie Yates as the only man in Texarkana naive enough to go up against Bailey and Sherman. I thought about McGaffney's order for me not to be touched, and saw that maybe he'd been trying to help me all along, behind the scenes.

Robinson pulled a cigarette from a pack in his jacket but never tried to light it, instead tapping it on the dash as he spoke, betraying his nerves. 'Then the week after Logan and Summerbell, the Anderson girl improved some, so Gaffy sent me down there to interview her – this is the Friday, right after you showed up. Gaffy said Jackie Sherman's gonna sit in on it, that Jackie had already spoken to her a few times, and they thought she knew more than she was letting on and maybe she'll open up to me. Beforehand, Gaffy tells me to lead her, to get her to say she didn't know the man attacked her, but that she thought he was a nigger. He said that was the best way to protect her. I didn't know my ass from the grass at that point; I did like Gaffy said because I was going out of my mind, but she wasn't having none of it. I remember it clear as I can see that drive-in screen now; Sherman wouldn't let up on her, kept yelling, "*What's his name, Alice? What's his goddamn name?*" She was on all fours on her hospital bed, screaming at me and Sherman that it was a white man attacked her, but she swore to Jesus she didn't know who he was.'

'*What's his name?*' – the exact words Alice Anderson spoke to me when I saw her in the hospital; the girl so traumatised,

327

she was recounting her encounters with Sherman, mistaking me for another cop. I couldn't believe he could do that to someone so vulnerable. 'But McGaffney made you change the story anyway, right?' I said. 'The interview you ran said she told you the killer was black.'

'Get it straight: I never changed a damn thing. I told Gaffy he could go to hell, but he went ahead and changed it anyway.'

It didn't make sense; if Sherman was in the room, he would have known the truth of it. 'But why bother to change it if Sherman heard what she really said?'

'Reckon only Gaffy could speak to that. I didn't care a lick by that point – that was when I first picked up a bottle, and I ain't stopped since.'

I turned away from him, stared blankly at the screen as the images played out across my eyes; Bogart pulling a gun on one of the villains, the lines between good and bad so clean in a way they never would be in Texarkana. Never really were in the first place. I felt overwhelmed, no idea how to take down Bailey and Sherman, make things right. And the biggest question of all still burned: why? 'So what now?'

He opened his door and climbed out. 'You got any sense, you'll drive north and don't stop until you cross the Mason-Dixon. You won't, but it's what you should do.'

'I meant you.'

His face creased and he let out a dry laugh. 'I'm gonna keep drinking until I get up enough courage to run Jackie Sherman over.'

'Jimmy—'

He slammed the door, and made for his car. But as I started my engine, he turned back. 'Oh, one other thing. Some girl been calling the *Chronicle* looking for you.' He was rustling through his pockets, looking for a message slip. 'Anna something . . .' He rummaged again, came up empty. 'I got the number on my desk somewhere. Said she had something more for you about the car – that mean anything to you?'

Anna Mendoza. The car that had been following Patty Summerbell. I turned the engine on and pulled away so fast, I sent Robinson sprawling.

CHAPTER FORTY-THREE

It was almost ten when I knocked at Anna Mendoza's door. Her brother opened it again, looking annoyed to have a caller at that hour. Anna must have heard my voice because she appeared next to him. She searched my face in the porch light, seeing the fresh cuts and scratches. 'Did you get hurt worse?'

'Another accident,' I said, trying to brush it off again.

'I tried to call you like you asked. The woman at the *Chronicle* said she didn't know where—'

'It's okay, it's okay.'

'I spoke to Darla, she was with Patty one time when she saw the car.'

My pulse spiked. 'She get a look at the driver?'

'No. It was in town, in traffic, and it was a few cars back. But Patty was sure it was the same one. Darla said she wasn't really paying attention because she thought Patty was just clowning around.'

Another dead end looming. 'She remember anything else about it at all?'

She pursed her lips, thinking, then said, 'Not really.'

'What about the model?'

'Darla didn't get a good enough look, but she thought Patty said it was a green Plymouth.'

It came to me all at once. Anna Mendoza read it in my face, reaching out and touching my arm and asking if I was alright.

The words sounded faint and distant, like she was on the other side of a tunnel.

The killer had been staring me in the face the whole time.

'Mr Yates? Does that mean something?'

I nodded, already backing down the drive. 'Yes . . .' I caught myself, just enough sense left to qualify it. 'I think so.'

I thanked her for all she'd done, sincerely, my mind racing ahead of my body. I ran back to the car and took off, the direction set, the plan anything but. A green Plymouth: the type of car driven by Richard Davis. The man who went to school with Vivian DeWitt, Patty Summerbell and Margaret Langley. The man who found a way to stay close to the case by cosying up to me. The man who first put me onto Randall Schulz, and was so determined to finger him as the killer. The man who followed me – in his green Plymouth – the night he first inserted himself into my life.

I was already halfway to his house, hearing Tom Walters's voice in my head telling me I was going off half-cocked again, not caring, doing it anyway. There were holes: there was more than one green Plymouth in Texarkana. I didn't have a motive. I couldn't link Davis to McGaffney or Alice Anderson . . .

Then a memory: Davis's face when he first saw Lizzie; an expression I mistook for lust – but Lizzie was the spitting image of Alice. Davis's expression was a man who'd just seen a ghost.

If I was right, the link to Alice would be there, somewhere.

*

There was one light on in Davis's house when I got there. I parked at the end of the street and tried to bring order to my thoughts, dredging up every bit of restraint I had so as not to storm in there and beat the answers I needed out of him. One thing nagged at me above all: why would Bailey and Sherman protect Davis if he was the killer? Unless he was working with them?

That would solve another problem: who had tried to kill me in that farmhouse. It wasn't Davis under the hood, I was sure of that much. The obvious answer was one of Bailey's men – maybe one of the deputies that helped Sherman beat me down at the Mason – but I couldn't figure out why they wouldn't come at me directly. Bailey hadn't been subtle in his first approach. If it was a cop posing as the killer, though, it meant they were waiting for me on the highway that night. And only two other people knew I'd be driving out there at that exact time. Winfield Callaway, and his secretary, Mrs Cornette.

As I was working through it in my mind, Davis forced my hand. He strolled out of his house and climbed into the Plymouth. He backed up, the car swaying on its shocks as he braked, threw it into forward gear and took off. One second to make a decision: search his house or follow him? I went with the second option, peeled away from the kerb in pursuit.

Davis's car was almost black in the night. There was little traffic around for cover, so I kept well back. He cut me a break by heading south-east, away from town and the cops, and we drove in a ragged two-car convoy. He took back lanes, no light anywhere, so I dropped back further so as not to be spotted. We crested College Hill and continued east.

We drove for another ten minutes, the landscape thick with pines now, before he cut off onto an unlit track. I stopped at the trailhead, unsure whether to follow; he'd see my headlights a

mile off. Every nerve in my body jangled; the darkness was op-
pressive, closing in around me. I thought about turning around,
searching his place instead. Even as the thought formed, I recognised it for what it was: cowardice. Running away again.
Everything I'd sworn I wouldn't do. I clicked my headlights off
and followed down the track.

*

The going was heavy and the terrain uneven, forcing me to go
slow even though every instinct told me to jam the accelerator.
I'd given him too much of a head start, so I didn't even have his
taillights to follow. Without lights, I couldn't see more than a
few feet in front of me, the trail just a narrow fire road cut into
the woods. The absurd thought hit me that if he'd stopped and
turned off his lights, I could drive right into his rear end before
I even saw him.

After a minute more, the trail took a sharp turn to the right
and I saw a cabin up ahead, Davis's car outside. I backed up so
my car was out of sight from his position, and stepped out. The
smell of wet pine was overpowering. It felt like the woods were
alive, animal sounds and rustling branches all around me, the
muddy ground shifting under my feet. I came off the trail and
went through the trees, using them as cover to get close.

I picked my way through the undergrowth until I was within thirty feet. The cabin looked like a small hunting lodge, a
narrow porch out front, the main door in the middle of it,
flanked by windows on either side. There were lights showing
in both. I stood there, the cold cutting through my filthy suit,
trying to make sense of it all. What if I was wrong? What if

Davis was just the screwy kid he seemed to be, and had decided to take off for his cabin in the woods for a couple days?

There was a movement, a shape at the window. A person. Not Davis – a woman. In silhouette at first, but then visible as she turned towards the light source.

Then it all fell away. The figure was Lizzie Anderson.

CHAPTER FORTY-FOUR

Lizzie's hair glowed in the light. She looked pensive, her arms folded, and her gaze jumping from place to place, never landing on one spot for long. I couldn't see Davis.

Seeing her there was jarring, like a hard smack to the jaw that leaves you struggling to see straight. Conflicting emotions hammered me: relief that she was alive and within reach – as if she'd be safe, so long as I could lay eyes on her; annoyance that she hadn't cleared out of Texarkana; confusion, jealousy even – the connection between her and Davis lost on me; and concern – a nagging sting that this scene was all wrong. I watched for a few seconds but then she was gone, the cabin still again. I waited for her to reappear, fighting the urge to break cover and go to her.

Nothing moved, so I started to creep towards the edge of the clearing, slowly, listening for any sounds. And then it dawned on me, the possibility I'd overlooked: that she wasn't there by choice. If he'd taken her . . .

The thought chilled me, the feeling like ice water filling my chest. I leapt up from my crouch and headed for the cabin, half-cocked for sure, but too scared to do nothing.

I was at the edge of the tree line when the lights inside went out. The shift left me blind, my eyes taking time to adjust to the total darkness. I heard the front door open and someone step out. There were only a few branches to hide me from view.

I froze, certain I'd played this hand as badly as possible, but couldn't lay it down now.

The footsteps were heavy boots – a man's walk. Davis. My eyes started to come back, and I could see him heading away from the house and towards his car. He climbed in, started the engine, and then the clearing was lit up again, me out of his beams' field by luck only. He made a three-point turn and set off slowly down the trail, back towards the road.

Thoughts hit me all at once: I was too late. He'd killed her and left her there.

No – there was no gunshot, and it was too quick for him to have strangled her. Then: my car – parked just around the bend. He'd see it and know someone was here . . .

I raced towards the house. Whatever I was going to do, it had to be quick. I jumped the steps onto the porch and crashed into the door. I tried the knob but it was locked. I ran to the window and cupped my hands around my eyes, but it was pitch black, couldn't see anything.

I went back to the door and tried to shoulder it. There was a muted scream from inside. The door held.

'LIZZIE?'

Another scream, all the other emotions gone now, only fear for her safety left in me. I stepped back and booted the door with the flat of my foot. It rattled but held. A second time. A third – it crashed open with the sound of wood splintering. I ran my hand along the wall next to the doorframe, fumbling, no light switch.

'LIZZIE?'

There – in the corner, a shape. I ran over, my eyes adjusting just enough to make her face out. She was in a chair, a strip of fabric in her mouth as a gag. I tried to pull her up but she was restrained. She was bucking, straining at the gag, trying to shout something. I got down to her eye level. 'Lizzie, look at me—'

She kept trying to speak.

I gripped the gag and ripped it out of her mouth. 'Lizzie, it's me—'

The gag came free and she bolted forwards against the restraints. 'Charlie, run, it's a trap . . .'

A light went on behind me. A flashlight beam, pointed at the side of my face. Blinded by darkness, now blinded by light. Lizzie screamed, full blooded this time.

Richard Davis was in the doorway. I could just make out the gun he was pointing at me, and the black gloves he wore on both hands. 'Nice to see you, Charlie.'

He looked from me to Lizzie and back again. 'You a little ahead of time, but ain't no matter.'

Lizzie thrashed at the chair, held back by the rope I saw now around her neck, the skin underneath it red raw. Her arms were handcuffed behind her, attached to the backrest. It all came clear now, too late to be any use: he'd used her as bait, put her in the window for me to see. Which meant he'd known I was out there all along; known I'd tailed him.

I moved so I was between Lizzie and the gun. 'What the hell?'

He stepped closer, into the middle of the room, the gun trained on me as he crouched down. There was a click and the room was illuminated – a battery lamp on the floor. The cabin was just one room; there was an unmade camp bed along the wall opposite where Lizzie sat. Under the far window was a small table, a gas stove and dirty tin plate on it. Every wall had the same carving cut into the wood, repeated over and over: *tXk*. Same as I'd seen cut into the trees in the woods where Alice Anderson and Dwight Breems were attacked.

Davis motioned for me to get on the floor. 'On your knees, please, Charlie. Ain't about power, you understand, I just need to know I got you under control. Hands behind your head too.'

I did as he said, thinking it would buy time if nothing else. 'What are you doing, Davis?'

He stared at me as if he was thinking about it. Then he said, 'I told you I got a story to tell.'

'A story? Killing all those people?'

He looked to one side, disappointment on his face. 'Ain't as simple as that. You mistaking the means for the end.'

'Lay it out for me then.' I stared him down, determined not to show the fear I felt. 'Help me understand how you justify it to yourself.'

'Who the hell has to justify anything? Ain't no-one else in this town operates in terms of right and wrong. The police? The people with the power? You crazy if you think they give a damn. I squared all this with myself a long time ago, don't you concern yourself with that.'

'So you're just another rat in the sewer?'

He laughed. 'Ain't how I'd put it, but it'll work. We all just doing what we got to do.'

Lizzie spat at him. 'You're an animal. You're lower than a rat.'

'Put the gag back on your belle, Charlie. She's got a dirty mouth, I don't want to hear no more from her.'

I didn't move. 'Do it your damn self.'

He stepped towards Lizzie, taking a wide circle around me. He put the gun to her head, staring at me. He tried to force the gag back into her mouth; Lizzie fought it, biting at his hand, so he pulled on the rope around her neck, choked her until she had to open her mouth and gasp for breath. Then he stuffed the gag back into place. She cried out again, the gag muffling it.

He stepped back so he was by the wall, Lizzie between us now. 'Look, you really need to have it in moral terms, I did it to save lives. "The Greater Good," ain't that what they call it? Now it's your turn to do your bit.'

I watched him as he spoke, but it was like looking at a stranger. I already knew I'd been played, but now I was seeing the depths of his madness. 'What do you want from me?'

'I want you to write the story. You gonna blow the lid on this town. And one other small thing, but we'll get to that.' He scratched his nose, his manner like he was asking me for a light. 'You do that, I'll let you both be on your way.'

I held his stare, shaking my head as the words registered. Then I looked at Lizzie; I could see she was afraid, but there was steel in her eyes too, some reserve of guts she was still able to draw on. 'You think I was born yesterday, Davis?'

'Try me. You an arrogant sum'bitch, but I ain't need to kill you, long as you write it all down.'

My knees were numb and I had pain shooting up and down my legs, the patched-up bones aching under my weight. 'Let me stand up.'

He walked around behind me and kicked me forwards. I only just got my hands out in time to break the fall, found myself prostrate on the floor. 'Hands behind your head again and you can lie flat. See, I know how to compromise.'

The floorboards were bare, splinters needling my cheek. All I could see were Lizzie's feet, Davis now a disconnected voice behind me. I kept him jawing while I scrambled for a plan. 'What's your damn story then? What do you want me to write?'

'Who. Not what, *who*.'

'Don't lead me, Davis, make your point.'

'Winfield Henderson Callaway.'

Not a name I was expecting, but somehow not a surprise either.

'Or daddy, as his other son gets to call him.'

CHAPTER FORTY-FIVE

Lizzie had stopped squirming, now sitting in silence, as stunned as I was at what he was saying.

'Callaway's your father?'

Davis scuffed a heel on the floor. 'He'd never admit as much, but that's the truth.' There was a fast patting sound – Davis tapping his toe as he spoke, some form of tick. 'My momma was a maid for him back in twenty-two. He beat on her for months, until one day he got the notion he could take any liberties he wanted with her. She let him do it, thinking it would make him stop, maybe endear her to him, but instead he got shot of her when he found out she was in the family way. Yours truly is the culmination of that sorry tale. You think my life might've turned out different if my name was Richard Callaway?'

I wondered if it was all in his mind; Davis the fantasist coming to the fore again. 'I'm supposed to take your word for all this?'

He sniffed. 'Ain't matter whether you do or you don't. I ain't here to prove nothing to you.'

I turned my head to ease the pressure on my neck. I told myself to ignore his words, the shock, and think only about escape. The battery lamp was five feet away; Davis had put his flashlight in his pocket – figure if I could get the room dark again, it might level the playing field for a few seconds. I pictured bundling Lizzie into the car . . .

Then I remembered. The image of the car triggered it: Jimmy Robinson's gun was still in my glove compartment. So dumb – I could have carried it with me. I wanted to shout, cuss myself out; instead I grit my teeth and tried to concentrate. Keep him talking. 'All this is because you got a hard-luck tale that your daddy didn't care for you? Have you any idea how pathetic that is, Richard?'

'Can't help but notice how it's "Richard" when you address me now. That's how it started, then it went to "Davis", now it's back to "Richard". That mean we're friends again, Charlie?' He snickered as he finished the sentence. 'Point I'm making is that you're as transparent as glass, and never more so than when you think you being smart. So you can try and make me feel guilty or ashamed or small, or whatever the hell else you wheedling for, because I ain't give a damn what you think. Only what you write.'

I lifted my head and craned my neck, trying to see him. I saw Lizzie out of the corner of my eye, doing the same. 'She leaves safely before I do anything.'

'Don't talk simple, Charlie. You so desperate to be a martyr for the cause, I let her go you'd most probably love to take a bullet from me. The deal is, you write or I shoot her in the head.'

I exhaled through my nose. 'Then I need to get up. And I need a pen and paper. Make some notes.'

'No, sir. You'll remember the important parts.' He took a deep breath, theatrical like always. 'Starts with Vivian DeWitt; that's the one thing you done that impressed me, Charlie. How'd you hear about her anyway?'

'Just tell your damn story.'

There was a scraping sound as he slid down the wall onto his haunches. 'Vivian DeWitt was murdered by Jefferson Callaway. Winfield covered it up. Don't know the ins and outs, but the story at the time was her fella did it and vanished. That ain't true, 'cause Jefferson murdered him as well.'

The words he reeled off made it feel like the floorboards were shaking. He talked as though he were reading out baseball scores, his nonchalance making what he said all the more shocking. Davis was a liar, a fantasist and a lunatic, but even as he ran his mouth, some things started to make sense. Callaway was the one man with the power to orchestrate a cover-up on that scale; with the power to make Bailey, Sherman and McGaffney do his bidding. Even so, it was a wild set of claims. 'You've got proof?'

'Nope. Ain't no proof because that was the point. He covered it up real neat.'

'Then how in the hell do you know this?'

He scratched. 'Jefferson told me. How you think?'

'Why would he tell you that? Of all people?' I said.

'Winfield was desperate to keep him away from me, but he never told Jeff who I was. Jeff loved slumming, so he palled around with the kids from Texarkana High behind Winfield's back; thought it made him real brave and rebellious, so I made sure we got close on the QT.' He coughed. 'Could have knocked me over with a raccoon's fart when I found out what he done.'

'You weren't such a fool, you'd have gone to the police right then.'

Davis ignored me. 'Anyway, Jefferson's tale had me steaming mad. I mean here's me, ain't never done nothing like that in my life, ain't never been given an even break, and old Winfield won't so much as acknowledge me. Whereas Jeff's out there killing folk, and Winfield moves heaven and earth to make sure he skates on it. Admit it, Charlie, that'd make you mad as a mule chewing on bumblebees, right?'

'Not to the point of killing people.'

'We'll get to that too. Ain't as clear cut as you paint it.'

I could hear Lizzie's breathing coming faster now, the dread anticipation of him talking about Alice. I didn't want her to have to hear it, but I had to keep him yakking. 'I still don't see what you were trying to accomplish.'

'Callaway.' He pounded the wall. 'Goddamn Callaway . . .' He pounded again, emphasising his point. 'I had to stick it to him so he felt it.'

McGaffney's note, coming into focus now. 'Red River,' I said.

'Red River.'

'You went after people that worked there.'

'The day I found out he was chasing the contract to run that place again, I knew I had a weapon. Had a way to hurt him.'

Blood rushed to my head at the insanity of it all.

I had an impulse: call his bluff, stand up and get myself mobile. He needed me, might mean he wouldn't shoot me. I took my hands off my head and pushed myself upright.

I heard him scrambling behind me. 'What you doing, Charlie?'

I got the rest of the way to my feet and turned around with my hands held up. 'I ache, and I'm sick of lying on the floor. So I'm gonna stand here, and if you really want to shoot me, have at it.'

He put the gun against Lizzie's skull. 'Told you, I'll shoot her.' She wrenched her face away from the barrel, eyes screwed shut.

I was assailed by the same feelings as back in the farmhouse with the killer, the thought of losing her terrifying to me, worse this time because it was her life in the greatest jeopardy. I steeled myself to what I had to do. The sickening idea of what he might do after – cutting her like he did Alice and the others – clinched it. I'd get her free of him, no matter what. Even at the cost of my own life.

I stretched my shoulders, got the circulation flowing again, my legs like broken stilts. 'No you won't. Because if you do, every damn bullet in that gun won't stop me ripping you apart, piece by piece. And then you don't get your story.'

His face contorted through a couple expressions, settled on indifference. 'Have it your way.' He jerked and I thought he'd pulled the trigger.

'NO—'

He grinned, still holding the gun to Lizzie's head, the movement a feint. She was shaking, eyes clamped shut, but otherwise stoic. 'Fine, stand there, suit yourself. But I will shoot her, Charlie, and you. You ain't the only newsman in town you know.'

I locked my eyes on his, the anger inside me as intense as any I'd ever felt. 'Get back to Red River. How does killing his employees hurt Callaway?'

He coiled a strand of Lizzie's hair around his finger, uncoiling it and coiling it again. 'Works two ways. First is I made damn sure I left enough pointers to make it look like Jefferson was up to his old tricks again. You imagine the scandal when that gets out?' He was gesticulating with the gun, and he let it drop without realising. 'The other is, you kill enough of them, eventually someone figures it's Red River folk getting themselves killed. Who the hell gonna work there then? Place would fall apart – right as Callaway gets his hands on it again. Work of genius, if you'll allow my pride.'

I swiped my hands over my face. 'Why didn't you just tell someone about Jefferson? Why kill innocent people?'

He was red in the face now, exasperated. 'Who the hell you want me to tell? The cops? They're the ones covered it up – they'd kill me and bury me next to that poor bastard Suter.' He waved with the gun again as he talked, the barrel pointing in all directions. I started to see an opportunity. 'Who else?' he asked. 'The newspapers? He's got them sewn up too. The Texas Rangers? Callaway's had them on his payroll since his bootlegging days – why you think you ain't seen hide nor hair of them?' He spread his arms. 'I had to do something serious to bring folk to their senses, else this just carries on. Lot more people would've died if I'd done nothing.'

He held the pose to underscore his point, not realising that his gun was pointed at the wall, and my heart raced. The lamp was behind me in the middle of the room. My legs tensed; I braced to make my move . . .

Too slow; he aimed at Lizzie again. 'When you write it down you'll understand.'

I turned around and flattened myself against the wall so the lamp was directly in front of me. The anticipation had adrenaline running strong in my veins. 'You lured Margaret Langley to Spring Lake Park that night. The night you killed her.'

'Yes I did.'

'You knew her from school.'

346

He nodded. 'Also knew her old sweetheart, Myron. Told her I had a message from him. I was gonna kill her solo, but when she turned up with that other boy to look out for her, I knew that was god's way of telling me I was on the right track. I mean, you credit that kind of luck? I needed a sign by then, too. Ain't easy cutting them girls up like that.'

Lizzie wrenched her hands to try to get free, the ropes holding fast. Her eyes blazed.

'Then why do it?'

'Had to, ain't I? Had to look like what Jefferson done to Vivian DeWitt.'

I wanted to ask him about Alice, why he let her get away, but I didn't think Lizzie could bear it. 'If I write your story, you'll get the electric chair. That what you want?'

He wagged a finger at me. 'You still underestimating me, Charlie.' He ran his forearm over his face, smearing a sheen of sweat. 'Ain't gonna be me's the killer. I already gave you the man for the job.'

I looked at him in disbelief. 'Randall Schulz?'

He smiled. 'Got all the evidence you need. And I got the last piece – right here.' He held up the gun. It looked like the picture of a Colt .22 the papers had carried at Bailey's behest.

I understood his intentions right away, the look on his face too pleased with himself to mean anything else. 'You're going to frame him?'

He shook his head. 'You are.' He smiled. 'That's the other part of our little bargain. You gonna take this gun, get his prints on it and leave it in his house. And then you kill him.'

My blood ran cold. 'Out of the question.'

His features twisted, genuine surprise. 'Why not? You

wanted to kill him before. What's different now?'

As the words sunk in, I saw more of his lies that I'd swallowed as truth. 'He never went to where Patty Summerbell died, did he? You sold me a line.'

He shrugged, nodding, and the gun dipped towards the floor again. Every muscle in my body tensed. I cut odds on the chances of my plan working: one-in-ten sounded generous. It was still higher than if I waited around to die. One more time . . .

'Care to hear what I think?' I said.

He looked confused, a sudden shift in the dynamic. 'No, and I don't—'

'I think you're a thousand times worse than Winfield Callaway ever was.'

He rolled his eyes again. 'I told you to quit trying to needle me.'

'I think you made every mistake a man can, ruined your life, and the only way you sleep at night is by telling yourself you're something special.'

His jaw tightened hearing the words. The gun started to sag.

I stabbed the air. 'The truth is, nothing you've ever done means a thing to Callaway.'

It sagged further.

'The TRUTH is—'

The gun hung limp at his side.

'You're the worst goddamn thing ever happened to this town.'

I pushed off the wall, a one step run up, and punted the lamp. It smashed against the opposite wall and the room went black. Davis shouted my name, but I was already at the door. I ripped it open and dived outside. I kept on going, half-stumbling, half-running for the car. I listened for a gunshot from the cabin, hearing nothing and praying I wouldn't. A sickening thought struck me: if he shot her now, Lizzie would die thinking I'd run out on her. Charlie Yates, true to form, a coward to the end. The notion was unbearable and I almost turned back – better to have her know I tried, than for her to die thinking I'd abandoned her, saving myself. But the instinct to press on was stronger, and I knew going back unarmed was the wrong play, selfish. That getting the gun was my best chance. I ran harder, ignored the pain in my legs.

Davis had parked his car right behind mine. My car had two flats, the back tyres slashed, a frog stabber on the ground next to the left rear – Davis a step ahead of me again. I threw the passenger door open. The gun was in the glove compartment where Robinson had left it. Hiding behind the car for cover, I flipped the barrel open, checked there were bullets in all six chambers. I shut my eyes and tried to think, push back the despair that was gnawing at me. The wind rushing through the pines, sounding like Lizzie choking. Davis was delusional, and I knew he was crazy enough to kill us both if he felt it was his only way out.

I started back, forging a path through the undergrowth to the edge of the clearing. I paused to check for him when I got there, not wanting to walk into a bullet.

With no sign, I broke cover and ran across the open ground and up onto the deck. I pressed against the side wall, knowing he'd have heard my footsteps on the wooden planks.

The windows were dark and no noise came from inside. My

heart was running triple time, but the thought of Lizzie being alone with him drove me on. I crept sideways, moving towards the front of the cabin and the door, staying flat to the wall. The boards underfoot creaked. I paused again. Still no sound from inside or out. I started to panic, fearing again that he'd already shot her, the sound masked by the wind while I was at the car. I crouched low and peered through the side window. It was pitch black inside, couldn't make out anything. My mind was a maelstrom of thoughts and images.

I crept under the window and carried on around the side of the cabin. The gun was slippery in my palm; I had no experience with weapons, and it felt foreign and unwieldy. I stopped at the next corner, the area in front of the cabin partially in view. I took a deep breath and poked my head around the corner to scope the front porch.

'Ain't no need to hide, Charlie.'

I ducked back out of sight. Davis was by the front door. I stuck my head around again, held just long enough to see.

He had his arm around Lizzie's throat, the gun to her temple. He was using her as a shield, only the left half of his face in view. Lizzie had her eyes closed, her head tilted forward like she was waiting for the bullet.

'Impressed you came back for her, Charlie. Thought you was long gone by now.'

I rubbed my face and tried to figure what the hell my move was. 'Let her go, Davis. Trade her for me and I'll do whatever you want. But you let her go.' Lizzie tried to say something when she heard my voice, but his choke hold cut it off.

'We've been over this, ain't gonna happen,' he said. 'You go back inside and lie face down, then we'll talk this out.'

I thought about doubling back around the house to get up behind him. Even if I got the jump on him, any shot I took could hit Lizzie. I had two bad choices: do nothing and he kills her, or do something dumb that gets her killed. Which would feel worse?

Frustration overtook me and I kicked the cabin with my heel. 'Why the hell didn't you just kill Callaway, Davis?' I kicked it again, everything boiling over. 'Tell me that. You hate him so much, why didn't you act like a man and go after him?' I was shouting now, my voice cracking. 'You had no need to kill all those people.' I hammered on the wall with my free hand.

There was silence for a moment. The wind was cold on my face. Then: 'You hate anyone, Charlie?'

The question brought the faces of Randall Schulz and Horace Bailey and Jack Sherman to my mind. As much as I despised them all, none of them made the grade. 'Not enough to kill them.'

'Then you can't understand. Ten years I known about him, Charlie.' A pause. 'Know what I remember from being a kid? Being dirt poor. That's all. The others at school used to pick on me something fierce on account of it. Because I'd turn up in the same dirty pants and shirt every day, 'cause they was the only ones I had. Winter mornings, I had to take the axe up to the pond and smash the ice on it just so our hog could take a drink.' He grunted. 'Hungry all the time. My momma didn't weigh but eighty pounds when she died; she never got over what he did to her. All the while, he's living in his mansion.' He hocked the phlegm out of his throat and spat. 'He coulda put a stop to it all any damn time he wanted, but he wouldn't even look at me. His own flesh and blood. Everything he did for that

351

murdering son of his, and he just left me for the dogs. Had the cops beat me up and try to run me out of town. Ain't words for how unfair that is. Killing him ain't enough.'

'So you took it out on innocent people.'

'Ain't no innocents in Texarkana, that's what I'm telling you. They reaping what they sowed where I'm concerned.'

I heard them jostling on the porch, Davis fighting to keep Lizzie under control. Then Davis spoke again. 'We done talking, Charlie. I'm gonna count to three and then I'm gonna shoot her. You want to stop that, you step out here onto the porch and show yourself. One.'

Nothing left to say. A fanatic with a grudge against a whole town. No words that could mollify him, a mind so warped by violence that he knew no other way. Maybe death was the only end for Davis, and he didn't care who he took with him.

'Two.'

I put my gun down and went to kick it away, rushing him my only option left. I heard more jostling, frantic now. Davis grunted and Lizzie screeched like a banshee. I chanced a look around the corner, saw the two of them swaying, Lizzie forcing him off balance. They staggered across the porch, crashing against the side of the cabin, Davis clutching Lizzie as she bucked.

Their momentum carried them all the way across the porch, then over the edge. They disappeared from view, a wet thud as they hit the ground. I snatched my gun up and ran across to where they fell, holding it out in front of me.

The drop was no more than five feet, but they'd landed in a pile, Lizzie on top of Davis. She was already scrambling to her feet; she broke away from Davis and limped clear of him. He was on his side, reaching for his gun that had landed three feet from his left hand.

I aimed at his head. 'Stop.'

Lizzie was clear. She fell to her knees, choking up, then screamed at him. At first it wasn't words, just guttural sounds. Then she shouted, heavy sobs coming between every word. 'You murdering bastard . . .'

He gazed up at me, mouth agape. He had blood on his teeth, looked like black tar in the dark. He reached for the gun again, wincing, his fingertips grazing the butt.

Lizzie shot me a look, her whole body imploring me. 'Shoot him, Charlie. Please, just shoot him—'

'DAVIS—'

He turned to me again, his fingers resting on top of his gun now. 'You not gonna shoot me, Charlie. Ain't what you're made of.'

'Do it, Charlie. For Alice.'

I looked from him to her and back again, watching him down the barrel of the gun, my arm feeling like it was made of stone.

'You ain't worked it out yet, have you?' he said.

Lizzie looked at me, wild-eyed. 'Don't listen to him—'

'What's to work out?'

He lifted his head, but something hurt him when he did it and he flopped back down. 'Come on, Charlie. You know I didn't kill this one's sister. Or McGaffney. You know that, right?'

I climbed down the steps at the front of the porch, kept the gun pointed at his head as I went. I stopped on the bottom stair, him on the ground a few feet away. 'I'm through with your lies, Davis.'

'Come on. COME ON.' A thick vein throbbed down the middle of his forehead. 'I admit I tried to kill the girl's sister, but she got away on me. That was my first, and I didn't have the stones to do it clean. I froze up for two seconds, and she took off like a deer through them trees.' He grimaced. 'Now Patty Summerbell and her knucklehead man, the fool that was with this girl's sister, them two in Spring Lake Park – all me, Charlie. I done them all. But the others weren't. I got no reason to lie to you.'

I saw blazing anger in his eyes.

Lizzie beat me to it. 'Who then?'

'Who you think?' He closed his eyes and laughed to himself. 'Same bastard as always.'

The name came off my lips the same time I thought it. 'Callaway.'

He opened his eyes and met mine, then stared into the barrel of my gun. 'Reckon you got the guts then, Charlie?'

'Doesn't take guts to kill, Davis.' I lowered the revolver. 'You can stay here for Bailey and his men. Figure you earned whatever they do with you. You all deserve each other.'

I told Lizzie to go inside and get the cuffs to lock him up with. Davis laughed. Then he gripped his gun and lifted it off the ground.

Everything slowed down. I raised my gun. I was faster than him. I sighted his head, had him point blank.

I hesitated. Davis swung his gun up in an arc.

I couldn't do it, my finger frozen.

Davis swung his gun past me. He put it to his own head and fired.

My finger wasn't even on the trigger.

CHAPTER FORTY-SIX

We rode in Davis's car back to town. Took me twenty minutes to convince Lizzie to come with me – she didn't want to even touch it, the thought of sitting in the green Plymouth so repulsive to her.

As soon as Davis had pulled the trigger, Lizzie had sprung up from the floor and gone after him, chasing her own piece of revenge. I jumped off the porch step and blocked her off, wrestling her away from him, knowing no good could come from it, a memory to haunt her later. She tore at my back until she went limp in my arms, crying.

I held her tight and in that moment, it was just the two of us in the whole world. I pushed her hair out of her face, the strands damp with tears. 'You're safe now.' I kissed her on the forehead. I felt relief like nothing I'd ever known before, a physical sensation that made my legs tremble. I wanted to get her away from the body, the horror, but there was also an impulse to stay where we were, certain that alone with me in that grim clearing, nothing could harm her now. To never see her in danger again.

I looked back over my shoulder and saw Davis lying there, eyes open and smiling, the Colt still in his hand. A trickle of blood ran down the side of his head; it was the only indication anything was wrong with him. Standing there, his story fresh in my mind, it was clear to me that Davis had started out as a victim himself. The fact didn't excuse him or his actions. It just made it worse knowing that it all could have been avoided.

*

'You should go to the hospital, get yourself seen to.'

Lizzie was staring out the passenger window, had barely spoken since we started driving. I repeated myself, knowing she'd say no.

'I don't want to go to hospital. It was no help to Alice.'

I had nothing to say to that.

She pressed her hand against the window glass. 'What he said, about Alice. Do you think that's true?'

We came over the top of College Hill, and the red sign atop the Mason was visible in the distance. It was the same question I'd been asking myself. 'Davis had no reason to lie, but that doesn't mean he didn't. He lied about everything else.'

'I don't understand what he said about Callaway. What reason would he have to do that to Alice? She was nothing to him.'

I had none of the answers she wanted. We travelled in silence again as the town came closer. I watched her face reflected in the windscreen, the image blurry and unclear. 'What happened?' I said. 'How'd he get you out to that cabin?'

'He tricked me.' She turned to look at me now. 'I got a call at home from someone saying you were passed out in the street, and he didn't know who else to call. I didn't know who it was then, but—'

'Why did you—'

'It was the same voice. The one that called me when they left you for dead at the Mason. He was right last time, so I had no reason to doubt him – what else was I supposed to think? I thought they'd killed you for sure this time.'

An ache ran down my spine, the memory of the beating Bailey and Sherman put on me still vivid and intense. 'Davis was the one called you then?'

She nodded once. 'Must have been. I recognised the voice. I didn't know what else to do.'

'He had to have been following me the whole time.' I wondered if we'd only uncovered the tip of the iceberg when it came to Davis.

'When I got there he told me you'd got up and walked off, and to get in his car. I'd never seen him before and no way I was going to go anywhere with that man. I could tell something was wrong from the look of him. I tried to leave, but he put a gun to my side and said he'd shoot me if I didn't go with him.' She was gripping a strand of hair, stroking it. 'He threw me in the trunk of his car, and when he got me out again it was pitch black. He tied me up in that horrible cabin, told me he was going to use me to get to you.' She tangled her fingers together and pulled them apart again, trying not to break down at the memory. 'I could smell him on me all the time I was in that chair. Cigarettes and sweat. I thought I was going to die.'

I stared at the road, not wanting to look at her, overwhelmed by thoughts of what could have happened. I had total clarity about my feelings for her now, any uncertainty or hesitancy stripped away in the face of a loaded gun. The fact that she'd nearly died made me queasy.

'What are you going to do now?' she asked me.

Robinson's gun was on the seat between us. I put it in my jacket. 'I don't know.'

357

'Charlie, stop the car for a minute.'

We came to the city limits sign. TEXARKANA U.S.A. is TWICE AS NICE. I pulled over to the side of the road just past it.

She put her hand on my arm. 'We don't have to go back to Texarkana. There's nothing there now. I thought about what you said before. I was about to leave, like you told me.'

'You still should.'

She touched my face. 'You could come with me. I've a cousin in Arizona, we can go anywhere—'

'Don't say it.' I took her hand in mine and kissed it lightly. Her touch was like nerve tonic, all my fear and anger draining away as I felt her skin on mine. But a bitter realisation had started swirling in my mind, relief turning to dread, and the contact seemed to solidify it. The realisation that it wasn't over yet. That she'd never truly be safe until Alice's killer was brought to justice. 'It's not as easy as that. You can't hear everything we heard and just ignore it.'

'So you believe him.'

'I don't know, but I have to find out. I can't just walk away.'

She gripped my fingers tighter and held my gaze. I kissed her hand again and drew it to me but looked away, the fear in her eyes too painful to see.

*

She dropped me at the lake in front of Callaway's house. I told her to ditch the car when she got to wherever she was going. 'Just drive and don't come back.'

'What are you going to do to him?'

I closed my eyes so she couldn't see my trepidation. 'Ask him if it's true.'

'And what if it is?'

I couldn't bring myself to say it. I opened the car door.

Lizzie gripped my arm. 'If he did it, will you kill him?'

'Is that what you want?'

She covered her face. 'I don't know. I thought so.' Her hands were trembling now. I took them in mine.

'But?'

She slumped in her seat. 'It seems too easy on him. And they'll kill you for it.' Her voice broke as she said it.

'They'd never arrest him. Not here. He can't just skate.'

'I'm scared to lose you. I can't stand the thought.' She was quiet for a moment. Then she said, 'What you did back there . . . No-one's ever looked out for me the way you have.' She blinked and a tear ran down each cheek. 'After my parents died, I felt like my life was over. I tried to cut myself off from the world – to never get too close to anything. I couldn't bear the thought of going through that again, so it was easier that way. You've been so kind. You're the first person that's made me think . . .' She stumbled, the words not coming easily. '. . . that it doesn't have to be that way.' She took my hair and pulled me close, kissed me on the lips – soft but urgent. 'You don't have to do this. Not for me, it won't bring Alice back.' She kissed me again. 'Let's leave. Come with me.'

The words were everything I wanted to hear – and the hardest, with what I knew I had to do. In my mind I saw a road fork in front of me, one path offering the prospect of being with her. Everything I thought I'd lost when I arrived in Texarkana. Lizzie and I, a new life, a fresh chance to be happy for both

359

of us. But I also saw the shadow that would always loom over that life. Glancing over our shoulders, the fear that Alice's killer might one day come back to tie up the loose ends. The resentment I'd feel for myself that I'd backed down, taken the easy way out instead of seeing justice done.

The other path led past the lake to Callaway's door. I didn't know what waited for me at the end of it, or if I'd return along it, but it was the one I had to walk. 'If I don't put a stop to this, they all died for nothing. This has to end.' I took her face in my hands and kissed her again, swearing to myself I wouldn't let it be the last time. 'Go. I'll find you, I promise.'

I patted my jacket pockets, made sure both the guns were there, and stepped out into the night.

CHAPTER FORTY-SEVEN

Dawn was breaking as I rounded the lake, the horizon behind me a brilliant blue band of sky bleeding up into the night. Saying goodbye had left a stabbing ache in my chest. Lizzie's face as she pulled away was fresh in my mind, her eyes laced with red veins, no tears left. But there had also been a determination about her that reassured me. As much as it hurt to see her go, it engendered a sense of calm in me knowing that, every second, she was getting further from Texarkana. From harm.

Just me and Callaway left.

His house was still in shadow; I crossed the grounds towards the French doors of his study, curving my path around the deck of the summer house. I didn't expect anyone to spot me at that time of day, but I was coming even if they did.

The French doors were locked. I took Robinson's gun from my pocket and used the butt to smash the pane nearest the lock. The glass shattered and fell to the floor; the noise was jarring in the quiet surrounds, but the silence swallowed it up as fast as it started. I covered my hand with my jacket sleeve, reached inside and twisted the lock. The door came open when I tried the handle, and I stepped inside.

The room was dark, the dawn's light not yet reaching it. I flicked on the reading lamp on the desk. The drinks tray was to my right. I poured a large measure of whiskey into a tumbler and set it down on the desktop, placed Robinson's gun next to it. Then I sat down in Callaway's chair.

I tried the drawers in the desk. I was there to confront Callaway, not burgle his office, but I had time to kill – all the time in the world in fact – so figured I'd do it anyway. I worked down from the top. Only the bottom drawer was unlocked; I pulled it out and looked through the contents – stationery, bank letters, a ledger of some kind. As I flicked through his mail, the door to the study opened and the main light went on.

'I had a feeling you'd be back.'

Winfield Callaway was standing there in a thick mauve dressing gown. He looked relaxed, like he'd come down and found his breakfast laid out same as any other morning; a man in complete control of his surroundings. 'I'd offer you a drink, Yates, but I see you've helped yourself. Little early for me, but you look like a man who's had a long night.'

'I have had that. But it's been illuminating.'

He walked to the centre of the room and stood with his hands on his hips. 'The time of night and your method of entry suggest you have a grievance.' He looked at the gun on the desktop, his eyes lingering on it for a second, then meeting mine again to show me he'd seen it and wasn't intimidated. 'Get to it.'

Brass-balled bastard was calling my bluff. 'Vivian DeWitt.' I watched for a reaction. 'Lawrence Suter.'

His face was impassive. 'What about them?'

'Is it true Jefferson killed them?'

He turned and paced to the far end of the room. I moved my hand to the gun, half-expecting him to pull a concealed pistol from his robe or one of the bookshelves, and try to make it a shootout. But he walked with the same air of confidence about him – swagger even – that said he wasn't going to do anything as rash as that. Made it worse in some ways. 'Remind me, you don't have children, do you?' He leaned on an ornate cabinet and looked back at me, eyebrows arched to emphasise the question. I shook my head. 'Jefferson lost his mother when he was two years old. I'm the first to admit I was never the best father, but what he really lacked was a woman's hand in his upbringing.'

I noted it wasn't a denial. 'Your point being?'

'People see the trappings of wealth and assume it makes everything perfect. Easy even. It's not the case; Jefferson had a troubled childhood. Even when he was older, he used to cut school to try to ingratiate himself with the worst of his peers from Texarkana. That's where he met the DeWitt girl.'

My heartbeat jumped; it felt like he was on the verge of admitting it. 'If that's meant to be an excuse—'

He pointed at me, the lecture starting. 'I've no need for excuses. I'm not about to explain anything to you.'

'Then what?'

He wrinkled his eyes as if the question had made him think. 'I've carried this with me a long time. It's good to air it a little. Even if the circumstance is . . . odd.'

'Why did he kill her?'

He cocked his head, again thinking about it. 'Jealousy, I think – I don't know. It's not the sort of thing a father wants to delve into.'

The way he talked about it – matter-of-fact, like it was nothing – made me screaming mad. 'You're not even a little bit repentant, are you?'

He closed his eyes and turned his face to the side, like he was fielding a child's question. 'Repentant . . . no, I'm not repentant.

That's for the devout and the naive. I don't class myself as either.' He walked back towards me, hands in his pockets. 'I wish matters had gone differently, yes, but I'm not going to waste any time worrying about it. I'll be dust in the ground soon enough, and what good will it do me then?'

His words took my breath away. So bold and so open about it. A presence so cold and malignant I wanted to kill him and run, find Lizzie and get as far away from him and that house as I could. I gripped the gun tighter. 'What about Alice Anderson? The McGaffneys?'

He took a deep breath and exhaled slowly, a slight wheeze coming from his throat. 'You have to understand, I tried to stop Jefferson. He's safe now, he won't cause any more trouble. I blame myself to an extent. I thought we'd resolved it all three years ago – I paid for counselling, the best doctors. When it all started again, I just . . . I didn't want to believe it of him at first.'

I wasn't following. 'You're telling me Jefferson killed them?'

He looked down at the floor.

I pressed him, checking he was saying what I thought he was saying. 'All of them? Summerbell, Logan, Langley, Breems—'

'Enough. Don't make me say it, Yates.'

The hair on my arms stood and my guts turned somersaults. I jumped up. 'Jefferson didn't kill those people. Richard Davis did. He admitted as much to me two hours ago.'

Callaway's head shot up, and he fixed me with a stare.

I kept going. 'Davis killed them all, except Alice Anderson and the McGaffneys, he says. Want to explain to me what the hell you're talking about?'

Callaway looked shell-shocked, his face turning white. 'You're lying.'

I shook my head, the picture becoming clear, the terrible mistake Callaway had made. 'You knew Jefferson killed DeWitt and Suter in forty-three, and you assumed it was him again this time around?'

'He . . .' He started coughing; he pulled a tissue from his pocket and spluttered into it. He grabbed my whiskey and took a mouthful, let the alcohol soothe his throat before he tried to talk again. 'But . . . he told me it was him. I didn't realise what was happening at first, but I confronted him after the Summerbell girl was killed and he told me he did it. The same when the two were killed in Spring Lake Park. He taunted me with it for god's sake.'

I could only wonder at how broken the relationship between father and son was that Jefferson had taken some awful pleasure in telling the lie. On the outside I stayed calm, but I couldn't believe what I was hearing – that the old man had got it so wrong. 'So even when he told you he did it, the first time, you did nothing about it?'

'Of course I did. Jefferson was confined here from the second I found out. You saw the orderlies, they were watching him around the clock.' The men I'd mistaken for gardeners. 'But he managed to slip out a handful of times – including the night of the murders in the park. The day you saw us, I was re-buking him for it.'

'So you failed on all fronts.'

He slammed his hand down on the desk. His face was hateful but defiant. 'No. Jefferson must have done it. It's obvious – the similarities.'

'You'd rather Jefferson killed five people than you be wrong? You're a goddamn madman. No wonder your boys are the pits.'

'Boys? I only have one son.' He straightened up, an attempt to regain his authority. 'Richard Davis is nothing to do with me. He's a mistake I should have rectified as soon as it was made.'

'Have it your way – but he got you believing in a lie, didn't he? Destroyed your precious Jefferson in the process too.' I glugged down the rest of the whiskey, accepting now what I had to do. I had no evidence for any of it, and I knew that Callaway would never be arrested in Texarkana. I couldn't just let him walk though; everything came back to him, and it had to end here. Someone had to see justice done. 'Where's Jefferson now? You kill him?'

Callaway slumped into the chair behind him. 'Don't be absurd.'

'So?'

'He's safe and he'll be cared for as long as he needs it. Well after I'm gone, if necessary.'

'He's still here, isn't he?'

Callaway looked away.

'Goddamn, he is, isn't he? So he gets to go on roaming around his mansion, and you get to run Red River again, everything else swept under the carpet. That how this goes for you? Who pays the price, Callaway?'

'You don't sit in judgement over me.'

I stormed around the table and stood over him, pointed the gun at his chest. 'The hell I don't. Don't you see that's what this is? This is your trial.'

He looked up at me, his chest barely moving when he drew breath. 'Such melodrama.'

I pulled back to hit him, but an image of him backhanding

366

Jefferson in the same spot stopped me. I kicked the chair next to him instead, sent it flying. He didn't even flinch. 'Why did you kill Alice Anderson? It wasn't Jefferson and it wasn't Davis. Tell me.'

'What reason would satisfy you, Yates?'

'Goddammit, this isn't a game.'

'Isn't it obvious?' He covered his face. 'I was trying to protect Jefferson. She'd seen him, and I couldn't risk her identifying him. Nothing more complicated than that.'

My face burned up 'She'd already said she couldn't identify anyone.' I grabbed the front of his robe. 'She wasn't a threat. And it wasn't even Jefferson. You madman.'

I was inches away from him now, my eyes locked on his.

And he shrugged.

I punched him straight in the face. He fell backwards, the force of the blow toppling him out of the chair, sending him sprawling on the floor. He didn't move at first and a part of me hoped I'd sparked a heart attack – save me having to do what was coming.

Then he stirred; rolled onto one side and held his jaw. There was blood trickling from his bottom lip, a thin line running down his chin and neck. 'What would you have me say, Yates?' He tried to get to his feet but couldn't manage it. 'You won't get remorse, or repentance, I've told you that. Is it money? Is that what you want?'

'That's how you've done it all these years, isn't it? Buy your way out of every problem.'

He pulled himself up on his elbow, only just able to support his own weight. 'A smart man would be seeing dollar signs if he was in your position. Give me a number.'

I ignored him. 'You had McGaffney killed because he knew about Jefferson.'

He wiped the blood away with his hand, leaving it smeared across his cheek. 'You can claim your share of the credit for that. I was wavering until you showed me his note, but once I saw that . . .'

My hands shook. 'The note was anonymous—'

'It had to be him. McGaffney found out about Jefferson and the DeWitt girl years ago. I thought I'd contained it, but I was never sure with him. I had him leaned on at the time to get him to let it all alone, but he carried on digging surreptitiously. I found out about it just in time to buy him off in forty-three. He came cheap – the house down the road from here, some cash; maybe that's why he liked to torture himself about it. That's what always made me nervous about him. When I saw your note, I knew he had to be removed this time.'

My mouth was dry. I could barely form the words. 'What about his wife?'

He made it to his feet, leaning heavily on the desk to help him up. 'It had to look right, didn't it?'

'What?'

'It had to be a couple. In a car would have been ideal, but the timing was more important than the place, so I had to have it done in their home.'

An innocent woman killed for the sake of it. For context. To dress it up as just another murder in a string of them. A tragedy so senseless, the thought overwhelmed me. I walked to the drinks tray and drank straight from the crystal jug, the liquor burning my throat, still easier to swallow than the poison coming from his mouth.

'Well now you know it all,' he said. 'Feel better for it?'

I took my lips from the decanter, whiskey running down my chin and soaking into my collar. I heard a noise somewhere in the house, a door opening and closing.

He looked at me in the mirror on the wall. 'You know I can't let you leave now, don't you? Not that you can prove any of it, but I won't risk you running your mouth.'

I heard another sound, closer now. I looked at the gun in my hand and then back at Callaway. 'You don't have a say in the matter.'

Callaway looked through me, dead eyes. Then he looked at the door to the study. As he did, Jack Sherman walked into the room, Horace Bailey right behind him.

CHAPTER FORTY-EIGHT

The two men nodded at Callaway and stationed themselves on opposite sides of the room from each other. I got wise to Callaway's game too late – keep talking to buy time, the call already placed to his thugs. Shouldn't have come as a shock, and yet I hadn't seen it coming.

Bailey spoke first. 'What are you doing here, Yates?'

I turned to face him, the gun pointed at the floor by my side, the whiskey jug in my other hand. 'Some business with Winfield.'

Callaway came around the desk and sat down in his office chair, right next to me.

Bailey hooked one thumb through his belt loop. 'Strikes me ain't nothing you can say Mr Callaway needs to hear.'

Sherman: 'Put the gun down.'

I took one more drink, wanting to keep my wits about me, then put the flask down on the tray, wondering if they'd shoot me in the back. 'You here to kill me, Sheriff?' I watched them all in the mirror to my side.

Callaway chimed in. 'You're supposed to be dead already. Horace's boy should have seen to that the other night.' He glared at Bailey, who showed no reaction.

'You set me up,' I said, speaking to Callaway. 'The employee list, the fifty thousand – the whole time you were just stringing me.'

'Simplest way to keep tabs on you, Mr Yates.'

It was said without emotion, eliminating me just another transaction to him, as easy as cutting a cheque. I turned to look at Bailey. 'So what now?'

Bailey met my stare. 'Armed man breaks into Mr Callaway's house. In the dead of night. Assaults him.' He grunted. 'You understand me, Yates? Ain't no-one gonna question it when you go down.'

I wiped my mouth on the back of my hand. 'How much did you know, Bailey? Did you know from the start? All those briefings, *Johnny Lawman doing his best to catch a killer*. And all the time—'

Sherman drew his gun. 'McGaffney was helping you. Who else?'

I thought about this and got the picture: the only thing keeping me alive was their need to know who else to silence. And that gave me a wedge. 'Too many to name, Jack. But your biggest problem is Jefferson Callaway.'

Winfield Callaway whipped around to look at me. Sherman looked at Bailey; Bailey said nothing.

I stepped sideways so Callaway was between Sherman and me – made sure Sherman didn't have a clean shot. 'That's the part you don't know, Bailey. Jefferson's not your killer. But he opened his mouth to the wrong person, and that's what started all of this.'

Sherman looked to Bailey again, but Bailey was staring at Callaway. 'What's he talking about?'

Callaway held his hand up to call a halt. 'I've heard enough. Get him out of here.'

Neither cop moved.

'He's not going to tell you because it means everything you did was wrong.' Sherman bristled, desperate to tear into me. 'Richard Davis is your killer – Winfield's other boy. Jefferson told him what he did to Vivian DeWitt three years ago, so Davis decided to frame him for more bodies. To get back at pops here.'

Callaway's head sank.

Bailey's mouth parted slowly. 'And how is it you know all this?'

'Davis told me. Right before he killed himself.'

'This true, Winfield?' Bailey said.

Callaway sat upright, tried to come out fighting. 'Who the hell knows? All we've got is his word for it, and that's worthless.'

'I haven't got a horse in this race,' I said. 'I've no reason to lie.'

Callaway scoffed. 'You've every reason to lie. You burst into my house with a gun and now you're trying to talk your way out of here.'

I stayed fixed on Bailey. 'So what are you going to do about Jefferson, Sheriff? He told a bad apple like Davis what he did – it's only a matter of time before he finds someone else to get it off his chest to. Think they'll all keep quiet what you did?'

Callaway slapped the arm of his chair. 'Jefferson is safe and he is contained. That is the end of it.'

'You asking me to put an awful lot down to faith there, Winfield,' Bailey said. His voice had a new hardness to it now, as clear as a siren going off in the room.

'I'm not asking you to, I'm telling you,' Callaway said.

Bailey raised his eyebrows and put his hands on his gun belt.

I watched Bailey, thinking I could force the wedge in deeper. 'Jefferson's still here. You know that?'

His eyes flicked to me, the only part of him that moved, then back to Callaway. 'You told me you put him in a rest home.'

Callaway sighed, as if an explanation was beneath him. 'I can control him better here, if he's close.'

'That's what you told me in forty-three, and look where we wound up . . .' Bailey said it softly, the end of the sentence trailing off, like it was tinged with regret. He whipped his gun out before I could move. I twitched, went to raise mine, but he was aiming at Callaway's chest. 'Where's he at?'

Callaway bolted forward in his chair, incandescent with rage. 'What do you think you're doing?'

Bailey's voice was level again, almost tired. 'We gonna straighten this out right now. Where is he?'

Callaway regarded Bailey with a look of pure contempt, his jaw shaking from being clamped so firmly shut.

Then Sherman nudged Bailey, pointed towards the picture window overlooking the grounds. There was a light on in the summer house. Bailey nodded, and Sherman hustled past me, threw open the French doors and stalked outside.

Callaway leapt up. 'Don't you dare—'

Bailey raised his gun so it stayed level with him. 'Sit down, Winfield.'

The air in the room crackled, Bailey and Callaway staring daggers at each other, neither man backing down. Sweat was pooling in my gun hand but I didn't move, transfixed.

Sherman reappeared thirty seconds later, coming out of the dawn light and dragging a figure with him by the hair.

Jefferson.

Sherman manhandled him through the doors and flung him onto the floor of the study. Sherman faced Bailey. 'Wasn't no-one else in the place. No nurses, no guards.' Bailey blew out a breath through his nose.

Jefferson tried to stand, but Sherman kicked him back down with the flat of his boot. 'Stay down, boy.' Sherman re-took his position across from Bailey, his gun trained on Jefferson.

Winfield Callaway grimaced at the kick, as if he'd taken the blow himself.

Jefferson looked around the room from face to face, startled, finally settling on Bailey. 'Sheriff? What's going on?' He wore only a vest and a pair of underpants, his hair like a bird's nest – Sherman must have dragged him straight from bed.

'Who killed them, Jefferson?' Bailey said.

Jefferson was shaking. He looked to Callaway for help. The old man stepped between his son and Bailey. 'You've lost your mind, Horace.' Spittle flew from between his teeth. 'You would point a gun at my son? At me?'

Bailey ignored him, looked past him to Jefferson. 'I already know it wasn't you, son, so why don't tell me what you think you playing at?'

I watched Bailey's face, nothing present behind his eyes. Seeing him like that, I knew I wasn't getting out of the study alive.

Bailey shouted, 'SPEAK OUT, BOY.'

Jefferson pulled at his own hair, as if trying to pull it over his face like a mask. 'He made me do it.'

'Richard Davis,' I said.

Jefferson nodded, his whole body rocking. 'He said I had

to tell pa it was me and it would be okay because he'd have to cover it up. Like last time. Otherwise . . .' He hung his head. 'Otherwise he said he'd tell everyone what I'd done.'

Bailey looked at Callaway, all the blood draining from his face. Callaway closed his eyes and held his head in his hands. Sherman looked from one man to the other, the confirmation dawning on them: Davis had duped them all.

Part of me was amazed by Davis's smarts. He'd waged war on Callaway by killing his employees, and at the same time found a way to get Callaway to cover the crimes up for him. The man was something else. 'You said "last time" – you're talking about Vivian DeWitt.'

Jefferson whipped around to look at me. 'Don't say her name to me. What's this got to do with you anyway?'

'Wise up, kid. Everyone in this room wants you dead but me.' I saw him eye the gun by my side. 'Why'd you tell Davis about DeWitt?'

Jefferson's mouth gaped. 'It . . . We were drinking, I barely remembered after. It slipped out.'

Sherman was getting twitchy, impatient for something to happen. He started towards Jefferson, but Bailey signalled for him to stay put, watching what was unfolding.

I could picture Jefferson telling Davis about the murder, trying to impress his no-good friend from the wrong side of the tracks. 'You must have been real buddies.' I looked at Callaway as I said it, saw the horror register on his face at the realisation the two knew each other.

Jefferson saw it too, and a dirty smile played on his lips. 'Even you would admit it was a good plan, pa.'

The room seemed to freeze. Callaway said, 'What?'

'Blackmailing you. Davis told me you'd buckled and agreed to pay.'

Callaway's forehead creased. 'What is this drivel?'

Jefferson looked around the room from face to face, settling on Bailey. 'That's right, Sheriff. Winfield Callaway, brought low by a cheap extortionist. What do you think about that?'

Callaway's face was caught between fury and confusion. 'There is no such scheme. You're deluded.'

'Deny it all you want, pa. He showed me the notes he sent you.'

I started to see it, and I sensed Bailey did too – Davis's last masterstroke. 'Is that what he told you was his purpose? To get money out of your father?'

Jefferson's smile faltered. 'What—'

Bailey delivered the knockout punch Jefferson never saw coming. 'Richard Davis was your brother, son.'

Jefferson's face changed, twisting in shock. 'You're lying.' He looked at Callaway to back him up, but the old man was drawn and grey. Jefferson stepped towards him. 'Say he's lying. We're friends, he wouldn't do that . . . he would've said something.'

'He was using you to get back at your father,' I said.

Callaway's right eye twitched; in a whisper, he said, 'Dear God, what did you do?'

Jefferson crumpled, his chest deflating and his eyes sunken in his head now. 'He would've said something.' He fell to his knees, planted his fists on the floor.

'You were had, Jefferson,' I told him. 'He made you take the rap for his crimes; what's a little lie next to that?'

Jefferson looked up at Callaway. 'Why didn't you tell me about him?' He made it to his feet, clawing himself up on his father's gown, and shouted in the man's face. 'Why didn't you tell me?'

'You betrayed me.' Callaway slapped him. Then again. Jefferson tried to grab his wrist but Callaway hit him again, harder. 'The hell you've put me through, you worthless swine . . .' Jefferson fell backwards and Callaway was on top of him, raining blows down, pummelling his head and chest.

Bailey stepped in and pulled Callaway off Jefferson. Callaway was gasping, looked like a heart attack in progress. Bailey moved him aside and hefted Jefferson to his feet, blood dripping from his nose.

Callaway took a deep breath before he spoke, his face tomato red now. 'I never told you because I wanted to protect you . . .' His lungs ran short and he bent over double, sucking down air.

Bailey positioned himself next to Jefferson. He reached into his boot and pulled out a small pistol – a throwdown piece. He held it out for Jefferson to take. 'Here. You heard what he thinks of you, now's the time to get even.'

Callaway looked up, eyes on Bailey, full of hate. 'You treacherous son of a bitch. After everything I did for you.'

'Everything you made me do,' Bailey said. 'I've carried enough water for you, Winfield.' He forced the pistol into Jefferson's chest, motioned again for him to take it. Sherman watched on, emotionless, like a soldier who'd seen death too many times.

Jefferson took the gun and turned to Callaway. His eyes were unblinking, not focused on anything, the blood from his nose trickling over his mouth.

Callaway looked up to him, imploring. 'Jefferson . . .'

'Mother knew, didn't she? That's why she did it. Your dalliance with the help.'

'Jefferson, I only ever wanted to protect you. Please . . .'

Jefferson looked down at the pistol in his hand.

Callaway closed his eyes. His face was resigned to what was coming and I thought about that line again, Alice Anderson's words to me – *You think death's the worst thing can happen, but you're wrong.* She wouldn't sympathise with him, but facing a gun held by a son who despised him so much, I felt sure he'd share her perspective on that belief now. 'If you're going to do it, get on with it.'

Jefferson stared at Callaway, his hand swaying from side to side. 'Christ almighty . . .' He blinked and dropped the gun. 'I can't.' He put his hands to his mouth and heaved.

Bailey tilted his head, looked on in disappointment. Sherman and Bailey exchanged glances, and Bailey nodded once.

Sherman raised his gun and shot Jefferson in the heart.

Before I knew what was happening, he aimed again and shot Callaway in the head.

Jefferson crashed to the floor, his arm landing on his father's forehead. His last two breaths came as ragged gasps, blood filling his lungs, and then he was quiet.

Bailey looked at the two men in turn and then clapped Sherman on the shoulder. He bent down and picked up the throwdown piece.

Then still on one knee, he turned and snapped off two shots at Sherman. The first missed, wood panelling splintering behind him, but the second hit him in the neck. Sherman toppled sideways.

CHAPTER FORTY-NINE

'Jesus Christ.' Took me a second to register that they were my words.

Smoke swirled around the room, and the gritty smell of gunpowder cloyed in my nose and throat. Callaway and Jefferson were both still. Sherman was on the floor, kicking one leg in the air like he was trying to get up, but making no sound, blood pooling under his neck. Bailey just watched him writhe. Sherman kicked three more times and then was still, his eyes open but lifeless. I almost dropped my gun in shock.

Bailey switched his gaze to me. I read his eyes and knew what he was thinking straightaway. He went to raise his gun, but I got mine up faster and had it aimed at his chest. He stopped and let his hand hang by his side.

My arm shook; I gritted my teeth to keep my jaw from doing the same. When I spoke, it was like my mouth was packed with cotton wool. 'You shot Sherman.'

Bailey shook his head. When he spoke his voice was calm, almost soothing. 'Jefferson did.'

He held his arms high and climbed up off his knee. He stepped over Jefferson's body and placed the throwdown piece in his hand. 'Callaway's staff will have heard them shots, they'll be calling for reinforcements right now. Depending on how I tell it, you can walk or you can go down for murder. I'm the only one can help you here, Yates.'

I couldn't take my eyes off Sherman's corpse. 'Why?'

Bailey flared his nostrils. 'Was only a matter of time before Jack would've done the same to me. I know he was angling to get my spot from Callaway. Besides, it's nice and clean this way. All you gotta do is go back to New York and keep your mouth shut.'

'And you'll just let me?'

'They's all killers, this is justice done, right here. You should be pleased.' He raised his eyebrows, earnest. 'What's between us is past, I got no beef with you now.' He pointed at the bodies on the floor. 'You right about Jefferson, couldn't trust that boy. But I couldn't do nothing about it long as Callaway was alive.' He gestured at his body. 'Besides, I been taking out his trash for him too long now.'

'Meaning?'

'Yates, you need to shut your mouth and listen to me, ain't time for this—'

I cocked the hammer. 'Meaning?'

He stopped moving, eyed the gun in my hand. Then he blew out a long breath. 'Meaning I cleared up Jefferson Callaway's mess three years ago, and I been paying for it ever since.'

'Vivian DeWitt.'

He nodded, his head tilted back, looking at me past the point of his nose. 'Was me came across Jefferson on the highway that day. He was in the middle of the road when I got there, holding what I thought was a knife – turned out to be a big piece of broken glass – blood all up his arms, in a daze. The car was parked a little way further down, his one up against it. Jefferson done killed them both, and they was still in they car when I got there. Found out later he'd shot them in the head, then did a number on the girl with the glass.

380

I looked at the bodies on the floor, too shocked and disgusted for words.

'Jefferson was wailing and begging me to call his old man, said he'd be able to square everything away. To this day I don't know why I made that call, but I did, and that was when Winfield came into my life.'

'You hid Suter's body.'

He nodded. 'Burned him up with a pile of trash on wasteland inside Red River. Winfield organised it all for me, got me in there and such.'

'Why only get rid of one of them?'

'Look, this ain't matter now, Yates. You running out of time—'

'It matters.' I swallowed. 'I want to hear you tell it. Explain it.'

He exhaled again, exasperated. 'You get rid of both, people gonna be looking for her forever. White Christian girl disappears, no-one's ever gonna let that lie. You get rid of him, you got a ready suspect and a reason he can't be found nowhere – because he's on the run. That's the kind of thing gets mothballed eventually.' He pinched the bridge of his nose, rubbed his eyes. 'Besides, Suter was the motive.'

'What does that mean?'

'It means Suter was the reason Jefferson was out there in the first place. Jefferson was infatuated with the DeWitt girl, they been fooling around, but he didn't know she was carrying on with Suter behind his back. When he found out, he lost his head. Told me that night that's why he done those things to her. His idea of revenge.'

I looked down the barrel of the revolver at Bailey's face, saw something approaching regret. I got the feeling he'd known for three years there was a reckoning coming. 'What did you get out of it?'

He touched his chest, the star pinned to his uniform. 'I was a career deputy. Been spinning my wheels for eighteen years. Three months after, I was elected Sheriff. Except turned out that all that meant was I was deeper in Callaway's pocket.'

I studied the lines on his face. 'The photograph you showed me, the dead body. Was that Suter?'

He held my stare. 'No. Suter was my first time to the dance, but there been others since. Always Callaway's orders.'

The room was in daylight now, the first rays of sunlight glimmering off the lake behind us, the light dancing on the far wall of the study.

'You could have put a stop to this at any point,' I said.

He shook his head. 'You got no idea how powerful he is. Was.'

'You killed Alice Anderson for him, didn't you? Your goons snatched her from the hospital that day – that's why that cop was hanging around her room.'

'What good's it do raking over all this, Yates? You and me can still come out of this just fine if you put the gun down and listen to me.'

I took a step closer to him, the gun steadier in my hand now. 'So did you just accept it when Callaway told you Jefferson was the killer?'

'Course not. We looked into it, but all the evidence kept coming back to him. Same gun, same wounds, same everything.'

'You knew about Davis?'

'That he was Winfield's boy, yeah. Not the rest of it. That would have killed the old sum'bitch even if Jack wouldn't have. He was off the deep end where Jefferson was concerned. Since his wife committed suicide.'

My face must have shown my surprise.

'Didn't know that part, huh?' He nodded. 'Suffocated the infant daughter and took an overdose the day she found out Callaway had a bastard by his maid. Way they tell it, Winfield changed after that. From the day he got me the badge, he had me doing his bidding – like a hunt dog. We caught Davis trying to talk to Jefferson a couple weeks back – should have realised something was up then. Callaway told me to run him out of town, but whatever else he was, that kid was tough as boot leather.'

It all came back to Callaway. Three years and a dozen dead bodies, two of them his own sons. To protect his reputation. His wealth. His power. And despite all of it, he ended up dead in his own study, shot by a badge-wearing thug he helped create. 'I'm calling the FBI. When they get here, you're going to tell them everything.'

Bailey rubbed the side of his face, nudging his hat as he did it. 'You making a mistake. Besides, means you explaining the fact you broke in here with a gun and then this happened. I can dress this up any way I need to.' His eyes were wide, emphasising his point. 'Now you go ahead and put that gun down and we can put a whole different look on this before anyone shows up.'

'And then what? Everything gets forgotten and it goes on like it was before?'

He took a step towards me. 'Not like before.' He pointed at Callaway, still looking at me. 'He's dead now. Can't pull no more of his tricks.'

'No.'

'You being stupid, Yates.'

'My conscience is clean.'

'The hell's that got to do with it?' He scratched his eyebrow with his thumbnail. 'Where's Davis's body at?'

I understood then, realised the whole conversation was just trying to warm me up to this. 'That's what you want out of me, isn't it? The last piece of the puzzle you need.'

He looked at me through half-closed lids. 'So I can square this all off, correct.'

'You're lying.' I used my sleeve to wipe the sweat running down into my eyes.

'Yates, whatever differences we had, ain't matter now. You need my help, goddammit.'

I cocked the gun. 'I don't need a damn thing from you.'

He stared at me, incredulous. Then his face changed, the aggression flooding back. 'Well good for you. But I'll be damned if I'm gonna let you do that to me the same day I got him off my back at last. No chance.'

He reached for his holster.

'Don't do it.'

He raised his eyebrows. 'Or what? You think you can pull that trigger, son? At best you gonna think on it two times, and I ain't need that long to put you down.'

'Stand still.'

'You looked like a scared rabbit when Jack started shooting. You a coward. You ain't got the steel to gun me down.' He took another step towards me.

'STOP.'

'Besides, I taken a bullet before—' He pulled his pistol.

I shot him in the chest. I pulled the trigger again, two more times, sent him spinning away from me. He crashed into a cabinet as he fell, leaving a splattered bloodstain on the cherry wood before he crumpled to the floor.

It took a minute for the ringing in my ears to subside. Somewhere in the distance I heard a siren, then more behind it. I felt calm, no sense of victory or revenge or redemption – none of the feelings I expected. Just calm. Finished.

I heard the sirens again, closer now, and they were like an alarm call. I snatched up the telephone on Callaway's desk and called the *Chronicle*, asked to speak to Jimmy Robinson. The secretary said he was out; I left him an urgent message: get to Winfield Callaway's place. I made her read it back to me and promise she'd get it to him as soon as she could.

I dipped my hand into my jacket pocket and pulled out the other gun I'd brought with me, Davis's Colt .22, covered with a cloth. I unwrapped it without touching it and placed it in Callaway's hand, curling his fingers around it with the rag.

Ballistics would show it was the gun used in most of the murders over the past three weeks. It wouldn't be enough to prove his involvement, and any decent scene-of-crime man would see through the plant if they looked hard enough. Didn't matter; the gun was a message to whoever found it that Callaway was at the heart of everything that had gone down. The fact that it wasn't the gun used to kill Bailey or Sherman or Jefferson would raise questions, hopefully about what they were doing there, and what exactly had happened in that study. Or maybe that was all a forlorn hope. In the end it didn't matter. They were gone now. Four men who deserved to die, vengeance for all those that didn't.

That was enough for me.

EPILOGUE

Bailey's keys were on the dash – thinking no-one would be dumb enough to steal his wheels.

I'd taken his cruiser as far as Broken Bow, Oklahoma – a shot straight north along 71, then back roads west until I got over the state line. I'd driven all through the morning, determined to get away from Arkansas and Texas as fast as possible. I'd stopped just once, at Lake Fort Smith, where the road came within fifty yards of the shore. I wiped Robinson's gun down and pitched it far out into the calm blue water.

When I'd got to Broken Bow, I'd ditched the cruiser at a truck stop to the east of town, then thumbed a ride with a trucker heading north to Wichita. I hadn't felt safe until I crossed into Kansas. It felt like every lawman this side of the Mississippi would be looking for me, even though I knew they had no reason to be; no-one alive could place me in Callaway's study that morning.

I drifted westward for the next week, a meandering path determined by whoever stopped to give me a ride. My aim was to get to Arizona, remembering Lizzie saying she had a cousin there. I knew it was a long shot, but I had to try. I'd fled Texarkana thinking of nothing but her, and I'd be damned if I'd give up on that now.

Being on the road gave me time to think. Wasn't usually a good thing. Most nights I woke with a start at least once, shaking, transported back to that study. It played out different ways in my dreams: I fire wide at Bailey and he shoots me down. I'm not quick enough. Or I can't pull the trigger. The thought of having killed him already seemed unreal to me, like something that had happened in a previous life.

With time, the intensity of the memories faded enough to let me think everything over rationally. I'd started to fill in some of the gaps. I thought about Winfield Callaway, how he'd manipulated everything from the get-go. The reward he put up had to have been a ploy, the purpose to flood the cops with false leads and tips, hope that any real information that came their way was lost in the noise. At the same time, he got his face plastered over all the papers, the local saint who'd do anything to catch a killer – right at the time he was gunning for the contract to run Red River again.

Good ink aside, I couldn't think of any other reason he'd done it – but it only made sense if he didn't completely trust Bailey to get the job done for him. Turns out he had more reason to worry about Bailey than he ever knew.

McGaffney's motivations took some unpicking too. He'd changed Alice Anderson's story in the paper even though Jack Sherman was in the room to hear her say it was a white man that attacked her. I eventually figured it had to be a public message to Winfield – *she's taken care of/she's saying it's a nigger/ you can leave her alone.* Turned out it wasn't nearly enough – Callaway had her killed anyway.

Just in case.

The realisation still made me retch.

*

I ran out of money after nine days. I'd had to lay out for new clothes, new shoes, food, motels, everything. My checking account was empty; no more paychecks from the *Examiner*, my expense account cut off. I was in Fort Collins, Colorado, six hundred miles from Arizona and the hope of picking up Lizzie's trail.

The operator came on the line to tell me my call to New York had been placed, and then I heard Sal's voice.

'Where you been, Chuck? Had me worried.'

'Running, Sal.'

'What's that mean?'

I looked west, the Rockies visible in the distance, didn't answer him.

'You know they fired you, right?'

'Figures.'

'Everything you did, and you know what clinched it? They got a two-thousand dollar invoice to replace the rental car you lost. How the hell you manage that little doozy?'

A half smile crossed my face. 'Tell them to mail the bill to my apartment if it makes them feel better.'

'Yeah, didn't think it'd bother you, so it didn't bother me none. Except to see that goof Walters get what he wanted. He was like a kid in Santa's grotto.'

'There's worse things than him in the world.'

'You alright? Sounds like you had a real come-to-Jesus moment down there.'

'I need a favour, Sal. Last one, I promise.'

He clucked his tongue. 'What is it?'

'I need some money. Can you wire me a hundred bucks? I'll get it back to you.'

He chuckled. 'I'll stand you two. But only if you tell me what happened down there. Maloney and McGill came back and told the story the same way all the papers reported it – some fella in the woods was killing all them kids 'cause he was bullied at school?'

'That's what they're saying?'

'It's all over the news, where you been?'

I hadn't touched a newspaper since I left Texarkana. Apparently the cover-up was in place. 'You're not buying that then?'

'Maybe, maybe not. It's the side story about the two cops and the high-stepper and his kid they found dead in the mansion at the same time. That came through pretty much as a footnote – burglary gone wrong they're saying. And I'm saying it smells like last night's fish; you know anything about that?'

The words were like pins in my skin. Everything that had happened, all swept away with a few lies. I wondered who was behind it now; Bailey's old buddy, Ward Mills, perhaps? Or maybe the cops who found Bailey and Sherman in the study that morning. Protecting their secrets above all else. As far as I was concerned, I just wanted to be shot of it all. 'Sorry, Sal. I don't know anything about that.'

He was quiet for a moment, then laughed, sensing there was more and I didn't want to talk about it. 'That's a whole lot of nothing for two hundred bucks.'

'Thanks, Sal. I owe you. I'll see you sometime.'

'Hey, Chuck, before you go?'

'Yeah?'

'Got a message here for you. Broad called Lizzie, said to tell you she's in Phoenix, Arizona, and to look her up sometime. That mean anything to you?'

I looked at the mountains again, the sunlight glinting on the snow-caps in the distance. 'Yeah, Sal,' I said. 'That means something.'

*

The square in Phoenix was nothing much more than a fountain and a small stone plaza with a bench on each side, carob trees providing some shade.

Sal had given me the telephone number Lizzie had left with him. When I called and arranged to meet her, the feeling was like the first morning after a storm, waking to find the sun beating down from a clear sky.

The bus dropped me on the eastern side of the square, and Lizzie saw me step off. She wore a white summer dress with floral print, a size too big for her – maybe borrowed from her cousin. She ran across to me and threw her arms around my neck, whispered, 'I'm so happy to see you,' and for a time we just held each other.

*

It was only later, sitting in a diner over coffee, that a shadow came over her face. She asked me to tell her what had happened.

'They're all gone. You don't have to give them a thought any more.'

'Did you . . .'

I clasped my mug with both hands, hiding behind it, wanting to spare her the details.

'Charlie?' She moved it aside, gently. 'I need to know. Please.'

Her eyes were pleading with me, and I understood that if I didn't tell her, it would always be between us. The mistake I made with Jane, uncertainties and unspoken words, festering until they poison everything. I set my mug down and told her all of it.

She wept when I told her about Alice, but by the end she was stony-faced. When I stopped talking, she took my hands in hers, across the table, mouthed, 'Thank you.'

*

The next day, she took me for a walk through Encanto Park. The sun glinted off the water in the lake, and for a moment I was reminded of Callaway's house when I left that morning. Then I felt Lizzie's hand in mine, felt the warmth of the sun on my face, and the memory receded, the future the only thing that mattered to me now.

'I love watching the water,' she said.

I looked at her, her smile infectious, making me beam like a goof. 'Ever make it as far as the ocean?'

She shook her head, still gazing out at the shimmering ripples. 'Never. I imagine it's breathtaking.'

'It is that.' I felt a tremor in my gut, the opening I'd been waiting for in front of me, feeling like she was willing me to say it, nerves making me falter. In the end, it just blurted out. 'What if I took you? See the Pacific?'

She looked at me as if she wasn't sure I was serious.

I figured I was already neck-deep, may as well plunge my head under now. 'California, I mean. We could be there in a few days. It's beautiful, you'd love it.'

We walked a few paces in silence, my heart beating like a drum. At length, she said, 'What would we do there?'

I jutted my bottom lip out, the question catching me off guard. 'My old editor in L.A. would put a word in for me – plenty of small town newspapers that need reporters. Somewhere by the ocean. Watch the sun melt into the water at the end of every day. Eat oranges.' I looked over and she was still staring at me, and I figured I'd blown it. 'Well, something to think about.'

She stopped and turned to me, my heart in my mouth. Then she nodded, a light in her eyes I'd never seen before, and she broke into a grin wide enough to make me sweep her up off her feet. 'I don't need to think about it, Charlie.'

Acknowledgements

I owe a debt of gratitude to more people than I could list here, but in particular I would like to thank:

My fantastic agent, Kate Burke, whose vision and insight helped make this a better book than even I could have hoped it to be. Also, the team at Diane Banks Associates, who have been so supportive from day one.

My editor at Faber, the brilliant Katherine Armstrong, whose patience and expertise honed this book, and made the editorial process such a pleasure.

The team at Faber, who understood the book I wanted to write and brought it to life so perfectly.

My family – Margaret, Dawn, Shelly, Josh, Paige and Kyle, who have always believed in me.

Everyone at City University, particularly Claire McGowan and Laura Wilson, whose input and guidance were invaluable in shaping this story, along with the crew from James' flat, who've read it almost as many times as me – Steph, David, Seun, James, Laura and Rob.

The amazing people at Maxus, in particular John Maloney, Tim McGill, Danny Maguire and Tim Grayburn.

The boys who've been there from the start – Peter Blackwell, Patrick Booth, Patrik Ewe, Richard King, Paul Ryan, Emmanuel Wedlock.

Awesome people – Tom & Jana, Emma P, Cecilia, Amy,

Anna, Vik, Jerome, Sammi, Paul S, Bryn, Chris E, Chris R & Ned.

And my wife, Claire, without whose love and belief, this book would never have been written.